A Dream for Tomorrow

MELODY
CARLSON

HARVEST HOUSE PUBLISHERS
EUGENE, OREGON

Scripture quotations are taken from the King James Version of the Bible.

Cover by Koechel Peterson & Associates, Inc., Minneapolis, Minnesota

Cover photos © Koechel Peterson & Associates, Inc. / Hemera / Thinkstock

Backcover author photo Ruettgers Photography

A DREAM FOR TOMORROW
Copyright © 2013 by Melody A. Carlson
Published by Harvest House Publishers
Eugene, Oregon 97402
www.harvesthousepublishers.com

Library of Congress Cataloging-in-Publication Data
    Carlson, Melody.
    A dream for tomorrow / Melody Carlson.
    p. cm. — (Homeward on the Oregon Trail series ; bk. 2)
    ISBN 978-0-7369-4873-9 (pbk.)
    ISBN 978-0-7369-4874-6 (eBook)
    1. Women pioneers—Fiction. 2. Widows—Fiction. 3. Wagon trains—Fiction 4. Oregon National
Historic Trail—Fiction. I. Title.
    PS3553.A73257D74 2013
    813'.54—dc23
                                                        2012026064

Printed in the United States of America

13 14 15 16 17 18 19 20 21 / LB-CD / 10 9 8 7 6 5 4 3 2 1

List of Primary Characters

THE DAWSON PARTY

Elizabeth Anne Martin
    JT (12) and Ruth Anne (8)

Asa and Clara Dawson, *Elizabeth's parents*

Matthew and Jess Dawson, *Elizabeth's brother and sister-in-law*

Brady, *Elizabeth's farmhand and a freed slave*

IN OREGON COUNTRY

John and Malinda Martin, *Elizabeth's brother-in-law and his wife*
    Todd, Emily (13), Bart (12), and Suzannah (9)

WAGON TRAIN LEADERS

Captain Brownlee, *wagon master*

Eli Kincaid, *scout*

FELLOW TRAVELERS

William Bramford, *a widowed lawyer from Boston*
    Jeremiah (18), Belinda (17), and Amelia (16)

Hugh and Lavinia Prescott, *friends of William Bramford, also from Boston*
    Julius (19), Evelyn (16), and Augustus (13)

Bert and Florence Flanders
    Mahala (18), Ezra (16), Hannah (13), Walter (11), and Tillie (8)

Horace and Jane Taylor

Henry and Gertrude Muller and their four children

Ruby Morris (*Jess Dawson's aunt*) and her friend Doris

Paddy and Fiona McIntire

Dr. Nash

Abner Stone and his son Robert

Chapter One

Mid-June 1857

For the third time in one morning, the wagon train came to a complete halt. With reins held tightly in one hand, Elizabeth used her teeth to tug one of her leather driving gloves up higher before she firmly pulled her wagon's brake handle. Listening to the creak of wood grinding against wood and the squeak of the straining harnesses, she was thankful that her father had insisted on giving her wagon and team a complete inspection earlier in the morning. He'd urged everyone in their unit to do the same, but the Mullers had not taken his suggestion to heart. Consequently they'd had the first breakdown of the day. As councilman of their unit, Father had not been pleased.

Shading her eyes from the sunshine with her prairie bonnet, Elizabeth peered upward at the intensely blue sky. Maybe it was the elevation or the time of year, but she couldn't remember when she'd seen sky this shade of blue. The position of the sun indicated that it was nearly noon, but she suspected they'd only traveled a mile or two, maybe less. Although she was relieved to give her weary team another chance to rest, she couldn't help but feel concerned about the travel time they were losing.

Elizabeth understood these delays were due to overly burdened teams and mechanical breakdowns. The stress of driving heavily laden wagons up this rugged trail was taking its toll on many of her fellow travelers. As a result, a number of bulky items had been abandoned alongside the trail in the past few days. Most had been large pieces of furniture, and some appeared to be family heirlooms. But no material goods were valuable enough to threaten the lives of people and livestock. And seeing the Taylors' wagon up ahead and the worn-looking team, she figured Reverend Taylor and his wife would soon be forced to leave their beloved piano behind as well. The way Mrs. Taylor clung to that instrument mystified Elizabeth. It was out of tune and was obviously putting a severe strain on their mule team. To risk injuring an animal for a piano made no sense.

Captain Brownlee had warned all the units that ascending the treacherous South Pass would be slow going this week. He'd strongly cautioned a number of wagons to lighten their loads before beginning their ascent. Some had heeded his advice. Lavinia Prescott even left behind the solid cherry bedroom furniture she had brought all the way from Boston. Others, like the Mullers and the Taylors, had not listened.

Several days back, Eli Kincaid, the wagon train scout and Elizabeth's good friend, had shared the welcome news that they were nearly in Oregon Country and were more than halfway to their final destination. "Of course, the hardest part is yet to come," he had said lightly.

"So I've heard," she admitted. "But at least the landscape is beautiful."

He nodded, looking up toward the foothills. "Beautiful…and treacherous."

Elizabeth looked past her sturdy pair of mules to the glistening black backs of her Percheron horses, Bella and Beau. So far this team combination had worked well together. However, crossing the prairie had been relatively easy. Elizabeth hoped that with the flat plains and weeks of travel behind them, the animals would be accustomed to each other and continue to pull their weight. She also hoped that she hadn't been mistaken not to go with oxen teams like the rest of her family.

"What stopped us this time, Mama?" Ruth poked her head out from the covered part of the wagon. "Another breakdown?"

"I'm not sure. I hope it's not Grandpa or Uncle Matthew." Elizabeth peered up the trail to where Brady and JT were walking back toward them. She had offered to take the morning shift of driving the wagon. Brady and JT would take over in the afternoon. JT removed his hat and waved it high as if to signal that all was well.

"It's someone up in unit four," JT explained to her as he paused by Beau, stroking the horse's glistening black flank.

"Your ma and pa and brother and his new bride are all jus' fine," Brady told her. "No problems there."

"But the Mullers' team is looking poorly," JT said quietly. "Grandpa is talking to them right now. I heard him telling Mrs. Muller that if they didn't unload some things, he didn't want to see her or her children riding in the wagon."

"Oh, dear." Elizabeth shook her head. Gertie Muller was a big woman, and she did not enjoy walking along the trail. "Hopefully they'll lighten their load before it's too late."

"What'll they do if'n their team gives up the ghost?" Brady asked Elizabeth with concern.

"I honestly don't know, Brady." She sighed. "I suppose we'd all have to take them in or try to replace their animals with some of our extra livestock."

"That don't seem fair, Ma." JT scowled. "Would you really let the Mullers use one of our cows to pull their wagon?"

She pressed her lips tightly together. The truth of the matter was that she would resent this as much as her son would. But she was the grown-up here, so she'd have to hide her emotions. "I reckon it'd be our Christian duty, JT. It's not as if we could just leave the Mullers all behind, could we?"

"As contrary as they've been toward us?" JT looked unconvinced. "I don't see why not."

Elizabeth forced a smile for the sake of her children. "Jesus said we need to love even our enemies, son. Besides, don't you think Gertie needs friends as much as anyone else?"

JT's brow creased as if he was considering this. "You want us to take over driving for you?" He brightened as if the prospects of driving were better than walking.

"Don't you think we'll be stopping for dinner soon?" she asked.

"Grandpa said we're not supposed to stop for another mile."

The idea of stretching her legs was appealing. She glanced back at Ruth. "What do you say? Want to walk now?"

Ruth nodded. "I think Flax wants to walk too."

Elizabeth handed the reins to Brady and JT, relieved to get down from the firm wagon seat, and she and Ruth and their energetic yellow dog made their way up the trail. They soon reached her parents' wagon, but only her mother was with it, and her head was bowed as if she were praying.

"Everything all right?" Elizabeth called up.

Clara blinked in surprise. "Oh, Elizabeth, you caught me unawares."

"Were you sleeping, Grandma?" Ruth giggled.

"I reckon I was." Clara gave them a sheepish, tired smile.

"How are you doing?" Elizabeth asked.

Clara's smile strengthened. "I'm a little worn out but no more than the rest of the travelers. Your father is checking on our unit…trying to talk some sense into certain emigrants."

"Like the Mullers," Ruth offered.

"Ruth." Elizabeth gave her daughter a warning look. "Remember your manners."

Clara pointed to a large wooden dresser alongside the road with vines growing over it. "Look at the poor old thing. It appears to have been sitting there for some time."

"Do you think there's anything in it?" Ruth asked curiously.

"I'm sure others have already gone through it," Clara told her.

"But you go ahead and have a peek if you like," Elizabeth said as she climbed up in the wagon to sit next to her mother. Then as Ruth and Flax hurried over to investigate the old dresser, Elizabeth turned to peer at her mother, looking into her eyes. "You look extra tired today. Is everything all right? Have you been sleeping well?"

"I'm sure I sleep better than most." Clara shook her head. "When I think about some of the mothers, like our friend Flo, sleeping with all three of her girls in the back of one crowded wagon...well, I can't help but feel a mite selfish."

"Well, if you're that worried, you could always invite a couple of the Flanders girls to come over and sleep with you and Father." Elizabeth laughed. "For that matter, I'm sure Ruth would willingly join you."

Clara chuckled.

"Do you want to walk with Ruthie and me a spell?"

Clara pursed her lips and then shook her head. "No thank you, I think I'll stay here with Asa until we stop for dinner."

Elizabeth reached over and squeezed her mother's hand. "Go ahead and grab a few more winks while you can get them," she said as she climbed down.

She continued up to Matthew and Jess' wagon, which was just one ahead of her parents'. She still felt a little awkward around them. She supposed it wasn't easy being newlyweds on a wagon train, where privacy was hard to come by.

"Hello there, Jess," she called out when she saw that her new sister-in-law was the only one seated in the wagon. "Is Matthew off helping his fellow travelers?"

Jess nodded and smiled. "It seems only fair after our recent breakdown."

Elizabeth climbed up to sit next to her. "It makes me glad we're traveling in a big group. More hands to help out when someone is in need." She had watched the men working together to replace Matthew's broken wagon wheel the day before. Not only did it look extremely difficult, it had appeared dangerous as well. It was one thing to make wagon repairs on flat ground but something else altogether to do it on a hillside. Still feeling like a protective big sister, she was relieved that Matthew hadn't been forced to deal with it on his own.

"I think we should be good from here on out," Jess told her. "It helped to move some of the load into your father's wagon."

"Yes, now that our food supplies are diminishing, it was time to redistribute some of the weight."

"And with Soda Pass only a day or two ahead..." Jess pulled out a book with a map, pointing out where they were on the trail. "And with an elevation of seven thousand feet, we need to take it as easy as we can on the animals." She stuck the book back under the seat. "Which is why I'm going to get out and walk after Matthew returns."

"Maybe you can walk with Ruth and me later." Elizabeth hopped back down. "In the meantime I want to go see who broke down up there."

"Yes, I'll be curious to hear about it too."

"Find anything in the dresser?" Elizabeth called out as Ruth and Flax came over.

"Nothing but dust."

She grasped her daughter's hand, quickening the pace. "Well, let's go see what's wrong up ahead. We'll find out what's holding us up."

They discovered the trouble about ten wagons up. The Spencers in unit four appeared to have broken an axle. Not only that, but unless she was mistaken, Elizabeth thought they had team trouble as well. She knew enough about livestock to recognize a mule was seriously injured. With his big boxy head hanging straight down and one hoof lifted off the ground, the poor animal was clearly suffering.

"It's a shame," Belinda Bramford said as she and her sister came over to Elizabeth and Ruth. "We've been watching for a while, and it's not good at all."

"They're going to have to put the mule down," Amelia informed them.

"Mr. Spencer is getting his gun," Belinda said quietly.

"They're going to *shoot* him?" Ruth asked with wide eyes.

"Look at that front left leg," Elizabeth told her daughter. "You can see it's broken. He must have fallen when the axle broke."

"But can't it be fixed?" Ruth asked.

"Oh, Ruth…" Elizabeth sadly shook her head. "You're a farm girl. You know the answer to that. There's no way that poor animal can go on. The only kind thing to do is to put it down."

Ruth turned to face her mother, covering her eyes with her hands. "I don't want to watch it."

"No," Elizabeth told her. "Nor do I."

"Me neither," said Amelia.

"Let's keep walking," Elizabeth told them.

So now with the two teen girls joining them, they hastened on ahead. But they'd only gone about fifty yards before they heard the gunshot. Ruth's grasp tightened on Elizabeth's hand, but she said nothing. Her head hung down as they walked up the rutted wagon trail. Because of their fast pace, they soon caught up with the slow-moving wagons. Naturally, there were questions regarding the gunshot. Fortunately the Bramford girls didn't mind sharing the sad news. Meanwhile, Elizabeth and Ruth continued walking.

"Grandma said we have to go a mile before we break for dinner," Elizabeth told Ruth. "Maybe we can get far enough ahead to go off the trail a bit to look for wildflowers or strawberries or gather firewood." She knew Ruth still felt confused and saddened over the injured mule and its untimely demise. And although it would be easy to sweep this under the rug and speak about something else, Elizabeth decided to use it as a teaching moment, and she silently prayed that God would help her.

Chapter Two

Elizabeth led Ruth away from the main trail. Still holding her daughter's hand, she picked their way through a clearing in a forested section, even breaking off some small branches the way Eli had shown her to do just in case she forgot the way she'd come, which didn't seem likely.

"I understand how upset you feel about seeing that mule," she began. "And knowing he had to be put down like that." She paused by a tall evergreen. "And I remember how I felt the first time I saw a horse put down. I was about the same age as you."

"What happened?" Ruth looked up with sad brown eyes.

"Well, you know how your grandpa loves a good fast horse, don't you?"

"Yes." Ruth nodded with interest and perhaps a tiny bit of pride. "I remember back home in Kentucky…Grandpa had some of the finest horses thereabouts. Everybody used to say so."

Elizabeth couldn't help but smile. "And Grandpa would agree with you on that account."

"So what happened?" Ruth asked.

"When I was a girl, your grandpa had a beautiful gray stallion named Storm. That horse was Grandpa's pride and joy, and Storm was valuable too. He had been siring some very fine foals for a couple of years by then. As I recall, Storm was about eight years old that summer—I can remember because he was almost the exact same age as me. Storm wasn't just beautiful, he was fast too. And he had won the Fourth of July race three years in a row. So naturally, Grandpa entered him that last summer too."

Elizabeth paused to pick up some branches near a dead tree, bundling them together and tucking them under her arm for kindling to use later. Ruth did likewise, making a smaller bundle.

"So what happened?" Ruth asked again as they continued strolling.

"Grandpa decided to let my Uncle Jake ride Storm that Fourth of July."

"*Old* Uncle Jake?" Ruth looked confused.

"Well, he wasn't old back then. And Uncle Jake had been begging and begging to ride Storm in the big race. And since he was Grandma's favorite brother, Grandpa finally gave in."

"What happened?" Ruth asked curiously. "Did Storm win the race?"

"He would have won. He had a solid lead, and the race was nearly over with. But then Uncle Jake decided to show off, and he veered Storm slightly off course. Everyone knew Storm was a good jumper, but Uncle Jake took Storm over a fence that wasn't even part of the race." She shook her head to remember what happened next. "Storm took the jump, but he must have been tired, and he caught his hind leg halfway over. He stumbled and broke a front leg. Uncle Jake suffered some too because the fall injured his back."

"And Storm?" Ruth looked worried.

"Poor beautiful Storm had to be put down. And sadly, your Grandpa had to be the one to do it…" She sighed sadly. "I was with him, and I had to watch." Elizabeth felt the old lump in her throat just to remember how crushed she'd been to see the big handsome stallion reduced to a quivering heap. "It was the hardest thing I'd ever seen. I loved that beautiful horse too. Seeing him like that…well, it was just devastating."

"Oh, Mama!" Ruth gasped. "That's horrible. Did Grandpa want to shoot Uncle Jake too?"

"Yes, it was horrible, and you can bet your grandpa was upset. Your grandma used to say it was a clear-cut case of pride coming before the fall. Uncle Jake's pride...Storm's fall. But on the way home that day, Grandpa talked to me, and I learned another important lesson. A lesson I'm still learning. And a lesson you'll continue to learn as well."

"What's that?"

Elizabeth paused from walking and looked down into her daughter's concerned brown eyes. "I learned that death is a part of life, Ruth. It's something that happens to everyone and everything...eventually. There is no escaping it. Death is part of God's plan for this world. We live our life here on earth as best we can, but we know that someday God will say it's time to go."

"Like when Pa and Uncle Peter died from the cholera?"

Elizabeth nodded sadly. "Yes. Like that."

"I don't want you to ever die, Mama." Ruth looked like she was about to cry.

Now Elizabeth wrapped her free arm around Ruth, pulling her close. "I don't plan on dying anytime soon. And I feel like you do—I don't want anyone in our family to die either. And I honestly don't think that's going to happen for a long, long time. But it's entirely possible that some people on this wagon train might die before we're done. And I can't pretend that it won't happen. Just like we saw that mule today ending his life, it's possible that could happen to some of our fellow travelers too. And if it does happen, we just have to trust God, Ruth. We have to believe that God is our heavenly Father and that he knows exactly what he's doing. We also need to remember that God is preparing a place for us...for after we die."

"You mean in heaven?"

"Yes. If we believe what the Bible says, we will live with God forever after we die...in heaven."

"With Pa and Uncle Peter...and that poor old mule too?"

Elizabeth wasn't sure what to say about the mule, but she simply nodded. "So death on earth isn't really the end, Ruth. It's just God's way of moving us to the next place. And that's why we don't have to feel afraid when someone dies."

"I thought Jess was going to die when she fell in the river that day," Ruth said solemnly. "But she didn't."

"No, she didn't." Elizabeth smiled. "It wasn't Jess' time to go, and God knew that."

"Because God must have known that Uncle Matthew needed her to be his wife."

Elizabeth laughed. "Yes, I'm sure that must have been why." Now she looked back in the direction of the wagon train, realizing that they'd wandered a little farther than she intended. "We better get back to the group," she said, taking Ruth's hand.

"Because of the Indians?"

Elizabeth shrugged. "I'm not that worried about Indians, Ruth. According to Eli, they're honoring their peace treaty through these parts. But rules are rules, and the captain would probably say we were too far away."

"What would *Eli* say?" Ruth asked.

Something about Ruth's tone made Elizabeth turn to study her eight-year-old daughter. "I don't know, Ruth. What do you think Eli would say?"

"He'd probably say…" Ruth lowered her voice as if she were a man. "He'd say, 'Let me walk you two pretty ladies back to the train.'"

Elizabeth couldn't help but laugh. "You think so, do you?"

Ruth nodded. "You know what else I think, Mama?"

"I have no idea what all goes through that funny head of yours."

"I think Eli likes you."

"Well, I think Eli likes you too." Elizabeth didn't care for the direction this conversation had taken. "In fact, I think Eli likes everyone on this wagon train. It's his job to help take care of us and keep us safe. Kind of like how a shepherd takes care of the sheep."

"I think Eli likes you more than he likes all the other people on the wagon train," Ruth persisted.

They walked together quietly until they were finally close enough to hear the rumbling of the wagon train. It sounded like the back section was finally moving again as well. Elizabeth didn't want to think of what had become of that injured mule, but she knew that many of the emigrants were low on provisions, and some of them weren't opposed to eating roasted mule.

Elizabeth glanced at Ruth to see that her daughter was still peering curiously up at her, and she realized that this was another topic she shouldn't be sweeping under the rug. She paused by a fallen log, switching her bundle of branches to the other arm. "And what makes you think that?" she asked. "Why would you say Eli likes me more than the other people on the train?"

"I saw how Eli looked at you at Uncle Matthew and Jess' wedding... and when you two were dancing together."

"Really? And how was that?" Elizabeth gazed back toward the trail, purposely avoiding Ruth's intense stare.

"Eli was looking at you...looking at you...like you hung the moon." Ruth giggled.

Elizabeth was too stunned to respond coherently. "*Wh—what?*"

"That's what Tumbleweed Tillie said that Mahala said when she saw you and Eli dancing at the wedding." Tumbleweed Tillie was Ruth's best friend and Mahala Flanders was Tillie's big sister. And Elizabeth could imagine them saying something like this.

"She did, did she?" Elizabeth tried not to act too shocked at Mahala's observations and comments. But she knew that eighteen-year-old Mahala was just one of the older girls who had enjoyed flirting with the handsome trail scout. Perhaps even more so since Matthew and Jess got married. In fact, Elizabeth felt certain that the recent wedding had stirred up plenty of romantic daydreams. Or maybe it was the month of June or the moonlit nights, or perhaps it was simply the clean mountain air.

But Elizabeth had noticed how the girls had become overly aware of the various eligible bachelors on this train. And even the girls still in their teens seemed unconcerned that Eli was nearly twice their age. Even the more sensible Bostonian city girls, Belinda and Amelia Bramford and Evelyn Prescott, seemed to pause whenever Eli passed by on his horse. She'd observed how they preened and smiled, sweetly calling out greetings. Maybe it was Eli's fringed buckskins and knee-high moccasins that attracted them. Or maybe it was his fine-looking Appaloosa. But more than likely it was Eli himself... his clear blue eyes and rugged good looks and easy smile and—

"Mama?" Ruth tugged on Elizabeth's arm.

"What?" Elizabeth blinked in embarrassment.

"Didn't you hear me talking to you just now?"

"I'm sorry." Elizabeth felt her cheeks growing warm. "I guess I was thinking about something else."

"I was asking you a question."

"What was your question?"

"Do you like Eli too?"

"Oh, well... of course I like Eli. He's been a good friend to our whole family and—"

"No, no. I don't mean like *that*, Mama. I mean do you *like* Eli the way Uncle Matthew likes Jess?" Ruth looked up with intense interest. "Would you ever marry Eli?"

Elizabeth glanced over to the wagons moving nearby. She spotted her brother's wagon and knew it wouldn't be long until her own wagon passed. Naturally, no one could hear this conversation over here, but it was a bit unsettling just the same.

"Why would you ask that?" Elizabeth questioned.

"Because Tumbleweed Tillie heard her mama saying she thought you and Eli should get married."

"Oh, Ruth." Elizabeth shook her head with disappointment. "You shouldn't repeat things like that. Don't you know that's just a hop, skip, and jump away from gossiping?"

Ruth's eyes grew wide with worry and she pressed her lips tightly together.

"I'll tell you what, darling." Elizabeth lowered her voice as if disclosing a deep dark secret. "If I ever think there's the slightest chance of something like you just mentioned happening, you and JT will be the very first ones to know about it."

"Really?"

"I give you my word on it."

Ruth smiled in relief. "Now, don't you forget that promise, Mama. JT and me will be the first to know if you're going to get married."

"Don't worry, I won't forget!" Elizabeth threw back her head and laughed. "And don't worry, I have no intention of getting married— at all!"

Of course, as they continued to walk, Elizabeth could think of nothing but Eli now. And the truth was, even if she did feel attracted to Eli, she could not for the life of her imagine marrying him ever. Or anyone else for that matter. James had been gone for nearly four years, but she'd only given up her widow's weeds six months ago. And she knew she could never let go of her memories of him.

Certainly, it was one thing to enjoy the company of a man or to dance at a family celebration—and both these activities still felt a bit foreign to her—but it was something else entirely to entertain the idea of marriage. It was inconceivable. Besides—and this thought was surprisingly reassuring—she felt relatively certain that Eli had no intention of marrying her or anyone. If she'd ever met a confirmed bachelor before, Eli seemed to fit the title perfectly.

In their conversations, which had been few and brief, Eli had always made it clear that he loved his outdoor job and independent lifestyle. Nothing pleased him more than sleeping under the stars and cooking over an open fire. He loved hunting and fishing, and after dwelling with the Indians for a few years, he was perfectly comfortable living off the land in a very rustic sort of way. Indeed, Eli Kincaid was what Elizabeth would call an independent soul. And she had no intention of tying him down or saddling him with two children.

Chapter Three

Weather could change abruptly in the mountains. One moment the sky could be clear and blue, and just minutes later a herd of menacing gray clouds could roll in. Elizabeth was accustomed to summer thunderstorms, but in the past she and the children had always sought the shelter of the barn or the house during a bad one. It was altogether different when their only refuge was their canvas-covered wagon.

"Don't be afraid," she told JT and Ruth in the back of their wagon, waiting out a storm and peering out the round opening to watch the lightning flash across the sky. Although it wasn't yet suppertime, the sky was the color of slate and as dark as dusk. Because of the threatening storm, the wagon train had stopped early to make camp for the night. And after seeing an uncomfortably close strike, everyone had retreated to the safety of their wagons, waiting for the danger to pass. Brady and Flax were hunkered down beneath the wagon now. And as Elizabeth witnessed another strike followed immediately by a clap of thunder that shook the wagon, she wondered if they might be safer down there too.

"That was so close I could feel my teeth rattling," JT said.

"*Oh, my!*" Elizabeth tightened her arm around Ruth, who was trembling in fear.

"Can we sing?" Ruth asked in a tiny voice.

"That's a very good idea." Elizabeth turned to JT, noticing that even his usual bravery seemed slightly shaken. "Why don't you get out your guitar, and I'll light a lantern."

The golden glow of lamplight and the soft strumming of JT's guitar improved the atmosphere immensely, and soon the three of them were singing "Camptown Races." And it didn't take long for Brady to join in with his harmonica. The happy lilting tones of the silly song lifted everyone's spirits, and it wasn't long until big fat raindrops began to fall. After a good thorough soaking, the storm moved on and the sky began to lighten again.

"That was fun," Elizabeth said as she climbed down from the wagon, helping Ruth to get down. "But now we have supper to fix."

"Can we have music again after supper?" Ruth asked hopefully.

"I don't see why not." Elizabeth reached for a pair of water pails and the carrying yoke. "JT, you let Brady tend to the team while you gather firewood or buffalo chips. Grandma said we were running frightfully low on fuel." She turned to Ruth. "And you go help Grandma get supper started while I run over to the creek to fetch us some water."

Ruth leaped over a rain puddle. "Looks like there's plenty of water right here."

"If we'd had time to put up the awning, we might have collected some too." She called out to JT. "Why don't you and Brady get our awning up after your other chores are done, son."

"Sure, Ma."

As they all set out their various ways, Elizabeth felt surprisingly light and happy. Perhaps it was a result of their unexpected sing-along, or the passing of the bad weather, or simply knowing the arduous day of travel was done and that everyone, to her knowledge, was still alive and well. But she felt a bounce in her step as she headed down toward the creek.

"Good evening."

She turned to see Will Bramford approaching with his own pair of water buckets in hand. "Oh, hello," she called to him. "It looks like we're after the same thing."

"Yes." He sheepishly held up a pail. "If anyone had told me a year ago that I'd be out in the wilderness foraging for water like this, I never would have believed him. But alas, here I am."

"Don't your girls usually fetch your water?"

"Usually. But they're trying out a special new recipe for supper…I believe it's one your mother shared with them. And since Jeremiah is tending the animals…" He swung the buckets playfully. "The important task of carrying water was left to me."

She smiled. "It is an important task."

He nodded. "Yes, and from what I've heard it becomes more and more important as we journey westward. I've read some grim tales about places like Devil's Backbone…" He made a slight shudder. "I don't even like to think about it."

Elizabeth didn't care to think about it either. "Wasn't that a glorious storm we just had?" she said as they walked together toward the sound of the nearby creek.

"Some of those last lightning strikes were awfully close to camp," he said.

"JT said he could feel his teeth rattling in his head."

Will laughed. "I think I felt the very same thing."

She knelt down by the creek, getting ready to dip a bucket when to her surprise, Will took it from her and filled it. "Here you go." Then he stooped to fill the other.

"Well." She stood, suddenly feeling uneasy. "I'm not used to such chivalry."

He chuckled. "I wonder when filling a bucket with water became chivalry."

"Still…it wasn't necessary." Now she watched as he filled his own buckets. After his unexpected help, it seemed only polite to wait. Then once he was ready, she arranged her full buckets on the ends of her yoke. "Carrying water always makes me feel like a true pioneer," she admitted as they made their way more slowly back toward camp. Now several others were walking their way, and as polite greetings and exchanges were made, she could tell that some of them were watching her closely, curious as to why she and Will Bramford were transporting water together.

To her dismay, partly because it was unnecessary and partly because it was drawing even more attention, Will walked her all the way back to her wagon and even helped her to unload the heavy buckets. "Thank you," she murmured meekly.

"Not at all. My pleasure." He grinned at her as if her discomfort amused him.

"I should get to—"

"I wondered if I might have a word with you." He glanced around her camp now as if to see if anyone was near enough to overhear them.

"A word?"

"Actually I'd like to offer you some legal counsel."

"Legal counsel?" She blinked and then adjusted her bonnet, folding back the wide brim.

"It's regarding Brady." He lowered his voice. "I've been meaning to say something for some time, but I couldn't quite think of how to put it."

Now she glanced around. She was certain that Brady would still be caring for the animals, but just the same, something in Will's demeanor made her uneasy.

"I overheard Brady talking to your brother about his plans for a small farm in Oregon Country."

"Yes." She nodded. "Brady is saving his wages in the hopes of developing his parcel of land."

Will cleared his throat. "That's what worries me. I can only assume that you and your family are unaware of the legalities in the Oregon Territory."

"What legalities?"

"First of all, despite a recent push to legalize slavery in Oregon, it is illegal."

"What is that to me? As you know, Brady is a free man. We have his papers to prove it."

"Therein lies the problem."

"What?" She frowned.

"Slaves are allowed temporary residence—I believe it's up to three years—all other Negroes are excluded."

"Excluded?" She blinked. "What are you saying?"

"I'm saying that Oregon voters voiced their opinion just this year. The majority voted to oppose slavery."

"Good." She nodded. "They should."

"They also voted to restrict residency to Negroes in Oregon Country. By quite a margin, I'm afraid. Eight to one is what I believe I read."

"I don't understand."

He set down a bucket and rubbed his chin. "I must agree...it's not an easy concept to grasp. Opposing slavery is admirable, but opposing a free man due to his race...well, in my opinion, that is plain old bigotry."

"But surely there are other free Negroes already living in Oregon. I'm certain that I've read of it somewhere. And I've heard of Negro explorers too. JT read something about it to us. Back in Kentucky."

"Certainly, there are Negroes in Oregon. But according to the recently created law, they are not living there legally now."

Elizabeth felt as if the dark clouds had rolled in again. But glancing up at the sky, she could see it was blue and clear. "I...uh...I don't even know what to say about this...or how to respond. I'm stunned."

"And I am terribly sorry to be the bearer of such bad news. I only felt you should know."

Now JT was returning. "I just took Grandma a bunch of buffalo chips," he told her. "Shall I put our awning down now?"

Flustered, she looked from JT to Will. "No, I don't think so. Not now that the weather has passed. You go and help Brady with the livestock first."

He just nodded but looked curiously at Will as he left.

"I'd better get this water to the ladies at my camp." Will smiled in a congenial but apologetic way. "I just wanted you to be aware of these things, Elizabeth. I'd been looking for the proper chance to tell you for some time, but it just never seemed to come up."

"As hard as it is to hear, I do appreciate knowing this." She shook her head. "But I'd also appreciate it if you kept this news under your hat."

"Of course. There's no need to talk about it to others. Certainly we have enough prejudice on this wagon train already."

"Although there are those who seem to like Brady."

"Yes, most assuredly. Speaking for myself and my family, we do like Brady. It's because of my fondness toward him that I'm telling you this."

"So let me ask you one more thing, just to be clear. Are you saying that if Brady were my slave, he would be legally accepted in Oregon?"

"Apparently. But even then it would only be for a few years." He held up his hands in a helpless way. "Although, to be honest, I am uncertain of how this law will be actually enforced in a territory like Oregon. Still, I suspect that some of the citizens will make an attempt."

"Oh, my…" She frowned as she considered the implications.

"And let's not forget what happened in Kansas a couple years ago."

"The Kansas Riots?"

"Yes. Not unlike Oregon, the majority in Kansas wanted to be a free state, but their pro-slavery neighbors stirred things up." He shook his head sadly. "It all turned rather nasty."

"Is that why Oregon has voted like this?"

"I'm not sure." His brow was furrowed. "And quite honestly, it seems to be in conflict with the Dred Scott decision."

"What is that?"

"A case that was tried in early March. I was following it before we left Boston. The question was whether or not slavery should be allowed in the West."

"And?" She waited eagerly.

"Dred Scott was a slave whose owner had lived in Illinois, a free state, as well as Wisconsin, also a free territory."

"Wouldn't it be illegal to own a slave in areas where slavery has been abolished?" Elizabeth felt confused.

"That was the point of this case. Actually, it was only part of the point since there was much political motivation as well. But on the surface, the question was to determine whether or not it was legal to own a slave in a free state. Unfortunately for Dred Scott, with five out of nine justices hailing from Southern states, the Supreme Court was stacked in favor of pro-slavery states."

"So what did they decide?"

"The court ruled that Scott was *not* free." Will let out a frustrated sigh. "Not based on his residency in either Illinois or Wisconsin. The opinion of the justices was that according to our constitution, Negroes were not considered citizens and therefore could not be considered free men."

"But that makes no sense. Many Negroes live as free men in the North. Even Brady has his freedom papers. Is he not free?"

"Lawmaking is puzzling, Elizabeth." He gave her a weary smile. "Our government must be proven and tried with each legislative step of the way. But on this complicated issue of slavery and states' rights, our laws are conflicted and convoluted and confusing. To be perfectly honest, I am greatly relieved to be removed from it for a while. I fear that this issue can only tear our country apart."

Elizabeth was trying to grasp all of this—trying to sort through and determine what needed to be done to protect Brady's future. "So perhaps it would be in Brady's best interest if we maintained a pretense when we settle…if we acted as if he is still our…our *property*." The word tasted bitter in her mouth.

"It seems a safe course of action. Except that most folks on this wagon train are already aware that Brady is a free man. You and your family have made that much clear. It might be difficult to turn back the hands of time now."

She let out a long sigh.

"Again, I regret being the bearer of bad news today. And, please know that if you have any questions or need legal counsel, I am always at your service." He tipped his hat, smiling as he picked up his water pails. "As you can see, I am occasionally of more value than simply that of a water carrier." He chuckled as he walked away, swinging his full buckets so that some of the water sloshed out.

But Elizabeth did not feel like laughing now. Not in the least. This news was greatly disturbing. So much so that it seemed almost unbelievable. But surely Will wouldn't tell her a falsehood, and certainly not regarding such a serious subject. But if it were true, why hadn't her father been aware? He was an avid reader. Surely he would have warned her that Brady would be unwelcome in Oregon, wouldn't he? But then...Will had mentioned it had been put to a recent vote. Perhaps Father, like her, had been oblivious. And it wasn't as if they'd originally planned to bring Brady along. He had made that choice in the eleventh hour.

Even so, this legislation was so unfair and unjust. In some ways it seemed even worse than the opinions of those who openly supported slavery—those whom she and her family had taken a stand against by becoming abolitionists. But for Oregonians to vote to oppose slavery on one hand and then turn around and vote to oppose residency to Negroes on the other...truly, it made no sense. And it made her angry. One reason she and James had originally planned to emigrate from Kentucky to Oregon was to escape all this. But suddenly it felt as if she had leaped from the frying pan into the fire—and taken poor unsuspecting Brady with her. What was to be done?

As Elizabeth filled the water barrel, she knew she would have to tell her father and Matthew about this. They had a right to know. Still, what could they do about it? It wasn't as if they could simply abandon their loyal employee and friend out here on the Oregon Trail. And the few settlements and forts along the way weren't welcoming to Brady's situation either. It hurt to think about Brady's high expectations for his new life in Oregon Country. To consider his hopes of having his own land to work, his dreams of living his last days as a free man in a free land...well, it made her stomach ache and put a rock-hard lump in her throat.

As she walked to her parents' camp, she silently prayed for divine guidance. God would have to lead her, she decided as she rounded a corner, spotting her mother and Ruth bent over the cooking fire. Just as God had led them through all the other steps of this journey, he would have to lead them in the best ways to help Brady.

"Is something wrong?" Clara asked as Elizabeth joined them.

Elizabeth pressed her lips together, giving a slight shake to her head—her clue to her mother that this was something she didn't want to discuss in front of Ruth. Fortunately Clara understood. "Eli brought us a nice piece of bison roast." She removed the lid from the Dutch oven so Elizabeth could spy the chunk of meat nestled with wild leeks.

"Looks good." Elizabeth nodded.

"It won't be done for another hour or so," Clara said.

"And since supper will be late, Matthew and Jess want to go fishing," Ruth said, "They asked me to come with them as soon as they're done tending to their livestock. May I go, Mama?"

"Only if you promise to catch us a big trout to have for breakfast." Elizabeth grinned at her.

"I'll do my best." She frowned with uncertainty. "But I might not catch one."

"I know, sweetheart." Elizabeth tweaked one of her braids and then waved at Jess, who was just coming into camp.

"Ready to go fishing?" Jess called out.

Ruth was off like a flash, and Elizabeth utilized the moment to tell her mother about what Will had just said.

"Oh, no!" Clara's hand flew up to her mouth. "Is that really true?"

Elizabeth sighed and then turned to begin measuring the dry ingredients for the biscuits. "I wish it weren't. But Will seemed to know what he was talking about. After all, he is an attorney."

Clara nodded. "Of course. I'm sure he wouldn't tell you this if he didn't know it was fact." She shook her head. "But it is so strange...that Oregonians would oppose slavery and then oppose Negroes as well. So very strange...and sad."

"I don't want to bring it up in front of Brady. Not yet. So if you could tell Father about it...he needs to know." She threw some salt into the bowl. "Not that there is much to be done about it."

"And you did say that slaves are allowed in Oregon?"

Elizabeth nodded as she began to stir. "For a few years. But most of these folks know Brady is a free man. And some of our fellow travelers plan to settle near us."

"Even if that were not the situation, it would be such a shame for

Brady to put on the pretense that he is a slave just to appease a foolish new law." She poured a cup of rice into a pan. "*Pish-posh!* To think we're out here in the middle of nowhere, assuming we have escaped the tomfoolery of divisive politics, only to hear of news like this…"

Elizabeth put an arm around her mother's shoulders. "I'm sorry to share bad news, but I must admit it's a comfort to know that my mother thinks as I do."

Clara gave her a sad smile. "I wonder, Elizabeth—not that I think it will ever happen…probably not in my lifetime—but I wonder if women ever got the vote…do you think that would change these things?"

"If all women believed as we did, it might." Elizabeth added a bit more water to the dough. "But to be fair, Father and Matthew think as we do, and that doesn't seem to change these things."

"Some folks…they say that only war will change these things." Clara sighed. "Your father says that war may be unavoidable—a war between the states, splitting our country right down the middle."

Despite the warm summer air, Elizabeth felt a chill run through her at her mother's words. Oh, it wasn't the first time she'd heard such rumors, but it was the first time she felt that they might be more than just idle talk. And although Will's news about Brady was disheartening and unwelcome, she still believed they would all be better off in the West. She hoped they would be.

Chapter Four

The uphill travel seemed to get more rugged with each passing day. And the weather was not helping. Afternoon thunderstorms came almost daily, sometimes accompanied by hailstones the size of large peas. Naturally this would turn the already challenging trail into a muddy streambed. Teams occasionally lost their footing, and numerous breakdowns occurred. But the wagon train pressed steadily onward, trying to place as many miles behind them as possible.

Due to the recent afternoon storms, Elizabeth had switched driving shifts with Brady. It wasn't that she didn't think he could manage her team during foul weather, but if anything happened to one of her animals, she would prefer to be at the reins. Then she would have only herself to blame. Not that she was expecting calamity exactly…but it was hard to know.

Besides her own concerns, she felt worried that this trip was taking its toll on some of the older folks, including Brady and her parents. Oh, they didn't complain, bless their souls, but sometimes her mother looked bone tired and had dark shadows beneath her eyes. And by the end of the day, Elizabeth couldn't help but notice that her father's usual spark and energy were missing. Sometimes he even snapped at the children, which was so unlike him. But she knew he was carrying a lot of pressure. It wasn't easy leading his unit. And some emigrants seemed intent on making it much harder.

"The Taylors are going to have trouble," Elizabeth quietly told her father after they finished their midday meal. He was helping her to check the hooves of her team. "Their wagon is far too heavy." She glanced over her shoulder to the wagon that had been traveling in front of her the past few days. "Their team is struggling. It's just a matter of time."

Asa stood straight and removed his hat and wiped his brow. "I know."

"I keep a safe distance behind them," she said. "But it pains me to watch them, Father. Isn't there something we can do?"

He shoved his hat back on his head and nodded. "Come with me." He took her by the arm and began walking. "Let's see if we can talk some sense in them together. I'll speak to Mr. Taylor." He gave her a sideways glance. "You talk to his wife."

Elizabeth nodded grimly.

"Afternoon," Asa said loudly to the Taylors. "Mind if we have a word with you?"

"Not at all." Mr. Taylor made an uneasy smile. "Is something wrong?"

"Not yet." Asa put his hands on his hips. "But it's just a matter of time. You folks are putting our unit at risk, and it's my job to tell you."

"What are you saying?" Mrs. Taylor demanded.

"I'm saying your wagon is too heavy," Asa told them.

"Our wagon is our business," Mrs. Taylor shot back.

"I've told you once and I've told you twice..." Asa shook his finger at the wagon. "You must get rid of that piano before it's too late."

"The good Lord is watching over us," Mrs. Taylor spoke in a superior tone. "There is no need for you to be concerned for our welfare."

Asa looked as if he was about to sputter.

"I disagree with you, Mrs. Taylor." Elizabeth spoke in her firmest tone, almost as if she were addressing one of her children caught in an act of disobedience. "My wagon follows yours, and your trouble could soon become my trouble."

"We are having no trouble." With narrowed eyes, Mrs. Taylor looked over to where her husband was focused on adjusting the harnesses.

"I see your team struggling more and more each day," Elizabeth persisted. "It's unfair and inhumane to make them pull such a load."

"Our team is strong enough. The good Lord made animals to serve man, not the other way around."

Asa exchanged glances with Elizabeth, encouraging her as he went over to speak quietly with Mr. Taylor.

"Again, I disagree with you. I believe God expects us to take good care of our livestock." She pointed to their team. "These mules are being overworked to the point of endangering lives. You may have noticed I've been keeping a safe distance from your wagon while we're on the inclines. It's because I'm afraid you're going to have serious trouble."

"The good Lord has brought us safely thus far, and I have the faith that he will continue to protect us."

"I believe in God's protection just as much as you, Mrs. Taylor." Elizabeth tried to keep the anger building up inside of her in check. "But I also believe that God expects us to use the good sense that he gave us. To ignore wise counsel is both foolish and dangerous."

"Mr. Taylor and I both use all of our good senses to serve our Lord." Mrs. Taylor gave her a disdainful expression. "Sometimes I feel as if we are among a minority in our religious beliefs. But we are used to our solitude. The good book says that the road to heaven is straight and narrow, and only a few will choose to travel it."

Elizabeth knew this had to do with the fact that her family did not attend the Taylors' Sunday church services, but she wasn't going to let this woman bait her with this distraction. "The road to heaven may be narrow, but the road to Oregon is filled with peril for unwise travelers," she warned. "Please listen to us, Mrs. Taylor. Lighten your load before it's too late. Do you want us to take our concerns to Captain Brownlee?"

Mrs. Taylor glared at Elizabeth now. "I'm sure the good captain has other matters to attend to." Now she made what seemed a mocking smile. "And I'm sorry you don't share my strong faith in the power of the good Lord to get us to our destination. But you are still a young woman, and I'm sure that the good Lord will continue tempering you and increasing your faith with maturity."

"This is not about faith or maturity." Elizabeth could see the wagons starting to move up ahead, and she was fresh out of patience and thus raising her voice. "This is about common sense, Mrs. Taylor! And it is not fair for you to put your team and all of us at risk just because you refuse to part with your precious piano!"

"The good Lord gave me my piano in order to worship him. Neither you nor anyone else can force me to leave it behind."

Elizabeth pulled her driving gloves out from where they were tucked in her belt, tugging them on in anger. She pointed a finger at Mrs. Taylor. "The very least you can do is to get out of this wagon on the upgrades and walk," she said loudly. "It won't make up for the weight of the piano, but it might help."

"Oh, ye of little faith." Mrs. Taylor's lips curled into a smug smile.

Elizabeth watched speechlessly as Mr. Taylor climbed onto his wagon with a somewhat grim expression. With her fists tightly clenched, she watched as the clergyman grasped the reins. What had her father said to him—and why had it made no difference? She glanced over her shoulder to see that Asa was storming off toward his own wagon. He looked as frustrated as she felt. She could just imagine what he'd say to her mother.

Elizabeth peered up at Mr. Taylor. "Can't you please talk some sense into your wife?" she pleaded. "Before you injure your team with this overly heavy load?"

He turned now, looking down upon her with surprisingly compassionate brown eyes. "I'm sorry, my dear, but my wife's mind seems to be made up on this matter. Now, if you'll please excuse us..." He gave her a weak smile as he released the wagon brake. "We do not want to keep the rest of the wagons waiting. Do travel safely, Miss Elizabeth."

How could he treat this so lightly? Too angry to respond in a gracious manner, she turned on the heel of her boot and marched back to her own wagon. As she climbed into the seat, untying the reins, she was thankful that her children had already left with Brady and Flax. They planned to walk up ahead, hunting for wild leeks and strawberries and collecting firewood for the evening meal.

"*Dear Lord!*" Elizabeth spoke loudly. "I am so angry I could *spit!*" Then, embarrassed at her unwomanly confession, she asked God to help her to control her unbridled anger toward the Taylors. Perhaps in time she'd be able to forgive them, but right now she was still too vexed. She knew she would be unable to pray for their safety as she'd been doing the past few days. But according to Mrs. Taylor, they didn't need anyone's help or advice—God would take care of everything for them. Maybe God would send a team of angels to carry the Taylors over the North Platte when it was time to cross too. Seeing the Taylors were several wagon lengths ahead of her, Elizabeth released her brake and snapped her reins. Thankfully tomorrow was Sunday, and they would change the wagon order in their unit on Monday…and then someone else could follow the foolish Taylors!

She could hear the rumble of thunder in the distance as the usual afternoon clouds gathered on the western horizon. In a couple of hours, just like clockwork, there would probably be another downpour. Until then, she hoped they would make good time. Her father had told her that the first hour would be on fairly level ground, and then they would have a rather steep climb with some switchbacks alongside the river. But if all went well, by the end of the day they should reach the Red Buttes, where they would camp for the night. And the plan was that their unit should complete their final crossing of the North Platte River by tomorrow afternoon or Monday morning at the latest.

Elizabeth knew that the North Platte was running fast right now due to the rains, but Matthew had assured them that this was normal for this time of year. "Nothing to be worried about," he'd said last night. "Not as long as we do it right." He'd pointed at his new bride. "And no jumping into the river this time."

Jess had simply laughed, but Elizabeth could see a trace of fear in her eyes. And truth be told, river crossings made Elizabeth nervous too. Ever since Jess' frighteningly close call when she was swept down the South Platte River, Elizabeth had insisted that Ruth and Flax were to ride in the back of the wagon when fording even the smallest of streams.

And although Elizabeth did the actual driving, Brady always rode next to her, ready to assist if needed. And always before crossing, a prayer for safe passage was said by her father.

Elizabeth's anger toward the Taylors had mostly evaporated by the time they began to ascend the switchbacks. Now she focused on her own team, patiently urging them forward as she maintained a safe distance from the Taylors. She was determined not to pay much heed to the wagon ahead of her. She obviously could do nothing about it now, and there seemed no point in fretting over it. At least Mrs. Taylor was walking. A small consolation, but it was something. Perhaps Captain Brownlee would talk some sense into them before the river crossing.

With one eye on the gathering clouds and occasional flashes of lightning, and the other eye on the backs of her faithful team, she continued to speak to Bella and Beau as she always did on the roughest parts of the journey. Praising their good work, she used her voice to calm them and offset the rumbles and booms of thunder, which steadily grew louder and closer. She knew that the elegant black Percherons were by nature sensible horses, and as long as they remained calm and steady, the less predictable mules should follow. Not all teams were this dependable, especially in thunderstorms.

Elizabeth was relieved that her children had become somewhat accustomed to these mountain storms now. JT actually enjoyed them. And for her brother's sake, Ruth tried to appear brave. The captain had assured everyone that they were just as safe outside their wagons as hunkered down in back. Perhaps more so. As long as they avoided standing under a lone tree, their chances of being struck by lightning were slim to nil.

Elizabeth's wagon began turning into a switchback. She usually didn't allow herself to look down at the raging river below them. Nor did her team seem too interested. Thankful that the surface of this road was still dry and somewhat stable, she looked ahead in time to see that the Taylors' wagon was just approaching the next switchback.

As usual in these challenging climbs, the Taylors' wagon was moving awkwardly. It lurched and jerked, moving forward a bit and then stopping abruptly. It even rolled backward at times, which meant that

Mr. Taylor wasn't handling the brake correctly and that the team was stressed. Hearing the constant crack of Mr. Taylor's whip, whether it was on the backs of the animals or just over their heads, was unsettling. In her mind's eye she could see the nervous mules jerking and pulling against each other, sweating and stumbling, with their ears pressed flat and the look of fear in their eyes.

Despite her anger at the Taylors, she felt pity for their overworked animals, and with her focus back on her own team, she began to pray. She asked God to help those poor mules to survive their foolish owners' ignorance. Elizabeth had been raised to respect livestock, particularly equines. Certainly she knew animals were not superior to humans, but she took her responsibility of caring for them seriously. And certainly, being a farmer, she also understood that animals were expendable. Cows, sheep, pigs, chickens…all were sources of food and income, and when the time came to butcher, she didn't weep or cringe. However, she did insist it be done humanely.

Elizabeth was distracted from her own team by a woman's loud scream. When she looked up, she could not believe what she was seeing in front of her. The Taylors' wagon was teetering on the outer edge of the switchback with two wheels hanging over the side and crumbling rock falling down the ravine.

"Dear God!" Elizabeth snapped the reins, urging her team forward.

"Help us!" screamed Mrs. Taylor as she lifted her black skirt, running toward the wagon as it slowly tumbled over the edge of the road and disappeared with a loud crash…and then an eerie silence.

"Oh, dear God!" Elizabeth continued pressing her team forward at a steady pace. "Please, help poor Mr. Taylor!"

When she reached a safe stopping place on the road, Elizabeth firmly pushed on the brakes, tied off the reins, and jumped down, running breathlessly to Mrs. Taylor, who was standing on the edge of the precipice, peering down with her hands clasped to her chin and a look of horror in her eyes.

"Oh, *no!*" Elizabeth peered down to the bottom of the gorge to see a jumble of broken wagon and debris spread along the rocky bank of the fast-flowing river.

"*Horace!*" screamed Mrs. Taylor. "Horace, can you hear me? *Answer me!*"

The only sound was the rushing water and the *thump* of footsteps as others in the wagon train ran up to join them.

"What happened?" Matthew demanded breathlessly.

"The Taylors' wagon!" Elizabeth gasped, pointing down to the wreckage. "Mr. Taylor...his wagon...*they fell!*"

"Help him," pleaded Mrs. Taylor. "Please, send someone down to help him. *Hurry!*"

"Take her to your wagon," Matthew instructed Elizabeth.

"Come on," Elizabeth said gently to Mrs. Taylor.

"*No!*" Mrs. Taylor said. "I can't go."

Matthew began shouting orders at the other men now, telling them to get ropes and winches and horses. Suddenly everyone was scrambling.

"Come on," Elizabeth urged her again, this time wrapping her arm around Mrs. Taylor's shoulders and moving her away.

"I can't leave him," Mrs. Taylor muttered.

"Get her out of here," Asa shouted at Elizabeth.

"We need to get out of their way." Now Elizabeth firmly guided her away from the edge of the precipice. "So they can rescue Mr. Taylor."

Mrs. Taylor looked at Elizabeth with frightened eyes. "They *will* rescue him?"

"Of course," Elizabeth said soothingly as she led her to the wagon. "Come with me...we can pray together."

"Yes, yes...we will pray." Mrs. Taylor was shaking now. By the time they reached the wagon, the old woman's face was as white as chalk, and Elizabeth could tell she was close to fainting. Leaning her against the wagon to steady herself, Elizabeth lifted down one of the chairs, helping Mrs. Taylor to sit. Then she got a tin cup and filled it with water. "Here, drink this."

Clearly in shock, Mrs. Taylor said nothing as she slowly sipped the water. Elizabeth could hear the men's voices yelling back and forth as they tried to figure out what to do and how to do it. Matthew sent one of the boys to get Elizabeth's riding horse, Molly. It wasn't long until Elizabeth's mother, worried that something had happened to her daughter, joined them as well. Elizabeth quietly explained to her about what had happened.

"Oh, you poor dear," Clara said to Mrs. Taylor.

Elizabeth pulled down another chair for her mother. "Here, you sit with her. You can both pray while I go find out how they are doing."

"Yes," Mrs. Taylor said eagerly. "Go and see if Horace is all right."

Elizabeth just nodded, but it seemed unlikely that anyone could survive such a fall. Even so, she prayed as she walked over to the crowd of women and children who were watching as their men used ropes and teams.

"Your brother is at the end of that rope," Flo Flanders informed Elizabeth.

"Oh, dear!" Elizabeth didn't like to think of Matthew dangling over the edge of that precipice. But seeing her father and Bert Flanders managing the horses that they were using to lower her brother, she felt a little more confident.

"Matthew is so brave," Mahala said.

"I sent Walter to get the captain," Flo told Elizabeth.

"Good thinking."

"Do you think he survived?" Flo quietly asked her.

Elizabeth just shook her head.

"It's because of Mrs. Taylor and that stupid piano," Mahala said bitterly. "If her husband is dead, it's her own fault."

"Mahala!" Flo frowned at her eldest daughter.

"It's true." Mahala pointed at Elizabeth. "Hannah said she heard you and Asa talking to them earlier. But they wouldn't listen."

"We did encourage them to leave the piano behind," Elizabeth admitted. "Many times. But it's unkind to blame Mrs. Taylor for this...especially considering she has lost everything...perhaps even her husband."

"Even if he survived that fall, which seems unlikely, he'll be severely injured." Flo shook her head. "Too bad they didn't dump that piano when they had the chance."

Belinda and Amelia Bramford joined them now. Mahala filled them in on the accident with descriptive details, but when the girls started to go over to see, Elizabeth stopped them. "We need to stay out of the way of the rescue team."

Just then Captain Brownlee arrived on horseback. First he surveyed the wreckage and the rescue efforts, and then he came over to the women. "Although this is all very unfortunate, just as I've told the men, all those who aren't directly helping with the rescue need to get back to their wagons and continue on over the pass." He pointed to the darkening sky. "That storm will be here soon, and the going doesn't get any easier with a downpour." He turned his horse toward the back of the train, yelling a command for all to hear. "*Wagons ho!*"

"I need to go to my wagon," Elizabeth told them. To her relief, she saw Brady and her children rushing back to find out what happened. Without going into much detail, she filled them in and then instructed the children to hurry. "JT, you go and ride with Jess," she told him. "Tell her that Matthew is helping rescue Mr. Taylor. And Brady, can you drive for my mother while my father helps with the rescue?"

"Sho 'nuff." He nodded eagerly as they hurried back to her wagon, where Elizabeth explained the captain's instructions to her mother.

"Mrs. Taylor can ride with me," she told Clara.

Mrs. Taylor tried to object, stating she didn't want to leave her husband behind, but she was clearly in no condition to remain there.

"Help me get her into the back of the wagon," Elizabeth said to Brady and Ruth and her mother. It wasn't easy, but they eventually got Mrs. Taylor settled on the bed and covered with a quilt with Ruth sitting faithfully by her side. And before long Elizabeth was back to driving her team around the dangerous switchbacks, trying not to look down and praying for the safety of her family and for poor Mr. Taylor. However—and she hoped she was wrong—she had a strong suspicion that Mr. Taylor was already making his own appeals to God in his maker's presence.

Chapter Five

Elizabeth was driving her wagon around the last switchback when the dark clouds broke open and big fat raindrops began to strike the canvas so loudly it sounded as if handfuls of gravel were being pelted down on them. Lightning flashed and thunder crashed, but her team plodded steadfastly along, following the Schneiders' wagon up the trail toward a high meadow. Although the animals' heads were down, it was almost as if they sensed their workday was nearly done. They knew they'd soon be fed and watered and allowed to rest for the night.

"We're almost there," she called back into the confines of the wagon, peeking to see that Mrs. Taylor still appeared to be resting quietly. Ruth, with her doll in her lap, was sitting patiently nearby, ready to play nursemaid if needed. Whether the old woman was merely asleep or actually unconscious due to the shock of her ordeal, Elizabeth was unsure. She was simply grateful that she wasn't giving Ruth any problems.

As she drove she tried to imagine the implications of today's disaster.

Mr. Taylor seemed likely to be deceased. In that case, someone would have to look after Mrs. Taylor. And if by some miracle Mr. Taylor had survived that horrible fall, he would need even more care than his wife—and they would both need food, shelter, and transportation. As sorry as she felt for the Taylors, she also felt fresh anger simmering inside of her. Their foolishness had put everyone in a very difficult position.

Even now, as she pulled on James' old oilskin barn coat and then maneuvered her wagon into the circle that was slowly forming for their unit, she thought of Matthew and her father out there risking their lives in a thunderstorm on a dangerous ravine…and for what? To pull out a dead man's body? To rescue a few food supplies for Mrs. Taylor's benefit? All because a foolish, stubborn woman had refused to relinquish an out-of-tune piano?

"You stay here with Mrs. Taylor," she called to Ruth as she put on the brakes. "I'll see to the team." She climbed down, pulling the oilskin coat more tightly around her as she started to remove the heavy harnesses from the team. It was still raining steadily, but the lightning and thunder had moved on by now. She tried not to feel angry as she cared for her animals. Normally, JT and Brady would be available to help with this chore, but now they were busy helping Jess and Clara… all because of Mrs. Taylor's selfishness.

As she struggled to free the horses from the gear, Elizabeth silently prayed to God, asking him to help her to get over her anger toward Mrs. Taylor. As she led the pair of Percherons over to a line that Jeremiah Bramford was just setting, she tried to remember what Mrs. Taylor was going through. Elizabeth knew what it was like to lose a beloved husband.

"Let me help you with those," Jeremiah offered.

"Thanks," she told him. "But I'm sure you have your hands full too." She had noticed that Will and Hugh remained at the scene of the accident to help as well.

"It's no problem," he assured her as he took her horses, nodding to the other animals that were already secured to the line. "Julius and I worked together."

She smiled at him. "Thank you."

"I've always admired this team." He stroked Bella's damp coat. "They're the most beautiful horses I've ever seen."

"Well, thank you very much. I like them!"

"Dad says you and your family raised horses in Kentucky."

She nodded. "Yes, but mostly we were farmers."

He lowered his voice now. "Do you think Mr. Taylor is dead?"

She sadly shook her head. "I don't know. But I am praying for them both."

"Well, go ahead and get the rest of your team," he told her. "I'll take care of these two."

Fortunately, JT and Brady soon arrived, and Elizabeth learned that JT had ridden with Clara and Brady when it was decided that a wagon should remain behind and Jess volunteered. Elizabeth was glad to have help with the end-of-the-day chores. Whether it was the rain or the aftermath of the accident, everything seemed to take longer than usual, but eventually Elizabeth and her mother had a fire going and supper cooking. Ruth was still playing nursemaid to Mrs. Taylor, who was either sleeping or simply unable to move. Clara took a cup of chamomile tea to her and returned with a worried expression. "Mrs. Taylor seems unwell."

"I would imagine she is very unwell." Elizabeth scooped a cup of rice from the barrel. "She's been through a shocking experience."

"More than just that," Clara said. "She has a very gray look about her. The same sort of coloring Aunt Beatrice had before she passed on last winter."

Elizabeth frowned. "I know there's a doctor in unit three. Should we send JT for him?"

"Perhaps."

After JT left to locate the doctor, Elizabeth felt even more guilty for her ill feelings toward Mrs. Taylor. What if the poor woman was dying? "Maybe we can use some of this gravy to make soup for Mrs. Taylor," she suggested to her mother. "Perhaps mash some rice into it?"

"Yes, that's a good idea."

Elizabeth was just filling a bowl with some buffalo and rice broth when JT returned with Dr. Nash in tow. "I'll take you to her," she told the doctor. "I made her some soup."

"Your son told me that her husband, Mr. Taylor, is most likely dead?"

"We don't know for sure, but I doubt he survived the fall."

"I didn't hear of the accident until we were making camp. I could take a horse back there…to see if I can be of any help."

She paused by the back of her wagon. "Right now, you might be of more help with Mrs. Taylor." She pulled the canvas back. "Ruth, please help Grandma with supper now."

Ruth looked glad to be relieved of her nursemaid duties. Elizabeth and the doctor climbed into the wagon, where she lit a lantern and assured Mrs. Taylor that there had been no news regarding her husband while the doctor began to examine her. He listened to her heart and checked her pulse and a few other things, including asking her some questions, which she answered in a weak, tired voice.

"I suspect you are simply overwrought over today's ordeal," he finally proclaimed. "It's certainly understandable." He turned to Elizabeth. "I would prescribe a good deal of rest and soups and tea like you've made here. As well as…" He lowered his voice. "An occasional dose of spirits to build up her blood."

Elizabeth blinked. "A dose of *spirits*? Where am I to get that?"

"I believe Ruby Morris still has a small supply. I've sent a few others her way." Dr. Nash gave her a sly smile. "Strictly for medicinal purposes, of course."

"Of course."

"Now if you'll excuse me, I'll head back down the trail and see how Mr. Taylor has fared."

"Yes," Mrs. Taylor said weakly. "Please do."

As he climbed out, Elizabeth held the bowl of soup in front of Mrs. Taylor. "And while the doctor is seeing about Mr. Taylor, you can sit up and eat this soup. It'll help to build your strength back up."

Mrs. Taylor reluctantly complied, and with Elizabeth's help and encouragement, she managed to get the full bowl down. "Now I want you to obey the doctor's orders and continue to rest." Elizabeth helped her to lie back down.

"But…Horace…" Mrs. Taylor's looked helplessly up at her.

"As soon as we know something, we will tell you. In the meantime, just rest." Elizabeth took the empty bowl and climbed out of the wagon. Instead of returning to her parents' campsite, she went directly to Ruby's wagon.

"Elizabeth." Ruby smiled to see Elizabeth approaching. "Welcome!"

"How are the Taylors?" Doris asked eagerly. "We heard of their troubles."

Elizabeth was surprised at how compassionate these two women were, especially after the Taylors had practically accused them of running a brothel during the first part of this journey. Mrs. Taylor nearly managed to get them kicked out of the wagon train. Putting that behind her, Elizabeth gave her the latest news, which wasn't much. "My mother was worried that poor Mrs. Taylor might be having heart problems as a result of her shock, but Dr. Nash from unit three just examined her."

"And she is all right?" Doris asked.

"I think so. But he did recommend that she receive a dose of spirits." Elizabeth made an uncomfortable smile. "That's why I'm here."

Ruby laughed loudly. "The doc wants you to give Mrs. Taylor some whiskey?"

"He said it would be good for her blood."

"I don't doubt that. But do you honestly think she'll willingly imbibe?"

Elizabeth frowned. "Probably not."

"She will if you tell her it's just medicine," Doris suggested. "I'll go find a bottle to put some in. What the old gal doesn't know won't hurt her."

"I never liked the Taylors," Ruby admitted as Doris was fetching the whiskey, "but I never wished them no ill. Nothing like this anyway."

"Here you go." Doris handed Elizabeth a tall amber bottle with a cork on top. "Medicine."

"Thank you." Elizabeth slid the bottle into a pocket of her oilskin, and feeling a bit like a bootlegger, she hurried back to her wagon. "I got the medicine Dr. Nash recommended," she told Mrs. Taylor as she opened the bottle and filled the soup spoon with the strong-smelling liquid. "Open wide." Mrs. Taylor complied but then wrinkled her nose at the taste.

"Ugh! That is horrible."

"Never mind. I just hope it will help you to rest," Elizabeth told her.

"Horace?" Mrs. Taylor asked quietly as Elizabeth was leaving.

"No word yet. The men haven't returned."

It was nearly dark when Asa and some of the other men returned on horseback. JT and Brady jumped up to help with the horses. Looking hungry and tired, Asa came into camp looking as if he were carrying the world on his shoulders. "Are you all right, Father?" Elizabeth led him to a chair by the fire, and as she got him a cup of hot coffee, Clara hurried to fill him a plate with food.

"Mr. Taylor is no longer with us," Asa said sadly.

"Oh, dear." Clara wrung her hands. "I was afraid that was the situation. Poor Mrs. Taylor."

"Where is she?" Asa asked.

"In my wagon," Elizabeth supplied. "Ruth is staying with her." She sat down on a chair by her father, waiting for him to continue his story.

He nodded, slowly forking into his food. "It's been a long day. Matthew and Jess are on their way now. They're bringing the body and a few salvaged goods. Will and Jeremiah are riding in front of the wagon with lanterns."

"Oh, my!" Elizabeth shuddered. "That stretch of road is bad enough in daylight. I can't even imagine it by dark."

"At least it's not raining now," Asa assured her. "And you know your brother. He'll be careful. And Jess had the good sense to fix him a hot meal, so he's not driving on an empty stomach."

"Should we tell Mrs. Taylor?" Clara asked timidly.

Asa sighed. "I s'pect we'll have to."

Without speaking, they all looked at one another.

Elizabeth knew her parents were both worn out. "Why don't I tell her," she offered. "Maybe I can offer a token of comfort…after all, I do know what it feels like to lose a husband."

Clara placed her hand on Elizabeth's head. "You are an angel, child."

"You two get some good rest tonight," she told them.

"What about you?" Clara asked. "Do you plan to keep Mrs. Taylor with you all night?"

"Where else can she go?"

Asa just shook his head.

"Why don't you send Ruthie over to sleep in our wagon," Clara offered. "That way you'll have more room."

"I'm so tired, I might just throw a bedroll beneath the wagon tonight," Asa told her. "Your mother and Ruthie will have plenty of room." He gave her a weary smile. "Hopefully my snoring won't keep them awake."

"You go see to Mrs. Taylor," Clara told her. "I'll finish cleaning up here. You'll have your work cut out for you in your wagon."

Elizabeth knew that was true. She sighed as she stood, pausing to plant a kiss on her father's and then her mother's cheeks, bidding them each good night and realizing how thankful she was that they were not the Taylors. Then she picked up her lantern and slowly walked to her wagon, trying to concoct a plan for how she would tell Mrs. Taylor this most unfortunate news. But she truly believed that deep down, Mrs. Taylor must already know. One glance at the wreckage today had convinced Elizabeth that no one could have survived.

Ruth, already in her nightgown, was reading a book that Jess had given to her by the golden lamplight. Such a sweet scene…until Elizabeth saw Mrs. Taylor watching them with a worried expression. Then the sweetness was gone. "Ruthie, Grandma invited you to sleep in her wagon tonight."

"What about Grandpa?" Ruth asked curiously.

"He's going to make a bed under the wagon." Elizabeth assisted Ruth with her shoes and then helped her down from the tailgate. Then with lantern in hand, she proceeded to walk Ruth over to her grandparents' wagon. On their way, they met JT and Brady. "I might as well tell you all at once," Elizabeth said quietly. "Mr. Taylor has passed on."

They expressed their sorrows, and then Elizabeth explained that she had yet to tell Mrs. Taylor. "This will be very hard on her, and we'll all need to do what we can to be helpful and understanding."

Finally, with everyone settled for the night, Elizabeth climbed back into her wagon. The irony that she was sharing her bed with the same woman she'd been enraged at earlier today did not escape her. And although she felt guilty for her anger, she was more concerned with how Mrs. Taylor was going to receive this sad news. For a moment, she almost thought that Mrs. Taylor was sleeping. But then she opened her eyes, staring at Elizabeth with such a deep and lonely longing that Elizabeth felt tears gathering in her own eyes. Mr. Taylor was probably this woman's only real family...and now he was gone.

"Mrs. Taylor," Elizabeth began slowly, "the men have returned. Unfortunately they did not return with good news."

"Horace?" Her voice broke.

Elizabeth nodded somberly. "He has passed on."

Mrs. Taylor tightly closed her eyes, her face contorted into a twisted mass of grief and pain. Then she rolled onto her side, facing away from Elizabeth, and curling up like a small child, she let out a long, low guttural sound—like a wounded animal. Elizabeth shuddered at the haunting sound. After a brief silence, Elizabeth was preparing to say something of comfort when Mrs. Taylor began to loudly sob. She continued like this for some time, sounding as if she might never stop.

Everything in Elizabeth wanted to run...to escape the unhappy confines of this crowded wagon, a spot that had been her family's refuge these past few months. She longed for a place of peace and quiet, a reprieve from the tortured sounds of this poor woman's heartache. At the very least, although it was discouraged, she was tempted to go outside and take an evening stroll. Instead, she moved the kerosene lamp closer to her and reached for her Bible, opening the old book to the place where she used a faded hair ribbon as a bookmark. She knew the twenty-third psalm by heart, but at the moment she felt the need to have something solid in her hands...and so she read.

The LORD is my shepherd; I shall not want.
He maketh me to lie down in green pastures:

he leadeth me beside the still waters.
He restoreth my soul:
he leadeth me in the paths of righteousness for his name's sake.
Yea, though I walk through the valley of the shadow of death,
I will fear no evil: for thou art with me;
thy rod and thy staff they comfort me.
Thou preparest a table before me in the presence of mine enemies:
thou anointest my head with oil; my cup runneth over.
Surely goodness and mercy shall follow me all the days of my life:
and I will dwell in the house of the LORD for ever.

Chapter Six

The next morning Captain Brownlee delayed the wagon train's departure for an hour to attend to the funeral and burial of Horace Taylor. At Mrs. Taylor's request, the captain was chosen to perform the solemn ceremony. Elizabeth felt dismayed that her father hadn't been invited to provide this service, because she knew his words would have provided more hope and spiritual encouragement than the captain's. However, the captain had clearly done this before…probably many times.

"Ashes to ashes and dust to dust," the captain proclaimed as he dropped a handful of dirt onto the faded patchwork quilt that had been salvaged from the wreckage of the Taylors' wagon and was now Mr. Taylor's shroud. The dirt landed in a dull thud, and the captain turned and walked away. Naturally there had been no time to make a casket, although Elizabeth had overheard one of the young people suggesting that someone should have salvaged the piano and remodeled it into a coffin. Unkind words perhaps, but the irony was inescapable.

"And now we will sing Horace's favorite hymn," Mrs. Taylor declared in a shaky voice. "If you will all join me in 'A Mighty Fortress Is Our God.'"

Elizabeth had offered her family's assistance with some musical accompaniment for the service, but Mrs. Taylor soundly rejected this idea. Now as the old woman bravely led the group in song, many of the voices stumbled over the melody as well as the words, but Mrs. Taylor's voice boomed out loud and clear, if not slightly off-key. By the time they came to the last verse only a few continued singing—with Mrs. Taylor still leading, still off-key. Elizabeth sang quietly along with her, but she nearly stopped singing as the appropriateness of the last few lines hit her. She turned to see Mrs. Taylor, still singing with eyes closed and two streams of tears sliding down her weathered cheeks.

> Let goods and kindred go,
> This mortal life also.
> The body they may kill,
> God's truth abideth still.
> His kingdom is forever.

Although there was great relief to have reached Red Buttes, many travelers were sorely disappointed when they learned that the North Platte River was so swollen with rain that their crossing would be delayed. However, Elizabeth and her family decided to make use of this unexpected break. Because of the muddy water of the North Platte, it was impossible to wash clothes in the river and get them clean. As a result, they were forced to carry buckets of water back to camp. They let the water sit until the silt settled to the bottom, and then they scooped water off the top to pour into the washtubs. This made doing laundry a challenge, but Clara, Elizabeth, Jess, and Ruth were determined to get it done, and working together made the task more enjoyable.

They took turns scrubbing and rinsing and finally hanging the clothes to dry in the morning sun, but when the afternoon rain came they scurried to move the nearly dry clothes into Asa's large tent to continue drying. The mixed blessing of the rain was that they were able to use their tarp awnings to collect drinking water that tasted much better than the river water. Besides, Clara had heard rumors of cholera on this river. She insisted on boiling any water they used for cooking or dishwashing.

During this waiting period, the men tended to mechanical repairs and wagon maintenance. Matthew insisted on applying fresh coats of tar to the undersides of the wagons. After all the rough roads, he wanted to ensure they were still watertight. And Asa hired Bert Flanders to replace some horseshoes and do a few other blacksmithing chores to strengthen the wagons and gear for the second half of their journey. In exchange for Bert's labor, Asa and Clara shared food supplies, which the Flanders were always grateful to receive.

During the days following her husband's demise, Mrs. Taylor kept to herself, saying very little to anyone. Despite Clara and Elizabeth's numerous attempts to draw her out, inviting her to take walks or to join them for family mealtimes, Mrs. Taylor insisted on staying holed up in Elizabeth's wagon. The bedding even began to smell as stale as the old woman, and Elizabeth felt more trapped than ever.

"What am I going to do with her?" Elizabeth quietly asked her mother on her fourth day of hosting Mrs. Taylor. The children had gone exploring with Asa, leaving the two women to wash up after their midday meal.

"You mean your guest?" Clara absently dried a wooden bowl.

Elizabeth added more hot water to the washtub. "I don't want to complain, and I do feel great pity for her, but I don't understand why she's become my personal responsibility."

Clara reached for a dripping plate. "Because no one else wants her?"

"Yes, I know…but…" Elizabeth glanced over to her wagon, which no longer felt like her wagon, and sighed.

"I know it isn't fair for you to be saddled with her for the duration of the trip," Clara stated. "However, it seems unkind to start moving the poor woman around against her will. She already feels lost and displaced. I can't even imagine what that would be like. No family. No friends. Hardly any possessions for that matter."

"I know...I've considered all that."

"And you've heard me ask her again and again. I've encouraged her to stay with us in our wagon, but she's worried about displacing Asa."

"She doesn't realize Father is already somewhat displaced by Ruth sleeping in your wagon."

"Asa doesn't really mind so much. Matthew is letting him use his old hammock."

Elizabeth scrubbed a scorched pot with vexed vigor. She didn't want to say the question that was really on her mind—was she going to be stuck with Mrs. Taylor for the duration of the trip?

"Your father and I discussed this topic this morning. He suggested that the wagons with the least occupants should help out. That would be us, the McIntires, and Ruby and Doris."

Elizabeth set the pot down with a clang. "I can just imagine Mrs. Taylor's response to sharing a wagon with Ruby and Doris."

Clara chuckled. "It might prove interesting."

"And the sweet McIntires. They barely have enough food as it is. And poor Fiona is still getting over losing her baby. I'd hate to foist Mrs. Taylor on them."

"So what are we to do?" Clara wiped her hands on her apron.

"Just what we're doing now." Elizabeth shrugged. "Maybe I just needed to let off some steam."

Clara slipped an arm around Elizabeth's shoulders. "I don't know that it makes any difference, but your father and I are very proud of how you're handling this, Lizzie. Asa was just saying how this trip has shown him what fine children we have raised. The hardships seem to bring out the very best in both you and Matthew. We couldn't be prouder."

Elizabeth hugged her mother back. "So I guess we'll just keep doing what the good book says then."

"That would be...?"

"Live one day at a time. Like Jesus said, tomorrow has enough worries to take care of itself. No use fretting over it today."

"How true."

"Speaking of the future, I wonder when we'll be able to cross the river."

"You must have been tending to Mrs. Taylor...your father announced that Captain Brownlee told the councilmen that if we have two days in a row with no rain, we will probably attempt it."

"It didn't rain yesterday." Elizabeth peered up at the clear blue sky. "And I don't see any thunderclouds today."

"Perhaps tomorrow." Clara hung the damp dishtowel on a nail. "I must admit it's been an unexpected luxury to have this break and to catch up on laundry and things. But already I'm itching to travel."

Elizabeth smiled. "It's funny, isn't it? How we've all gotten so accustomed to being on the road. What will we do when we reach our last stop in Oregon?"

"Get down on our knees and kiss the ground?"

Elizabeth threw back her head and laughed at the image of her mother kissing the ground.

"Sounds like someone is happy."

They both turned to see Will Bramford and his two daughters approaching. They greeted them and were surprised to see that the girls wanted to share some wild strawberries with Mrs. Taylor. "We thought it might help to cheer her up," Belinda said.

"What a lovely idea," Clara told her.

"She's in my wagon. Go ahead and take them to her," Elizabeth encouraged them, lowering her voice. "She's been a bit reclusive, but she might enjoy the company of you sweet young girls."

Belinda and Amelia exchanged looks as if they were uncertain.

"Go on," their father urged them. "Take your gift to Mrs. Taylor."

As the giggling girls approached Elizabeth's wagon, Clara excused herself to her own wagon, leaving Will and Elizabeth standing there.

"It must not be easy having Mrs. Taylor in your care," Will began carefully. "How are you holding up?"

She untied her apron, hanging it up to dry. "I'm all right."

"Have you spoken to your father about the legal issues facing Brady in Oregon?"

"I mentioned it to him." She unrolled her sleeves, adjusted her skirt, and pushed the stray hairs from her face. She tried not to imagine her mother, who was probably listening attentively on the other side of the canvas.

Will gave her a sympathetic smile. "You look weary, Elizabeth."

She frowned, unsure of how to respond to that.

"A pretty sort of weary," he added cheerfully.

Now she felt her cheeks blushing, and tried to think of someplace to excuse herself to, but certainly not to her own wagon.

"I know of a beautiful spot by the river," he said suddenly. "Quiet and serene…with wildflowers abounding. In fact, that's where the girls found the strawberries yesterday. Would you like to take a walk there with me?"

The idea of a place like that was very enticing…and yet…she wondered what Eli would think if he saw her with Will. And then she wondered why she wondered that. What difference should it make? Besides, she still had some legal questions concerning Brady for him. Why not?

"Come with me, Elizabeth. I know you'd enjoy it." He gave her a wide smile. "I've seen you and your family toiling so hard while others are enjoying a short holiday. I think you deserve some time off as well."

She glanced over at where the girls were still standing by the tailgate of her wagon. Perhaps they had managed to engage Mrs. Taylor. And even if they hadn't, she had no intention of spending such a glorious day cooped up with her. With resolution, she reached for her prairie bonnet.

"I do believe I will take you up on that offer." Elizabeth called out to her mother now. "I'm going to walk down to the river with Mr. Bramford, Mother."

"Have a lovely time, dear," Clara called back.

Elizabeth did her best to make small talk with Will as they walked toward the river. At the same time, she tried to suppress the nagging concerns over what Eli or anyone else might think to see her out like this, alone in the company of a man. But being part of a wagon train seemed to break a lot of conventional rules. And after all, hadn't her own mother sounded pleased to send her on her way? Besides, she reminded herself, Eli hadn't been around to see her in days. In some ways she felt as if he were purposely ignoring her.

"Excuse me?"

She turned to see Will looking curiously at her.

"What?" She paused, trying to figure out what she had missed.

"You seem to be lost in your own thoughts."

"Oh…" Her hand went to her mouth. "I'm sorry. Did you say something that I completely missed?"

He chuckled. "I know that we legal types have been known to put our listeners to sleep sometimes. At least that's what my children say. But I must say it doesn't usually happen while walking."

"My apologies." She focused her attention on tying her loose bonnet strings.

"You seem to have a lot on your mind, Elizabeth."

She nodded. "I suppose I do." Now to distract him from guessing what she'd really been daydreaming about, she brought up the subject of Mrs. Taylor, briefly explaining her dilemma. "It's not that I would throw the poor woman out," she said finally. "It's just that I was unprepared for such a burden." She sighed. "I have my children to think of, and then there's Brady with this unfortunate legal news. And of course, I must stay focused on all that pertains to having a successful journey to Oregon."

"You certainly have more than enough to occupy your thoughts."

"I know we're not supposed to fret about tomorrow…"

"According to whom?"

"The Bible, of course."

"Oh, yes, of course."

"But it's hard not to want to figure out a few things in advance." She glanced at him, hoping for some wise counsel. "For instance, how long am I supposed to care for Mrs. Taylor? Should I encourage her to depart the wagon train at the next post? Will my family need to pay for her passage back to the East?"

He nodded, rubbing his chin as if taking this all in. "Good questions, all of them. First of all, I must ask why you are caring for Mrs. Taylor in the first place. She's a grown woman. She chose to come on this journey. She stubbornly refused to part with her piano, which is greatly responsible for her husband's untimely death. But none of that is your fault."

She let out a long sigh of relief. "Yes, that's how I feel too."

"It was kind of you to take her in. But I do not see why you should hold yourself responsible for her indefinitely. Mrs. Taylor has shown herself to be a strong woman. If she plans to survive in the West, she will need to pull herself up and take charge of her own circumstances."

"I agree. But at the same time, I realize that she is a widow who is still grieving the loss of her husband."

"You and I both have some understanding of grief, Elizabeth. But I have found that the tighter one holds onto one's grief, the longer it takes to get beyond it."

She nodded, considering this. "Yes, but everyone is different when it comes to grieving. I've known those who remarry within six months of losing a spouse. Yet I only gave up wearing my widow's weeds last winter—after three and a half years of being bereaved."

"I suppose those who love deeply also grieve deeply."

She wanted to ask how it had been for him, but that felt too personal. And it might give him the wrong impression of her interest.

"However, in the case of Mrs. Taylor…due to the circumstances of being halfway to Oregon, she lacks the luxury of being able to grieve at her own leisure." He paused at the edge of a stream, offering her his hand as they balanced on the rocks to pass over it.

"This truly is beautiful out here," she told him as she gazed out to the small green meadow they were approaching. As usual in these parts, there was an abundance of mosquitoes. She swatted them away as they walked. Fortunately they thinned out some when they reached the muddy river. "Oh, my. Do you think we'll really be able to cross that tomorrow?"

"I hope so." He pointed to a smooth large rock that jutted out over the fast-flowing water. "That's my favorite place to sit and think." He jumped onto it and then, for the second time, extended his hand, pulling her up to the top of the boulder.

Soon they were both settled on the rock, and once again she began to feel uncomfortable. Had this been a mistake? Instead of dwelling on this, she returned to the safe subject of Mrs. Taylor. "So what would you recommend I do?" she asked. "In regard to Mrs. Taylor."

"In my opinion, you've already proved yourself a good friend and neighbor by taking her in. However, I do not see that you need to continue feeling as if you must care for her."

"Should I throw her out?" Elizabeth tossed him a sideways glance.

He chuckled. "Oh, I'm certain you won't do that."

"What then?"

"Discuss with her what her plans for the future are."

"I've attempted to do this, but she simply shuts down. Or else she turns away. And sometimes she cries." Elizabeth bit her lip. "It's very frustrating."

"Perhaps someone else should speak to her."

She nodded eagerly. "I agree. But both of my parents have tried."

"Perhaps Mrs. Taylor needs some legal counsel."

She looked hopefully at him. "Would you be willing to speak with her?"

"For your sake, I would."

She looked down at her hands in her lap. As much as she appreciated his help, she didn't want him to intervene with Mrs. Taylor just because of her.

"I'm sorry," he said quickly. "That wasn't fair. I will be glad to speak to Mrs. Taylor because it's the right thing to do."

She looked up at him and smiled. "Thank you. I appreciate that."

They continued to talk about Mrs. Taylor's situation, and then they discussed Brady and some reasons that Will thought she might not need to be overly concerned. "Laws regarding slavery and abolition are constantly changing. Especially in the frontier. I suspect that citizens in Oregon Country will be so busy carving out civilization and livelihoods that these racial laws will not be of utmost concern. Not for a while anyway."

"Really?" she felt hopeful.

He nodded. "Perhaps I was amiss to bring it up with you at all."

"No, I'm glad you did. I don't believe that ignorance is bliss."

"Where ignorance is bliss, 'tis folly to be wise."

"Thomas Gray," she supplied.

His brown eyes lit up. "You know that poem?"

"I remember it. It always seemed a sad one to me."

He nodded. "It seems like a young person's sort of poem. I had to memorize it as a lad."

"Do you still know it?"

"Only the last few lines."

"Say them," she challenged.

He laughed uncomfortably as he looked up at the sky. "Let me see..." And then in a deep orator's tone, he began to recite.

> To each his sufferings: all are men,
> Condemned alike to groan;
> The tender for another's pain,
> The unfeeling for his own.
> Yet ah! why should they know their fate?
> Since sorrow never comes too late,
> And happiness too swiftly flies.
> Thought would destroy their paradise.
> No more; where ignorance is bliss,
> 'Tis folly to be wise.

Despite the warm sun overhead, she felt gooseflesh on her arms. "I haven't heard that poem in years...I'm astonished at the meaning of it now."

"In some ways it seems to typify your life at the moment...don't you think?"

She simply nodded. "The part about feeling another's pain..."

"And how sorrow never shows up late...and happiness too swiftly flies."

"But you don't agree with Gray, do you?" she asked. "Certainly, you wouldn't trade wisdom for bliss?"

He rubbed his chin in a thoughtful way. "Sometimes I would."

She was surprised by this and didn't try to conceal it.

"But most of the time I wouldn't," he assured her. "The truth is I believe that happiness and wisdom can be compatible. At least I hope so." He removed his hat, running his fingers through his dark wavy hair with a faraway look in his eyes. "That's why I decided to go west. I hoped I might eventually find happiness…and I hoped to use my wisdom along the way."

"And so far?"

He looked at her, and his serious expression was absorbed by a smile. "So far…so good."

Chapter Seven

That same evening, after supper, Will came to Elizabeth's camp and paid a visit to Mrs. Taylor in the back of Elizabeth's wagon. He stayed for the best part of an hour. Elizabeth and Ruth were just finishing up the supper dishes when he finally emerged.

"How did that go?" she asked as she set a cast-iron skillet on the fire to dry.

"I'm not sure." He glanced over his shoulder back toward the wagon. "She is a stubborn woman."

Elizabeth couldn't help but chuckle over this. "But sometimes stubbornness is a good quality."

"Sometimes." His brow creased as he patted Ruth on the head. But Elizabeth sensed this wasn't a conversation he wanted to have in the presence of children.

"Thanks for your help," she told Ruth. "Now you can go over to Uncle Matthew's wagon and listen to the music if you like."

"That sounds like a good idea," Will said. "I'll bet that's where my children are headed by now. We certainly have some fine musicians in our unit."

After Ruth left, Will quietly told Elizabeth a bit about the conversation. "She feels like she's reached the end of her rope," he explained.

"What?"

"She wants to die."

"Oh…" Elizabeth wasn't very surprised.

"I got her to admit that she really has no one to go back to in the East."

"I was worried that might be her situation."

"And now she is afraid that she will be a burden to the mission in Fort Walla Walla."

"I can understand that." In fact, Elizabeth couldn't help but think Mrs. Taylor was a burden right now. But she wouldn't voice this aloud.

"I tried to make it clear to her that she is responsible for herself and her own well-being. And I told her it was impolite for her to continue taking unfair advantage of your hospitality. I told her that you have enough on your hands with your children and this trip without having an invalid to care for as well."

"You said that?" Elizabeth's hand flew to her mouth.

"I did." He smiled. "Perhaps a bit more gently. But I wanted her to grasp the gravity of her actions…or rather, her inactions."

"You actually called her an invalid?"

"Not in those words. But I told her that she needs to get up tomorrow. She needs to do some walking. She needs to help you and your mother with the chores. I told her that if she doesn't do these things, she will most assuredly turn into an invalid. And you do not need an invalid on your hands."

"No." She grimly shook her head. "Not at all."

"So it will be up to you, Elizabeth. Tomorrow morning, you must hold her accountable to these things. See that she gets up and gets dressed and gets outside. You will do her no favors by continuing to cater to her this way."

"You're right." She nodded eagerly. "Thank you so much!"

"And I made her tell me her age."

"Really?"

"I told her it would help me to assist her in the plan for her future."

"How old is she?" Elizabeth whispered.

He chuckled. "How old do you think she is?"

"I'm not really sure. I've assumed she's about ten years older than my mother. I'd say at least sixty. Maybe even sixty-five."

He laughed. "She is forty-six."

Elizabeth blinked. "Are you jesting?"

"Not at all. She told me her date of birth."

"She's younger than my mother." Elizabeth couldn't help but compare the two women. Her mother was so active and helpful and engaged. So unlike Mrs. Taylor.

"And I hate to admit it, but she's not that much older than I am. I even pointed that out to her."

Elizabeth just shook her head. "Well, I never…"

"To my way of thinking, the old girl should still have a lot of life left in her."

"There you are, Dad!" Belinda came dancing into their campground. "We need more dancers for a reel." Now she grabbed Elizabeth's hand as well. "Come on, you two, this is our last night on this side of the river. We need to celebrate."

And celebrate they did. Late into the night. Most of the people from their unit had gathered to enjoy the warm summer evening. Out of respect for Mrs. Taylor's bereavement, they had relocated their evening sing-alongs from Asa's camp to Matthew's several days ago. And the past few nights they had tried to keep the noise level down. But Elizabeth felt certain Mrs. Taylor could hear their music and laughter tonight. And perhaps that was a good thing. Even if the sound of merrymaking enraged the pious old woman, who wasn't that old, it might also help to shake her out of her mire of gloom and despair.

Elizabeth danced with her father and Will and young Jeremiah and several others. But the whole while, she found herself glancing over her shoulder, searching along the sidelines, hoping to spy a man in fringed buckskins. Often Eli had been lured to their campsite by the music. But he was nowhere to be seen tonight. Even so, Elizabeth was enjoying herself, and each time her thoughts strayed to Eli, she reprimanded herself.

"May I have your attention, folks," Asa waved his hands, quieting the musicians. "As enjoyable as this is, I must insist this is the last dance. We all have a big day ahead of us tomorrow, and it's getting late. We all need a good night's rest."

Although the young people complained, Elizabeth knew they would comply, and for the last dance, the musicians played another reel. She wasn't too surprised when Will asked her to dance. Still grateful for his help with Mrs. Taylor, and realizing how much she valued his friendship, she gladly agreed. They had just begun to dance when she noticed some of the young people pointing in their direction and laughing.

Elizabeth looked uneasily at Will, wondering why they had suddenly become such a spectacle. But then she realized that Will was staring over her shoulder with a shocked expression. She stopped dancing and turned in time to see a woman in a rumpled white nightgown with long gray hair flying behind her dancing wildly toward them with a crazed look in her eyes.

"*What on earth!*" Elizabeth gasped, unable to believe her eyes. "*Mrs. Taylor?*"

"It most certainly is." Will looked on with amusement.

The musicians, oblivious to this new development, continued to play, and Mrs. Taylor continued to dance in a clumsy, uncontrolled sort of way.

"What do you think is in that bottle?" Will asked her.

Elizabeth's hand flew to her mouth when she spied the amber bottle in Mrs. Taylor's hand. Ruby's whiskey! Was it possible Mrs. Taylor had drunk all of it? Letting go of Will's hand, she rushed over to Mrs. Taylor, trying to put an arm around her, hoping to lead her back to the wagon.

"Lemme go," Mrs. Taylor yelled at her as she pulled away. "I wanna dance with the rest of the heathens!"

"Let her dance!" one of the youths called.

"Yes, let her dance!" yelled another.

Elizabeth looked over at Will, hoping for help.

"Come on, Mrs. Taylor," he began. "Let's get you back to—"

"Dance with me!" she yelled. Then she tipped the bottle to her lips and, seeing that it was empty, gave it a toss that narrowly missed Asa's head. By now the music had stopped, and everyone was staring at Mrs. Taylor as she held onto Will's hand, demanding to dance with him.

"Strike up the band," he called out. "Mrs. Taylor wants to dance."

Matthew and the others couldn't help laughing but once again began to play.

"What has gotten into her?" Asa asked as he and Clara came over to join Elizabeth.

"Ruby's whiskey," she quietly confessed.

"*What?*" Asa looked truly shocked.

"The doctor recommended it as medicine on the day Mr. Taylor died. But she hated the taste of it so much, I couldn't get her to take it again. She must have found the bottle tonight."

"Goodness! Was the bottle full?" Clara asked with concern.

Elizabeth just nodded. "Do you think it will hurt her?"

"Well, it doesn't look like she's hurting right now," Asa chuckled.

"But if she drank all of it, Father, could it hurt her?"

He glanced over at the discarded bottle. "I don't think so. However I suspect she will be feeling the effects in the morning."

Elizabeth watched in disbelief and horror as Mrs. Taylor continued to dance all over the place, dragging poor Will along with her. The young people continued trying to do the reel but eventually gave up and simply watched, giggling among themselves.

"Mercy me!" Clara put a hand on her cheek. "I never would have believed this if I hadn't seen it for myself. Mrs. Taylor…drunk as a skunk."

"Since the old girl has a taste for moonshine, maybe we can convince her to travel with Ruby and Doris after all." Asa winked at Elizabeth.

"Oh, Asa!" Clara just shook her head.

"I'm only jesting." His eyes searched the crowd of onlookers. "I wonder what became of Ruby and Doris."

"I believe they turned in," Clara told him. "Which is what we should all be doing."

"What I want to know is how much more of that moonshine Ruby is carrying." He frowned. "I'll talk to her in the morning."

All Elizabeth wanted to know was how she was going to get this drunken old woman to settle down enough to stop dancing and go to bed. Thankfully as the song ended, Mrs. Taylor appeared to be running out of steam. And with the help of Will and Hugh and their sons, they all managed to get Mrs. Taylor back to Elizabeth's wagon. The old woman's head had barely touched the pillow before she fell deeply to sleep, where to Elizabeth's dismay she snored loudly for most of the night.

Poor Mrs. Taylor had a bear of a headache in the morning. But Elizabeth showed her little mercy as she reminded her of their expectations for the day. "You must get yourself dressed and outside for a little walk, and then you can have some coffee," she told her.

They didn't see Mrs. Taylor until after breakfast was finished, and when Clara offered her some coffee, Mrs. Taylor held up a limp hand and slowly shook her head.

"Here." Elizabeth handed Mrs. Taylor her washrag. "You can help my mother and Ruth finish up these dishes and pack up the kitchen gear. I have plenty of chores at my own camp to attend to now." She turned to Ruth. "You stay here and keep helping Grandma. There's much to do to get ready for the crossing."

"Maybe Ruth would like to ride with us," Clara offered.

Elizabeth glanced at Mrs. Taylor. "Unless Mrs. Taylor would care to."

"I am fine to remain with you, Elizabeth," Mrs. Taylor muttered as she washed a plate.

"All right then. Ruth, you ride with Grandma and Grandpa." Elizabeth was relieved that Mrs. Taylor was cooperating with them this morning. She didn't know how much Mrs. Taylor remembered from the previous night, but Elizabeth felt she should be made aware of her behavior. Perhaps it might even motivate the old woman to set aside her pride and judgment and begin interacting with her fellow travelers.

Elizabeth glanced at her mother. "I'm sure you and Ruth can fill Mrs. Taylor in on the *activities* last night." She tried not to smirk. "I think she might find it enlightening."

Ruth giggled and Clara just shook her head.

"Wha—what happened?" Mrs. Taylor asked in a shaky voice.

"Well, it's bit of a long story," Clara began.

"A funny story," Ruth added with a twinkle in her eyes.

Elizabeth couldn't help but laugh as she walked over to her wagon. The image of Mrs. Taylor dancing in her nightgown would probably provide her with chuckles for years to come. She knew that her mother's version of Mrs. Taylor's embarrassing debacle would be told gently. And she could count on Ruth to be polite about it as well.

It was a relief to be able to move about in the back of her wagon without Mrs. Taylor's imposing presence. She aired the bedding in the sunshine while she tended to organizing and packing and securing—readying her wagon for fording the river. It felt good to know they would be moving again and getting closer to their goal. The break had been somewhat welcome, but she knew that time was critical. They were more than halfway there, but the easy part of the journey was behind them. According to her father, the worst was yet to come.

"Getting ready for today's crossing?"

She paused from shaking dust out of a blanket and smiled at her brother. "I'm working on it."

"I just told JT and Brady to start getting your team ready. Eli just stopped by to tell Pa we'll be the third unit crossing today, and the first unit is already halfway through."

"So it's going well?"

"So far. The river is still pretty high, but Eli said that's in our favor. He said the key is to keep your team moving. Don't stop, or you risk getting your wagon wheels stuck in the silt."

She nodded as she folded the blanket. "How is Eli? I don't think I've seen him for more than a week or so."

Matthew eyed her curiously. "Does that mean you've been missing him?" His teasing tone reminded her of their childhood days.

"No." She reached for another blanket. "I was simply curious."

"Well, it seems he's been scouting along the river, trying to find a better place for us to cross in case the rains didn't let up. He also did some Indian scouting. And some hunting. Gave Ma another good buffalo roast." He smacked his lips. "Supper will be good tonight."

She gave the blanket a shake. "That's nice."

"Do you want me to tell Eli anything for you?" Again with the mocking tone.

"No thank you, Matthew." She gave him a stiff smile and he just chuckled.

"Happy crossing, sis."

"You too, Mattie." She smirked at him. "Don't be letting your bride fall out today."

His grin faded some. "If need be, I'll tie her into the seat next to me."

Now Elizabeth laughed. "I have a feeling Jess would have something to say about *that*." Their sparring was cut short by JT and Brady bringing the team over to hitch, and Elizabeth had to scurry to finish up her chores.

"Grandpa said I can ride Molly and help get the livestock across the river," JT informed her.

Elizabeth frowned. "He did, did he?"

"Please, Ma. I know I can do it."

She took in a slow breath. "JT, I'm sure you *can* do it." She glanced at Brady, who seemed a bit uncertain too. "But I would prefer to have Brady handle the livestock today. He will ride Molly."

"Yes'm." Brady nodded with a relieved expression.

"But, Ma—"

"I need you to help me drive the wagon, JT. Uncle Matthew said it has to be done just right. I need a good driver at my side."

JT brightened.

"I best go see to the animals," Brady said. "Your Pa wants them to get across ahead of the wagons."

"Yes." She smiled at him. "Thank you."

Elizabeth did a quick check of her team and then asked JT to go and fetch Mrs. Taylor. "We need to load up and be ready to go."

"Does she still have to ride with us?" he complained.

"*JT.*" She gave him a warning look.

"I know, I know. She's a poor widow and we should be kind to her…" He wrinkled his nose. "But she smells funny."

Elizabeth pulled off his felt hat and ruffled his hair. "JT! Even if that's true, I don't want to hear you saying anything disrespectful like that about your elders."

"Sorry, Ma." He looked down at his feet.

"And I don't want you to say anything unkind about her…uh, her little escapade last night."

"Escapade?" His brow creased.

"It means adventure…a jaunt…an exciting incident."

He grinned. "*Mrs. Taylor's escapade.* I might write about that in my journal tonight."

She winked at him. "You won't be the only one."

Soon they were loaded and moving toward the river. To Elizabeth's relief, Mrs. Taylor chose to ride in the back of the wagon. Elizabeth suspected she wanted to lie down, probably still recovering from last night's antics. Because Father had rearranged the lineup, Elizabeth's wagon was now following the Flanders'. Theirs was the lead wagon for their unit. She tried not to feel worried for their welfare, but it concerned her that with Bert and Flo and their five children, the wagon was heavy. And despite Bert's attempts to strengthen the wagon, it wasn't the same caliber as the wagons Elizabeth's family had brought from Kentucky. She said a silent prayer for their safe crossing.

The river looked just as muddy as it had all week. However, it didn't seem to be moving as rapidly today, and it had definitely receded some. The wagon crossing right now, the last one in unit four, didn't seem to be having any trouble. But then it was a big sturdy-looking wagon with a strong team of oxen pulling. Even so, it was hard to watch. She knew that in the blink of an eye, something could go wrong.

Elizabeth tugged her driving gloves on tighter, redirecting her attention to a group of women and children, members of their wagon train who were drawing water from the river. She grimaced to see one of the mothers dipping a drinking cup into her bucket and allowing her little ones to drink that dirty water. Hopefully Elizabeth's mother had been wrong about the rumors of cholera on this river. Just in case, she said a silent prayer for those children and the other families, praying that God would keep them healthy.

Now it was time for the Flanders to cross. "Let's pray for them," she said to JT. And together they said a quick prayer for the Flanders' safety. Fortunately, Bert must have heard Eli's advice and taken it seriously because he drove his team fast and hard, and they made it through without incident.

"Time for us to go." JT pointed to Captain Brownlee, who was waving his hat at them—the sign to go.

She released the brake and snapped the reins. "Gid-up!" she shouted, snapping the reins again. "Let's go! *Gid-up!*"

"Gid-up!" JT yelled, slapping his thigh. "Go!"

The team moved with speed and dependability just as she expected them to. Even so, both she and JT continued to shout encouragement—as if the sounds of their voices alone were getting this wagon across the muddy waters. She glanced at JT. "I'm glad you're paying attention. Next time you might be driving."

"Gid-up!" he yelled loudly, nodding.

After what seemed like an hour but was probably mere minutes, their wagon began to emerge from the river, water pouring from the team and the sides of the wagon. "Good job!" Elizabeth called to her animals. "Well done!" Now she handed the reins to JT. "You can drive from here."

Proud to be in charge of the wagon, JT drove as if he'd been doing this for years, catching up to the Flanders and following them down a trail made muddy by the dripping wagons and teams ahead of them. "We're on our way," Elizabeth declared happily.

Chapter Eight

After several uneventful but grueling days of travel, the travelers camped at Horse Creek. "This little old creek might not look like much," Asa told his unit that evening, "but compared to where we'll be traveling for the next three days, you will recall this place as heavenly."

"Some people call this stretch of the trail Devil's Backbone," Matthew added.

Asa nodded grimly. "Thirty miles of alkaline desert. No grazing grass for your livestock. No drinkable water. Nothing but long, hot, dry days."

"It sounds humanly impossible," Lavinia Prescott exclaimed. "How can we survive such a horrible ordeal?"

"Preparation," Asa told her. He'd just returned from a councilmen's meeting with Captain Brownlee. He held up his hand with four fingers splayed. "There are four things ya'll need to do in order to be prepared.

"One—draw as much water as you can today. Fill every bucket and barrel and pickle jar and teapot. You might even soak some blankets

73

and clothing in water too—that's what I plan on doing. And remember your water must be carefully guarded and rationed while we're crossing Devil's Backbone. And even though you'll be thirsty, do not forget that your first priority is to keep your team watered.

"Two—gather as much livestock feed as you think your animals will need for the next three days. As you can see, we have grass growing abundantly round here. Some of it's been cut near our camp, but if you wander out a spell, you'll find plenty more to be had.

"Three—see to your livestock and wagons. Check hooves and hitches and axles and wheels. Oil what needs oiling, fix what needs fixing. The last thing you want is a breakdown out on Devil's Backbone. We can't afford to waste any time out there. Time is water. We run out of water, and we run out of time."

"Four—check your wagon's load. I know, I know...we've been telling you this all along." Asa glanced at Mrs. Taylor. "Some of you listened and got rid of your weighty items. Some of you did not, and it has cost you dearly." He shook a feisty fist in the air.

"Hear me loud and hear me clear. You will be carrying extra weight due to the water, so you must do whatever you can to lighten your load now. Your animals are your only lifeline out here in this forsaken wilderness. If you've got them pulling too heavy a load, especially in a stretch like we're about to encounter, you are risking precious lives—and not just your own. Believe you me, there are plenty of emigrants' gravesites along Devil's Backbone. I don't want anyone in my unit to be joining them."

He paused to look across the crowd of serious faces. "And now I want you all to bow your heads with me while I ask the Lord's blessing on our upcoming travels."

For the rest of the afternoon and into the evening, everyone in their unit made trip after trip hauling water from the creek. "Do you think the creek will run dry?" Ruth asked as she and Elizabeth walked together with more full buckets.

Elizabeth laughed. "I don't think so. Not today anyway."

Back at camp they had supper and then took a quick inventory of their water supply, and Asa seemed pleased. "But we all need to go out and cut more grass," he told them. "By my estimation we have only half of what we need."

Even Mrs. Taylor went out to cut and bundle grass. It was back-breaking work, but they stayed at it until Asa was satisfied. "Good work," he told them. "In the morning, before we hitch up, the boys and I will walk all the livestock down to the creek for one last good drink."

Tired from a long day plus all the extra work, Elizabeth was glad to call it a night. She wasn't even too concerned that she was still sharing her bed with Mrs. Taylor. And she was determined to say something encouraging to her before she slipped off into slumber. "I appreciate how much you've been helping out," Elizabeth said carefully as she brushed out her hair as she did every night. "It's good to see you out there pulling your weight with the rest of us."

Mrs. Taylor looked up from reading her Bible, which was her nightly routine. "*Pulling my weight?*" Her voice wavered.

Elizabeth set her hairbrush aside, trying to determine what she'd said wrong. "It's good that you're working with the rest of us."

"You believe it's my fault, don't you?" Mrs. Taylor said quietly.

"What do you mean?" Elizabeth now began to braid her hair.

"You believe it's my fault that Horace died...because I wouldn't give up my piano. You and everyone else believe that, don't you?"

Elizabeth tied off the braid and let out a long sigh. "I'm not sure it's important what I or anyone else believes in regard to your husband's demise."

"I see them looking at me..." she continued in a shaky voice. "I know that they all blame me. I hear them whispering. They think I killed my husband." Now she was starting to cry.

"Mrs. Taylor, over the years I have learned that what people think of you is not nearly as important as what you think of yourself."

Mrs. Taylor pulled a rumpled hankie from her sleeve, wiping her eyes. "Do you know what I wish?" she said quietly. "I wish that I had been in the wagon with Horace. I wish that I had died with him. Then no one would be saying I killed my husband." She sniffed. "In a way we would be martyrs."

"*Martyrs?*"

"We would have both died for our faith." Mrs. Taylor stuck her chin out. "That would make us Christian martyrs."

Elizabeth was tired and longing for sleep, but something in her could not allow Mrs. Taylor to believe this without at least challenging it. "I'm sorry," she said gently, "but I do not believe that would make you martyrs."

"Well, of course it would. We would have both been killed on a mission for God."

"You would have both been killed because you refused to follow your councilman's orders. My father warned you, Mrs. Taylor, that piano was too heavy for your team. And you know it."

Mrs. Taylor pointed a bony finger at Elizabeth. "See! You do believe I'm responsible for Horace's death. You as much as admitted it. Tell the truth, Elizabeth Martin, you blame me, do you not?"

Elizabeth looked up at the canvas overhead, wishing there was some gentle way out of this. "Yes, it's true that I believe your stubbornness over that piano contributed greatly to your husband losing control of the wagon...I believe your overloaded wagon was partly responsible for the accident that took your husband's life." She let out a long sigh. There. She had said it.

And now Mrs. Taylor began to sob again. Even louder this time. Elizabeth could only imagine what Brady and JT, sleeping beneath the wagon, must be thinking.

"I'm sorry." Elizabeth placed a hand on her shoulder. "You demanded the truth from me."

"I know...I asked for it...and I'm sure you're right. It's what everyone else believes."

"But only God knows the full story." Elizabeth softened her tone. "Well, God and Mr. Taylor. There might have been other factors involved." She tried to think. "Perhaps a snake frightened your team and made your husband lose control. Or maybe the axle broke or a harness snapped. Or...perhaps it was simply Horace's time to go."

Mrs. Taylor looked at her with red-rimmed eyes. "Do you think so?"

"I honestly don't know. But I do know this..."

"What?"

Elizabeth pointed at her. "You will have to come to terms with this. It's obvious you feel guilty. And you should feel guilty. It was selfish to hold onto that piano."

"I know." She nodded sadly. "And I do feel guilty. Believe me, I feel very guilty."

"I find that reassuring."

Mrs. Taylor looked confused by this.

"It just shows that you're human," Elizabeth explained. "And it makes me like you more."

"Truly?" Mrs. Taylor looked surprised.

Elizabeth nodded.

"But what shall I do with all this guilt?" Mrs. Taylor held her hands up helplessly. "I feel as if I've been buried alive with it, as if I can hardly breathe at times. And I find myself wishing I were dead. I even considered jumping into the river the other day when you were crossing the North Platte. But I knew that would be a sin. Oh, dear, what can I do?"

"Being that you're a Christian woman, I should think you would know what to do, Mrs. Taylor. But perhaps it's a bit like the shoemaker's children."

"The what?"

"Surely you've heard the old saying that the shoemaker's children go barefoot."

Mrs. Taylor shook her head. "No, I have not. What does it mean? Their father is a shoemaker, so certainly they would have shoes."

"Yes…you would think so. But perhaps the shoemaker father, so weary from making shoes all day, came home so tired that he overlooked his own family's need for footwear."

"Well, yes, I can imagine that."

"And perhaps someone in the clergy…someone such as yourself… perhaps you have lost sight of who God truly is."

"What are you saying?" Mrs. Taylor seemed offended now.

"I'm speaking of the gospel—the good news. I should think you of all people would have great need of it just now."

Mrs. Taylor's brow creased as if Elizabeth was talking of some great mystery. But Elizabeth felt as if she were finally getting someplace. Was it possible that with all the Taylors' focus on serving God as missionaries, Mrs. Taylor had actually lost her grasp on God's true character—the simple truths that Elizabeth's father had taught his children from the cradle? Perhaps Mrs. Taylor had never understood them. And as Elizabeth remembered the Taylors' negative sermons, railing against everything, predicting hell and damnation for everyone, she knew it must be so. Mrs. Taylor had been so full of condemnation and judgment, she had been blinded by it. Elizabeth had never once heard Mrs. Taylor make mention of God's love or grace or mercy.

"Surely you are aware of the gospel," Elizabeth continued patiently, as if speaking to a small child. "You do know that God sent Jesus to take away the burden of sin and guilt."

"Yes…" she murmured, "of course."

"But you feel as if you're being buried in guilt and you even felt tempted to take your own life?"

She nodded. "I even imbibed and became drunk and danced like a fool for the whole world to see." She started sobbing again.

Elizabeth patted her on the back, suppressing the urge to chuckle. "Quite honestly, I think that is your most forgivable offense of all, Mrs. Taylor. No one here will ever hold that against you. In fact, it might have softened some hearts toward you. We all knew you were in pain over losing Mr. Taylor."

She just nodded, sniffling again.

"But you do need forgiveness for the guilt you're carrying in regard to Mr. Taylor's death. It's only natural that you blame yourself. And you're right, there are others who blame you too."

"I know…I know. But what can I do?"

Elizabeth reached for her own Bible now, flipping to the back. "I'm sure you're familiar with this scripture. It's from the first book of John, chapter one, verse nine." She began to read. "If we confess our sins, he is faithful and just to forgive us our sins, and to cleanse us from all unrighteousness."

"Yes. I am familiar with that."

"Just like the shoemaker was familiar with boot making." Now Elizabeth read the verse again, slowly and clearly. "Don't you see, Mrs.

Taylor? You need to confess your sin—you need to admit what you did wrong and take responsibility for it. Then you can hand it over to God so he can forgive you…and cleanse you."

She pressed her thin lips together as if she was trying to grasp this. Elizabeth suspected that this was a new challenge for Mrs. Taylor. She was probably unaccustomed to confessing any of her shortcomings. Before losing her husband, she probably didn't even realize she had anything to be forgiven for.

"I know you are a proud woman, Mrs. Taylor. At least you were before…but God wants you to be humble. He wants you to admit that you were selfish and stubborn about your piano. When you admit to these things, God will be able to pour out his forgiveness and mercy on you. God will give you a new beginning, but only if you admit to your own sins and shortcomings."

Mrs. Taylor sighed and with downcast eyes just sadly shook her head.

"I hope I haven't worn your ears out." Elizabeth turned the wick down on the lantern. "I know we're both tired, and we have a long hard day ahead of us tomorrow. If you want to discuss this further tomorrow, I am more than willing."

Mrs. Taylor remained silent.

"Good night." Elizabeth crawled into bed and closed her eyes, saying a silent prayer for this poor lost woman.

✦

The first day on Devil's Backbone was long and hard and hot and dry. The pale sun-baked alkaline soil seemed to suck the moisture out of everything around it. Nothing grew in this hellish wasteland. When they came across a small bog of brackish-looking water, Elizabeth knew from her father's warning that it was toxic, and the bleached bones of unfortunate livestock seemed to grimly confirm this.

Mrs. Taylor had continued being very quiet today. But at least she got out and walked for short spells. Elizabeth could tell the travel was hard on her. It was hard on everyone. Even the children seemed dull and slow as they plodded along. The sooner they all escaped this dangerous desert, the happier she would be.

Whether it was knowing that water was scarce or simply the hostile arid climate, she found herself feeling thirstier than ever. And despite her resolve to ration and control the water, she had difficulty forbidding her children from drinking when they were thirsty. She would rather give up some of her water than to see them suffer. By the end of the day, she couldn't even imagine how they would make it through two more.

"The good news is that we made nearly twelve miles today," Asa announced at suppertime. Their whole family was gathered under the shade afforded by the large tarp attached to her parents' wagon. Several of them were draping themselves in the damp cloths Asa had encouraged them to pack. But Elizabeth guessed even those would be dry by tomorrow.

"What is the bad news?" Matthew sounded slightly irritable, but he had helped Ruby and Doris with a minor breakdown in the heat of the day, only to find out he had guard duty tonight and wasn't too pleased about it.

"We still have two days to go." Asa made a weak smile.

"I can help you on guard duty," JT said to Matthew.

"Thanks, buddy, but I think you need to be eighteen."

"That's right," Asa told them.

"And male," Jess added, which made them laugh to remember when she had disguised herself as a young man.

"It seems unlikely that any Indians would venture out here," Elizabeth said as she began gathering some of the dishes. The plan was to first rub them clean with the alkaline soil to conserve water and then to rinse them in boiling hot water.

"You never know." Asa pointed a stern finger at Matthew. "Whatever you do, don't fall asleep. Someone in unit four got caught sleeping, and it resulted in a steep fine."

Matthew reached for the coffeepot. "Anyone mind if I finish this off?"

The second day on Devil's Backbone was worse than the first. Elizabeth was thankful she hadn't suffered a breakdown as had some of the others, but she knew her team was stressed. Horses were not as hardy as oxen and mules. For this reason she took over for JT and Brady by caring for the stock at the end of the day. She knew some people would think it silly, but she spoke to the horses as she curried their coats and checked their hooves. She told them they were doing a good job and that they only had one day of this hellish torture left.

"Talking to your horses, are you?" Will Bramford popped his head over the other side of Bella's back.

"Goodness!" She stood up straight. "You startled me."

"You startled me," he teased. "I thought your horses were actually conversing with each other."

"Ha-ha," she said sarcastically.

"Do you always talk to your animals?"

She held her chin high. "I believe if I take care of my animals, they will take care of me."

"Well, they are some fine-looking animals," he admitted. "Can't blame you for that."

"If you were smart, you'd be tending to your own team right now," she told him, "instead of wasting time talking to me."

"Are you suggesting I go speak to my oxen?"

She shrugged, continuing to curry Bella's coat.

"You have heard the expression, dumb as an ox?"

She stood up straight again, looking him in the eye. "Those *dumb* oxen are getting you and your family safely to Oregon. I should think that would win them some respect."

"They're just animals, Elizabeth. Besides, Jeremiah and Julius are seeing to them now. They're being properly fed and watered." He frowned. "You seem a bit irate. Is Mrs. Taylor getting under your skin again?"

She exhaled loudly, shaking her head. "I'm sorry. I didn't mean to sound so contrary. And to answer your question, no, Mrs. Taylor is just fine, thank you very much." Actually Mrs. Taylor had barely spoken to her since their late-night conversation about forgiveness. "The truth is I'm a bit worried about our water situation."

His dark brows shot up. "You're running out of water?"

"I don't want to tell my father because he's our councilman. But I'm afraid I've already gone through more than two-thirds of our water supply, and we still have a full day of travel through this…this fire and brimstone desert." She tossed the curry brush into the canvas bucket that no longer held water.

"Oh…" He rubbed his chin. "Do you think you have enough water to make it?"

She sighed as she pushed a strand of hair away from her face, tucking it into her bonnet. "It doesn't look good. And I know my brother and father will barely have enough. Maybe I shouldn't have brought so much livestock. I've considered getting rid of some hens, but they really don't drink much water anyway." She glanced over to the milking cow she'd brought from the farm. She'd long since dried up from giving milk, but the poor animal looked parched, and Elizabeth knew she was thirsty. She had so hoped to get this cow all the way to Oregon, but now she was uncertain. "I'm afraid I'll need to sacrifice Goldie."

He looked startled. "Who is Goldie?"

"Our cow. She was our best milk cow too."

"Oh." He looked over to the cow. "You would do that so your team can have more water?"

She nodded sadly. "It's the sensible thing to do. But it won't be easy."

"No, I should think not."

"Well, I suppose I should go tell my father the bad news. The sooner we do this, the better."

"Wait…" He held up a hand. "Give me just a moment."

"Why?" She turned to look at him.

His brow was creased in thought. "What if I adopt Goldie?"

"What do you mean?"

"Well, I hate to see her killed, and we seem to be all right with water. We still have enough for tomorrow and probably some to spare."

"That's because you don't have extra livestock."

"I don't really mean to say I'll take Goldie off your hands, Elizabeth. But how about if we share some of our water with her?"

Elizabeth tilted her head to one side, trying to determine his motives.

"Is it because you don't want to see her slaughtered? You know we would share the meat with everyone in our unit, including your family."

"It seems a shame to kill a perfectly good milk cow." He reached over and patted her on the neck. "And she seems such a nice cow."

Elizabeth couldn't help but smile. "Still, you can't just be giving me your water. Out here water is more precious than gold. What would you expect in return?"

He shrugged. "Well, my girls keep hinting that they want to follow your family to where you locate in Oregon. At first I thought it was because they were in love with Matthew. But now he's married." His eyes twinkled. "Maybe we'll be your neighbors and we can drop by and borrow a quart of milk sometimes. That would be a fair exchange for a bucket of water."

She was surprised. "You really want to go all the way down to the southern part of the Oregon Territory to live? I thought you planned to settle in Portland. Where we're going is a fair distance from there."

"We are a democratic family," he declared. "And my children have the majority vote."

"Even the females?"

"Yes. We are a very progressive bunch."

She chuckled but then grew more serious. "Are you certain you have water to spare for Goldie?"

"I think we do. But I'll check with my children first. Put it to a vote."

"Please, let me know directly," she told him. "This is a decision that should be made as soon as possible." She frowned at the sweet Guernsey. She had only given Goldie a smidgeon of water so far, knowing she should conserve it in case she really was forced to put her beloved bovine down.

"I promise to return shortly." He tipped his hat.

"And I'll understand if you choose not to do this, Will," she assured him. "You must look to the welfare of your own stock and family first."

He just nodded and then hurried away. She hoped that he was being honest with her. She would feel terrible if he was shortchanging his own family for her sake. But really, why would he do that? Oh, she knew that he was somewhat interested in her. But she had never done anything to give him the impression that she wanted anything more than friendship with him.

Now she had to ask herself why she was interested only in his friendship and not something more. Why didn't she consider him someone she could potentially marry and grow old together with? Will seemed to be a genuinely good man. And she liked him. He was intelligent and interesting. Certainly, many widows would see Will Bramford as quite a catch. Why didn't she?

She took a handful of grass over to poor Goldie, holding her flattened palm out as the cow hungrily munched. "I sure don't want to lose you," she whispered, looking directly into those liquid brown eyes. "But we have to do what we have to do."

Chapter Nine

William returned with the good news and a pail of water. "We took an inventory of our remaining water," he explained. "The vote was unanimous. Goldie will be spared."

Elizabeth was so happy that she threw her arms around Will and hugged him. "Thank you! Thank you!" Then feeling self-conscious and silly, she quickly stepped away. "Now I can give Goldie a drink, poor old girl."

As she was letting Goldie have some water—careful that she didn't drink too much—she noticed a familiar-looking Appaloosa passing by. She squinted into the afternoon sun in time to spy Eli waving their direction, but instead of stopping to say hello the way he used to do, he just continued on, leaving a cloud of alkaline dust in his wake.

With his back to Eli and apparently oblivious to him, Will continued talking to her. "After we decided to share some water, I made an offhand comment to my children. I told them that saving Goldie might ensure our family some borrowing rights should we run out of butter or cream next winter."

"Really?" She arched her brows. "And what did they say to that?"

He grinned. "The girls let out squeals of happiness, and Jeremiah mentioned reading that the climate down there was moderate—even in winter."

"That's true enough. But what about the Prescotts?" She moved the bucket away from Goldie now, pausing to stroke a silky golden ear. "I thought your families planned to settle together."

"Yes, I'm sure this will make for some lively discussion during the next few weeks." He shrugged. "But the Prescotts are a democratic family too. I'm sure they'll put this idea to a vote."

"Well, thank you again for your kindness to Goldie," she told him. "And if it turns out you don't settle near us in southern Oregon, I hope you will let me repay you in some other way. Perhaps you'd like a nice laying hen."

"Perhaps."

They continued the grueling climb up Prospect Hill—a hard haul across a bleak and barren landscape. As Elizabeth drove, her mouth became so dry that she had difficultly swallowing, and she was forced to take small sips of water just to wash down the alkaline dust. She hadn't mentioned her shortage of water to her family. But before they left in the morning, Will had sent Jeremiah with another bucket of water.

"Your family saved this animal's life," she'd told him as she showed him Goldie.

He smiled. "She's a pretty cow."

"She's a Guernsey."

"I'm sure she'll be valuable once you settle."

Elizabeth tried to imagine it now, what it would be like when they reached their destination—the Promised Land of southern Oregon. Malinda had painted such lovely word pictures in her letters. Rolling green hills, crystal clear springs and rivers, tall evergreens, mild winters…and the ocean was only a half a day's travel from them. It all sounded wonderful, especially compared to this horrible place. But thinking of Malinda's letters about Oregon reminded Elizabeth that she still had not heard back from her sister-in-law. Although she checked for mail at every possible stop—longing to get some kind of confirmation that John and Malinda knew they were coming, some reassurance that all was well—there was never a letter. By now more than enough time had transpired for Malinda to respond to the letter Elizabeth had sent back in January. Elizabeth tried not to dwell on this, but it was unnerving.

She had been careful not to reveal her concerns to her family. But sometimes, especially in the dark of night or driving through this wasteland, she felt very worried. What if something bad had happened to John and Malinda and the children? What if there had been an epidemic? Or, worse, an Indian raid? Father had mentioned that Oregon Country had experienced some incidents of Indian aggression during the past few years, but Malinda had never mentioned such goings-on in her cheerful letters, so Elizabeth had simply assumed those troubles were in another part of the territory. After all, Oregon was a vast piece of land.

To distract herself from fretting about their Oregon relatives, she tried to imagine what today's destination, the Sweetwater River, would look like. The name alone seemed to suggest heaven. And the thought of water made her thirsty again. She reached for the canteen, which was nearly empty—not because she'd been guzzling it, but because she'd poured less than a cup of water into it after their midday stop, convincing herself she could make it through this day with just enough droplets to moisten her mouth. The rest of their remaining water had gone to the livestock for the final leg of this journey, reserving about the last gallon for the children and Brady, minus her meager portion and a bit for Mrs. Taylor, who planned to sleep throughout the afternoon.

But Brady and the children needed more water since they were afoot in order to lighten the wagon's load. She'd considered asking Mrs. Taylor to walk along with them, but the poor woman seemed pitifully worn out after walking all morning. Elizabeth had felt sorry for her out there on foot, stumbling wearily along and sweltering in that heavy black woolen dress. It was ironic that Mrs. Taylor only wore black even before her husband's tragedy.

Trying not to feel too put out over the grieving woman's extra weight in the wagon, especially since her own children were walking, Elizabeth reminded herself that their load had lightened considerably after using up most of the water they'd started with at Horse Creek. Plus she'd told JT he could ride Molly if need be, and she'd encouraged Ruth to join her grandparents if she got too hot or tired. And rubbing his sore backside, Brady had assured her he was happy to walk.

Elizabeth peeled off her riding gloves and rolled up her sleeves. She then untied the strings of her prairie bonnet and even unbuttoned several top buttons of her shirtwaist, hoping that some stray breeze of stagnant air might cool her some. This was going to be a very long afternoon—perhaps the longest afternoon of the entire journey. She suddenly wished she'd invited Ruth to ride with her. Really, what difference would sixty or seventy more pounds have made? And Ruthie's chatter was always such a good distraction. If she were here, they might even be singing. Or maybe not. Elizabeth's throat felt so dry she wasn't sure she'd be able to croak out a tune.

Still, to pass the time, she decided to sing a song inside her head, but the only tune that came to her was the cowboy song Matthew and JT had played before bed last night, and it wasn't a very happy song. Even so, the lyrics from the first verse seemed to be stuck in her head now, and there she let them stay, running the lonesome tune through her head again and again.

"Afternoon, Elizabeth."

She looked over, surprised to see Eli and his horse walking alongside her wagon, curiously watching her. Maybe she'd been wrong to assume he'd been avoiding her after all.

"Afternoon, Eli." She nodded, giving him a polite smile.

"You appeared deep in thought…with a very troubling expression. Is something troubling you?" He waved his hand. "Something other than the last day on Devil's Backbone?"

"Truth be told, I was simply singing a song inside of my head," she confessed.

He grinned with interest. "Now what song would that be, I wonder...?"

"Just an old cowboy song."

"I happen to like old cowboy songs." His blue eyes twinkled, and the wrinkles on the edges of his eyes crinkled in a way that softened her on the inside. "Won't you share it with me?"

She considered refusing him but then wondered why. What did it matter if she sounded foolish? At least it would help pass the time. "I only know the first verse," she admitted.

"I'd love to hear it." He leaned forward with interest.

So holding her head high, she cleared her throat and sang.

> Oh, bury me not, on the lone prairie,
> Where the coyotes wail and the wind blows free.
> When I die, don't bury me
> 'Neath the western sky, on the lone prairie.

He took off his hat, slapped it across his thigh, and threw back his head, laughing loudly. "Well, if that's not an entirely appropriate song for this leg of the journey, Elizabeth. I thank you for sharing it with me."

She twisted the end of the reins in her hands. "You're welcome... I suppose."

"And since you were so kind to sing the first verse to me, would you like me to sing the rest of the song to you?"

"Of course, if you know it."

"I most certainly do." He put his hat back on then sang out in a rich baritone.

> "Oh, bury me not on the lone prairie."
> These words came soft and painfully
> From the pallid lips of a boy who lay
> On his dying bed, at the break of day.
> But we buried him there on the lone prairie,

Where the rattlesnakes hiss and the wind blows free,
In a shallow grave, no one to grieve,
'Neath the western sky, on the lone prairie.

To her surprise, she felt a lump growing in her parched throat. "That was beautiful, Eli. Beautiful and sad." She slowly shook her head. "I don't wish to see anyone else buried on this trip."

"Nor do I." He reached for his canteen. Fancier than her plain brown container, his was covered in black and white cowhide with a beaded leather tassel hanging down. "I'd almost forgotten that song altogether. I haven't heard it in a coon's age."

"If you'd been at our camp, you'd have heard it last night," she told him a bit sharply.

He slowly loosened the cap of his canteen. "That makes me wonder...am I still welcome at your campsite?"

"Why wouldn't you be?" She peered curiously at him.

"There's a rumor rumbling through this wagon train..."

"What sort of rumor?" Even as she asked this, she recalled how some of the older girls had been talking about her and Eli following Matthew and Jess' wedding. She also remembered how she had warned Ruth to be wary of gossip.

"It's the usual sort of rumor."

"Please, don't think I'm encouraging you to repeat rumors, Eli." She pushed a strand of hair from her face, tucking it under her bonnet. "I certainly don't appreciate idle gossip."

"Yes, that's wise." He took a short swig from his handsome canteen. As he put the cap back on, glancing over his shoulder, she suddenly felt worried he might leave without telling her why he'd been avoiding her.

"Although I am curious as to how a rumor would make you believe you're unwelcome at our campsite, Eli. Hasn't my family always received you with open arms? And JT and Matthew enjoy it immensely when you play music with them—although I must admit our singing was not with great enthusiasm last night. Everyone was very tired."

"I can understand that."

"But I'm still curious, Eli. Why would you be unwelcome at our campsite?"

"So you do want to know about the rumor after all?"

She shrugged then made a sheepish smile. "I suppose I do." She waved her hand to the vast emptiness all around them. "I've been so desperate for distractions that I am humming sad cowboy tunes in my head."

"There are worse ways to spend your time."

"Please," she insisted, "tell me this rumor. Perhaps I can dispel it for you."

"The rumor is that a certain attorney from Boston is courting you."

"Courting me?" She opened her eyes wide. "Will? Courting me?"

He simply nodded, but he studied her with an intensity that made her wonder.

"Well, hopefully you don't believe everything you hear, Eli."

"Are you saying it's untrue?"

"It's untrue as far as I know." She sat up straight. "I am being courted by no one."

He chuckled. "Don't be so sure of that."

She felt her cheeks growing hot. To distract him, she reached for her canteen and started to take a sip but then remembered that except for a few drops, it was empty. Flustered, she set it down on the seat beside her and fixed her gaze back on her team.

"*Are you out of water?*"

She shrugged, forcing a smile for him. "I am fine."

"*Elizabeth?*" He looked intently at her. "Tell me the truth. Are you *out* of water?"

"My livestock were all thoroughly watered on our midday break. My children, Brady, and Mrs. Taylor all have sufficient water. We are fine, Eli."

"I'm asking about *you.*"

She sighed.

Now he leaned over and reached for her canteen, leaving his in its place. "I'll exchange that back with you at the Sweetwater River," he told her in a firm voice. Then he turned his horse and trotted away. She waited until he was out of sight to pick up the canteen. It was nearly full. She slowly opened it, taking a long swig of cool refreshing water. As she recapped the canteen, she wondered when she'd ever tasted anything so perfectly delicious and satisfying.

By the time the Sweetwater River was within sight, Eli's canteen was as dry as her own had been. Between her and Mrs. Taylor, they drank every drop. She had felt sorry to pass several wagons that were unable to continue due to animal fatigue and thirst. Some of the animals looked like they might not even survive the day, but when she paused to inquire, their owners assured her that help had been promised.

"The captain said that a rescue team will be back here before dark," a woman from unit two told her. "With water and fresh animals."

"And you want to remain out here?" Elizabeth called back.

The woman nodded to the wagon behind her. "We must stay. Everything we have is in there. We'll wait for help."

"Good luck," Elizabeth told her. She wasn't sure that she'd remain behind if she were in their same position—not in this awful place. But it wasn't for her to decide. She was just thankful it wasn't anyone in their unit. That would mean that her father and brother would be forced to return. Fortunately, the wagons were only a few miles from the river. But each mile out here felt like a hundred.

Elizabeth had never thought much about the smell of water, but that is what first told her they were reaching the end of Devil's Backbone. She could smell something tangy in the air, something green and clean and slightly pungent. And then it hit her—it was water! Her team seemed to smell it too because they began to lift their feet a bit higher, hastening toward it along with the other teams.

The trees and green grass were just coming into view when JT came bounding up on Grandpa's riding horse. He had two buckets in one hand. "Grandpa told me to go to the river and get some water," he happily told her. "Brady will take Beau and Bella to the line first, and I'll be there to meet them with water."

"Bless you!" she called out.

It was amazing how everyone instantly became energized as they got closer to the Sweetwater River. Even though they hadn't actually tasted the sweet water of the river yet, Elizabeth was sure it would be true to its name, and she felt as if the very air had revived the weary travelers. The sounds of laughing and singing and happy conversations flitted through their campsites as people settled in for the night. Elizabeth parked her wagon in the space that Brady seemed to be saving for her. Then as he began to remove the harnesses from the team, she grabbed two buckets and ran straight down to the river, meeting JT coming toward her with his own two pails.

"The water really does taste sweet!" he told her.

"I can hardly wait."

He held up a pail. "Go ahead and have some, Ma."

"Not yet." She shook her head. "Take it to the animals. They deserve it."

It was like a big party at the river. Some of the travelers had jumped in with their clothes on. Some had taken parched horses to drink directly from it. She found a clear spot and dipped a bucket in, and holding it up, she stuck her entire face in and thirstily drank. It was true—the water was sweet! Sweet and cold and fresh and clean. She felt as if they'd walked through hell to get here, but this was indeed heavenly!

Chapter Ten

D espite some of our setbacks, we're making good time," Asa told the family later that evening. Tired but happy, they had just finished supper and were enjoying their campsite near the Sweetwater River.

"What about those poor folks who are still stranded out there on Devil's Backbone?" Clara asked.

"A rescue team went out hours ago, and the captain said they should all make it into camp before midnight," Asa assured her. "I'm sure relieved everyone in our unit made it with no problems. Otherwise I'd be out there now."

"How many people do you s'pose broke down by the end of the day?" Matthew asked.

"The captain said there were about a dozen wagons all together. Unit two had the most troubles." He cleared his throat. "Sounds like their councilman may get replaced."

"Did he do something wrong?" Clara asked.

Asa shrugged. "Not exactly. But I hear he's too easy on his folks."

He glanced at Mrs. Taylor, who was still picking at her plate of food. "The captain said he should have forced them to rid themselves of more weight before they crossed Devil's Backbone. One wagon was still carrying a maple dining room set that must have weighed near five hundred pounds." He shook his head. "Can you imagine the toll that took on those poor oxen!"

"Well, you can be proud that no one in your unit had a problem," Jess told him. "You are a fine leader, Asa."

He grinned at her. "How many times do I have to tell you to call me Pa?"

She looked slightly embarrassed but pleased just the same. "*Pa.*"

"If we keep making good time and pushing hard this week, Captain Brownlee says we should make Independence Rock by the Fourth of July after all."

Matthew let out a whoop. "*Independence Day at Independence Rock!*" He stood up and grabbed Jessica, and singing "Yankee Doodle," he led her all around the campsite in a joyous jig. Naturally JT and Ruth joined in as well, all of them singing loudly and joyously. Elizabeth hummed along, well aware that making this spot by this date was critical to the success of the wagon train. To arrive even a week later could be the difference between safely crossing the last mountain pass and getting trapped in an early blizzard.

Despite the warm evening, she shivered to remember the chilling tale of the Donner party. She and James had read a graphic account of this tragedy about ten years ago. It was a heartbreaking story of pioneers headed for California who perished in the mountains, and she had pushed this dreadful report far into the recesses of her mind—and never shared it with her children. But she had every confidence that with wise leaders like Captain Brownlee, Eli, and her own father, they would not be caught like those poor immigrants.

"Tonight we will have some real music," Matthew told them after they ended "Yankee Doodle" on the third verse. "We'll celebrate making it across the Devil's Backbone."

"What about the Fourth of July?" Ruth asked hopefully. "Will there be celebration at Independence Rock? Will we have fireworks and ice cream and horse races?"

Asa laughed. "Not likely, little one."

"Besides the cream," Elizabeth said, "where would we get *ice* way out here—and in the middle of summer?"

Ruth's mouth twisted to one side. "Then what about fireworks and horse races? Will they have those at Independence Rock?"

"I don't think it would be fair to race our horses," Elizabeth told her. "They're already working hard enough."

"According to the captain we'll reach the rock in midmorning," Asa told Ruth as she returned to collecting the dirty supper dishes. "And we can't stay there long. We'll have time enough to take a quick look around and inscribe our names on the rock if we so choose. But even if there *were* any fireworks to be had, it won't be dark enough for fireworks there. I have a feeling that fireworks are as scarce as hen's teeth—and ice—out here." He chuckled with a twinkle in his eye.

Elizabeth eyed her father as she washed a plate. Knowing his love for fireworks, he'd probably packed a little something for the Fourth. Not that she planned on mentioning this to her children, but it wouldn't surprise her a bit.

"Would you like me to take over the dishwashing for you?" Mrs. Taylor offered.

Elizabeth reached for the bar of soap and smiled. "No, thank you," she told her. "I'm actually enjoying this immensely. It's so nice to have my hands in warm soapy water again with no rationing."

Ruth handed her another dirty plate. "Isn't it lovely that we don't have to wash our dishes in the dirt anymore?" she said, and everyone laughed.

Before long, Matthew, JT, and Brady reappeared with their musical instruments, and soon they were playing a merry accompaniment while the women continued cleaning up after supper, tapping their toes as they washed and dried and stowed things away. Elizabeth had just finished scrubbing the last pot when some of their fellow travelers began showing up. Everyone was in good spirits. Some, like the Schneiders, just came to listen, tapping their toes and clapping. Others, like the McIntires, brought their own instruments or simply sang along. And some, especially the young people, started up some dances.

One thing was clear—everyone seemed exceptionally happy tonight. As Elizabeth tossed the dirty dishwater out behind the wagon, so glad she didn't need to save it, she whispered a silent prayer of thanksgiving. How wonderful that they would be traveling along the Sweetwater for the next hundred miles. As she used a rag to wipe out the washtub, she vowed to never take water for granted again.

It wasn't long until nearly everyone in their unit was present at Asa and Clara's campsite. Even Gert Muller set her chair on the perimeter of the impromptu party, smoking her pipe and looking on with interest. Elizabeth was grateful that their site wasn't large enough for everyone to dance tonight. She was content to simply sit around the fire, visiting with the other women as they watched the young people having a merry time. Meanwhile the men were gathered around Asa, smoking pipes and listening to the latest news—probably reports on the breakdowns on Devil's Backbone and the possibility of reaching Independence Rock in a few days.

"It gets surprisingly cool in the evenings," Elizabeth said as she pulled her shawl more snugly around her shoulders.

"I don't mind the chilly night air a bit," Ruby said. "But I suppose that has to do with my age."

"I'm afraid I was a bit hasty in getting rid of blankets and heavy clothing," Lavinia Prescott told them. "Hugh suggested we should reduce some of the weight we were carrying last week. It was so warm that day, I assumed we'd have no need of winter things. So I let him leave a whole trunk full of woolen clothing and blankets alongside the road."

"You didn't!" Flo Flanders' eyebrows arched.

Lavinia grimaced. "Evelyn doesn't even know yet—but her best winter coat was in that trunk. As well as a heavy woolen quilt that my mother made for our wedding more than twenty years ago. Not to mention the blankets and long johns and whatnot."

"What on earth will you do when winter comes in Oregon?" Mrs. Taylor asked.

"How will you and your children stay warm?" Flo demanded.

Lavinia's countenance suddenly changed and she looked unconcerned. "Oh, we've had a shipment of dry goods en route for nearly a year now. There are blankets and coats and all sorts of necessary supplies. They should arrive in Vancouver in early August."

"A shipment of goods?" Flo's brows shot up even higher. "Isn't that awfully expensive?"

"We are merchants," Lavinia reminded her. "We plan to open a store."

"A store?" Flo looked impressed. "Out in the wilderness. Well, well, that's a right good plan." She elbowed Elizabeth. "Sure wouldn't mind having a store where we settle. Say, Elizabeth, did your sister-in-law say if there's a store where you're going?"

Elizabeth shook her head. "Malinda hasn't mentioned it."

The women continued to chatter on about what it would be like when they settled and where they planned to be. It seemed that many of them were considering joining Elizabeth and her family. She was about to warn them that it would add additional travel time to their journey, but instead she was distracted by a certain someone who had just entered their camp. Dressed in his usual buckskins, Eli had his guitar with him. But he looked uncertain—as if he thought he might not be welcome. Naturally, and to her relief, he was warmly greeted by Matthew, and before long he was playing enthusiastically with the other musicians.

She tried not to be too obvious watching him as she tapped her toes to the lively music, but she was glad he'd come. Even more glad that he felt welcome. Still, it reminded her of his comment. Were people really gossiping about Will courting her? She glanced over to the group of men and was somewhat surprised to see Will looking directly at her, almost as if he'd been watching her the whole time. She simply smiled at him and then turned back to the women, where Mrs. Taylor was excusing herself to bed.

"It's been a long, tiring day," she told them. "Good night, everyone."

After she was gone, Doris began to snicker.

"What's so funny?" Ruby asked her.

"I was just wondering if Mrs. Taylor might be in need of some more medicine."

Naturally this got some of them to giggling, making more comments and observations—all at Mrs. Taylor's expense. Elizabeth exchanged uncomfortable glances with her mother, relieved that she seemed as concerned as Elizabeth. However, she didn't say anything but quietly kept on knitting. Elizabeth didn't want to chastise the women for their merriment, and yet she felt the need to speak up in Mrs. Taylor's defense.

"I know Mrs. Taylor has her faults," Elizabeth began quietly. "But she really is trying to make an adjustment…in her own way. I know from personal experience how difficult it is to lose a husband…the pain is still fresh for her."

"Oh, of course it is," Lavinia said with genuine sympathy. "And it's unkind for us to make fun of her. I have corrected my daughter for this very thing. You have my sincere apologies."

Elizabeth smiled at Lavinia. Sometimes this woman could be uppity and insensitive, but Elizabeth had never liked her so much as right now.

"I'm sorry too," Doris said.

Flo nodded. "I am too."

"I just think if we all continue being patient and understanding…" Elizabeth continued. "If we can show her true compassion and love, she may become stronger and grow from this experience."

Clara looked up from her knitting, giving Elizabeth a nod of approval.

"And I'll admit that I'm not always as patient with her as I'd like to be," Elizabeth confessed. "The truth is I sometimes feel put out, as if I've reached my limit."

"Which raises a question," Clara said soberly. "Is it fair that Elizabeth is the only one bearing this burden?"

"I've wondered about this very thing," Lavinia said. "How can we help you, Elizabeth?"

"I don't know." Elizabeth held up her hands. "My mother has offered to take her in, but Mrs. Taylor rejects the idea."

"She feels she would be putting Asa out," Clara explained.

"Although he is already put out since Ruth is sleeping with you."

Clara just nodded.

"I have an idea," Flo said eagerly. "Why don't we all take turns having Mrs. Taylor for meals? We could give her a roster for the upcoming week."

"That's a wonderful idea," Clara said. "And it would allow Mrs. Taylor to interact with families besides ours."

"And perhaps if she gets more comfortable with other families, she will consider some alternative arrangements," Lavinia suggested.

"What is she going to do now?" Doris asked. "Continue to Oregon? Or will she find a way to return back East?"

"She seems determined to continue," Clara told them.

"Really?" Elizabeth was surprised. "When did she say this?"

"Yesterday evening as we were preparing supper," Clara told her. "You were tending to your animals. But Mrs. Taylor told me she'd been giving it much thought, and she believes the mission where Mr. Taylor was headed can still use her help."

Elizabeth didn't want to question Mrs. Taylor's judgment on this, and certainly not in front of these women, but she had her doubts. What sort of Indian mission would welcome a lone woman to serve? Still, she felt slightly encouraged by this news—at least Mrs. Taylor was feeling stronger and was considering her future. That alone was worth a lot. Elizabeth was glad to hear it, especially since Mrs. Taylor had been rather close lipped these past several days. Elizabeth had attributed it to tiredness, but she still hoped to finish their conversation about forgiveness and guilt.

Despite the celebratory mood, it was plain that the travelers were weary after their past three days of harrowing journey, and before long some of them began to excuse themselves to bed. With only the music makers and the young people remaining, Elizabeth was about to turn in as well, but she remembered that she still had Eli's handsome canteen and hoped to return it to him, along with her sincere thanks.

"This will have to be our last song tonight," Matthew told the young people, who still claimed they were not tired. While they played,

Elizabeth retrieved the canteen and then, waiting for the song to end, handed it over to Eli. "I just wanted to thank you for helping me out today," she told him. "I needed that more than I realized."

He smiled at her. "But I don't have your canteen with me," he told her. "It looks like you'll have to hold onto mine until we can make a proper exchange. I wouldn't want you to be without a canteen."

"But we have other—"

"You hold onto it, Elizabeth." His eyes glinted with amusement. "I don't want to take it with me and forget about returning yours." Then he slung his guitar strap over his shoulder, waved goodbye, and left.

"That's a real good-looking canteen," JT told her with genuine admiration.

"Sure is." Matthew winked at her.

"Time for bed," she told them. "Tomorrow is another day." She could hear Matthew chuckling as she headed for her wagon. Sometimes it seemed little brothers never grew up!

⸎

As Captain Brownlee predicted, they reached Independence Rock by midmorning on the Fourth of July. And despite the lack of horse racing, ice cream, and fireworks, it was a busy place. Once again, everyone was in a celebratory mood. And although Elizabeth thought it a waste of money, Asa insisted on paying a stone carver, who appeared to make a good business there, to put the names of all the members of their family as well as Brady's into the rock. They watched for a few minutes as the rock carver began his work, but naturally, they couldn't stay to see it completed.

"Maybe the children or some of our descendents will come to this place and see it someday," Asa told them. "It's a part of our family's history now."

"I don't think I'll ever pass this way again," Clara assured him.

He laughed as he put an arm around her. "Nor I, my dear. Nor I."

Elizabeth couldn't imagine that she would either. But talk of their descendents and family history got her to thinking. "Father," she said as they were walking back to their wagon, "remember how Great-Grandpa used to tell us stories about the battles of the Revolution when we were kids?"

"I don't remember that," Matthew said. "I don't even remember Great-Grandpa."

"That's because he died before you were born," Asa told him. "But yes, Elizabeth, I remember your great-grandpa telling you and Peter the same stories he told me when I was young." He chuckled. "Well, not *exactly* the same. Some of the battles sounded bigger and bloodier than when I was a lad."

"I want to hear these stories too," Matthew said.

"Yes," Elizabeth told him. "I think we all do. Why don't you see how much you can remember, Father? Tell us about the role your ancestors played in that important part of our country's history."

"My ancestors played a part too," Clara said. "My grandfather fought alongside Daniel Boone."

"I forgot about that," Elizabeth admitted. "You both must tell your family's stories at supper tonight." She looked ahead to where the children were walking with Jessica. "These stories need to be handed down to the next generation."

So it was that both Asa and Clara reminisced over supper. "My grandpa fought the great battle of Germantown," he told them. "In Pennsylvania."

"Is that where he lived?" JT asked. "Not Kentucky?"

"My family moved to Kentucky following the Revolution," Asa explained.

"Mine were already there," Clara proclaimed with a spark of pride.

The children and everyone listened with interest as old stories of battles and heroes and sacrifices were shared over supper. "So you see," Asa said as the women began to clear the plates, "our *free* country—the United States of America—was not truly free. The lives and blood of many of your ancestors paid the price for our freedom today. And that is why we can follow our dreams—journey to new land and build new lives in a new frontier similar to how our ancestors did it many generations ago." Asa held up his coffee cup in a toast. "Here's to freedom and the Fourth of July on the great Oregon Trail."

"Can we do this every year on Independence Day?" JT asked eagerly. "I don't see why not." Asa grinned. "I think Grandma and I enjoy it every bit as much as you do."

"I'd like you children to write these stories down in your journals when you have time," Elizabeth told them. "It's as important to remember where we came from as it is to be prepared for where we're going."

But now their fellow travelers were showing up at their camp again, dressed up and ready for music and celebrating. Yesterday, the women in their unit had each agreed to make a special treat to share for a dessert potluck. By the time the dishes were spread on the table, it looked like a real party. Certainly it wouldn't compare with the fancy sweets that would be gracing an Independence Day party back in Kentucky right now, but Elizabeth had no doubt that it was being enjoyed every bit as much by their friends—possibly even more so.

However, everyone agreed that the real highlight of the evening was when Asa shot off several brilliant fireworks. No one had expected this. But when he persuaded everyone to walk out into the dark meadow with him, away from the campfires and lanterns, they all let out gasps and aahs as they watched colorful starbursts painting bright streaks against the velvet black sky. Some actually shrieked at the sound of the deep booms echoing against the mountains. And Elizabeth got a thrill that was beyond what she remembered from last year's fireworks—although she wasn't sure if it was simply the fireworks since her cheeks were still flushed from dancing with two handsome and attentive men tonight. She knew that people, including her family, were speculating and talking among themselves, but she simply acted nonchalant as she stood watching her father's fireworks with Eli on one side and Will on the other.

Admittedly, with only three different parcels of fireworks to shoot into the sky, it was a rather short display, but it was delightful just the same. And when it was done, they all sang "The Star Spangled Banner" together. Really, Elizabeth thought as she walked with her children back to the wagon, she couldn't imagine a more perfect day.

Chapter Eleven

Elizabeth thought that traveling alongside the beautiful Sweetwater River for a hundred miles sounded heavenly, especially after surviving Devil's Backbone. And although each day meant a long and strenuous climb for the hardworking teams, drivers, and walkers, their arduous ascent was made more endurable by the gracefully curving river that traveled with them. Elizabeth wished she were an artist and could capture the rich tones of the emerald green river, the vivid green shades of the aspen trees, and the snowcapped mountains against the jaybird-blue skies. Sometimes the view was so stunning it brought tears to her eyes. And knowing they were coming to the end of this leg of the journey was bittersweet. She was glad to be getting closer to Oregon but sad to leave this beauty behind.

"Look!" Elizabeth directed the women's attention toward a herd of antelope grazing in a distant meadow.

"I hope Bert has his rifle handy," Flo said eagerly. "Fresh meat sounds wonderful."

"I'm afraid they're too far away to get a good shot," Elizabeth told her. "Anyway, it's too late." The herd, hearing the wagon train rumbling toward them, had already begun to spring away.

"Isn't it lovely to have the river so nearby?" Elizabeth said absently. "Having good fresh water to drink every day…"

"Except for those durned crossings," Flo said. "I don't see why we have to keep going back and forth across the same river. It feels like we must be going in circles."

Elizabeth chuckled. "The river goes like this." She used her finger to draw an S in the air. "But we want to go like this." Now she drew a straight line.

"Oh." Flo slowly nodded. "I understand. Now why didn't Bert explain it to me like that?"

"I was surprised by the crossings too," Elizabeth admitted. "At least they're not too challenging…for the most part."

"I get aggravated at how much precious time each crossing takes," Lavinia said.

"At least you don't have as many animals as Elizabeth and her family." Flo shook her head. "That must get tedious."

"Brady and JT are becoming quite expert at herding the livestock across," Elizabeth said proudly.

"I heard Hugh telling the children we would need to cross over again before the day is done." Lavinia let out a long sigh. "I feel my patience is being sorely tried."

"My father said there might be up to nine crossings before we're done with this river," Elizabeth told her. "So you might as well get used to it."

"I used to consider myself a fairly adventurous person," Lavinia told them. "I thought nothing of loading up the carriages with tents and food and household goods, and taking the children to the beach, where we would stay for a whole week, living like gypsies."

"That sounds like fun." Flo nodded. "I'd like to do that too…perhaps in Oregon."

Lavinia continued. "So when Hugh and Will cooked up this plan to go west, I imagined it would be something like our beach visits. I was not intimidated in the least by their outrageous idea. I figured I was a strong and adventurous soul. I believed I would thoroughly enjoy all the challenges of this journey—that I would be a stronger more capable woman by the end of it."

"I believe that's true—you have already become stronger and more capable." Elizabeth was impressed with how much Lavinia had changed over the past weeks—for the better.

"But I am so fed up with all of it. I swear if our next stop was a town with a hotel and a bathhouse and a restaurant, Hugh would not be able to pry me out of it. I would simply stay put. I would open a store right there. Let my husband and children continue on without me."

Elizabeth couldn't help but laugh. "Oh, Lavinia, you wouldn't really do that."

"Oh, yes I would. I do believe I would."

Flo and Elizabeth were both laughing now.

"Yes, go ahead and laugh at me." Lavinia gave them a mockingly disdainful look. "But sometimes I feel that I have been the brunt of a cruel joke."

"Even on a beautiful day like today?" Elizabeth asked.

"Well, I must admit that it's lifted my spirits some. But there were moments on Devil's Backbone when I hoped we'd be attacked by Indians—with no survivors."

"Lavinia!" Flo shook her finger at her. "That's horrible."

"I'm sorry, Flo. But a swift death from an arrow through the heart seemed preferable to slowly drying up on a desert that never seemed to end." She held out her hands. "Just look how withered and dry my skin has become. I swear I will be a wrinkled old prune by the time we reach Oregon."

Elizabeth just smiled. Lavinia was indeed a character, but the more Elizabeth got to know her, the more she liked this outspoken woman. She enjoyed her dry wit and humor. Although no one had mentioned it lately, Elizabeth found herself hoping that the Bostonians would change their destination plans as Will had suggested. It would be interesting to settle near these colorful friends. However, at the same time, she was determined not to raise this issue. This was a very big decision, one that each family must make for themselves.

The river crossing came late in the afternoon, and being that it was an exceedingly warm day, Elizabeth thought the short trek through the water might be appreciated by all of the travelers—people and livestock alike. However, when she saw the river, she was dismayed that it looked deeper and wider than usual.

"This warm weather has melted the snow on the mountains," Eli explained to her. Still mounted on his horse, he had ridden over to talk to her as she waited for her turn to cross in her wagon. "That water is making the river run faster than we expected."

"Is it safe to pass here?" she asked with concern.

"Sure." He nodded. "But everyone needs to be careful…as usual."

She glanced over to where JT and Brady were getting ready to drive their livestock across. As usual, Brady was riding her father's mare, Penny, and JT was on Molly. "Do you think JT will be all right today?"

"I don't see why not. He's a good horseman. He and Brady are both doing a great job getting the livestock across."

With her eyes still locked on JT, she hoped he was right. JT had become much more competent in the saddle this year, and he'd grown in so many other ways. But in her heart he was still a boy…not to mention her only son.

"Don't worry, Elizabeth." Eli's tone was gentle. "JT can handle it."

She turned and smiled at him. "Thank you." Now she noticed her old canteen tied to the back of his saddle. She was tempted to point this out and offer to exchange with him. But the last few times she'd suggested swapping back, he'd made excuses as if he was turning this into a game, and she wasn't sure she wanted to play. One thing seemed clear—he was not eager to get his handsome canteen back from her. And the truth was she had grown attached to it. Because of the cowhide, it seemed to keep water cooler than her old one. Of course, she now felt guilty because it was so hot. He probably missed it. So she reached for his canteen, dangling it before him in a way she hoped was tempting.

"Your canteen sure does a nice job of keeping water cold..." She grinned at him. "I would think you'd be missing it on a hot day like today."

He grinned right back at her. "Matter of fact, I just filled your canteen up. It's plum full of ice-cold river water." He nodded to the canteen in her hand. "How about that one?"

She gave it a shake. "I filled it at the midday break. It's about half full now."

"No, thank you." He chuckled as he tipped his head then kneed his horse directly toward the river, quickly crossing—as if to show her that although the water was a couple feet deep, it was passable.

Now Brady and JT approached the river's edge, yelling at the herd and whistling loudly, keeping the animals together as they drove them into the water. If it were a more gentle crossing, Flax would have joined them, but these rapids were too deep and swift. Besides, today Ruth was in charge of the dog, and she was riding with her grandparents. Meanwhile Mrs. Taylor, after a vigorous morning of walking with Clara and Doris, was resting in the back of Elizabeth's wagon. Clara had made a roster for Mrs. Taylor, listing the days of the week along with different wagons. This way they could share the responsibility of caring for the widow among the wagons with the least occupants. But today was Elizabeth's turn.

Elizabeth felt proud to see Brady and JT working together so well. She knew that Brady's herding skills had actually earned him some respect from fellow travelers. But unfortunately, not everyone was tolerant to Brady's status as a freed slave. And it wasn't unusual to hear bigoted comments tossed his way occasionally. To her relief, Brady never reacted to these unkind remarks, but many a time Elizabeth had been thankful she wasn't a man, or it might have come to fisticuffs.

Now as Brady and JT were just beginning to cross, Elizabeth was dismayed to see that a youth named Robert Stone was driving several skinny cows right behind them. It wasn't that she disliked Robert, but seeing him reminded her of a scene she'd witnessed between Robert's father and Brady. It had happened months ago, back when they were still organizing the wagon train in Missouri, but Mr. Stone's hateful bigotry was still fresh in her mind. He'd picked a fight with Brady over firewood of all things. In Robert's defense, he hadn't sided with his father that day, but Elizabeth knew that when it came to racism, the apple often fell close to the tree.

It was plain to see that Robert was not nearly the horseman JT or Brady were. Not only that, but Robert's horse was acting quite skittish in the water. Distracted from watching her own son, Elizabeth couldn't help but keep her eyes fixed on Robert. Why had his unit allowed him to take on such a task when he was clearly not up to the job?

The thought had barely gone through her head when she saw the horse stumble, lurching forward and then falling sideways. Robert plunged headfirst into the water. "Oh, no!" she cried out.

"What is it?" Mrs. Taylor called from the back of the wagon.

"Robert Stone just took a bad fall!"

Mrs. Taylor stuck her head out in time to see. "Oh, my Lord!"

Elizabeth jumped down from the wagon, yelling for help, trying to be heard above the noise of the animals. Meanwhile Robert, facedown in the water, was being swept right through the herd. If he was not trampled to death, he would surely be drowned. "Somebody help him!" she shrieked as she ran to the water's edge. "*Brady!*"

Brady turned at the sound of her voice and saw the youth facedown and propelled by the rushing water yet somehow escaping all those hooves. Brady tried to maneuver his horse toward him. But now Robert, still unconscious, was being tumbled downstream like a ragdoll. Brady spurred Penny, urging her to go downstream after the boy. However, the water soon turned deep, and now Penny was forced to swim. Brady, clinging to the horse's mane, stayed with her, floating behind the horse until he suddenly disappeared beneath the water.

With hands over her mouth, Elizabeth watched in horror. As far as she knew, Brady did not know how to swim. Now she noticed a flash across the river and saw Eli riding his horse downriver as well. Would he be able to help them?

Matthew had hopped down from his wagon and run down to the river to assist JT, who was now all alone in getting the herd ashore.

Elizabeth knew all she could do was to pray. With eyes wide open, watching as JT and Matthew scrambled to keep the herd of startled animals together, she prayed for both Brady and Robert...and then for Eli.

Several other bystanders, including her father, who hadn't seen Robert fall, had gathered with her, pummeling her with questions. She gave them a quick account, explaining her fears for Brady.

"Let's get over to the other side and see what we can do," Asa told them. Then he hurried back to his wagon, which was leading their unit today, and quickly drove it across the water. Elizabeth ran back to her wagon, which was fourth in the lineup.

"Who was that in the river?" Mrs. Taylor's face was pale, and her voice sounded shaky. "Not JT?"

"No, JT is fine." Elizabeth released the brake. "Robert Stone, from a different unit." She watched as the wagon behind her father's forded the river. Slowly inching forward, she anxiously awaited her turn.

"One moment, all is well," she said to Mrs. Taylor, "and the next thing you know everything turns to chaos. That is just how it happened."

"Oh, dear." Mrs. Taylor put a hand on Elizabeth's shoulder. "I am just so glad it wasn't your boy."

"Thank you. So am I." Elizabeth blinked back tears. "But Brady went to rescue the boy. He went under. I'm fearful for his life too."

Mrs. Taylor let out a gasp. Then as Elizabeth got her wagon lined up to take her turn, Mrs. Taylor began to pray in a loud confident voice. "Dear Lord, we beseech thee to protect our dear friend Brady. Help him to make it to safety. Let him come to no harm. And we beseech thee on behalf of the boy Robert too. Protect him and help him to get safely to shore. We ask these things in thy holy name, dear Lord. Please, grant these requests to thy servants. Amen."

"Amen," Elizabeth echoed. It was a much more formal prayer than she normally prayed, but she was grateful all the same. But the time had come for her to cross, and she needed to focus her full attention on her team.

❧❦❧

Elizabeth knew that in times of high anxiety, minutes often seemed like hours. After what felt like many hours, some of the men who had gone downriver to see about Brady and Robert returned.

"What is the news?" Elizabeth eagerly asked Hugh Prescott.

"Both men are recovered." Hugh's expression remained serious. "We were sent to fetch the doctor to tend to the boy from unit four." He nodded to his son now. "Julius, you run and see if you can find Dr. Nash. Asa said he's in unit three." As Julius hurried away, Hugh turned back to Elizabeth. "The boy suffered a severe blow to the head. He is still not conscious."

"And Brady?"

"Brady is alive."

She let out a relieved sigh. "I'm so glad."

"But the poor old fellow nearly drowned before he dragged the boy out of the water."

"Brady rescued the boy?"

"That's what Eli said. And he was there to see it happen."

"But Brady is all right?" Elizabeth still felt concerned.

"Matthew and Asa are helping him back to camp right now."

"And my father's horse?" Elizabeth knew how much Father loved Penny.

"The horse is just fine. Made out the best of the lot of them."

Elizabeth noticed more of the group coming now. Squinting into the sun, she could see that it was Matthew and her father on foot, and Brady, slumped forward, was on the back of Penny. She ran to meet them but could tell immediately that although he was alive, he was not well.

"Oh, dear Brady," she exclaimed. "I was so worried."

He barely looked at her.

"Bring him to my wagon," she told her father and brother.

"What about Mrs. Taylor?" Matthew asked.

"Never mind," Elizabeth said. "Bring him to my wagon. Brady's traveling with me and he's my responsibility. Is he not?"

"But Clara can care for him," Asa persisted. "You know she is good at medicine. Let her deal with this, Elizabeth. You already have more than enough on your plate. Your mother will be glad to handle this."

As badly as Elizabeth wanted to help Brady, she knew her father was right. "Fine," she conceded as she walked beside them. "Let mother care for him." She reached up and patted Brady's leg. "You'll be in good hands, Brady. Mother has the healing touch."

"Yes'm," he mumbled in a gruff voice.

"You were very brave to rescue that boy," she said as she walked with them toward the long line of waiting wagons. "If Robert survives it will be due to your selfless courage."

His head barely bobbed.

"I'm going to run and tell Mother you're bringing him." She hiked up her skirts and scurried ahead. When she reached the lead wagon, she breathlessly relayed the story of Brady's rescue. "But he's not well," she said. "I wanted to take him in my wagon, but Father insists you're the best one to nurse him back to health."

"Your father might be right about that." Clara had already turned around and climbed back into the wagon. "I need to get the bed ready. Elizabeth, you and Ruthie run back and get some dry clothes for Brady."

"Yes," Elizabeth agreed. "And I'll send Ruth back with them. But I'll have her and Flax ride with me for the remainder of the day."

Elizabeth knew that no one in this wagon train—probably not even Dr. Nash—could care for Brady as well as her mother. He truly was in good hands. Even so, as the wagons started to roll, she thought about how he had looked slumped over like that on Penny. And she prayed once again for Brady, putting him in God's hands.

Chapter Twelve

It wasn't until the next day that Elizabeth's family learned young Robert Stone was recovering nicely from his near drowning. "Besides a goose egg on his head and a slight loss of memory, he seems just fine," Dr. Nash told them during their midday break. "But I thought I'd drop by and check on your slave."

"He's a *free man*," Elizabeth said.

"Oh, I'm sorry…" Dr. Nash looked confused. "I'm certain Abner Stone said he was a slave."

"That's not surprising." Elizabeth paused from slicing bacon. "But considering how Brady saved Mr. Stone's son's life, I would think he'd be a little more gracious."

"Your man *saved* the boy's life?" Dr. Nash looked doubtful.

"What?" Elizabeth stopped slicing.

"Brady rescued the boy," Asa told him.

Dr. Nash cleared his throat. "That is not what Abner Stone says."

"What is he saying?" Elizabeth demanded.

"Well, I don't like to repeat gossip. But Abner Stone seems to be under the impression that Brady was responsible for his son's accident."

"*What?*" Elizabeth shook the butcher knife in the air. "That's a flat-out lie. I saw the whole thing. Robert's horse stumbled. Robert fell headfirst, and he was swept down the river. Brady left our animals and risked his life going after that boy."

"And Eli saw Brady drag the boy out of the river," Asa added.

"Abner Stone is a bully and a bigot and a liar," Matthew said. "He had it out for Brady right from the get-go—and to say this now."

"Keep your voices down," Elizabeth urged them, nodding toward the wagon behind them.

Now Dr. Nash held up his hands. "I'm not trying to get in the middle of this feud. I only stopped by to check on your...uh...your man. Did you say his name is Brady?"

"Yes," Clara told him. "Right this way, please."

As Clara led him to the wagon, Elizabeth exchanged glances with her brother and father. "Can you believe that?" she quietly demanded.

Matthew shook his fist. "It makes me want to go over to unit four and straighten that man out."

"That's not how we handle our problems." Asa sat down with a perplexed expression.

"Are you saying we should take this lying down?" Matthew demanded.

"No." Asa removed his hat and rubbed his temples.

"Well, I won't go looking for trouble, but if it comes knocking on my door, I'll answer." Then he stormed away.

"Oh, dear." Elizabeth returned to slicing bacon. She was thankful that Jess and the children had gone out gathering kindling and buffalo chips. She sure didn't want JT and Ruth seeing any of this. And it was convenient that Mrs. Taylor was traveling and dining with Ruby and Doris today. She hadn't even protested when Elizabeth let her know that was the plan.

"Matthew will cool down," Asa assured her. "And I do understand his frustration. As a younger man, I might have gone over there to talk some sense into Abner Stone myself." He chuckled. "With my fists."

"Oh, Father." Elizabeth shook her head. "You've never been a violent man."

He stood now, coming over to see how their midday meal was faring. The beans, which had soaked all night, were bubbling, and she'd just begun frying up the bacon. "Do you think I have time to run down the captain and get his opinion on this situation?"

"Sure." She handed him a leftover biscuit from last night. "And don't worry, we'll keep your food warm till you get back."

She gave the beans a stir and then turned the bacon, trying to figure out what made some people so mean. To tell bald-faced lies about Brady! Why would someone do that?

"Keep giving him fluids," the doctor said as he climbed down from the wagon. "And lots of rest."

"What do you think it is?" Elizabeth asked him.

"I'm afraid he got some water in his lungs," Dr. Nash grimly informed her. "It could turn into the old man's friend."

Elizabeth frowned. "You mean..."

"I mean time will tell."

"Do you want some dinner?" Clara offered. "In exchange for your time?"

"No, thank you. The wife has some soup waiting for me."

As she tended to the cooking, Elizabeth couldn't stop Dr. Nash's insensitive comment about "the old man's friend" from running through her head. She knew he was really saying that Brady's lungs might become so congested that he would never recover—that he would quietly die in his sleep.

"Don't worry," Clara told her. "I think Brady is improving. I've been giving him my garlic and honey remedy. And now I'm going to make him some chamomile tea. We'll get him back to his old self. You'll see."

Elizabeth forced a smile. "If anyone can help him, Mother, it's you."

❦

After a couple days of Clara's thoughtful treatment and remedies, which even included an occasional tablespoon of Ruby's spirits, Brady became strong enough to get out of the wagon and walk in the sunshine for a few minutes at a time. He even offered to go back to his old sleeping arrangement of the hammock underneath Elizabeth's wagon.

"I just hate putting Mr. and Mrs. Dawson out of their wagon," he told Elizabeth as she walked alongside him. "Just don't seem right."

"Don't worry about it. Father says he's enjoying sleeping outside. And my mother is perfectly content to sleep with Ruthie and me." She lowered her voice. "And believe me, it's much better than when I had Mrs. Taylor sleeping in my wagon."

He made a weak smile and then coughed. "I sho' appreciate all you folks has done for me. Treatin' me almos' like family. I am truly obliged."

"We are your family," she told him.

"I been dreaming 'bout my farm in Oregon while layin' there in the wagon." He paused to catch his breath. "How I'm gonna plant me some peas and corn and collards and okra." He rubbed his stomach. "Just thinking about it makes me hungry."

"That's a good sign, Brady. Getting your appetite back. Maybe you're ready for something besides soup tonight."

He nodded but then bent over coughing and hacking so hard that Elizabeth gave him her arm to balance himself. Then, knowing he was getting tired, she waved to her father, calling out that Brady had probably walked enough for the time being.

As she and Asa helped him back into the wagon, she was glad that she hadn't told Brady what Will had shared with her a few weeks ago. Just hearing how Brady was dreaming of his own farm, how it was helping him to grow stronger...well, she just didn't think she'd ever be able to tell him the truth. Not while they were on the road anyway. And maybe it didn't matter so much. If they settled far enough from others, who would be the wiser as to Brady's true status?

Naturally, this reminded her of the other thing they were keeping from Brady—Abner Stone's mean-spirited claims that Brady caused his son's accident. Just thinking of this made her feel angry inside. But Asa had explained the situation to the captain, who also listened to both

Eli's and Elizabeth's accounts of what had really happened that day and then offered to intervene on their behalf.

"Robert Stone seemed a bit confused," the captain explained to them yesterday morning after he took the two of them aside for an update. "All the boy remembers was crossing the river with all the live-stock and Brady and JT. After that, he's unclear. I suspect that his pa has filled his head with his own stories and now Robert isn't quite sure what actually happened."

"Would it help if we spoke to him?" Eli offered. "Elizabeth and I could testify to him regarding what we saw that day."

"I suggested that very thing. But Stone claims his boy isn't ready for that. Says he's still getting over the blow to his head."

"I think Mr. Stone's the one who's not ready for that," Elizabeth said. "He doesn't want to know the truth."

"I did give Stone a stern warning," the captain told her. "If he goes around starting rumors or stirring up trouble against Brady, he will have me to answer to."

Elizabeth just nodded. However, she knew that it was impossible for the captain to be in all places at all times. And this was a big wagon train. Just the same, she thanked him for his help.

After the captain continued on his way, Eli remained. "If I get a chance to speak to Abner Stone, I will have no problem attempting to set him straight in regard to what happened to Robert that day."

"Thank you. I appreciate that. And I'm sure Brady would too, although he's unaware of Abner Stone's attempts to sully his name."

"That's probably good." He tipped his hat. "Please give Brady my best. Tell him I look forward to making music together again."

She smiled. "I'll be sure to let him know."

❧

"Today we'll make it to Devil's Gate," Asa told everyone over breakfast.

"Devil's Gate?" Ruth got a worried look, and Elizabeth understood her concerns.

"I hope it's nothing like Devil's Backbone," Elizabeth said quickly.

Asa just laughed. "Don't fret, girls. Devil's Gate is just a big ol' rock. Nothing to get worked up about."

But as she stood there at the end of the day, looking up at the giant arched piece of stone with the sun behind it, she knew it was more than just a big ol' rock. "It's beautiful," she said quietly.

"How did they make it?" Ruth asked.

"Nobody made it," JT told her. "It just happened."

"How did it happen?" Ruth asked. "What made the big hole?"

"The river," Elizabeth explained. "See how it flows right through? Hundreds of years of the powerful water have worn away at the stone, carving a hole right through it."

"Why didn't the river just go around it?" JT asked. "Wouldn't that have been easier?"

"That's a good question," Elizabeth pointed out. "I'm not sure myself. I think rivers normally do go around things like this."

"But I'm glad it didn't," Ruth said happily. "I like it just how it is. I think it's very pretty."

"So do I," Elizabeth agreed. "And it reminds me of us."

"Of us?" JT looked confused.

"How?" Ruth asked.

"We wanted to go west," Elizabeth began. "Some people said it was too hard. But we really wanted to go…so we just pressed onward. We have pressed on and on, just like this river. And like this river, we're carving our own way through the wilderness."

"I wish they'd change the name of this rock," Ruth said suddenly. "Instead of calling it Devil's Gate, they should call it God's Gate."

"I agree." Elizabeth nodded. "Much better."

"Because God is getting us to the West," Ruth proclaimed. "And this is like his gate."

So the three of them agreed, from that point on, they would refer to it as God's Gate. And that night, when Elizabeth insisted they all write in their journals, she described God's Gate in detail. And JT drew a nice picture of it. And Ruth wrote a sweet little poem.

❧

"We should make it to Split Rock tomorrow afternoon," Eli announced a few days later. It was the first day that Brady had felt well enough to walk for most of the day—and the family and Eli were celebrating his recovery with a little music. Asa had let others in the unit know it would only be a small gathering. And when Matthew noticed Brady getting winded on the harmonica, he suggested they take a break. Now Clara was insisting that Brady drink some tea and honey.

"Is Split Rock like God's Gate?" Ruth asked Eli.

"*God's Gate?*" Eli tipped his head to one side.

"We renamed Devil's Gate," Elizabeth explained. "After suffering Devil's Backbone, we were weary of the 'devil' name." She laughed. "God's Gate just seemed more appropriate."

"I have to agree with you on that." He chuckled. "Well, Split Rock isn't nearly as spectacular as Devil's—I mean *God's* Gate. But it is interesting for other reasons."

"What is it?" JT asked.

"It's a notched rock in the Rattlesnake Range."

"Are there lots of rattlesnakes up there?" Ruth looked concerned.

"Not any more than most places. Do you remember my warning about rattlers, Ruth?"

She nodded soberly. "Watch out around rocky places. And they like shady holes on hot days. And if you hear a rattler, don't scream or jump. Just slowly move away."

"Very good." He nodded.

"So what's special about Split Rock?" JT asked him.

Eli held his fingers like a V then peered through it. "It has a notch kind of like this, and if you look out of it just right, you will have South Pass in your sights."

"South Pass?" JT's brow creased. "Isn't that in the middle of the Great Continental Divide?"

"Sounds like someone's been doing his geography." Eli winked.

"Mama makes us," he told him.

"Yes. South Pass is in the easiest place to cross the Great Divide."

"Does that mean we'll be in Oregon then?" Ruth eyes grew wide.

Eli nodded. "We will officially enter Oregon Territory soon."

"But it's still a long way to where we plan to settle," Elizabeth reminded her. "You've seen the place on the map—near the Pacific Ocean."

"But we will be in Oregon." Ruth danced with excitement now. "Really truly in Oregon. Will it be beautiful there like Malinda wrote us?"

"I better warn you," Eli told her. "South Pass is not nearly as pretty as some of the territory we've just gone through. It'll be mostly flat barren land, with some sagebrush, bunchgrass, and lots and lots of sky. Although it can be a good place to hunt sometimes."

"Oh." Ruth nodded, trying to take this in.

"Also, there's a town up there."

"A real town?" Elizabeth felt hopeful. "Not a fort?"

"South Pass City is a real frontier town. They discovered gold in those parts a dozen or so years ago," Eli explained. "Naturally a town sprouted up." He frowned. "To be honest, it's not the best sort of town. And they've had their share of troubles." He went on to explain how the mining was said to have ruined the river and how that had angered the Indians. "As a result there's been plenty of skirmishes round those parts."

"Is it dangerous?" Elizabeth asked.

"I don't reckon you need to worry much. But just to be sure, I'll be scouting around for the next few days. Want to make sure the Indians are acting friendly to emigrants."

"The best news about South Pass," Asa told them, "is that it's considerably flat up there. We'll still be at high elevation, but it'll be fairly easy traveling for the next week or so. We should be able to make good time."

The next day, they began their ascent into Rattlesnake Range, and late in the day, they stopped at Split Rock, where just as Eli had said, similar to a big stone gun sight, they could spot South Pass right through the notch. They all took turns looking and then, eager to make camp, continued on their way.

During the first couple of days traveling over South Pass, Elizabeth tried to hide her disappointment for the sake of her children. As Eli had said, this country was not nearly as attractive as along the Sweetwater River. Though they were now in Oregon Country, which was often referred to as the Promised Land, everything for as far as she could see looked bleak and dry and hot. Certainly, it was not as bad as Devil's Backbone, and there was water to be had at regular intervals, but other than the flatness, which made for smoother traveling, it was not very enjoyable.

However, by the third day, she began to see this place differently. She began to appreciate the vastness of the sky, the formations of the constantly changing clouds, and the occasional herd of buffalo or antelope moving across the land. She decided that in its own way, this landscape was beautiful too. However, she was extremely thankful that she and her family were not settling in this part of the country.

As usual, Elizabeth either walked or rode Molly in the cooler part of the morning. Today, she was walking with several other women friends again. Up ahead of their group, Jess was walking with Fiona and, it seemed, enjoying an animated conversation. It was nice seeing those two young wives forming a friendship. And Paddy and Matthew seemed to get along as well. So much so that Elizabeth secretly hoped the McIntires might consider settling along the southern Oregon coast too. But as usual, she wasn't going to mention this. Everyone needed to make their own decisions.

"Look at those rugged looking mountains." Flo pointed toward the northwest.

"That's the Wind River Range," Elizabeth told them. "Father was just talking about them at breakfast."

"But just look at all that snow," Flo continued. "It must be frightfully cold up there. Just like winter."

"What does that mean?" Lavinia frowned up at the mountains. "Is winter coming early? Are we in danger of being snowed in? I've heard stories about—"

"No, no," Elizabeth assured her. "It's not like that at all. My father said that snow is perfectly normal. He said that some mountains out West have snow on them year-round."

"Oh, my." Flo sighed. "It makes me cold just to think of it."

"I certainly hope I'll be able to purchase a few more blankets and things in South Pass City," Lavinia said. "To make up for the ones I left on the other side." She shook her head. "What a foolish thing that was."

"Don't be so sure," Elizabeth told her. "That extra weight could have meant the difference between a serious breakdown and being here right now."

"Yes, don't forget Mr. Taylor," Flo reminded her.

"And a number of other unfortunates," Elizabeth said.

"Hugh told me that more than a dozen emigrants have been laid to rest on our journey so far."

Already aware that the death toll had just reached fifteen, Elizabeth simply nodded.

"Hopefully, the worst is behind us now," Flo said with optimism. "Bert said we have lots of downhill traveling ahead. I reckon that'll be much easier on everyone."

"Not necessarily," Elizabeth warned. "Going downhill can be hard on a team, and it requires great concentration and expertise on the part of the driver. I'm not sure I'll allow JT or even Brady to do much of the driving when we start going down."

"I didn't realize that," Lavinia admitted. "I do hope that Hugh and Will grasp this. Our boys have been doing a fair amount of driving too. But they have no experience going down a mountain range such as this."

"I'm sure my father will give our unit a good lesson before we begin our descent," Elizabeth told them.

"Thank the good Lord for Asa," Flo said. "Speaking of Asa, I've a mind to ask him to speak to my Mahala for me."

"Mahala?" Lavinia asked.

"I'm afraid she's caught the eye of a young man in unit one."

"That's not surprising," Elizabeth said. "Mahala is a very pretty girl."

"And eager to wed," Lavinia said.

"Well, she *is* eighteen," Elizabeth reminded her. She looked up past Jess and Fiona to where the younger girls in their unit were all walking together, scurrying about and stooping down at regular intervals to collect buffalo chips. Hearing that some folks were running short on fuel, Asa had announced a contest this morning. "The youngin who finds the most chips wins a prize." Of course, no one knew what the prize would be, but Ruth had borrowed Elizabeth's old apron to collect the chips in. "It's like an Easter egg hunt," she'd said with enthusiasm.

"Believe me, I know she's eighteen." Flo sighed. "Hannah teases her constantly, calling her an old maid. An old maid at eighteen?"

"So tell us, Flo, what's wrong with this young man in unit one?" Lavinia inquired.

Flo scowled. "I don't like to pass judgment on anyone. But there is something about this man that bothers me."

"How so?" Elizabeth pressed.

"Well, my first impression was that he has shifty eyes. But it's more than just that." Flo held up a finger. "For one thing, he is traveling alone."

"What difference does that make?" Elizabeth asked.

She held up a second finger. "And two, he is traveling very light."

"Oh…" Lavinia got a knowing expression. "Do you think he's running from the law?"

Flo had a grim expression. "And three, he just acts plain sneaky."

"What kind of sneaky?" Elizabeth asked.

"Instead of coming around to visit Mahala in the light of day and politely acquainting himself with her family, he sneaks around. He meets up with her behind our backs. The man reminds me of a slippery snake. I wouldn't be surprised if he plans to run off with Mahala and marry her on the sly." She shuddered. "If he even intends to marry her!"

"Oh, dear." Elizabeth felt very concerned now. "What does Bert say about all this?"

"Bert is so durned busy in his spare time. Oh, I shouldn't complain, because all this blacksmithing work is going to feather our nest once we settle. But all the same, I just hate to trouble him with this. After all, I might be all wrong." Flo let out a loud sigh. "And one thing I forgot to mention about the young man…"

"What's that?"

"He's devilishly handsome. Dark curly hair, dark eyes."

"Oh…" Elizabeth and Lavinia exchanged glances.

"Will you tell me this young man's name?" Lavinia asked. "I certainly don't want to see him trailing around any of our young ladies."

"He goes by Jack Smith." Lavinia scowled. "But I wonder if that's his given name."

"Jack Smith in unit one," Elizabeth said slowly. "I'll let my father and brother know to be on the lookout for him."

"And I'll tell Hugh and Will and our boys too," Lavinia said.

"With all these fellows watching out for Mahala, she should be safe."

"'Ceptin' that she seems to like the attention...and, as I said, he is devilishly handsome."

"Have you tried just talking with her?" Elizabeth asked.

Flo laughed. "Until your Ruth gets a few more years on her, I reckon you have no idea what it's like to talk to a daughter Mahala's age." She turned to Lavinia. "Do you understand my meaning?"

Lavinia chuckled. "My Evelyn's only sixteen, but she thinks she's all grown up. She likes to tell me what to do."

"Mahala thinks I don't know what I'm talking about half of the time."

"Even my sweet nieces, Belinda and Amelia...they do give me a bit more respect than Evelyn, but they don't heed my advice the way they used to."

"I suppose I should be thankful that Ruthie is still young."

"Count your blessings," Flo told her.

"Well, I probably shouldn't say this..." Lavinia spoke cautiously.

"Say what?" Flo asked eagerly.

"Can I trust you not to repeat it?" Lavinia eyed them both.

"Certainly." Flo nodded. "You have my word."

"Well...I happen to know that your Mahala caught the eye of my Julius months ago, back when we first started out on this journey."

"Truly?" Flo looked hopeful.

"However, besides being partners for an occasional dance, I don't know that Mahala has given my poor boy any encouragement. And poor Julius...well, he's a little shy around the ladies. Especially the ones he's fond of."

"Julius is a very nice young man," Elizabeth intervened. "Both he and Jeremiah are well spoken and polite."

Lavinia nodded. "I'd be the first to agree with you on that."

"How old is your Julius?" Flo asked.

"He'll be twenty in November."

Flo looked hopeful. "I sure do wish that Mahala would look his direction instead of batting her eyelashes at that slimy Jack Smith."

"But what if you're wrong about Jack?" Elizabeth tried. "It's so easy to misjudge people. Remember when everyone thought Jess was a man?"

They all laughed. Just the same, Elizabeth was determined to inform Matthew and Asa to be on the lookout for this notorious Jack Smith. She hoped Flo was wrong about his character. But it wouldn't hurt to do some quiet investigating. In fact, the next time she saw Eli, she would ask him his opinion on this matter. He seemed a pretty fair judge of people.

Chapter Thirteen

By the end of the next day, the landscape had changed dramatically. They had entered a very wet grassy area that was perfect for grazing the livestock. Even the air was moist and cooler than usual.

"I wish we could camp here for a week," Clara said as she and Elizabeth set up their outdoor kitchen. Asa had taken the children for a walk. Naturally, their initial reaction to walking at the end of the day was not enthusiastic.

"It's to see an interesting sight," he'd told them with a twinkle in his eye. And that was all it took to get them on their feet. Then, like the Pied Piper, Asa stopped by other campsites in their unit, inviting all the other children to join him. Even some of the young people went along as well.

Out of habit, Elizabeth almost called out to remind the children to pick up buffalo chips on their way. But then she remembered they were still well stocked from yesterday. Ruth had been the winner of Asa's "Easter egg" contest. Elizabeth wasn't sure if it was due to Ruth's persistent diligence or if the older girls had helped her when they saw how hard she was working to win. But to Ruth's delight, the prize was a half dollar to spend as she liked in South Pass City on Saturday. A virtual windfall.

Supper was nearly ready by the time Asa and the children returned to camp. But the way they were giggling and carrying on over something in a bucket made Elizabeth very curious. "Did you children bring home a frog?" she asked.

"No," JT told her. "Something even better."

"You both have to guess," Ruth said.

"Is it a turtle?" Clara asked as she dished out a plate.

"No."

"Berries?" Elizabeth ventured as she poured Asa a cup of coffee.

"No. But we might want to have some for dessert," Ruth said.

"What is it?" Elizabeth demanded, coming over to peek in the bucket.

"Ice!" both children said at once.

Sure enough, it did look like a big chunk of ice. Elizabeth touched it. "Where on earth did you find this?" She eyed her father.

"Captain Brownlee told us about Ice Slough a few days ago," he explained. "That's what this place is called. And over in the ice caves you can find ice year-round."

"Oh, my." Clara came over to see for herself. "What do you know!"

"Can we make shaved ice with sugar for dessert?" Ruth asked hopefully.

"We can do even better than that," Clara told her. "But first let's eat our supper before that wonderful ice melts."

Elizabeth covered it in towels to help keep it cold while they ate supper. Then, while Elizabeth and Clara cleaned up afterward, Asa helped the children to make bowls of shaved ice, topped with sugar and some berry juice that Clara had preserved on the trail. The results were cool and delicious.

Unfortunately, their stay in Ice Slough was brief, and the next day they were moving through dry, hot, barren land again. But at least it was easy traveling. Elizabeth had decided to ride Molly this morning.

Feeling surprisingly refreshed from their short stay at Ice Slough, she'd even taken the time to put on her full riding outfit. As well as her best hat.

"Don't you look nice," Clara had told her when she rode past where her mother was walking with Ruth and Jess. Elizabeth thanked her and waved. She also waved at where JT and Brady were driving her wagon. Then she nudged Molly into a trot and then a canter. It was fun feeling the cool morning air in her face. And Molly seemed to enjoy this bit of freedom as well.

Elizabeth continued riding on up, hoping to get ahead of the wagon train, where she could ride without breathing the dust the wheels and hooves stirred up. She was nearly to the front when she observed a young woman walking alongside one of the wagons and talking to the driver. Upon closer inspection, she realized the young woman was Mahala Flanders. And of course, she must have reached unit one by now because they were in front this week.

Slowing her horse, Elizabeth reined Molly closer to Mahala, hoping to get a peek at what she assumed could only be the mysterious Jack Smith. And sure enough, the man had dark curly hair and dark eyes. But he didn't appear as young as Elizabeth had assumed he would be. In fact, unless she was mistaken, this man was probably in his thirties.

"Mahala." Elizabeth feigned surprise. "My goodness, what are you doing way up here?"

Mahala looked up with a startled expression. "Oh, hello, Elizabeth." She made a stiff smile. "I was just out walking this morning. I didn't notice that I'd gone so far ahead of our unit."

"I was just enjoying a ride." Now Elizabeth slid down from the saddle, and holding the rein, she walked next to Mahala. Then looking up at the attractive stranger with what she hoped seemed a natural interest, she smiled brightly. "I don't believe we've met. I'm Elizabeth Martin and a friend of Mahala's."

"Pleased to meet you, Elizabeth." He smiled back at her. "Name's Jack Smith."

"Pleased to meet you too. Are you traveling with your family?"

He shook his head. "No, I'm not that fortunate. I'm traveling alone."

"Oh." She nodded with sympathy. "And where is your final destination, if you don't mind me asking?"

"California," he told her. "Off to find my fortune like everyone else."

"So you're one of those who will be parting ways with this train before too long."

"Yep. I'll be heading south soon."

Elizabeth eyed Mahala. "You probably know that Mahala and her family are headed for Oregon."

"So I've heard." He glanced down at Mahala and then back at Elizabeth with what seemed growing interest. As if he was really looking at her—but in a way that made her truly uncomfortable. Still, she was determined not to show it.

"Well, I'm sorry I only just met you, Jack, especially seeing how you're traveling alone," she told him. "But this is a big wagon train and it's hard to get to know everyone."

"It certainly is."

Although Elizabeth hated playing coy, she felt she'd been presented an opportunity to get this man to show his true colors—and in front of Mahala. "California certainly sounds like a pretty place," she told him. "I hear that you can grow almost anything down there. My children and I are headed to southern Oregon to start a farm there."

"You and your children?" His dark brows arched with interest. "What about your husband?"

"Sadly, I'm a widow."

"I'm sorry." Unless she was mistaken, his eyes lit up at this news.

"I sold my farm in Kentucky so we could set out for a new life," she continued. "Some think it was foolish for a young widow to come on a trip like this, but the lure of new land and new fortunes…" She smiled. "Who could resist?"

"So you're an adventuress." He looked at her in a way that made her skin crawl, almost as if she'd come upon a snake on the trail. Perhaps she had.

"I suppose I am." She patted Molly's neck. "Well, I guess I should be on my way. I promised my mare a good ride this morning."

"That is one fine-looking horse. Very fine." He glanced past her and she watched him carefully eyeing her horse, taking in the fine English saddle and silver-trimmed bridle. She felt sure she had this man figured out. No doubt he was a fortune hunter, which left only one explanation for why he was toying with Mahala's affections.

"Thank you." She smoothed Molly's mane, determined to pour it on thick. She wanted him to think she was wealthy...and silly. "My family was known for raising some of the best and fastest horses in Kentucky. My father used to race them too. Anyway, I hope to continue the tradition in Oregon. And I brought some of my finest livestock with me."

As she removed her riding gloves, tucking them into her belt, she could feel Mahala's eyes on her—and her fury. Not that Elizabeth cared so much. If she could spare this girl from a future of pain, what did it matter? Jack planned to part ways at South Pass, which was less than two days away. What if Mahala was considering going with him?

"Hearing you speaking of Oregon...I wonder if I have made a mistake," he told Elizabeth.

"A mistake?" Elizabeth tipped her head to one side. "What do you mean?"

"I mean—well, it seems as if the prettiest women in the wagon train are headed for Oregon. Why on earth am I going to California?"

Mahala spoke suddenly. "But Jack, I asked you about coming to Oregon with us and you said you couldn't—"

"I reckon a fellow can change his mind if he wants to, Mahala." His tone just now was much sharper than the honey-coated one he'd been using with Elizabeth.

"Does that mean you *will* come to Oregon?" Mahala looked up hopefully.

He looked past her, smiling directly at Elizabeth as if Mahala had disappeared. "I'm sure I could be enticed to change my plans."

Elizabeth nudged Mahala. "What do you think, should we entice him or not?"

Mahala's cheeks were flushed pink, and she looked flustered and confused, as if she were playing a game where someone had changed all the rules. "I...uh, I'm not sure."

"Perhaps we should invite Jack to come visit our unit tonight," Elizabeth told her. "He could meet our fathers and—"

"*Fathers?*" It was Jack who looked uneasy now. "I thought you were traveling alone, Elizabeth. Alone…with your children, I mean."

She made an innocent smile. "Oh, didn't I mention my father and mother are traveling with us as well? Naturally they have their own wagon. As do I. My father is councilman of our unit. And my brother and his new bride are traveling with us as well. And Mahala has both her parents and lots of brothers and sisters with her." She laughed. "If you are tired of being alone, you would certainly enjoy all the family and entertainment we can provide for you in our unit." She grinned at Mahala. "Isn't that right?"

Mahala appeared to be speechless.

"So please, Jack, do feel free to visit us this evening." She gave him a coquettish smile. "Can we expect you for supper?"

"I…uh…I'm not sure."

"Oh?"

"I'll give it some thought."

"All right. You know we're in unit five." Elizabeth turned back to Mahala. "Do you want to walk with me for a spell?"

Mahala didn't answer. She just looked from Elizabeth to Jack and back to Elizabeth again. Then without saying a word to Jack she turned away from him and, to Elizabeth's delight, she continued to walk with her. Elizabeth slowly edged them away from the trail, watching as Jack's wagon, moving just a bit faster than they were, moved on ahead.

"What were you doing just now?" Mahala hissed at her.

"I was visiting with you and Jack," she told her.

"No…you were up to something. I could tell. What was it? And why?"

"Just being neighborly."

"*Elizabeth.*" Mahala stopped walking, locking eyes with Elizabeth.

"All right." Elizabeth put her hand on Mahala's shoulder. "I'm sorry, but I was concerned for you when I saw you visiting with Jack."

"*Why?*"

Elizabeth shrugged. "You seemed in intimate conversation, Mahala.

But something about it did not feel right to me. I care about you, and as your friend, I wanted to be sure you were all right."

"You *care* about me?" Mahala turned to stare at her. "It looked to me like you cared more about Jack than me."

"I'm truly sorry about my little charade." Elizabeth shook her head. "I was just curious, Mahala. I wanted to see what Jack was made of."

"What did you *think* he was made of?"

"Unfortunately, I could feel the way he was looking at me. The way he took inventory of my horse and reacted to my words gave me the impression that he thought he could snare a wealthy widow on her way to the West—that he would take full advantage of the situation. Couldn't you see that?"

"You don't even know him, Elizabeth." Mahala sounded angry now.

"I think you're wrong. I do know him. Rather, I know what sort of a man he is. You saw how warm he was toward me…and how he changed when he heard I had family to back me. His interest in me completely vanished. The idea of my father and brother scared him off. Didn't you see that?"

Mahala bit her lip.

"Why would my father—one of the sweetest men around—scare off a man like Jack?"

"I…uh, I don't know."

"Did Jack ever offer to come around and meet your parents, Mahala?" Elizabeth looked directly into her eyes.

There was a long pause. "No…"

"Do you honestly think Jack was courting you?"

"I don't know."

"Did he ever mention marriage to you?"

Another long pause. "No…"

"Did he ask you to go to California with him?"

Mahala said nothing, but Elizabeth saw silent tears building in her dark brown eyes. She saw her chin beginning to quiver.

"Oh, Mahala." Elizabeth reached over and hugged the girl, holding her tightly as she spoke. "Don't you know you are worth so much more than that? You are smart and kind and beautiful. And yet Jack would only take advantage of you…for his own selfish purposes. I can assure you that Jack Smith has some deep dark secrets. I know you are a good and decent girl. Jack Smith is looking out for himself above everyone else—including you. Trust me, you would be making the biggest mistake of your life if you went to California with him. He would use you and then discard you as soon as his next opportunity came along."

Elizabeth released her, but now the tears were pouring down Mahala's cheeks. "I was such a fool," she said. "But I wanted to believe him."

"I know you did. But I just don't know *why* you did."

"Because…because…" She let out a loud sigh. "It's just that I…well, I don't want to be an old maid."

Elizabeth threw back her head and laughed.

"That's what Hannah keeps saying I am, Elizabeth. An old maid. She tells me that all the time. And it's true. Hannah will probably find a husband before I do."

"That's nonsense. Listen to me, Mahala. We are headed to country where men outnumber women by a great deal. Believe me, no one as smart and pretty as you has the slightest chance of being an old maid."

"Really?"

"Of course." Elizabeth pulled out a handkerchief and handed it to her. "Not only that, but there are nice young men right here on this very wagon train—and not Jack Smith, thank your lucky stars. But there are decent young men like, say, Julius Prescott…young men who would be over the moon to be able to court a girl like you."

"Oh, go on." She waved her hand. "Why would a wealthy Boston boy notice a girl like me?"

"Can you keep a secret?" Elizabeth knew she might be stepping over a line, but it seemed the right thing to do at the moment.

"What?" Mahala wiped her wet cheeks and then gave the handkerchief back.

Elizabeth held up her hand like an oath. "Promise you won't tell anyone if I tell you this?"

Mahala held up her hand. "I promise."

"All right. The secret is that you, Mahala Flanders, caught Julius Prescott's eye the very first day he met you."

"No!" Mahala looked truly stunned. "Are you teasing me?"

Elizabth shook her head. "Not at all. I heard it from a very reliable source. The trouble is that Julius is very shy around girls. Especially if he likes them."

"Oh...?" She slowly nodded. "My brother Ezra is like that too."

"So, you understand what I'm saying?"

"I think I do."

Now they both walked along in silence for a while, and Elizabeth could tell that Mahala was deep in thought. Perhaps she was even planning her wedding with Julius. Elizabeth didn't even care. She was just relieved that Mahala was not going to be trapped by the likes of Jack Smith...if that was his real name. Flo had been right. The man was a snake.

"Elizabeth?" Mahala's voice sounded worried.

"Yes?"

"Please, don't tell my mother about any of this."

Elizabeth chuckled. "I won't tell if you don't tell."

Mahala stopped walking and stuck out her hand. "It's a deal."

As they shook on this, Elizabeth was greatly relieved to know that this morning's strange conversation with Jack Smith would remain their secret. Despite the happy results, Elizabeth wasn't the least bit proud of the role she'd played in order to reveal that man's slimy character. She was just as glad to bury it.

Chapter Fourteen

I don't know how it happened or when it happened, but you'll hear no complaints from me," Flo quietly told Elizabeth the next afternoon. They had met on their way to fetch water for the evening meal, and Flo was all lit up.

"What are you talking about?" Elizabeth hooked one of the full buckets on the end of the yoke, balancing it while she put the other one in place.

"*Mahala,*" Flo whispered.

"Oh?" Elizabeth decided to act oblivious. "How is Mahala?"

"She seems to have forgotten all about that nasty Jack Smith."

"Has she?" Elizabeth adjusted the carrying yoke over her shoulders, waiting for Flo to join her with a sloshing bucket in each hand.

"At first I feared she was hiding something from me. For all I knew she was planning to run off with the snake."

"But she's not?"

Flo shook her head. "No. She seems to have put him completely behind her." She lowered her voice again. "And unless I'm mistaken, she has set her sights on the Prescott boy."

"Julius?" Elizabeth feigned surprise.

"Yes." She nodded eagerly. "Julius Prescott."

Elizabeth smiled. "Well, he should be pleased."

They were catching up with some of the young women, and Flo changed the subject. "I hear we'll make it to South Pass City by tomorrow afternoon. Bert's been making enough money with his blacksmithing that I plan to do some shopping. We're right low on flour and beans and bacon."

They continued to visit as they walked back to camp. Flo seemed exceptionally happy as she chatted. It was probably due to her relief that Mahala had come to her senses, or perhaps it was something more. Elizabeth remembered back to when she first met Flo on the riverboat. Certainly, she seemed happy enough then. But it was a giddy sort of gladness that bordered on silliness. At the time, Elizabeth had assumed Flo wasn't a very deep person, and she didn't fully trust her. But after all these months on the trail together, watching Flo working hard, caring for her children, being a good wife to Bert…well, Flo seemed to have changed in some good ways. Certainly she was still a fun-loving person. But she also had a little more grist to her. And Elizabeth was proud to call Flo her friend.

"Are you and Bert still set on going all the way to the southern Oregon coast to settle?" Elizabeth asked. "In Elk Creek, like we are?"

"Oh, yes. Bert's mind is made up on it." Flo frowned. "However, that means we'll have to part ways with you folks."

"You won't travel on to Vancouver with us?"

"No. Bert says we can't afford passage for our whole family and all our belongings on a ship. He wants us to take the Applegate Trail. I reckon it'll take us a while longer to get there. But in due time we'll catch up with you. And if this place is as pretty as we've heard, we will be most grateful to get there."

"And we will be most grateful to see our dear friends again."

"Do you reckon the Bostonians will settle there too?"

"They seem to be leaning that way."

"Oh, good. That will please Mahala to no end."

Later, as Elizabeth was working with her mother and Ruth to pre-pare supper, she was thinking on these things, wondering over all the relationships that had been established on this wagon train.

"You're very quiet this evening," Clara said after Ruth went to their wagon to get a sweater. "Is anything wrong, dear?"

Elizabeth pushed the pan of nearly baked biscuits back into the heat. "No, Mother, I'm fine. Just thinking." She told her that the Flanders planned to take the Applegate Trail to join them in Oregon. "And the Prescotts and Bramfords seem to be changing their plans to do the same."

Clara gave her a sly smile. "Well, I think that Will Bramford has his own special reasons for wanting to follow you."

"Oh, Mother." Elizabeth waved her hand.

"Anyway, I think it's wonderful we've made such fine friends on this trip." Clara stirred the stew and then replaced the lid. "Won't it be a delight to have them settling in Oregon with us?"

"Yes...of course." Elizabeth set the plates and silverware out. "I just hope we haven't been too influential in their decisions."

"Oh, I don't think you need to worry. These are strong-willed peo-ple, Elizabeth. I doubt that we'd be able to influence them to do any-thing they didn't want to do." She smiled. "Fiona told me that she and Paddy want to join us there too."

"Oh, that will be so nice for Matthew and Jess. To have a young cou-ple..." She sighed. "Won't it be sweet to see them raising their children together?"

"At this rate, most of unit five might wind up being our neighbors in Oregon." Clara poked the fire with a stick.

"Well, except for the Mullers and the Schneiders. They are still deter-mined to settle farther south in Oregon." Elizabeth chuckled. "And I do not plan to encourage them to do otherwise."

"And Mrs. Taylor is still set to go to the mission near Fort Walla Walla."

"Yes...I know."

"It won't be long before this wagon train starts to part ways." Clara sighed. "I suppose it will be sad in some ways."

ᘒ⁓ᘒ

The women were in high spirits as they walked into South Pass City together. The men, tending to livestock, were not far behind. And the young people, eager to explore this town, were not far ahead. They all knew they had only two hours before they must be on the trail again. And so they walked quickly, chatting happily among themselves as they went.

"How many letters did you write?" Flo asked Lavinia with wonder.

Lavinia held up her large bundle of letters. "I want all my friends in Boston to know what a delightful time we're having," she told her. "I'm hoping they'll want to follow our example and come out themselves next year."

Elizabeth laughed. "Did you tell them the truth, Lavinia? Did you describe the hardships? Or all the times you wanted to turn back? And your plans to stop right here in South Pass City and check into the best hotel and never come out again? Did you tell them that?"

Lavinia chuckled. "Certainly not. That is something they'll have to discover for themselves." She pointed to the top envelope now, holding it up for Elizabeth to see that it was addressed to Fort Vancouver. "And this letter is to instruct our shipping company to send our goods on down to Empire City in Coos Bay and to secure us passage on the same ship that your father has booked for your family."

Elizabeth glanced at her mother.

"So the decision is made," Clara said happily. "I'm so glad to hear it."

Flo pointed to the young people ahead of them. Most of them were laughing and making merry, but Mahala and Julius seemed deep in conversation. "I know that news will make one of my children very happy."

As they came into the dusty little town, going their separate ways, Elizabeth felt unimpressed. Why would anyone choose to live in such a bleak and desolate place? Of course, she knew it was the gold that brought these people here. Fortune seekers. But was it worth it? As they searched for a mercantile, they passed a number of saloons, and Elizabeth tried not to pass judgment on the inhabitants of South Pass City. It was hard not to feel pity for them. No one looked very happy. Oh, folks might be laughing, but they didn't seem truly happy. She glanced at some ill-clad women lingering outside of a dance hall and flirting with a group of tough-talking men. Such empty lives. And all for the pursuit of gold and fortune? The city seemed to testify that the love of money really is the root of all evil.

While the women were searching for the post office, a fistfight broke out in front of a saloon, and two men tumbled into the dust right in front of them. Elizabeth grabbed Ruth's hand and her mother's arm, hurrying them both over to the other side of the street. She wished she hadn't brought Ruth to this rough mining town, and she hoped Father was keeping a close eye on JT. The sooner they left here, the better.

"Maybe we should have discouraged Brady from coming here today," she said quietly to her mother. "I hope he doesn't run into any trouble."

"Oh, I'm sure your father and brother will see that he doesn't."

They found the post office, but to Elizabeth's dismay, there was no letter from Malinda and John. She tried to conceal her disappointment as they took care of their other errands. At their last stop, the mercantile, Ruth was unable make up her mind about how to spend her half dollar. Tired of this noisy town, Elizabeth felt her patience dwindling, and she was about to tell her indecisive daughter to simply get the candy. Never mind that she had discouraged sweets earlier.

"I will get the colored pencils," Ruth announced.

Elizabeth smiled. "Excellent choice."

The final purchase made, they hurried back to camp. Elizabeth knew they hadn't used up their full two hours, but she was relieved to get out of South Pass City just the same.

"We seem to be the first ones back," Clara said as she sat down in the shade of the wagon. Ruth was already looking for her tablet, ready to try out the new pencils.

Elizabeth loosened the strings on her bonnet. "I'm sure the others will be along soon," she told her mother.

"That town was disappointing."

"Such sad, empty lives." Elizabeth filled a drinking cup with water, sharing it with her mother.

"I've heard that gold rushes bring out the worst in folks." Clara handed back the tin cup. "I think we saw that with our own eyes today."

Elizabeth nodded and then took a sip.

"Are you worried about not receiving a letter from John and Malinda yet?"

She hung the cup back up and sighed. "I really thought Malinda would have written to me...and that I would have received it by now. I sent her a complete list of the posts along the way. She's familiar with how wagon trains work. Why hasn't she written?"

"I'm sure she did write, Elizabeth. But there's no telling how dependable the mail service is out here in the frontier. There are robberies and Indians and...well, there must be a dozen ways that a letter could get lost."

"I suppose." Then she excused herself and set off to saddle up Molly. With only two more hours left on the trail today, her plan was to ride.

She was just cinching up Molly's saddle as their fellow travelers began to return from town. Everyone was busily getting into the wagons and preparing to leave, and JT, eager to drive, already had the reins in his hands. Elizabeth had just climbed onto her horse when she looked around. "Where's Brady?" she asked her son.

He shrugged. "I haven't seen him since we went to town."

"He didn't come home with you and Grandpa?"

"Nope. All he wanted was to get some socks. I thought he came back with you."

"Wait here while I go ask around." First she went up to where Matthew's wagon was just starting to roll. "Have you seen Brady?" she asked.

"Not since town," he told her.

She looked at the empty seat next to him. "Where's Jess? Is she missing too?"

He grinned. "Nah, she's walking with Fiona. They took off a while ago."

Waving, she turned the horse around, certain that Brady must be with JT by now. But as she rode back, she could see he wasn't. She hurried over to her parents' wagon, which was also starting to move forward, but neither of them had seen Brady either.

"What should I do?" she asked her father.

"I don't know." He grimly shook his head, slowing his wagon to a stop. "I can't very well ask the whole train to wait for him."

"I know." She glanced over her shoulder toward town, wishing that she'd spot her old friend slowly walking toward them. "JT wants to drive anyway. I'll head back toward town to look for him," she said quickly.

"*By yourself?*" He looked alarmed. "I'll come with—"

"You can't leave Mother alone to drive the wagon," she told him.

"Get your brother then."

"He's alone too." She made a brave smile. "Don't worry, I'll be fine. Can I take your horse so Brady will have something to ride? We can catch up with you."

"I don't like this, Elizabeth."

She was already untying Penny and hoping that Brady wouldn't mind riding bareback. "Don't worry," she said again. "We'll be back in no time. I'm guessing Brady just got tired. He probably sat down to catch his breath." She said *gid-up* to Molly and gave a cheery wave to her parents. "See you soon!"

But as she rode Molly toward town, she didn't feel nearly as confident as she had put on. The last place she wanted to be right now was back in that horrid little mining town. Still, she couldn't leave Brady behind. She wouldn't! She just hoped that no harm had come to the dear old friend. And so, as she rode, she prayed for his safety and welfare.

She was nearly in town when she heard the sound of hooves thundering up from behind her. Startled and preparing herself for trouble, she said "Whoa" to Molly and peered over her shoulder, bracing herself for horse thieves, drunken miners, or Indians.

To her relief it was Eli. "Elizabeth," he called out. "What are you doing heading into town again—and all by yourself?"

She quickly explained her dilemma. "It's not my father's fault. He didn't want me to come alone. But I can't just abandon Brady."

"No, of course not. I'll help you look for him."

Exceedingly grateful for his company, Elizabeth held her head high as the two of them rode into town, Penny trailing slightly behind.

"You don't think Brady decided to leave the wagon train, do you?" Eli asked her.

"No. I'm certain he didn't."

"He wasn't hankering to become a gold miner?"

"I cannot even imagine that."

Once in town, Eli took the lead, asking everyone they met on the street if they'd seen a Negro man passing through. Although some unkind jokes were made at Brady's expense, no one seemed to have seen him. They went from one end of town to the other with no luck. Finally they stopped in the middle of town, trying to decide what to do next.

"We're burning daylight," Eli told her. "And don't forget we still have a long ride to catch up with the train."

"But how can I just leave him?"

"What about your children and your family, Elizabeth? If we don't go back, you'll be leaving them." They were having this difficult conversation in front of the dance hall. Several ill-clad women were still loitering about in the late afternoon sunshine. One of them, a flashy-looking redhead, started to flirt with Eli, commenting on his fringed buckskins.

"Why don't you come on inside and cool yourself off, cowboy," she called up at him. "Come on down from that big horse and have a drink with me."

Ignoring the loquacious redhead, Elizabeth turned to the sultry looking dark-haired woman next to her. "Excuse me, ma'am," she said in a friendly tone. "Have you seen an old man—"

"What kind of old man are you looking for?" the redhead asked in a teasing tone. "We get all sorts in here. I'm sure I can find someone for you."

"He's a Negro man," Elizabeth said in a stiff voice.

The dark-haired woman's eyes glinted like she knew something, but she still kept quiet.

"You mean Brady?" the redhead asked.

"Yes!" Elizabeth said eagerly. "Have you seen him?"

The redhead jerked her thumb over her shoulder toward the dance hall. "He's in there."

"Brady's in *there?*" Elizabeth exchanged a glance with Eli, and he looked uncertain. But Elizabeth was already sliding out of the saddle, tying her reins to the hitching post.

"Your slave ain't feeling too smart right now," the redhead told her as she pushed open the door to the dance hall.

"He's not my slave." Elizabeth locked eyes with the woman. "He's my employee."

The redhead nodded with a curious expression. "Well, your *employee* got himself beat up good today."

"Is he all right?"

Now Eli was coming inside.

"He's back here." The redhead pushed open another door, revealing a small windowless room with a narrow bed pushed against the wall with Brady lying on it with a bloody towel draped across his forehead.

"Brady!" Elizabeth rushed to his side. "Are you all right?"

He opened his eyes, and a slow smile of relief washed over his swollen face. "Miss Elizabeth," he gasped. "Am I glad to see you."

"What happened?" Eli asked as he joined them in the stuffy little room.

"Did someone in town do this to you?" Elizabeth demanded.

Brady's smile evaporated. "No, ma'am. No one in town done this."

"Who did it then?" Eli asked quietly.

Brady winced as he pushed himself up to a sitting position. "I had just got my socks at the mercantile. Then I figgered I'd best get myself back to the wagon train." He reached up to touch his bruised head. "I was just cutting down the alley when I saw a man from the wagon train…he came at me, swinging his fists, saying he's gonna kill me. But that boy was with him…you know, the one I pulled from the river. Robert Stone's his name. He yelled out, 'Don't kill him, Pa.'" Brady looked confused. "Was that man Robert's pa?"

Elizabeth looked at Eli. "Abner Stone," she said.

He nodded.

"Brady," Elizabeth said urgently. "Are you strong enough to travel?"

"Sure." He reached for her hand and slowly stood, wavering a bit as if dizzy.

"Easy does it." Eli came over to steady him.

"I brought my father's horse for you," she told him. "Do you think you can ride?"

"Sure, I can ride." He smiled, revealing a broken front tooth. Probably the handiwork of Abner Stone. "Druther ride than walk."

"Let me help you." Eli wrapped an arm around Brady, guiding him to the door and out.

Now Elizabeth turned to the redheaded woman, who had been lurking by the door, watching them the whole time. "What do I owe you?" Elizabeth asked. "For caring for Brady like this."

The woman waved her hand. "Nothing."

"I don't have any money on me right now," Elizabeth admitted. "But I could send you something in the mail. At our next stop."

"I said you owe me *nothing*." The redhead rolled her eyes upward. "I was just trying to be a good neighbor to the poor old man. Wasn't looking to get rich from it."

Elizabeth went closer to her and, looking directly into her eyes, she reached for her hand. "Thank you, ma'am. You are truly a good Samaritan."

The woman looked confused, pulling her hand away. "I don't know what you're talking about. I don't even know what a Samaritan is."

"God bless you," Elizabeth said as she walked through the dance hall, pausing at the front door. "God bless you for your kindness to a stranger."

Now the woman laughed. "Well, now, that's a new one."

"Come on, Elizabeth," Eli called from outside. "We'll have to take it slow and easy for Brady's sake. But we need to get moving if we're going to catch up with the wagon train before dark."

Chapter Fifteen

Abner Stone and his family were removed from the wagon train in Fort Bridger. No one was sad to see them go. Elizabeth felt a little pity for Robert. But there was nothing they could do for the boy. Maybe he would learn an important life lesson from all this—maybe he would grow up into something vastly different from his dad. She prayed he would.

The going continued to be rough in these parts. There were numerous breakdowns on the rugged mountain trail and many a stream and river to cross. Teams and emigrants were pushed to their limits, and at the end of the traveling day, there was little energy left for anything more than wagon repairs, chores, and bed. And the next day they would get up and do it all over again.

Elizabeth knew they were in Blackfoot country now. She also knew that the Blackfoot tribe was in a peace treaty with the government. So when they passed by a tepee village one morning, she was more interested than concerned. As she rode Molly alongside the wagon train, looking out toward the village, she wondered what it would be like to live as they did. Would it really be that much different from how the emigrants were living right now? To her surprise, it looked intriguing… from a distance. However, she had no idea what it would be like if she were actually there. She supposed that Eli could tell her about that. But from her vantage point here, it seemed peaceful and orderly, and the idea of being stationary instead of constantly rolling along was highly appealing.

"Good morning, Elizabeth."

She turned to see Eli riding his horse toward her. Because of the rumbling noise of the nearby wagon train, she hadn't even heard him approaching. She waved and greeted him. "I was just thinking of you."

A smile lit up his face. "Me?"

She pointed to the tepee village. "I was wondering what it would feel like to live like that." She sighed, pulling the reins to stop Molly. "It looks so peaceful and calm from here."

He chuckled as he stopped his horse next to her. "Well, it's not so different from any other village where families live next to each other. You'd hear kids playing and letting out happy squeals. Dogs barking. Neighbor women arguing over who picked the last of the chokecherries."

"Chokecherries?" She eyed him. "That doesn't sound good. Are they poisonous?"

"No, they're delicious."

"Really? Why are they called chokecherries?"

He laughed. "I have no idea." He untied a buckskin bag from his belt. "Hold out your hand," he told her.

She held out her hand, and he poured a powdery-looking substance into it. "What is that?"

"Pemmican."

"What is that?"

"Mostly it's dried venison and bison that's been ground into powder. But this pemmican is my own special recipe." He pointed to some dark red flecks in her hand. "I added dried chokeberries to it. Go ahead, give it a try."

"Just eat it?" she asked.

He nodded. "You wondered what it was like to be an Indian. Just eat it."

So she dumped the powder from her palm into her mouth. It had an interesting taste—a mix of salty and sweet. "Not bad," she told him.

"It's saved my life more than once," he said as he poured some into his own palm and ate it.

She looked back toward the tepee village. "Do you think you'll ever live like that again, Eli? I mean with the Indians?"

"I don't know…"

She turned back to him, watching as he gazed toward the village. "Do you miss it?"

"There were many things about the village that I will never miss. But I do miss my family."

"Oh…" She tried to imagine him with his Indian wife and child. "How old would your son be now?"

"About the same age as JT."

"Oh…" She wished she could think of something besides "oh" to say.

"I have to admit there are things about village living I do miss," he continued.

"What sort of things?"

"I miss the comforts of family and community. I spend so much time traveling around the country that I sometimes stop and realize how I have no roots…nothing to keep me in one place." He nodded back to the wagon train. "You folks are traveling too. But you have a strong feeling of community. Especially in your unit. And of course, you have your family with you."

"I don't know what I'd do without that," she confessed.

He pointed back to the Blackfoot village. "In some ways you're more like the Indians than I am, Elizabeth."

"How so?"

"They are very connected to the tribe. Everything in their lives surrounds family and community. To be exiled from the tribe is a fate worse than death."

"Is that how you feel?" she asked him. "As if you are exiled?"

He smiled. "Not exactly. If anything this is my own doing. I have turned myself into an exile by choice. I always tell myself I can return to civilization anytime I want." He looked into her eyes, almost as if searching for something. "I'm just not entirely sure if I want to."

She felt her cheeks growing warm. "I wouldn't be able to live like that," she said quietly. "To travel endlessly, never having a home, never having neighbors or family nearby." She shook her head. "Even now, I'm longing to end what feels like a never ending journey. I long to stop moving and to put down roots. I want to build a home, hang curtains in the windows, plant crops, raise animals…" She looked defiantly back at him. "I will not settle for less."

They remained like that for a long moment, eyes locked while seated on their horses. It was almost like a contest…who would look away first.

"And you shouldn't settle for less," he told her quietly. Then he turned and looked away. "I wouldn't want you to."

She took in a slow breath, trying to steady the fluttery skittish feeling inside of her, hoping he could not see it.

"Excuse me," he said. "It looks like there's a breakdown near the front of the train. I should go and lend a hand."

"Yes, of course." She stayed put, watching him ride away, a pale cloud of dust rising up behind him. And somehow she knew that this moment was like a crossroads for them. He was riding away from her now, and that was how it was meant to be. They were too different. She wanted a home, family, community, security. He wanted his freedom, adventure, independence. It was like the old story of the fish falling in love with the bird…where would they build their home?

As they traveled through Soda Springs and along the twisting Snake River, the going gradually grew a bit easier. At least on some days. On other days it seemed that nothing went right. Wagons would break down or an animal would need to be put down. Sometimes the wagon train was delayed by a burial service and sometimes by a birth. Sometimes, following a less challenging day, the travelers in unit five gathered for music and merriment. However, Eli seemed noticeably absent of late.

Elizabeth wasn't sure if it was her imagination, but Will appeared to be making the most of Eli's absence. He seemed to take for granted that his company was welcome. And it was undeniable that Will Bramford was a good companion. A perfect gentleman, intelligent, interesting, witty...what more could a widow hope for? At least that's what Flo and Lavinia liked to tell Elizabeth every time they got the chance to!

"Have you heard the latest news?" Will asked her one night. Everyone was in good spirits because they would reach another milestone the next day—Fort Hall.

"What sort of news?" she asked as she tapped her toes to the music.

"Well, it's not actually news yet." He lowered his voice as he led her away from the area where the young people were dancing a reel to the lively music. "In fact, it is a secret. But if you promise to keep it under your hat..." He chuckled. "Or under your bonnet, I'd like to share it with you, and I'd appreciate your opinion."

She nodded, suddenly curious as to this news.

They were a good distance away from the crowd now. Will leaned close to her and whispered into her ear. "Julius is planning to propose matrimony to Mahala."

"Truly?" Elizabeth blinked. She knew the two had been spending time together, but she'd not heard a single word of this. Yet she walked with Lavinia and Flo nearly every morning. Were they keeping this away from her?

"Furthermore, their parents don't even know about it yet."

This was even more surprising. "Then how did you find out?"

"Julius is my godson. He came to me first, asking me my opinion."

"Of course. What an honor for you."

"Yes...but it's also quite a responsibility. I wouldn't want to misguide my only godson."

Now she felt worried. Her first impression, back in March, was that these Bostonians were awful snobs. And the Flanders...well, they were good hardworking people, but they were not the sort that the highfalutin Bostonians would normally include in their circle of friends back in Boston. In fact, they had taken some time to bridge that social gap. But the wagon train was a good place for forging new relationships.

Even so, Elizabeth sometimes wanted to laugh out loud at the strange irony of befriending both Lavinia and Flo. She could hardly imagine two women more different. And yet for the most part, they got along.

"As I said, I am honored Julius asked for my advice." Will was watching the young dancers with an intense expression.

"And how did you advise him, may I ask?"

"It's my opinion that if Julius loves Mahala, and if Mahala loves Julius, then why should anyone stand in their way?"

Elizabeth nodded. It seemed the only fair response. But now she was considering this relationship from another angle. Certainly Mahala was a dear girl, but the way she had shifted her affections so swiftly from the disreputable Jack Smith to sweet Julius Prescott...well, it was a bit disconcerting.

Part of Elizabeth had been relieved that Mahala so easily forgot Jack, but another part of her was bewildered by this rapid change of heart. Was it truly possible to fall in and out of love so quickly, so easily? Perhaps for the young. But what if Mahala truly didn't love Julius? Or what if she didn't love him quite as much as Julius appeared to love her? Of course, Elizabeth knew this wasn't her concern. And she would never voice these questions. Not to anyone. Besides that, she had made a promise to Mahala and she intended to honor it—the incident with Jack Smith would remain undisclosed. Still, it was unsettling to harbor such a secret.

"What do you think?"

"What?" She looked at him. "Think about what?"

"Do you think it's wise for Julius and Mahala to become engaged?"

"Oh...well...I don't see why they shouldn't...if their love is genuine." She felt a bit nervous now. "However, I do wonder why you are telling me about all this...why you'd care about my opinion. What difference does it make what I think?"

He looked into her eyes with tenderness. "I've taken you into my confidence because I have no one else to discuss this with. Certainly not Julius' parents. Not yet anyway. And not my own children. Belinda and Amelia wouldn't be able to keep quiet about it. Do you mind that I shared it with you? Am I out of line?"

"No...no, not at all. I was just curious. I hadn't thought of it like that."

"Because I feel that you're my friend, Elizabeth. I know I can trust you."

She smiled back at him. "Yes, of course, we're friends, and I'm honored you confided in me. And I do think Julius and Mahala will make a fine couple. I'm sure they'll be very happy together."

He let out a sigh. "It's a relief to hear you say that." He rubbed his chin. "I really do trust your judgment, Elizabeth."

"I'm sure both sets of parents will be pleased to give their blessing."

"Even Lavinia?" His brow creased slightly as if, like her, he was well aware of the social differences of these two families.

"Even Lavinia." She gave him a confident smile. "I'm sure of it."

"That is a huge relief. You have no idea." He let out an even bigger sigh. "I'm surprised I've found this so worrisome, but it's because I want the best for Julius. And for Mahala too, of course."

"Of course." Elizabeth pushed thoughts of Jack Smith to the back of her mind.

"Now I just hope that my own children aren't planning matrimony anytime soon."

"Nor mine."

Will laughed. "I should think not!"

Elizabeth had difficulty imagining that JT or Ruth could grow old enough to wed. Oh, she knew it was a fact of life, but the idea of her children marrying, leaving her alone, starting families of their own... it was all rather unsettling. And yet JT was only seven years younger than Julius. And it wasn't unusual for girls just eight years older than Ruth to marry. What would her life be like if she was completely alone in fewer than ten years?

"You seem deep in thought."

Elizabeth shook herself from her dismal imaginings, forcing her attention back on Will. "I'm sorry. Truth be told, I was feeling somewhat disturbed to think that Ruth and JT will be old enough to marry one day...and that they will leave the nest." She forced a smile. "I know it's inevitable, and I would want it no other way. And yet I cannot imagine my life without my children. It made me feel so lonely."

"Oh, I doubt you'll ever need to concern yourself with that, Elizabeth."

"Why not?"

He waved his hand over to where various members of her family were either making music or dancing or visiting with others from their unit. "Your family seems to have a special bond. And I suspect your children will always want to live near you. Also, you seem to adopt new family members wherever you go. I doubt you'll ever be alone."

Her smile grew more authentic now. "I suppose you're right."

"Quite frankly, I cannot imagine you ever living alone." His dark eyes glimmered with what seemed genuine affection. "I know I would be distressed by the thought."

She felt her cheeks growing warm at what seemed his obvious insinuation. But instead of responding to it, she pointed to the dancers. "Oh, look, they need another couple for a square."

"What are we waiting for?" He grabbed her by the hand, and they hurried over to join the young people in a square. But as they went through the dance moves, Elizabeth felt Will's eyes fixed more firmly on her than ever before. As they performed the do-si-do and the promenade, she felt as if she were stepping into a whole new kind of wilderness—and it wasn't just the Oregon Territory.

Chapter Sixteen

Captain Brownlee called a midday meeting in Soda Springs, which was a beautiful spot. To preserve travel time, which was always their top priority, he asked the emigrants to bring their lunches with them. And so they gathered in a sweet green meadow for what felt like a very large picnic.

"First of all, I congratulate all of you on making a fine journey thus far," his voice boomed out across the meadow. "As you know, some of us are soon to part ways. Those of you who are bound for California or the Applegate Trail will be heading south with Major Thompson in a few days. As planned, I will lead the rest of the train northward on the Oregon Trail. For those purposes I must reorganize the train, and I want all councilmen to meet at my wagon after we stop for the day. The councilmen will meet with their units later this evening."

The captain paused, looking out over the crowd. "I wish I could tell you that the hardest part of the journey is behind us, but that would be a severe falsehood. Long and difficult traveling days lie ahead for us. I pray that the strength and savvy you have acquired from the first part of our journey will fortify you to successfully finish this race." He took off his hat, waving it. "And to the travelers heading south, you will be in good hands with Major Thompson. I wish all of you Godspeed and safety for the remainder of your journey." He replaced his hat, and as he walked away, everyone in the meadow clapped and cheered loudly.

But even in the midst of this merriment and celebration, even as they were sitting in this sunny lovely meadow, Elizabeth felt a chill run down her spine. She sensed that the captain was warning them—the hardest part of the journey was still ahead. She looked at her children, cheering loudly with everyone else, and silently prayed that the good Lord who had brought them safely thus far would continue to do so.

Everyone remained in high spirits for the remainder of the day. And indeed, the traveling was relatively easy and the weather pleasant enough. There was no reason for anyone to be glum. At the end of the day, Elizabeth's foreboding feelings seemed to have evaporated. Or perhaps she'd imagined them.

As she and Clara were setting up camp and getting ready to fix supper, she was surprised to see Gert approaching them. She and Gert hadn't been the best of friends, but they had reached a place of mutual respect. At least Elizabeth had assumed as much. But as Gert approached, her expression was grim.

"Evening, Elizabeth." Gert nodded with a somber expression. "Evening, Clara."

They both greeted her, pausing from their preparations. "Is something amiss?" Elizabeth asked.

"No, no, nothing's wrong. I just wanted to come over here and have my say," Gert abruptly told them.

"Your say?" Clara's brows arched.

"Mostly I want to say thank you and I'm sorry."

"Really?" Elizabeth tried not to act too shocked.

"We'll soon part ways, but before we do, I thought I should say something. I made no secret that I didn't think much of you folks at the onset of this journey. I saw ya'll coming in here late, with your fine horses and your fancy wagons and...well, I reckoned you were a bunch of greenhorns. I thought for sure and for certain we'd all end up picking your sorry remains off the side of the trail and that ya'll'd be charity cases." Gert sighed. "But you folks proved me wrong. It's been an honor to travel the trail with ya'll and to be in your unit."

Elizabeth and Clara exchanged smiles.

"Thank you very much," Clara told her. "It was a pleasure getting to know you, Gert."

"Oh, I doubt that." Gert pulled her corncob pipe from the dirty bib of her apron. "I know I can be a real pain when I speak my mind the way I do. And my boys, thanks to their pa letting 'em run wild, are unruly."

"Well, we wish you and your family a safe and blessed trip to southern Oregon," Elizabeth told her.

"Much obliged." Gert twirled the pipe between her stubby fingers. "And if you'd convey my gratitude to Asa, I'd be much obliged. Tell him for me that he's as fine a councilman as any and I am honored to say I was in his unit."

Clara reached out and grasped Gert's hand. "I will do that."

"That's all I come to say." Gert nodded with finality, turned on her heel, and left.

"Well…I'll be." Clara slowly shook her head. "I did not see that coming."

"Now I'm almost sad to part ways with her." Elizabeth measured some saleratus into the cornmeal. "But I'll keep her and her family in my prayers."

"So will I." Clara poured water into a pot. "Even though we're parting ways, I feel that they're like family. Everyone from unit five will remain in my prayers."

Asa returned from meeting with the captain just as supper was getting done. "Something smells good." He sniffed the air.

"Oh, Grandpa, it's just beans and bacon again," Ruth told him.

"And cornbread," Elizabeth added as she moved the cast-iron pan from the fire.

"I happen to like beans and bacon and cornbread." He smacked his lips.

"I asked Matthew and Jess to join us tonight," Clara told him. "I figured they'd want to hear about your meeting with the captain."

He nodded as he sat down. "And Mrs. Taylor is dining with the Schneiders?"

"That's right." Elizabeth reached for the coffeepot, automatically filling a cup and handing it to him.

"Bless you, child." He grinned up at her.

"How was your meeting?" she asked.

He gave her a hard to read look. "Interesting..."

She nodded. "Yes...and I suppose I should wait for everyone to get here before I start peppering you with questions."

Soon they were all gathered at the table, and after Asa asked a blessing, he began to tell them about the meeting. "First of all, as he said, the captain has reorganized the train." Asa beamed at them as he reached for a chunk of cornbread. "We are now part of unit one."

"Unit one?" Clara blinked. "Why is that?"

"Who cares why—we are unit one now!" JT exclaimed.

Asa chuckled as he took a bite.

"Have we been promoted?" Ruth asked.

"What about our fellow travelers from unit five?" Jess frowned. "What about my aunt and Doris? Are we still with them?"

Asa nodded. "Yes. I should have been more clear. Unit five has become unit one. And starting tomorrow, we'll have only eight wagons in our unit. And only about half the original units are going north. Thirty-five wagons total, and that's counting the captain's wagon."

"We make these changes tomorrow?" Matthew asked.

"First thing in the morning," Asa told him. "The units who are going south are supposed to get up an hour earlier than usual to organize their train. They'll leave camp first, and our train will leave an hour later than usual to put two hours between the two trains. Eli will lead the southbound train until they meet up with Major Thompson just outside of Fort Hall."

"And then Eli will return to our train?" JT asked.

"I'm not right sure about that," Asa told them.

"Why not?" Matthew asked.

"It seems that Major Thompson hasn't secured a scout yet. According to the captain, he and Eli are friends from way back. Eli may continue south with them."

"But what about us?" JT asked. "Don't we need a scout too?"

"If Eli goes south, the captain will get us a new scout in Fort Hall. He said there will be plenty of good men to choose from there."

"Then why doesn't Major Thompson choose one of them?" JT asked.

Asa smiled. "I know you'll miss Eli, son. He's a good man, and he's been a right handy addition to our music. But he'll have to do as he sees fit. And Captain Brownlee assured us that we will have the best of scouts even if Eli does decide to go south."

Elizabeth poked at her supper, which had suddenly lost any appeal. Even so, she took a big bite of beans, chewing slowly as she attempted to conceal her disappointment at this news.

"You still didn't tell us why we became unit one," Clara reminded Asa.

"Most of unit one is heading to California, so the captain decided we should take over that honor."

"So it is an honor?" Elizabeth asked.

Asa grinned. "I'm not sure about that. But the captain did tell me privately that we have one of the strongest units on this train. And we will be in the lead starting tomorrow."

The children let out whoops of delight. It was always welcome to be at the front of the train, where there was so much less dust to eat. Elizabeth smiled, trying to act as happy as the rest of them, but all she could think was that Eli was leaving. For all she knew, starting tomorrow morning, he might be gone from her life for good.

"Is something wrong?" Jess asked Elizabeth as she helped her and Ruth clean up after supper. Clara had already retired to her wagon. "You seem awfully quiet tonight."

"No, I'm fine," Elizabeth assured her. "Just tired I suppose."

"Why don't you let Ruth and me finish this," Jess told her.

Elizabeth started to protest, but Jess insisted.

"All right." Elizabeth removed her apron. "Thank you."

As Elizabeth wandered back to her wagon with apron in hand, she felt strangely out of sorts, and she knew it had nothing to do with being excused from washing dishes tonight. She didn't want to admit it, and she knew it made no sense, but she was clearly upset about Eli. She didn't want him to go with the train to California. And yet she also knew that it was probably for the best for him to do so.

"Anything you need doin' tonight?" Brady looked up from where he was sitting in front of their wagon, whittling on a piece of wood.

"Nothing I know of." She gave him a weary smile. "How are your ribs feeling these days?" She knew he was still recovering from his beating in South Pass City.

"Not too bad." He nodded. "Gettin' better every day."

She hung her apron on a peg to dry and rolled her shirtsleeves back down, reaching into the wagon for her knitted shawl. The night air was cooling quickly this evening.

"You feelin' sad about Mr. Eli leavin' the train?" Brady asked quietly.

She turned and looked at him in surprise. "Why would you say that?"

He shrugged and looked down, turning the smooth piece of wood around and around in his weathered brown hands. "I dunno."

"Come on, Brady." She reached up for one of the chairs hanging on the side of the wagon, setting it down next to Brady, and sat in it. "Tell me why you said that."

He made a sheepish smile, revealing the broken tooth. "It's jus' that I see you and Mr. Eli talkin' sometimes. I watch how you looks at each other, like you seeing something more there than the rest of us. And that day when you and him fetched me from South Pass City, I heard you talkin' as we was goin' to the wagon train. You mighta thunk I was sleepin', but I was listenin' some too."

"Oh...?" She tried to remember exactly what they'd talked about that day. Mostly she'd been thankful he'd helped her. And as usual, she had appreciated being in his company. If she hadn't been so concerned for Brady's welfare, it would have been a most enjoyable ride.

"Are you sad, Miss Elizabeth?"

She nodded without looking at him, feeling a lump growing in her throat. "I don't want anyone to know it, Brady, but I am sad."

"I thought so."

"Please, don't tell."

"You can trust me," he assured her.

"I know."

He returned to whittling, and she slowly stood. "Thanks for listening," she told him. "I think I'll take a little stroll. It's such a pretty evening."

"You do that." He nodded. "Maybe you should take a stroll on up the front of the train…maybe you should be sayin' some farewells along your way."

"Maybe so…."

As she walked, she knew what Brady was telling her. At least she thought she knew. He was telling her to go speak to Eli while she still had the chance. But even if she managed to find him, which seemed rather unlikely, she had no idea what she would say to him. What was there to say? She thought again of the last serious conversation they'd shared while looking at the tepee village. Hadn't Eli made it perfectly clear that he had no intention of settling down…ever?

Even if he did want to settle down, what difference would that make to her? She wasn't even ready to consider marrying again. Was she? At least that was what she'd been telling herself these past few years. But if she were to be completely honest with herself, she knew that had been changing. She knew that the prospect of being alone after her children grew up and married was grim. So grim that she had briefly considered the possibility of a life with Will Bramford. Certainly, she could do worse. She suddenly remembered the way Jack Smith had leered at her. Far worse.

But Eli Kincaid? Well, that made no sense whatsoever. A match like that would be perfectly ridiculous, and the man was not interested anyway. He had made that plain right from the start. And truly, that was what she needed to come to grips with tonight. Not the fact that Eli Kincaid was leaving, but the fact that Eli Kincaid was not the marrying kind. Certainly, Eli might have enjoyed the distraction of her company and perhaps even her friendship—if only for a short spell—but it was plain as day that he had no intentions of settling down with her for good.

To be truly practical, she told herself, she should be exceedingly grateful that Eli was leaving the train. In fact, she hoped that he really was choosing to go with the California train. That would force her to get beyond these foolish schoolgirl feelings and start acting like a grown-up and responsible woman—the mother of two children. She didn't have room in her life for a reckless romance with an irresponsible, wandering man. She didn't even need to tell him goodbye. If anything she should simply tell him good riddance. Not that she would be so rude if she happened to see him.

But turning around and hurrying back toward her wagon, she decided that she would rather not see him after all. It would be much easier to simply part ways. Surely, she wished him well, and she knew she would keep him in her prayers. But no good would come from her looking into those sky-blue eyes. Best to make a clean break and, like the wagon train, move on.

Unit five, or the new unit one, was just coming into sight when Elizabeth saw those familiar fringed buckskins ahead. She was tempted to turn and walk the other way, but where would she go? She sure didn't intend to wander away from the safety of the wagons at this time of the evening. Best to just hold her head high and act as if nothing was wrong. After all, nothing was wrong. She was fine. Just fine.

"Elizabeth," he said as they drew closer. "I was just looking for you."

"Looking for me?" Her resolve was unraveling.

"Brady told me you took a walk." He began to walk alongside her now. "Mind if I join you?"

She pulled her shawl more snugly around her shoulders. "Not at all."

"Brady said you were saying your farewells."

"Oh…yes…"

"Have you heard that Major Thompson has asked me to be the scout for the southbound train?"

She nodded. "My father mentioned it."

"So it appears that we'll be parting ways…for good."

She nodded again. That hard lump was returning to her throat.

"I hoped that I'd be able to speak to you before we part…privately." He gently slipped his hand under her elbow. "Do you mind if we walk this way?" He was directing her away from the train, away from curious onlookers, but she didn't resist.

"I must admit that I was surprised," she said quietly as he led her toward the nearby creek. "I thought you were our scout and that you would continue with Captain Brownlee all the way to Vancouver."

"I thought so too...originally."

"Why did that change?"

"It's partly your fault."

"What?" she turned to peer at him. "My fault?"

"You and your family have managed to lure quite a crowd to southern Oregon."

"I don't understand what that has to do with this change of plans."

"Because a number of families have decided to follow your example by settling in southern Oregon, we have more than thirty wagons that are headed for the Applegate Trail."

"I still do not understand."

He pointed to a large boulder. "Care to sit?"

After they sat, he continued to explain. "As you know, Major Thompson was hired to take a small part of this wagon train to California. But no one anticipated such a large group breaking off to travel the Applegate Trail. So the revised plan is for me to accompany Major Thompson until we reach the fork of the California and Applegate Trails. After that, I will lead the smaller train north on the Applegate Trail and safely into southern Oregon."

"So you'll be helping the Flanders and McIntires and Schneiders?"

"Along with all the others."

"Oh..." She nodded. "Well, that makes sense."

"Does it?" Eli was looking intently into her eyes, and she was having difficulty holding back the tears.

"Certainly. For the sake of our friends, I'm glad you're going to help them." Unwilling to let him see her tears, she turned to look away.

"And for your sake?" He reached over and, taking her chin in his hand, turned her to look back at him.

"My sake?"

"You seem very sad, Elizabeth. Did I do something to hurt you?"

"It's just that...well...we had become friends. I wasn't ready to say goodbye." She felt lost as she looked into his eyes. This was not at all how she had intended this to go. What had happened to all her strong resolve?

"I don't know if I'm ready to say goodbye either."

She felt a flash of hope, but in the same instant reminded herself that she had no right to hope. She knew better. Eli was an independent man. He had no roots...he wanted none. And then he leaned down and kissed her. And despite all her sensibilities, she kissed him back.

"I'm sorry," he said as he let go of her chin.

"Sorry?" She felt flustered...and unexplainably happy...and sad.

"I didn't mean to do that."

"You didn't?"

He looked away with a faraway and worried look.

Now she felt angry. How dare he—to kiss her like that and then act as if it were a big mistake. She stood. "I suppose I didn't mean to either," she said with irritation. "And now if you'll excuse me, it's getting late."

"Wait." He reached for her arm. "I'm sorry, Elizabeth. I didn't handle that right. I'm not good at these sorts of things."

She stood up straight, glaring back at him. "Nor am I."

"I just didn't want us to part like this...not saying a proper goodbye."

She squared her shoulders. "I'm sorry, Eli. Goodbye. I wish you Godspeed and safe travels." Now she turned away, hurrying back toward the train.

"And not like that either," he said as he caught up with her.

She didn't say anything but just kept walking as fast as she could without actually running. Why had she allowed him to lure her off like this? What kind of a fool was she? And what if someone had seen them? What would her family say? What would her children think?

"Elizabeth." He caught her by the arm, forcing her to stop. "I'm sorry."

"Sorry for what?" she asked in a defiant tone.

"I'm sorry that I'm not very good at this."

"Yes." She nodded. "You said that already. I'm sorry too, Eli." She reached out and took his hand, firmly shaking it with finality. "It's been a pleasure to know you," she told him stiffly. "I wish you well. And now I must go see to my children. Good night and goodbye."

This time when she turned from him, she actually ran, and she only slowed down when her wagon came into sight again. Then, despite the merry sounds of music coming from her parents' campsite, she climbed into the back of her own wagon. And in what little privacy the rounded canvas walls could provide, she quietly cried.

But when she was done, she wiped her eyes and blew her nose and headed out toward the sound of the happy music. Thankfully, many tears were shared at this impromptu going-away party. Many were unwilling to part ways after going through so much together. Hugs and farewells were exchanged all around. And no one was the wiser as to the real reason for Elizabeth's tears.

Except Brady. When they said good night later that evening, he looked at her with a somber, knowing expression—as if he truly understood her anguish. She knew she could trust him.

Chapter Seventeen

Being the lead unit in the wagon train was always a privilege, but according to Asa it was about to become an earned privilege. "I forgot to mention this yesterday…" he told them at breakfast. "Captain Brownlee said that for the remainder of the trip, the order of the wagon train will be determined by the performance of the units."

"What do you mean?" JT asked.

"The units with the fewest breakdowns will lead the train. Those with the most will be at the tail."

"So we don't have to wait for them anymore?" Ruth said.

"We'll still wait for them when we make camp," he explained. "But if they lose precious time on the trail, the whole train won't have to suffer with them."

"I feel sorry for the units who get stuck in the back," Elizabeth admitted. "Is it fair?"

"Captain Brownlee hopes that it will force all the units to take this last part of the journey very seriously. He said the trail is about to become very rugged—some of the worst terrain we've seen. We'll be crossing through mountains, dense forests, raging rivers and deserts where water is scarce. He said some wagons will still need to lighten their loads. He also said we need to make sure we've got enough food supplies. There won't be many places to restock between Fort Hall and Fort Boise. After that, civilization will be even more scarce."

"Maybe we should have taken the Applegate Trail instead," Elizabeth said.

"They'll have troubles of their own," Asa told her. "And once we make it to the Columbia River, we'll travel by rafts and make better time."

"We'll need to restock our pitch pots," Matthew told him.

Asa nodded. "You and I will sit down and make a new supply list before we get to Fort Hall tomorrow."

Again, Elizabeth was hit by the seriousness of this leg of the journey. It wasn't as if the miles behind them had been easy. They most certainly had not! But thinking that the roughest part still lay ahead filled her with dreading. Yet for the sake of her children, she knew she must remain brave. She also knew she needed to put all thoughts of Eli behind her—far behind her. Perhaps the demands of the trail would help her to do this.

They arrived at Fort Hall at midmorning, learning that the California section of their train had made their stop in Fort Hall the previous afternoon. "They're making good time," Clara said as she and Elizabeth walked with some of the other women into the fort.

"I miss Flo," Elizabeth admitted.

"And I miss Tumbleweed Tillie," Ruth said with longing.

"I miss Fiona," Jess added.

"And Julius misses Mahala," Lavinia told them. "He even wrote her a letter last night, although where he plans to send it is a bit of a mystery. I suppose he'll just wait and hand it to her in September." The couple had announced their engagement at the farewell party just two nights ago. The plan was for them to have a wedding next summer. Time enough for Julius, with the help of his family, to get a small cabin built for them.

But first, as Hugh and Lavinia had pointed out, Julius needed to help his own family to get settled.

Fort Hall, which was owned by the Hudson Bay Company, was said to be better stocked than some of the forts, but Elizabeth and Clara were dismayed at what they found. They hoped the men were faring better.

"Why don't we part ways?" Clara suggested as she tore her list in two, giving half to Elizabeth. "Jess and I will look for these items while you and Ruthie look for those. We don't have much time, so perhaps we should simply meet back at the train."

"And I need to stop by the post office too," Elizabeth reminded her.

With Ruth's help, Elizabeth managed to find most of the items on their list and even some that weren't. Elizabeth couldn't be more pleased than when Ruth found a burlap bag of potatoes nearly hidden on a low dark shelf. However, Elizabeth nearly got into a tussle over them when a bossy woman from another unit attempted to pry the potatoes out of Ruth's arms.

"Excuse me," Elizabeth said firmly, taking the bag from both Ruth and the rude woman. "I'll carry those for you, Ruthie."

"Oh!" The woman glared at Elizabeth. "I didn't know the little girl was really a shopper. I thought she was just playing with the potatoes."

"She is my shopping helper," Elizabeth told her. "And she found the potatoes."

"But that's the only bag of potatoes," the woman pointed out.

"Perhaps they have more in back," Elizabeth told her as she set the potatoes with their other items, waiting for the shopkeeper to tally the goods.

"Grandpa will be so pleased about the potatoes," she told Ruth as she counted out her money. "That was a good find."

They had a lot to carry now, but Elizabeth felt it was well worth it. Fortunately, she spied Jess and Clara coming their way. And since they weren't as loaded down as Elizabeth and Ruth, they shared the load among themselves.

"There's the post office," Clara pointed out. "You run in and check for mail while we wait."

"But hurry," Jess reminded her. "We don't have much time, and we're in unit one."

"That's right." Elizabeth ducked into the post office, quickly explaining who she was and inquiring about mail.

"You're with Captain Brownlee's train?" the man asked.

"Yes. That's right." She told him her name again.

"Let me go check on it."

She waited for what seemed a long time, and he returned with a letter. "Mrs. James Martin," he read the front of the envelope. "Ten cents due."

She gladly pulled out a dime, handing it to him.

"Here you go, ma'am." He handed her the precious letter.

"Thank you so much!" she declared. Then she hurried out to where her family was still waiting. She waved the letter in the air to show them.

"Is it from Aunt Malinda?" Ruth asked eagerly.

"We should start walking back," Clara said. "We don't want to be late."

"I assumed it was from Malinda, but now I'm not sure." Elizabeth examined the yellowed envelope. "Oh, dear! It's not from Malinda at all."

"Who's it from?" Clara inquired.

"It's from Mrs. Thomas Barron." Elizabeth frowned. "All the way from Kentucky!"

"From the Barrons who bought our farm?" Ruth asked curiously.

"Yes." Elizabeth shook her head in wonder.

"What did she write?" Ruth asked.

"I don't know." Elizabeth slipped the letter into the basket she was carrying. "But it will have to wait. We need to hurry."

"That's right," Clara agreed. "We're unit one now. It wouldn't do to be late."

"That's for sure," Jess said. "Not on our very first week of leading the train."

Fortunately the men were already at the wagons, and it looked like they were nearly ready to go. Elizabeth hurried to stow her basket of goods in the back of the wagon, but seeing the letter, she pulled it out and tucked it in her pocket. Although she was disappointed it wasn't from Malinda and John, she was curious as to why Mrs. Barron had written to her. She hoped it wasn't to complain about the farm.

"You wanna drive now?" Brady asked from where he was adjusting a harness.

"No, you and JT can continue to drive. We'll switch after the midday break."

He nodded, climbing slowly into the seat.

"*Wagons ho!*" Captain Brownlee yelled from the lead wagon. Sometimes the captain rode one of his horses. Sometimes he rode in the wagon with the cook. But once he yelled "wagons ho," everyone knew it was time to move.

Elizabeth began walking quickly, wishing to get ahead of the train as she and the other women had been doing lately. Walking up front wasn't merely invigorating, it allowed them to avoid eating trail dust. But to her surprise, none of the other women were walking up there. Perhaps they were either riding or just farther behind. All the same, she continued walking at a good fast pace, hoping to gain enough distance to walk more leisurely so she could read this mysterious letter from Mrs. Barron. Hopefully there was no bad news.

Finally, satisfied that she could slow down, she pulled out the letter and carefully opened the envelope. But to her surprise, it simply contained another envelope. She examined the inner envelope to see it was addressed to the farm in Kentucky, but it had Elizabeth's name on top— and the handwriting was familiar. She flipped it over to see that this letter was indeed from her sister-in-law Malinda. There was also a short note on the back that appeared to be written by Mrs. Barron, informing her that this letter had arrived shortly after Elizabeth and her family had departed from the farm in March.

Elizabeth thought back to that momentous day. It seemed like another lifetime. And indeed it had been nearly five months ago. Had it really taken five months for this letter to catch up to Elizabeth? And why was it sent to Fort Hall? She flipped the outer envelope over again, seeing that it was indeed addressed to Fort Hall.

Feeling slightly confused, she opened the second envelope, the one from Malinda. Why on earth hadn't Mrs. Barron forwarded this letter to one of their earlier stops so that she might have picked it up weeks and perhaps even months ago? Elizabeth had left her a full list of dates and places for mail forwarding. Perhaps Mrs. Barron had lost it.

Judging by the date on Malinda's letter, she had penned this shortly after receiving Elizabeth's letter announcing that they were migrating to Oregon. Elizabeth smiled to herself, thinking of how excited Malinda must have been to learn she had family coming to settle nearby. But as Elizabeth began to read what felt like a very hastily penned letter, she realized that something was wrong. Very, very wrong.

My dearest Elizabeth,

I was so very surprised to read your letter and so very taken aback that I had to read it twice and then thrice. Now I am writing to you with shaking hand and as quickly as my pen can move. Do not come to Oregon, Elizabeth. I beseech you, do not come. This is no place for you and your children these days. And this is no place for your aging parents either. Do not come! I realize my advice must be shocking to you because I have written such glowing praises of this gloriously beautiful but violent land. I wrote to you only of the splendor of this country because I did not want to discourage you or cause you to worry about our family and the travails of living on the frontier. I felt compassion for how you suffered when you lost your beloved James. I did not wish to trouble you with more sorrows. And I never dreamed that you, a widow with small children, would try to come.

I understand your bereavement even more now that I am widowed also. John died of influenza in November. His death was not the result of an Indian raid. However the Indian wars have been numerous and violent these past several years, starting with the Coquille Massacre in the fall of 1851 when five explorers were murdered.

This was followed by another bloody battle where fifteen Indians were killed as retribution. On it has gone, killing and bloodshed. Just last week we learned of the most recent incident at the Applegate River Camp, where Dr. W. Myers was killed. I am weeping as I write this, Elizabeth, because the good doctor did not deserve to die. Especially as this frontier has such great need of doctors. Perhaps my own John would still be alive if we'd had a doctor nearby. I pray this letter reaches you in time to deter you from making this most dreadful mistake. Even now I must decide if I should bring the children back to Kentucky. Perhaps we can stay with you on your lovely farm. I do hate to give up on John's dream. And it will be difficult to leave our home and this beautiful but treacherous land, but I fear the price is too high. I would write more, but I must get this letter posted as soon as possible. Please, dear Elizabeth, do not come. Stay where you are safe. Count your blessing that you have a home where people are civilized.

> *Most sincerely, your sister by marriage,*
> *Malinda Martin*

Elizabeth's hands were trembling as she read and reread this horrifying letter. It seemed too horrible, too frightening to be true. For a moment, Elizabeth thought perhaps she was simply asleep and suffering from a ghastly nightmare. Sometimes she had them, suffering fearful images of frontier tragedies. And yet here she was with the sun on her head and the ground beneath her feet...and this letter in her hand. She stared at it, wishing it were untrue or perhaps a cruel hoax. But the handwriting was clearly Malinda's. Perhaps the penmanship was not as smooth and controlled as usual, but considering the circumstances, that was understandable.

Elizabeth turned to look at the wagon train steadily moving toward her, followed by a low cloud of brown dust. Everyone she loved was represented in that slowly moving train—pressing onward step-by-step toward their final destination. Would they be met with bloody Indian battles, sickness, and perhaps even death?

Tears were streaking down her cheeks now. What had she done? What had she gotten them all into? Why had she ever encouraged her family and her new friends to follow such a dangerous path? Her stomach twisted as if she would be sick. And suddenly the sad news of James' brother's death overwhelmed her. John was dead! Both brothers had died of illnesses—within four years of each other.

Poor Malinda, like Elizabeth, was now a widow, trying to maintain her farm and raise her four young children in the midst of Indian battles on the Oregon frontier. It was all too unimaginable. Oh, why had Elizabeth been so persistent to pursue such a hopeless dream? Why had she involved so many others?

She pressed a fist to her mouth as she stared at the wagon train, which was quickly catching up with her. She didn't know what to do. Everything in her wanted to rush back to the wagons. To run to her father and insist that they must stop moving westward, to tell him that they must turn their wagons around and head eastward and return to Kentucky as quickly as possible. But that wasn't possible. Turning back like that would be to invite another sort of disaster—a deadly race against weather and provisions. Oh, what had she gotten them all into?

Instead of running back to the wagons, where she would have to divulge the awful truth, she continued to walk forward. And putting one foot in front of the next, she began to pray, fervently begging God to help her to sort out this unfortunate mess, begging him to lead her family to safety, begging for a miracle.

After an hour or so she realized that the rumbling sound of the wagon train had ceased, and for a moment she wondered if perhaps some miracle had transpired and the wagon train had decided to turn back. But when she turned around she realized the train, as usual, was simply stopping for the midday meal. She also realized that her family would wonder what had become of her. With fear and trepidation at the thought of sharing this grimmest of news, she hurried back toward the wagons.

"Where have you been?" Clara asked as Elizabeth joined them.

"I'm sorry," she breathlessly told her. "I lost track...of time."

"No matter." She handed her a stack of tin plates and utensils, and Elizabeth, grateful to be busy, tried to shove thoughts of Indian massacres into the recesses of her mind. However, after they finished their meal and after Elizabeth did her share of cleaning up and putting the last of the pots and dishes away, she set off to speak to her father. She could not keep this news from him.

Finding him examining his team and the harnesses, she impatiently waited for him to finish. "I need to speak to you," she said abruptly.

"Elizabeth." He stood up straight with a surprised expression. "Why aren't you attending to your own team?" His tone was terse.

"JT and Brady will see to my team."

"Don't forget that it's your job too." His expression softened. "I'm sorry, Lizzie. I didn't mean to scold. But the captain's warnings keep ringing in my head. We all must be on our toes or risk calamity."

"Father," she began in a shaky voice, afraid she was about to cry again.

"What is it, child?" He came over and peered at her face. "Are you unwell?"

"I'm a bit unwell—in spirit."

"What is it?" His brow creased. "Does this have to do with Eli Kincaid?"

"Eli?" She was shocked. "What do you mean?"

He shrugged. "Oh, just something your mother said."

She firmly shook her head. "No. This has nothing to do with Eli, Father." She pulled the rumpled letter from her skirt pocket. "It has to do with this letter from...from Malinda." She handed it to him. "It's too horrible to even speak of. Maybe you should just read it for yourself."

Asa looked at the letter and then up to where Captain Brownlee was just mounting his horse. The captain paused for a moment, removing his felt hat and waving it up and down—his signal that drivers should be in the wagons.

"No time to read it now." Asa tucked the letter into his shirt pocket and hurried toward the wagon seat, where Clara was already waiting. "I'll read it as we travel."

She nodded and hurried back to her own wagon, where Brady was waiting by the team and Ruth and Flax were seated. "You wanna drive now, ma'am?" Brady asked hopefully.

"Yes," she told him. "You take a break. Rest in the back if you like."

He shook his head. "D'ruther walk some, I reckon."

"JT is riding with Matthew," Ruth said as Elizabeth climbed up. "Jess is walking with Belinda, Evelyn, and Amelia." Ruth grinned. "And it was my idea. I told Jess that since Fiona was gone on the Applegate Trail, it was time for her to make some new women friends."

"*Wagons ho!*"

Elizabeth released the brake, and clicking her tongue loudly, she snapped the reins. She watched as Beau and Bella obediently moved forward, slowly leading the rest of her team...faithfully plodding one step at a time...steadily pulling the wagon closer and closer...mile by mile...to where she no longer wished to go.

Chapter Eighteen

Not wishing to worry Ruth, Elizabeth kept up the pretense that all was well, chatting and singing with her daughter for the remainder of the afternoon. She knew she should be thankful that the trail wasn't too demanding here, because based on her father's words and judging by the landscape ahead, it would soon get much rougher. Still, she thought she would rather face the worst rugged trail than the news in Malinda's letter.

When they finally stopped at the end of a long day, Elizabeth as usual sent Ruth to assist her grandmother. "I'm going to give a hand with the team," she explained. "Tell Grandma I'll be along soon."

At first Brady protested that he didn't need Elizabeth's help with the team, but she insisted. Then when JT joined them, she let the two of them take over and went off in search of her father. She could tell by his expression that he had read the letter.

"Elizabeth," he said as he led his team to the line.

Without saying anything, she helped him tend to the oxen. She could tell he was tired. And she suspected that the letter from Malinda had taken a toll on him too. She was thankful to see Brady and JT coming now as well as her brother. "Can you fellows take over for us?" she asked Matthew with a serious expression. "I need to speak to Father."

Matthew just nodded, but he looked curious.

"Come on, Father," she said. "Let's take a walk."

Asa didn't protest. And for a while they just walked in silence.

"That was quite a letter," he said finally.

"Yes." She sighed. "I'm still stunned by it."

"I let your mother read it too."

"I supposed that you would. How did she take it?"

He shook his head. "She cried for the loss of John."

"Yes...so did I."

"I had read of some Indian troubles in that part of Oregon," Asa said slowly. "But I thought that the army had moved in...that these troubles had been resolved."

"As I was driving this afternoon, I became quite angry with Malinda," Elizabeth confessed.

"Angry?"

"For not telling me the truth in her previous letters."

"Oh, yes...that..."

"Then I realized that she was only trying to protect me. And I remembered the great joy the children and I had each time we received one of her long, descriptive letters...how we would gather after supper and read it together. Malinda made Oregon sound like such a wonderful place, like a heavenly Promised Land."

Asa reached into his shirt pocket, removing the letter, and handed it back to her. "But not in this."

"No...not in that." She tucked it into her skirt pocket. "What are we to do?"

Asa stopped walking, and removing his hat, he rubbed his forehead. "All we can do is what we're already doing, Elizabeth. Continue."

"But what about her warning?"

Asa let out a long loud sigh. "I must admit that I'm perplexed by this news. I don't relish the thought of taking my grandchildren into hostile Indian territory. But there are always troubles in this world, Elizabeth. Our ancestors struggled against all sorts of adversities to settle our land. My grandpa defended his family against Indians. Even my pa when he was a boy. We knew when we chose to make this pilgrimage that it wouldn't be easy."

"And certainly, it's not. But the lure for me—the prize at the end of this arduous journey—was settling in the Promised Land."

"Even that won't be easy," he told her. "When we arrive, we'll have to clear land and build cabins."

"Yes, I know it will be hard." She nodded eagerly. "But I was looking forward to settling, Father. I wanted to build something new with my children...for my children." She held her hands in the air. "But not so they could perish in an Indian raid."

Asa put his hat back on and frowned.

"An idea came to me this afternoon," she began carefully. "While driving."

"An idea?"

"Yes. I know it will sound outlandish at first, but just consider it with me."

"Go ahead." Asa waited.

"The wagon train to California...what if we turned around and attempted to catch up with them?"

Asa just shook his head. "I don't think so. In the first place, they will be at least two days ahead of us by the time we backtrack to the fork and reroute. In the second place, I don't know that California is any safer than Oregon." He rubbed his chin. "I've read stories of troubles down there with Indians and Mexicans and even the gold miners. You saw South Pass City, Elizabeth. Imagine more of that."

"What do we do then?" She reached out and clung to his arm.

"As I said, we continue...just like we've been doing."

"But what about the others?"

"The others?"

"Friends from our unit—the Flanders and McIntires, already on their way to my Promised Land. And what about the Prescotts and Bramfords? Lavinia mailed a letter to have their shipment of goods sent down to Coos Bay."

Asa looked truly perplexed.

"I wish Eli were here," she mumbled.

His brow creased. "Eli?"

"He seems to understand the Indians. Perhaps he could advise us."

Asa's eyes lit up. "How about if we take this matter to Captain Brownlee?"

"Yes." She nodded eagerly. "Can we do that?"

"I know he's a busy man," Asa said. "But how about if I share your letter with him and ask for his opinion."

She handed him back the letter, glad to be rid of it because she knew she'd be tempted to read and reread it. Also, she didn't want her children to see it because she knew they'd be curious to hear Aunt Malinda's latest news.

When she returned to her parents' camp to help with supper, she could sense the quietness in her mother. However, Ruth and Jess made up for it by chattering happily. "How are you doing?" Clara quietly asked Elizabeth as the two of them stood by the cooking fire, tending to the pots.

Elizabeth made a forced smile. "Father took it to the captain."

Fortunately, Clara seemed to understand the cryptic meaning and now changed the subject to chokecherries. Elizabeth had told her about what Eli had said, and Clara thought perhaps she'd found some today. "I went into the brush to attend to my business a bit ago." She smiled. "And I saw these dark berries. I picked some, but I don't think we should eat them without knowing what they are."

"Yes, they could be poisonous."

"I put them in a cup over there. I was hoping that someone in the wagon train might be able to identify them."

Just then Asa showed up with the captain and another older man in tow. "Hello to the camp," Asa's voice boomed. "We have company for supper."

"Welcome," Clara told them. "We have more than enough."

"And we have potatoes," Elizabeth said.

"I've come to the right place." The captain grinned. "Now I'd like to introduce you folks to our new scout." He tipped his head toward the tall, lanky man. "This here is Jim McCall. Jim was a trapper for the Hudson Bay Company for better than twenty years. He knows the country we're headed for like the back of his hand."

"Pleased to make your acquaintance." He rubbed his scraggly beard as if he wasn't very comfortable. "And as much as I appreciate the offer of a hot meal, I was just getting ready to light out."

"You go right along," the captain told him. "I know you've been itching to get on down the trail. I just wanted you to meet some folks first."

Jim thanked him and then excused himself.

"We couldn't ask for a better scout," Captain Brownlee told them.

"Is he better than Eli?" Ruth asked.

The captain chuckled. "I reckon no one's as good as Eli. He speaks more Indian languages than anyone I know."

"I wish he hadn't left." Ruth's lower lip protruded slightly and Elizabeth knew just how her daughter felt. Not that she planned to show it.

"Well, those folks headed for the Applegate Trail are right lucky to have Eli." The captain smiled down on Ruth. "And aren't some of your friends in that group? Surely, you want them to get to their destination safely."

She nodded with serious eyes. "Yes, I do. Tillie and her family are going to meet up with us after the Applegate Trail. I'm glad Eli is helping them."

"And don't you worry, little lady, we're in good hands with Jim McCall." He tapped his chest. "And I'm still here to take care of you too."

"Say, Captain Brownlee, I'll bet you can identify something for us." Clara held the tin cup of berries out for him to see. "I found these nearby. Do you know…"

"Let me see." He reached into the cup and then popped some of the dark red berries into his mouth. "Yep. Chokecherries," he proclaimed.

"Did you know that *before* you ate them?" Clara asked. "Or after?"

He chuckled. "I would never eat a berry I didn't recognize." He reached in for some more. "They must be coming on early in these parts. But we've had a lot of mild and sunny weather these past weeks."

Now Clara tasted one. "They're a bit tart, but they would be delicious cooked into a cobbler or pie."

The captain smacked his lips. "Chokeberry cobbler sounds delightful."

Now Clara called Jess and Ruth over, showing them the chokecherries and explaining where she'd found them. She handed them a basket and a bowl. "Go and get us as many as you can pick."

"I'll mix the cobbler crust," Elizabeth offered.

"Supper won't be ready for at least half an hour...maybe longer," Clara called out as Jess and Ruth hurried away.

With only the adults left at their campsite, Clara gave Asa and the captain each a cup of coffee and invited them to sit.

"The captain read your letter." Asa handed the rumpled envelope back to Elizabeth.

She stopped from measuring flour. "And what did you think?" she asked Captain Brownlee.

Other than the snapping of the fire, the campsite grew quiet, and then the captain cleared his throat. "I can understand why you would be alarmed," he began. "But it's my opinion that your relative wrote that letter in a highly emotional state."

Elizabeth bit her lip as she poured a bit of sugar into the flour. Certainly Malinda was emotional. She had just lost her husband. There had been Indian raids. Why wouldn't she be emotional? Still, Elizabeth held her tongue as she sprinkled a pinch of salt and reached for the lard bucket.

"Anyone going west must accept that there will be Indian troubles. It is unavoidable. Sometimes the white man initiates these skirmishes. Sometimes it's the Indians. As a military man, I can assure you that the settling of a wilderness is never without bloodshed." He held a stick from the fire up to his pipe, pausing to light it.

Uncomfortable at the mention of bloodshed, Elizabeth glanced at her mother, but Clara seemed unruffled by this.

"Civilization does not come freely," he continued. "It is purchased with a price. A very costly price."

"Human bloodshed," Elizabeth declared sadly.

"I'm well aware that this can be offensive to some womenfolk," he said, "but if you want to successfully pioneer in the wilderness, you will have to put your female sentimentalities to rest."

Elizabeth couldn't help but feel irked by this statement as she mixed the cobbler dough. Even so, she continued to hold her tongue. After all, the captain's experience of the wilderness was much more vast than her own. And he'd been invited to share his opinion.

"So you're saying we should proceed with our plans?" Asa asked him. "Continue on to our destination and deal with the situation when we get there?"

"That is my advice." The captain shrugged. "Oh, certainly, you could choose another region to settle in. Oregon has much land to pick from. But wherever you go, you'll face some challenges. Best to accept this and simply move forward."

Asa glanced at Elizabeth with a slightly smug expression.

"And what of our friends?" Elizabeth asked the captain. "The ones who have changed their plans to travel with us to what I have been proudly proclaiming as a Promised Land."

"Oh, Elizabeth," Clara said, "I have never heard you make that claim to anyone. If anything, you've kept rather quiet, and sometimes you've even discouraged others. You can't lay the blame for this on your own shoulders."

"Even so," Elizabeth continued, "don't I have a responsibility to communicate this news of Indian troubles to the Prescotts and Bramfords and...shouldn't even Ruby and Doris be informed?"

"Ruby and Doris are determined to settle wherever Jess and Matthew go."

"And shouldn't they be advised too?" Elizabeth glanced around, realizing her brother wasn't here. He was probably still tending to the livestock with JT and Brady.

"Certainly, you should be free to tell others about what challenges lie ahead," the captain calmly said. "If they are unaware of the perils in the wilderness, it's about time they figured it out." He chuckled then took a pull on his pipe.

"Captain Brownlee is right," Asa told her. "Everyone here knows that this is a dangerous journey. Settling will be equally dangerous. Anyone who thinks otherwise is a fool."

Elizabeth chucked the wooden spoon into the bowl with a dull clunk. "Then I suppose I am the fool. Now if you will excuse me." She wiped her hands on her apron and marched off. Oh, she knew it was bad manners to storm away like this, but it would be worse manners to remain there and give Captain Brownlee a piece of her mind. Besides, she knew he was probably right. It just aggravated her that he could be so complacent about it.

As she walked, she knew exactly where she was going. It was her responsibility to let their Bostonian friends know about this news. Perhaps it wouldn't be too late for Lavinia to send another letter to the shipping company, preventing their goods from going all the way to Coos Bay.

"Good evening, Elizabeth."

Elizabeth was surprised to see Will and Hugh walking behind her. They had probably just finished tending to their livestock. "Well," she said. "I'm glad to see both of you. I have some news to share." She frowned. "Unfortunately it is not good news."

The men stopped walking, looking at her with curiosity. "Go ahead," Will encouraged her. "Please, tell us. Are we about to be attacked by Indians?"

"No." She shook her head. "Not yet." And now she pulled out the letter. "I have received word from my sister-in-law in Oregon…all is not well." Then she proceeded to tell them, without sparing any details, about what Malinda had written. "Here," she handed Will the letter. "Feel free to read it for yourself."

Both Will and Hugh looked slightly stunned. And suddenly she felt guilty. "However, Captain Brownlee is at our camp right now, telling my family there is no cause for concern. He thinks this is all simply routine…the price we pay for civilization." She frowned. "But I felt it my duty to share this grim news with you. Perhaps you and your families will want to reconsider your plans now."

"Do you mind if we share this letter with our families?" Hugh asked her.

"Do as you see fit," she told him. "Although I'm not sure I will be reading it to my own children. I do not want to give them nightmares."

Will nodded. "Sensible."

"I'm very sorry to have to be the bearer of bad news," she said.

Will put a hand on her shoulder. "And it seems this has taken its toll on you too, Elizabeth. What will you and your family do?"

"I'm not even sure." She sighed. "Although my father seems to agree with the captain—he keeps saying we will continue as planned."

"Thank you for telling us," Will said.

"I just wished I'd received this letter sooner." Now she excused herself and, feeling a little less vexed at the captain, returned to her own camp. Matthew and Brady were there now. And from what she could surmise, they were still discussing the contents of Malinda's letter.

"So what do you think of this new development?" she asked Matthew.

"It's not surprising." He simply shrugged. "Although I am sorry to hear of John's passing. I hadn't expected that."

"But you are comfortable taking your new bride into hostile Indian territory?"

"Oh, Lizzie." Matthew shook his head. "Isn't that overstating it a bit?"

"Wait until you read Malinda's letter."

He stuck out his hand, but she explained that she'd given it to Hugh and Will. "It seemed only fair they should know. They still have time to change their plans."

"What about the others?" Matthew asked. "The ones on the Applegate Trail?"

But now the chokecherry pickers were returning, loudly boasting about how many berries they had collected and who had found the most. Elizabeth was grateful to be distracted with the making of the cobbler. She poured the juicy chokecherries into the Dutch oven and then layered the cobbler crust evenly on top, finally getting it placed just so on the hot coals. "It should be done in about an hour," she told Ruth as she stepped away from the fire.

As they gathered around the table, waiting for Asa to say a blessing, Elizabeth no longer felt quite as upset as she had earlier. Then, as Captain Brownlee amused them with tales of adventure on the Western frontier, she slowly began to accept that, yes, they were going to a place that would be fraught with peril. There would be challenges and hardships. Perhaps some of her loved ones would perish. But how was that different from what they were doing right now? As the captain was just pointing out, the most difficult and dangerous days of travel were yet to come. Elizabeth recalled the Bible verse she had Ruth and JT memorize before starting on this journey. Perhaps it was time she reminded herself of its meaning.

Take therefore no thought for the morrow:
for the morrow shall take thought for the things of itself.
Sufficient unto the day is the evil thereof.

Matthew 6:34

Chapter Nineteen

It seemed that nearly every day, as they traveled along the Snake River, Elizabeth was reminded that the line "sufficient unto the day is the evil thereof" could not be more true. Each traveling day seemed to bring new challenges. The rugged terrain and hot August weather only added to their travails. Broken wagon wheels, cracked axles, split harnesses, injured animals...everyone on their train seemed to be suffering in one way or another. No unit was spared. And yet they pressed on.

The demands of the trail made it difficult to have much meaningful interaction with the other travelers. In a way, this seemed a blessing. Elizabeth was not eager to hear Lavinia's thoughts on the letter from Malinda. However, as it turned out, Lavinia had not been privy to it.

"Hugh and I spoke to Captain Brownlee about your sister-in-law's letter," Will told Elizabeth a few days later when they crossed paths while fetching water. "He reassured us that we should not be troubled by it."

Elizabeth studied his expression. Unless she was mistaken, he was not convinced of his own words. "What do you think?" she asked.

He sighed. "As you know, I'm a city boy. A city boy who was bent on having an adventure in the wild frontier. I suppose I'm worried I may have bitten off more than I can chew."

She smiled. "I appreciate your honesty."

"You do?" Will's frown transformed into a hopeful smile.

"I got aggravated at Captain Brownlee the other night," she confessed. "He's a good man, but his bravado and pompous speech about how bloodshed was how the West would be tamed and the price we pay for civilization...well, I found it rather unsettling. Then I reacted, and he made a comment about female sentimentalities." She let out a big sigh.

Will chuckled. "Oh, my. I'm glad the good captain wasn't giving his speech to my daughters. They would want to twist him by the ears."

"Your daughters are too well mannered to do that."

"Yes, but they would be just as vexed as you. As I mentioned, I have given them the vote...that leads to all sorts of troubles." He grinned.

"Speaking of the vote, have you asked them to vote in regard to the events my sister-in-law described in her letter?"

"Hugh and I gathered both of our families together last night. We didn't actually read the letter to them. But we did explain these new developments, tempered with what Captain Brownlee told us. We tried to paint a very fair and realistic picture of what lies ahead."

"What did they say?"

"Lavinia had some questions. First, she wanted to know what your family planned to do."

"What did you say?"

"Well, I'd had an interesting talk with your father just that morning. He assured me that your family was not changing your plans."

"That's true," Elizabeth confirmed. "My mother actually helped me to see this situation in a whole new light. She pointed out that poor Malinda will need us now more than ever. Malinda was my best friend before she and John moved to Oregon. Now I'm eager to be by her side and to comfort her and to help her with her children. I can hardly wait to see her."

"So I told Lavinia that you folks were pressing on. Then, of course, Julius was concerned about Mahala. He told us that even if we chose to remain in Portland, he would continue on to meet up with Mahala."

"He would be welcome to travel with us."

"That's not necessary. When put to the vote, it was unanimous. Even Lavinia, after first voting to oppose, eventually came around and voted to go."

"She did?"

"Well, you heard that she already sent the letter to the shipping company, didn't you?"

Elizabeth nodded.

"Lavinia is worried if she doesn't go, she will never see her goods again."

"Oh."

"And she is fond of you and your family too." He smiled warmly at her. "We all are."

Elizabeth looked down at her buckets of water, still sitting by the creek. "I must get this back to my mother. We were nearly out of water." He helped her to hook them onto the water yoke, pausing to push a stray piece of hair away from her eyes.

"There you go."

She thanked him, and despite the heavy load, her feet felt lighter than they had in several days. She wasn't sure if it was because of relief— that the Bostonians hadn't been scared off by Malinda's letter—or because of Will's sweet attentiveness. However, these kinds of thoughts toward Will simply reminded her of Eli. And the thought of Eli and how he had kissed her that last day…well, it was enough to scorch her cheeks with unwanted heat. Once again, she pushed all thoughts of that wandering man far to the back of her mind. Perhaps someday when she was an old woman, sitting by her fireplace in the winter, she would allow thoughts of Eli to sneak back out. But in the meantime, she planned to bury them deep.

ᏵᎧᎧᎧᎧ

"I am so very weary," Mrs. Taylor told Elizabeth at the end of an especially trying day. "I looked down in that steep canyon, down to that river below, and for a moment I thought it all looked very inviting."

Elizabeth tried not to show her shock. The canyon walls towered far, far above the river. The only way down there was to fall. "Inviting?"

"I thought to myself...if my foot stumbled...if I went tumbling down...well, it would be the end of my suffering."

Elizabeth put a hand on Mrs. Taylor's shoulder. "Perhaps you should go lie down in the back of my wagon." Mrs. Taylor had been staying with Elizabeth's family for the past several days. "Rest while we prepare supper."

"No." Mrs. Taylor shook her head. "I will do my part."

Still, it bothered Elizabeth to think that Mrs. Taylor had considered taking her own life like that, because she knew that was what she was saying. But at the same time, Elizabeth felt a smidgeon of relief to think that Mrs. Taylor had confided in her. Perhaps it was time for them to finish the talk they'd had weeks ago, after Mr. Taylor's untimely death. To that purpose, after the supper dishes were cleaned and put away, Elizabeth asked her mother if Ruth could sleep in their wagon tonight. "I think Mrs. Taylor needs to talk," she whispered.

Clara glanced over to where Mrs. Taylor was sitting in a chair, simply staring out into empty space. "Yes, I think you're right," she whispered back. "Ruthie," she called out, "why don't you spend the night with Grandma and Grandpa tonight."

Naturally, Ruth was pleased to oblige, and fortunately, Asa didn't complain about having to sleep outside of his wagon. Mrs. Taylor seemed oblivious. Or perhaps she simply didn't care.

Due to the demands of this difficult leg of the journey, most of the emigrants were turning in early at night. They hadn't enjoyed a musical evening for a week. Elizabeth was relieved to tell her family good night, and Mrs. Taylor had already gone to be bed. As Elizabeth walked to her wagon, she silently prayed, begging God to give her some kind of help or direction for poor Mrs. Taylor. She was obviously miserable. But what could possibly make her feel better? Part of her hoped that Mrs. Taylor would be asleep. Perhaps all she needed was rest. Didn't they all?

Elizabeth tried to be quiet as she climbed up the tailgate. Without even lighting the lantern, she unbuttoned her blouse, hoping that the even breathing she heard meant that Mrs. Taylor had already drifted off. But by the time she slipped into the bed, barely moving, Mrs. Taylor spoke up.

"I thank you for sharing your wagon with me," she said in a gruff voice. "I know I'm at your charity."

"You're welcome," Elizabeth said stiffly. Sometimes it was hard to react graciously to the way Mrs. Taylor said certain things. "And I know you didn't intentionally put yourself in a position to need our charity."

Mrs. Taylor simply humphed.

"But I do think it's good for myself and my family…as well as everyone on this train to practice charity. Don't you agree?"

"I suppose that's true."

"Mrs. Taylor," Elizabeth tried to be gentle. "I know you are hurting inside. I know that you're still grieving the loss of your husband."

"That too is true."

"But I'm concerned at what you said to me earlier…about ending your suffering."

Mrs. Taylor sniffed.

"However, I think I understand."

"You do?"

"Yes." Elizabeth sighed. "I remember my dark days of despair. I was buried in grief after losing my husband. I remember moments when I did not wish to live. But then I thought of my children…and I realized I had no choice. I had to live."

"You are blessed to have children, Elizabeth. And your family."

"I know. I'm sorry you don't have those same comforts."

"I did have children…once…" Her voice trailed off.

Elizabeth was shocked. It had never occurred to her that Mrs. Taylor had been a mother. "You did?"

"Miriam would have been twenty-seven…Jane would be twenty-five. Both of them were born in summer."

"You and Mr. Taylor had two daughters?"

"Mr. Taylor was not the father."

"Oh?"

"My first husband...Ephraim Miller. He was their daddy."

"You were married *before* Mr. Taylor?"

"Yes. That was before Mr. Taylor. Ephraim and I married long ago... when we were both quite young." She sighed. "We were so very happy in those days...back in Virginia. Miriam was born about a year after we were wed. Jane about two years later. Oh, such a pretty pair they were. Blue eyes and blond curls and pink cheeks...just like their daddy."

Elizabeth's imagination was stretched to its limits as she attempted to imagine Mrs. Taylor as a young energetic woman with two pretty little daughters. "What happened?" she asked meekly.

"The summer when Jane was five and Miriam was three, a new family had come to town—a widowed mother and her little boy. They'd come to our church seeking help. They were poor and in need. Ephraim and I decided to take them into our home. No one knew they were carrying typhoid fever. Not until it was too late."

"Your daughters got typhoid?"

"All of us got it. Ephraim, Miriam, Jane, and myself."

"Oh, my." This was familiar...painfully so. "I'm so sorry."

"I lost everything that summer."

"Oh, Mrs. Taylor, I am so very sorry. I had no idea your sorrows and suffering ran so deep."

"I didn't think I'd ever recover from that loss."

"I can scarcely imagine."

"About ten years after losing my family to typhoid, a missionary came to speak at our church. And when I heard him speaking of reaching out to the less fortunate, of preaching to savage Indians in the wilderness, I felt as if I had been awakened. As if something dead inside of me had risen from the grave. I decided that I wanted to do that too."

"Was that Mr. Taylor?"

"Yes. God sent Mr. Taylor to bring me back to life."

Elizabeth sighed. "And now you've lost him too. I'm so sorry."

Mrs. Taylor let out a choked sob. "And do you...do you want to know the truth, Elizabeth?"

Elizabeth didn't answer.

"The truth is that I'm to blame for all their deaths. All of them."

"Oh, Mrs. Taylor, I don't see how—"

"Ephraim did not want to take the widowed mother and her child into our home. He insisted from the beginning it was not a good idea. But I had already offered this to the reverend at our church. I had told him that we had plenty...plenty of food and plenty of room, which wasn't completely true. Even when Ephraim advised me against it, I stubbornly insisted upon taking the two in. I was too proud to back down, Elizabeth."

"You wanted to help them."

"No, I wanted to put on the appearance of helping them." Mrs. Taylor was crying harder now. "I wanted everyone to see what a good Christian I was by taking in these poor people. It was my pride...my foolish pride. And the same was true with my piano. My foolish pride insisted on holding onto that piano...the same piano that crushed the last breath of life from my beloved Horace." Now she was crying loudly.

With a lump in her own throat, Elizabeth just let her cry, knowing it would be pointless to say anything at this point. Just let her purge her grief with her tears, and perhaps this confession would help her to heal these old wounds. Finally, the sound of a lonely coyote's howling made Elizabeth realize that Mrs. Taylor had ceased to cry.

"Are you awake?" Elizabeth whispered.

"Yes." She sniffed.

"I do understand you better now," Elizabeth told her. "How you must be suffering. But I'm going to tell you what I told you before... I believe that God is just waiting to forgive you of these things. And I believe that until you let him do this, you will not be able to forgive yourself."

"How is that possible? How will I ever be able to forgive myself?"

"Perhaps you're getting the cart ahead of the horse," Elizabeth said. "Perhaps you just need to do your work of confessing your transgressions to God. If you truly believe that your pride caused these troubles, why not confess this to God...and ask him to forgive you?"

"You make it sound so simple."

"Isn't it?"

She sighed. "I don't know."

"Then ask God to show you, Mrs. Taylor. So that you *will* know."

"Oh, Elizabeth...you always give me so much to think about when I stay in your wagon."

"Are you saying you don't like spending the night in my wagon?" Elizabeth tried to insert some lightness into her tone.

"I must be a glutton for punishment...because I must admit I look forward to these times."

"Do you know what?" Elizabeth asked her.

"What?"

"The more I get to know you, the more I hear of your struggles and your mistakes and your weaknesses and your pain, the more I truly like you, Mrs. Taylor. All of this makes you seem quite human. And I think if you let others know you in this way, you would find yourself surrounded by a lot more friends."

"I've been trying," she said weakly.

"That's all you can do." Elizabeth let out a tired yawn.

"You go to sleep, child. And I promise I will think on all you've said."

❧

Two things remained with them for the next few days. The trail remained rough and rugged and cruel, and Mrs. Taylor remained Elizabeth's guest by asking if she could lengthen her stay for a few more days.

"You would tell me if I'm a great inconvenience..." Mrs. Taylor said on the third night. "Wouldn't you?"

"Yes," Elizabeth assured her. "And if it makes you feel any better, you do not kick nearly as much as Ruthie." She chuckled. "I do hope she's not being too hard on my mother."

"I don't think I'll ever be able to repay you for your kindness to me," Mrs. Taylor told her. "These late-night talks have helped me more than you will ever know."

"Hearing that alone is repayment enough."

"Today, while walking, I made my confessions to God. I laid my whole soul bare before him. And I asked him to forgive me."

"Good for you." Elizabeth smiled in the darkness.

"I'm not sure I won't have to do it all again tomorrow," she said a bit ruefully.

"At least you're moving in the right direction."

"And perhaps in time, if God is willing, I will be able to forgive myself. Although I've decided that if getting God's forgiveness is the best I can do, I should not complain."

"No, you should not. But it would be questionable to me, Mrs. Taylor, to think that if God, who is perfect, is able to forgive you, that you would be unwilling to do the same. Doesn't that seem ungrateful? Isn't it a bit like throwing the Almighty's forgiveness right back in his face?"

Mrs. Taylor let out a small gasp.

"I'm sorry if I spoke too frankly."

"No, no…that's quite all right." She sighed. "Again, you have given me something to think upon."

Elizabeth hoped that she wasn't giving her too much to think upon. Sometimes it was a relief not to think too much. There were certain unwanted thoughts in Elizabeth's mind…things she tried to bury or squelch or deny. But sometimes, especially if she was very tired at the end of the day, these disturbing thoughts seemed to run rampantly of their own accord, galloping freely past like a handsome Appaloosa.

Chapter Twenty

One day blurred into the next as they followed the twisting Snake River. So many times Elizabeth peered down the steep gorge, wondering how it would feel to dip her toes into that cool, clear water. But it was too far down for anything more than lowering a bucket on a long rope. Still, the water they pulled up was cold and refreshing.

Everything else was hot, dry, and dusty. And every day felt just like the one before it. She would walk in the morning, drive in the afternoon, and do chores at the day's end…again and again. Elizabeth didn't think this stretch of geography was quite as bad as Devil's Backbone, but it did feel unending. At least Devil's Backbone had ceased after three days. This barren wilderness just seemed to go on and on.

To make matters worse, Elizabeth heard a rumor of cholera outbreaks on the wagon train. This made the travelers, fearful of contracting the devastating illness, keep to themselves. Clara and Elizabeth, both well versed in disease prevention, insisted on boiling all their drinking water as well as rinsing dishes and utensils in boiled water. And so far, all of them remained healthy, though tired.

However, they'd had a couple of nasty breakdowns the last few days. First Ruby and Doris' wagon cracked an axle, and then one of the new families in their unit, the Petersons, had an ox go lame. As a result, unit three had taken over the lead position. Elizabeth didn't much mind. In some ways it took the pressure off. Besides, each wagon's place in the train didn't seem to matter—the dust did not discriminate. By the end of the day, everyone was coated with it. Every evening, Elizabeth shook out clothing and blankets and rugs, but it seemed to make little difference. She wondered if she would ever get the grit out of her teeth.

When the day came to cross the Snake River, Elizabeth felt a conflicting set of emotions. On one hand, she was hugely relieved to think they would be moving into more friendly terrain—or so she hoped. On the other hand, she knew that her father and brother were unusually nervous about this crossing.

"What's so different about this crossing?" she asked as she wiped out a frying pan. They'd just finished breakfast, and since their unit was now third in the train, they knew it would be several hours before their turn to cross. However, the men in their unit had been making good use of the time by sealing every crack they could find with pitch and tar, attempting to make their wagons as buoyant as possible.

"The captain says the Snake runs fast and deep," Asa told her. "And the current isn't always predictable."

"I think we should strap two wagons together," Matthew said as he coiled a rope around his arm. "Go across in pairs."

"I'm not so sure," Asa countered.

"What difference would it make to go in pairs?" Elizabeth asked.

"It gives more weight," Matthew explained. "To resist the current."

"That makes sense."

"I don't know." Asa's brow creased. "If it's not done right, it seems it could be a recipe for disaster."

"Let's go watch unit three," Matthew said suddenly. "They should be getting ready to cross by now. Maybe we can learn something."

"I've heard folks from unit three bragging," JT told them. "They say they're the best unit in the train."

"Well, it's true they haven't had as many breakdowns as the rest of us," Elizabeth pointed out. "But it's not polite to brag."

"You go on with the men and watch the others," Clara told Elizabeth. "You'll have to decide how you want to cross."

Elizabeth looked at Ruth. "You stay here and help Grandma." Then, seeing the disappointment in her daughter's eyes, she added, "And as soon as you're done, come join me by the river and we'll watch together."

"I'll stay to help too," Jess offered.

A large group of spectators were clustered along the rocky riverbank to watch as unit three gathered their livestock, preparing to swim the herd across. Elizabeth knew that each unit was expected to get all their animals across first and float the wagons afterward. As usual, Brady had volunteered to herd their animals. Elizabeth considered discouraging him as she recalled the unfortunate incident with Robert Stone, but seeing the hope in Brady's eyes, she knew she had to concede.

When JT insisted on going as well, she put her foot down. But Matthew, hearing mother and son going round and round about it, had intervened. "JT is as good in the saddle as any full-grown man," he defended his nephew. "Better than most on this train."

"And I can swim, Ma." JT stood tall, nearly looking Elizabeth squarely in the eyes.

"He'll be just fine," Matthew assured her.

And so she'd given in. Brady and JT as well as Julius and Jeremiah and two of the teen boys from the Petersons' wagon—all six would drive the team across the river. And Elizabeth would watch from the sidelines, praying the whole while for the safety of the men and animals.

"There they go," JT said as unit three began driving their animals into the river. "Look, Ma, they got boys my age herding too."

She just nodded, silently praying for the safety of the young men. She was surprised they only had three working the small herd, and she bit her lip when she saw one of the smaller calves beginning to drift downstream. Hopefully it would find its way back. It wasn't tidy and neat, but eventually the three young men got all the other animals onto dry land. The onlookers let out a loud cheer, and Elizabeth let out a long breath. "I'm not sure I want to watch all this," she told Matthew.

"But you can watch and learn," he said.

Now Jess, Clara, and Ruth were joining them. Elizabeth gave them a quick lowdown on the livestock crossing. "I hope the calf finds its way back to the herd."

"I'm sure he will," Clara told her.

"The first wagon is getting ready to go." Elizabeth pointed down to the river where a wagon was being pulled into the water. A taut rope was tied to the front of the wagon, and the oxen team was just starting to pull on the other side.

"They're going one by one," Clara observed.

"That water's moving fast," Elizabeth said with concern.

"What keeps the wagon from floating away?" Ruth asked.

"Captain Brownlee ran a line through the river," Elizabeth showed her. "See that rope in the water?"

"And remember there's the rope in back too," Clara pointed out. "To hold it steady."

The wagon was pushed and pulled with the current, and there were moments when the rope jerked so hard that Elizabeth was afraid it would snap, but eventually the wagon made it to the other side, easing out of the river with streams of water pouring down from it. Everyone on the other side let out another boisterous cheer.

"Maybe we don't need to go in pairs after all," Elizabeth said quietly to Matthew.

His brow creased as he watched the second wagon prepare to float across. Everything looked the same as with the first one, but the wagon was barely afloat when it seemed to get swept by a small rush of water that whipped the towrope so hard that it snapped in two. Suddenly the floating wagon turned sideways and then flipped over into the current, spilling people and boxes and supplies into the fast-moving water.

Screams of horror sliced through the morning as the overturned wagon now smashed into a nearby boulder, breaking into pieces. Men from unit three and others ran down the river, yelling and throwing ropes and attempting a rescue.

"I can't watch this." Elizabeth grabbed Ruth's hand, tugging her along. "Let's go back to camp."

"Will they be all right?" Ruth asked in a frightened voice.

"I don't know." Elizabeth shuddered as she hurried Ruth away. "But we'll pray for them."

Despite Elizabeth and Ruth's prayers, they later learned that only one family member, a small girl whose dress managed to keep her afloat, survived.

"She was taken in by another family," Jess told them more than an hour later.

"Unfortunately, that wasn't the end of it," Clara sadly reported.

"What?" Elizabeth demanded.

"Another wagon, the first one from unit two, suffered a similar fate." Clara shook her head with teary eyes. "I can't keep watching this."

"Go lie down," Elizabeth told her. Then, even though she'd already done it, Elizabeth went over her wagon again, checking it from one end to the other, making certain it was sealed as tightly as possible and that everything inside was as secure and low as it could be.

"I want to double up our wagons," Matthew said as he joined her at the front of her wagon. "I think the extra strength will get us across more safely."

She peered into his face. "Are you certain?"

He shrugged. "How can I be certain, Lizzie?"

She sighed. "I know...I know. And I trust you, Matthew. You've put a lot of thought into this so far."

"Are you willing to try it with my wagon? We could go first in our unit."

"Yes. Ruth can ride with Mother, and I'll—"

"I want to ride with you, Mama." Ruth tugged on her sleeve.

Elizabeth hadn't realized Ruth was even listening.

"Please, Mama. I want to ride with you."

Elizabeth reached for her hand. "All right. But we have to sit close together, and if anything goes wrong, you hold on to me, do you hear?"

Ruth nodded with wide eyes.

Elizabeth turned to Matthew. "What do we do?"

He explained his plan to remove the canvas coverings. "So they don't catch the wind like sails," he told her. "I'm sure that's what happened to the second wagon." Then he told her how they would bind their two wagons together like a large square raft. "We can't do it until we're at the river's edge," he told her, "and I also plan to run extra tow ropes. Maybe even four, just to be sure they're strong. And I'll run a couple extra lines across the river too. You and Jess can help to gather up all the ropes we've got. We're gonna need 'em."

While Elizabeth hurried to get ropes, she explained Matthew's plan to her mother. "It makes sense to me," she said.

"Now that you've explained it, I think it does make sense," Clara agreed.

"If it works for us, you and Father might want to try it too," Elizabeth suggested.

"Asa wants us to cross last so he can help everyone else in our unit," Clara told her. But perhaps we can plan to cross with Ruby and Doris." She frowned. "I worry that their wagon isn't as strong as it should be. I can see how it could help them to be strapped to a sturdier wagon."

"It's time for unit one to get our extra livestock down to the river," Asa began calling out to all the wagons. "And you drivers can get into your wagons and start lining up to cross."

Elizabeth hugged her mother and then told Ruth to get into the wagon. But just as she was getting in, Mrs. Taylor hurried over. "Elizabeth," she called out. "I know I'm supposed to ride with Ruby and Doris, but would you mind if I rode with you instead?"

Elizabeth quickly explained the plan to bind her wagon with Matthew's. "We're not even sure it will work," she said apologetically.

"Yes, so I've heard. It's why I want to go with you. I think it sounds like a good idea."

Elizabeth shrugged. "Feel free to join us."

Mrs. Taylor hurried over to the other side, climbing up and sitting on the other side of Ruth. Elizabeth released the brake and snapped the reins, urging the pair of mules to follow Matthew's wagon down toward the river. Her Percherons were already with the other livestock, waiting to be driven across the river. Brady and JT would remove the mules at the water's edge and take them to join the others.

Matthew helped her get her wagon into place, snugly up against his. Then, with the help of Asa and some other men who were curious to see how this was done, the two wagons were lashed tightly together. People from other units were looking on as well, some making comments that were less than kind.

"I don't know why they took the canvas off," a man said. "Seems like a lot of trouble over nothing."

Elizabeth stopped from tying an end of rope to glare at him. "You think wagons breaking to pieces in the river current and emigrants losing their lives is *nothing*?"

He gave her a surprised look and turned away, talking to the other men as if she weren't even there.

Elizabeth tucked the remaining rope into the wagon and stepped back, looking at the two wagons lashed together. "It really does look more like a raft now," she quietly told Matthew.

"Hopefully it will float like one too." Matthew had just finished securing the tow rope—a four-ply rope that would be pulled by the six oxen that Brady and JT had yoked together on the other side of the river. "All aboard," he told her with a twinkle in his eye.

Elizabeth got into her wagon now, joining Ruth and Mrs. Taylor as they crouched down in a small central space that Elizabeth had carved by moving boxes in the back of the wagon.

"Everybody ready?" Asa yelled out.

"Ready," Matthew yelled back. "Let 'er go."

Elizabeth held her breath as the oxen on the other side began to pull. Would they be able to handle the weight of two wagons? Would the ropes be strong enough?

"Look, Mama, we're floating," Ruth said happily.

"Yes." Elizabeth exhaled. "So far so good."

Mrs. Taylor had her eyes closed, but her lips were moving as if she was praying—and Elizabeth appreciated it. A few random waves splashed up against the side of the wagons, but they remained surprisingly steady and smooth as they cut through the water. Within only a minute or two, they were safely across.

She turned to look at Matthew and Jess now, and both of them were grinning. And all at once, they all let out a whoop of happiness, surprising Mrs. Taylor.

"We made it!" Ruth exclaimed.

"It worked!" Elizabeth told Matthew. "Well done, brother!"

It didn't take long for the others to follow their example, taking down canvases, binding wagons together, and crossing by twos. Soon their entire unit was safely across, celebrating at the river's edge.

"Unit one will now be the lead unit," Captain Brownlee hollered from across the river, where he'd remained to help the others. "Go ahead and join up with Jim McCall and the others, unit one. Lead the way!"

Elizabeth exchanged glances with Matthew as they all hurried to hitch their teams and prepare to travel. She couldn't remember when she'd felt so proud of her "little" brother. The Oregon Trail might be one of the hardest challenges of their lives, but it could be the making of them too. She was just stepping up to get into the wagon when she noticed a group of men carrying a bundle toward unit three, which was positioned nearby. A cold rush went through her as she realized it was a body wrapped in a blanket...one of the unfortunates from an overturned wagon. How many lives had been lost today? Would there be more? Yes, her family and loved ones would all be stronger and tougher at the end of this trip—she believed that to her core—if only they all survived it.

Chapter Twenty-One

"We'll make Fort Boise tomorrow," Asa announced as they lingered around the supper table. "The captain said we'll arrive there in time to make camp that evening. He doesn't recommend going to the fort at night, but he'll give us two extra hours to fetch supplies and look around the next morning."

"And I'll check the post office and mail my letter to Malinda," Elizabeth told them.

"Do you think she'll get her letter before we get there?" Ruth asked.

Elizabeth tried to appear less concerned than she felt. "It's possible."

"Sure, it'll get there," JT told Ruth. "The mail goes lots faster than a wagon train."

As her family visited about what they wanted to see and do in Fort Boise, making lists and plans, Elizabeth went to the wagon to get her shawl and a sweater for Ruth. It was probably her imagination, but she thought she could feel the nip of fall in the air. At first she'd tried to convince herself it was the elevation, but then she learned they weren't nearly as high up as they'd been a few weeks earlier. Still, she reminded herself, it was nearly mid August. Fall was only about a month away. And that meant the end of this trip was only about a month away as well.

While at the wagon, she lit a lantern and pulled out their well-worn map, carefully unfolding it and tracing her finger over the distance they'd already gone. It was impressive to see they'd traversed most of the continent by now. And it made the distance they had yet to go seem a bit smaller.

She pulled on her shawl and folded Ruth's sweater over her arm, blowing out the lantern to conserve kerosene. Then as she was leaving her wagon, she heard a rustling sound nearby. As always, she paused and listened intently and waited, prepared to grab her gun if necessary.

"I didn't mean to startle you."

She peered through the dusk darkness to see Will Bramford cautiously approaching. "Oh, hello," she said with relief. "I thought perhaps some kind of wildcat was about to leap."

"It is wise to be careful this time of night. I was walking, and thought I saw a light over here—and then it went out. I thought perhaps you'd gone to bed, although it seems a bit early."

She reached for the lantern again, taking a moment to strike a match. "I was trying to conserve lamp oil," she admitted. "But I think I'd rather have the light."

"Have you noticed how it's getting darker earlier? Those nice long days will get shorter and shorter as fall gets closer."

"So it's not just my imagination."

"What's that?"

"I felt like fall was in the air. But it's not even the middle of August."

"We're farther north now," he reminded her. "Probably close to the forty-fifth parallel. Back in Kentucky, you were below the fortieth parallel."

"I can barely remember latitudes and longitudes from geography," she admitted. "And I even had to teach it in school for a while…before I got married."

"You were a teacher?" He looked both surprised and amused.

"Not for very long." She smiled shyly. "James didn't think it proper for a married woman to teach school. I was only seventeen when I took over teaching for my friend Malinda when she got married..." She sighed sadly.

"The same Malinda who was recently widowed?"

She nodded. "Yes. She's a year older than me, but we were close the whole time growing up. Then we married the Martin brothers, and it was as if we became sisters."

"You must have missed her when she left."

"Oh, I did. I missed her dearly." Elizabeth reached back into the wagon, feeling around for the map again. "Anyway, I'm trying to remember where the longitudes and latitudes go." She unfolded the map, spreading it on the tailgate near the lamplight. "My map doesn't seem to have those marks on it."

Will reached past her, tracing his finger through the middle of the country, from just above Kentucky to California. "That's about where the fortieth parallel goes," he explained. Now he drew another imaginary line a bit higher up. "This is probably about where the forty-fifth would be. So you can see it's quite a bit higher. That would account for longer nights in summer and shorter days in the winter. Where we're heading in Oregon is about the same latitude as where we lived in Boston."

She nodded. "Well, thank you for the lesson." She folded up the map again. "How is it you know so much about geography?"

"I suppose it's not so much to do with geography as politics."

"Politics?" She was confused.

"The Kansas–Nebraska Act of 1854...forty degrees is where they drew the line dividing those states...the difference between North and South."

"Oh..." She nodded. "You mean if the country were to be divided. North and South."

"The country is already divided." The conviction of his words startled her.

"Well, I suppose it is. But surely it's something that can be worked out by our government." She fiddled with a shell button on Ruth's sweater.

"You truly believe our government, which is as divided as our states, can resolve this peacefully?"

"I don't rightly know. But I'd like to think they could."

"I wish you were right, Elizabeth, but I feel certain that this is going to be settled through bloodshed...similar to what happened in Kansas."

"So perhaps we're not really leaving civilization behind us after all?" She studied his creased brow. It was clear he was frustrated over their country's condition. "I mean, if states were to truly take up arms and go to war against each other..." She attempted a laugh. "Although I find that unimaginable."

He just shook his head. "I hope you're right."

"And since we have enough challenges of our own to consider out here in the untamed West, I suppose it's easy to push thoughts of a war like that out of one's mind." She smiled. "As the good book says, 'Sufficient unto the day is the evil thereof.'"

Now he smiled. "I like the way you think."

She suddenly grew uneasy about being out here like this, alone with Will in the dark. What sort of an example was she setting for her children? Or for his? "Perhaps you'd like to walk me to my parents' campsite," she suggested.

"Thank you," he told her. "I would like to."

"And if you're truly hankering after a political discussion, I am certain my father can accommodate you. I assure you he has plenty of opinions on this subject," she said as they strolled. "Sometimes he can argue quite brilliantly against slavery. But other times he can go on and on about the oppressions of the North. That's when the womenfolk tend to sneak away."

"Asa sounds nearly as divided as our country." Will laughed as they entered her parents' campsite. "I'll have to think twice before I start talking politics with—"

"*Politics?*" Asa looked up from where he was sitting by the fire, working on a broken piece of harness. "You want to talk politics?"

"Well, now...I'm not so sure."

"See what you started." Elizabeth chuckled as she took the sweater over to Ruth. "I thought you might need this."

"What kind of politics did you want to discuss?" Asa asked Will.

"Will was just telling me about the fortieth parallel and how it's becoming the dividing line between North and South," Elizabeth told Asa.

"I'll tell you what divides North and South," Asa began. "The North fails to appreciate that it needs the South."

Will sat down on a barrel across from Asa. "I agree with you on that."

Asa looked up from the harness in surprise. "You do?"

"I certainly do. Not only that, but I have to confess that I think the North sometimes acts superior to the South."

Asa nodded. "You got that right. Just because we Southerners are mostly farmers is no reason for Northerners to treat us as if we're inferior."

"So you consider yourself a Southerner?"

"Well, not anymore." Asa grinned. "But I am a farmer."

"So do your sympathies lie with the South?"

"I'm not rightly sure." Asa set the harness strap down. "But I fear Kentucky will be caught in the middle of the mess. And the more I think of it, I'm not sorry I won't be there to witness it. Nor do I want to choose sides."

"What would you do if you were forced to choose?" Will asked.

"Well...as you know, my family and I oppose slavery, which might make one think we were aligned with the North. But I'll be the first to admit I wasn't always in that camp. I owned slaves and felt justified in doing so."

"What made you change your mind?"

Asa glanced over to where Elizabeth was warming herself by the fire. "My children. It took me a while, but I finally came around."

"Did you know that Massachusetts has been abolitionist since 1780?"

"I reckon you folks don't have much in the way of agriculture either." Asa tied off a piece of leather, pulling it tightly with his teeth. "Now on account of me being against owning slaves, you might think I'm leaning to the North. But the truth is I do understand why plantation owners feel they need slaves. And I know some slave owners, including myself when I kept slaves, who treat their coloreds with more human kindness than some Northerners treat their own labor force."

"Perhaps, but our laborers up north are free to come and go at will. At the end of the day, they go to their own homes and families," Will pointed out.

"I've read about small children working up there in your Northern mills," Asa said with conviction. "I've heard tell of how them little ones toil away such long hours that they never see the light of day. I reckon that's not much different from slavery."

"I couldn't agree with you more." Will nodded. "I have lobbied for labor laws to protect children."

"Will Bramford!" Asa chuckled. "How am I to argue with you if you keep agreeing with me on every cotton-pickin' thing?"

"Now you just wait a minute. I'm sitting here listening to an abolitionist with Southern sympathies…I think you can produce a spirited argument all by yourself, Asa."

Asa slapped his thigh and laughed loudly. "You're welcome to my fire to talk politics anytime!"

After Fort Boise, where everyone tried to gather enough food supplies to get them through the next leg of their journey, they entered into some very rugged but handsome terrain. According to the captain, they were now in "real Oregon country," complete with mountains and forests and rivers and streams. Beautiful to the eye but difficult to travel—especially with a wagon.

"It's no wonder that mountain men travel light," Elizabeth said to Lavinia as the two of them walked up ahead of the train on the trail. "I'm sure they make much better time than we do with our wagons." She was thinking of a pair of trappers they'd seen earlier that day while waiting to ford a small river. The trappers had made a few jokes at the emigrants' expense and then had simply led their mules across the river and disappeared from sight.

"I can't imagine being able to live very comfortably with only what I could carry on the back of a mule," Lavinia said.

"Sometimes I think I could."

"Really?" Lavinia peered curiously at her. "Are you turning into a wild woman, Elizabeth?"

Elizabeth laughed. "I certainly hope not. It's only that I am so weary of the snail's pace we seem to travel in these parts. Waiting for the wagons to cross a stream that is easily passed over on foot. Watching with fear and trepidation as wagons are pulled by ropes up a steep ravine. Sometimes it feels so tedious and never ending. And just to get our goods to our destination. Do you not ever see the folly in it?"

Lavinia firmly shook her head. "What would you cook with if you didn't have pots and pans? Where would you sleep without bedding? And how would you build a house if you didn't have tools?"

"Yes…I suppose you are right." Even as she said this, Elizabeth wondered what it would be like to live like a mountain man. Was it really so different from what they were doing now? If anything, it seemed easier.

"Some of our fellow travelers are traveling lighter," Lavinia said quietly. "Have you noticed how many children are shoeless? Or how many women are wearing what appear to be rags? Do you think they didn't pack enough goods? Or have they simply ceased to care about appearances?"

"I fear it's both." Elizabeth bit her lip. "Sometimes I feel guilty and want to share goods with others. But my parents warn against this. My father is a generous man, but he says if I begin to give to some, how will I justify not giving to others?"

"Asa is a wise man."

Elizabeth sighed. "And my mother reminds me that what I've packed is for the welfare of my own children."

"That's true."

"But as good Christians, shouldn't we extend our hand to the poor?"

"Jesus said the poor would be with us always."

Elizabeth frowned.

"Besides, don't forget how your father and brother share game and fish with others in need. And Hugh and Will and the boys will be eternally grateful for all the hunting and fishing lessons your menfolk have given them. Do not underestimate the benefits your family has shared with many. Even Captain Brownlee uses you folks as examples of how to live successfully along the trail."

Elizabeth knew that was true. But she also knew that they could probably do more to help others. Lately she had felt torn. She'd see a painfully thin child, and if no one was looking, she'd slip the hungry waif a biscuit left over from breakfast. Then she'd beg the child not to tell anyone of her generosity—not because she was trying to do good deeds in secret as the Bible said, but because she was worried that she'd soon have a whole lineup of ravenous children begging from her. If that happened, she would be putting her entire family at risk. Life on the Oregon Trail wasn't only exhausting, it was a balancing act between generosity and survival.

Chapter Twenty-Two

They reached the mighty Columbia River on the third week of August. This was a crossroads where once again travelers would part ways. About half the wagons would cross the river and, led by Jim McCall, continue heading north. The rest of the wagon train, led by the captain, would continue west, following the river down to Dalles City. There they would transfer their wagons to a raft, which would transport them all the way to Fort Vancouver.

Mrs. Taylor planned to travel north with the Petersons and to eventually reach the mission near Fort Nez Percé, which was known to some as Fort Walla Walla. With her bundle on her back and her group readying to cross the river, Mrs. Taylor came to say her final farewells to Elizabeth and her family. With tears in her eyes, Mrs. Taylor hugged each one of them—a display of affection that surprised them all. Then she thanked them for their kindness and generosity, and finally she went to board the raft, where the Petersons were waiting for her.

Elizabeth watched Mrs. Taylor, silently praying that God would watch out for her and help her along her way. She admired her courage but was concerned about how a single woman would fare in a mission that was expecting a married couple. And then, just as the men were preparing to untie the raft, Mrs. Taylor, with her bundle still in hand, leaped off the raft and ran lickety-split back to where Elizabeth and her family were still gathered.

"Oh, please," Mrs. Taylor breathlessly begged Elizabeth. "May I travel with you? Might I join you on your journey to southern Oregon? I want to go to Elk Creek too!"

Elizabeth glanced at her father, but he simply smiled and nodded.

"Of course," Elizabeth grasped her hand. "You are part of our family now."

"Truly?" Mrs. Taylor blinked with tears in her eyes. "You mean that?"

"Certainly."

So Mrs. Taylor ran back to the raft, calling out to them that she had changed her mind and telling them goodbye. As the raft began to move, she remained there, a lonely figure in a dusty black dress, just watching and waving as the Petersons and their wagon were ferried away from her. Elizabeth wondered if Mrs. Taylor was also saying goodbye to her dreams of being a missionary.

Traveling along the south shore of the Columbia River had benefits as well as challenges. The benefits included plentiful game, good fishing, and easy access to water. The challenges were in the terrain. Uphill and downhill…again and again. And the air in these parts was dusty and hot and dry. But knowing the end of the trail was only days away, they pressed onward.

"Why can't we float down the river right now?" Ruth asked one afternoon. "Why do we have to wait until Dalles City?" Their wagon was stopped, waiting for their turn to cross over a stream that rushed into the river. But stretched out beside them, the river looked enticingly calm and peaceful and serene…inviting.

"Grandpa said there are some treacherous waterfalls ahead," Elizabeth explained. "Falls that would wreck our raft, and that would be the end of our trip."

"Oh." Ruth nodded with a serious expression.

Before the day was over, they saw Celio Falls for themselves. Thundering majestically over a cliff of rocks, they were loud and white and frighteningly beautiful. "See why we're still traveling on land?" Elizabeth asked Ruth.

She simply nodded. But they all stood there for a while, watching with interest at the way the barely clothed Indians speared and netted salmon among the rocks there.

"Looks like there's good fishing in these parts," Asa said. "Once we're on the river, we'll have plenty of time to catch some."

ᏣᎧᎦᎤᎾ

A day and a half later, they reached Dalles City and enjoyed a lively celebratory party that lasted all evening, complete with music and dancing and good food. But the next day they learned the unfortunate news. Although Captain Brownlee had prearranged for their transportation down the Columbia River, he was dismayed to discover that most of the rafts he'd commissioned, as well as the men to pilot them, had already gone downriver. Someone else had offered them more money.

"When I spoke to the captain this afternoon, he was fit to be tied," Asa told his family the next evening after supper. Mrs. Taylor and Ruth had gone to the wagon to read, but the rest of them were still gathered around the campfire, eager to hear Asa's report.

"Captain Brownlee told me that the wagon master who commandeered those rafts *used* to be a friend of his. And he said that this overland transport business is turning into a money-grabbing, cutthroat industry. In fact, he declared that this might be the last train he leads west."

"Poor Captain Brownlee." Clara shook her head as she refilled Asa's coffee cup.

"What about poor us?" Elizabeth said. "How will we make it to Fort Vancouver before our ship sets sail now?"

"Don't go flying off the handle," Asa told her. "Being that we're still the lead wagon, the captain assured me that our unit will get the first available raft. However, he also informed me that the raft is only large enough to accommodate six wagons. And he mentioned how a smaller raft is more maneuverable in the rapids."

"But we still have seven wagons in our unit," Elizabeth reminded him. "Even with the Petersons gone north, that's one wagon too many. Who gets left behind?"

"As luck has it, or not, depending on how you look at it, the Bentleys told me they can't afford the expense of transporting their wagon to Fort Vancouver on the raft."

"Oh, dear." Elizabeth felt badly for the young couple, especially since Matilda had just confided to her and Jess that she thought she was with child. "Will they have to go by land? I've heard that's a long and dangerous ordeal in a wagon."

"No," Asa told her. "They plan to leave their wagon behind and travel the river with us, only taking some of their goods."

"Well, it sounds as if we're set then," Elizabeth said.

"We're nearly all set." Asa cleared his throat. "Matthew, why don't you tell them your idea in regard to the livestock."

"I thought we were going to hire someone to drive the livestock west for us," Elizabeth injected.

"That *was* the plan." Matthew's expression grew grim. "Until I met the man this afternoon. The one we'd planned to hire."

"And…?" she waited.

"And if you want a drunken good-for-nothing caring for your prize Percherons and Molly and the other animals…" He shook his head. "Well, then Charlie Moore will not disappoint you."

"How do you know he's a drunken good-for-nothing?" Clara asked.

"Because when I met him, he couldn't even stand up straight, and he smelled like moonshine and horse manure. I can handle the horse manure, but I refuse to trust my animals to a drunk."

"Can we find someone else?" Elizabeth asked. "Someone reliable?"

"I've been looking," Asa told her. "It's slim pickin's around here."

"Which brings me to my idea," Matthew said. "A long trip floating down the river doesn't really appeal to me. Especially knowing it will be followed by an ocean voyage. Just thinking about all that confinement makes me feel restless already."

"I'm actually looking forward to it," Clara said wistfully. "To simply sit and watch the world float by…without all the backbreaking bumps…or the dust."

He gave her a tolerant smile. "I'm glad for you, Ma. But I reckon we're different. So anyway I got to wondering…what if I decided to go by horseback instead of by river? And while I was at it, how about if I drove our livestock along with me?"

"What?" Elizabeth felt alarmed at the idea of her younger brother out in the wilderness by himself.

"That way we can be sure of two things," he continued. "Our animals will make a safe journey, and we'll get them there on time to be shipped with us as planned."

Elizabeth glanced nervously at Jess, but she seemed perfectly at ease with this new plan as if it were nothing out of the ordinary.

"I already told Jess my idea, and she agreed," Matthew confessed.

"Can I go too, Ma?" JT's eyes lit up. "Please say I can. It would be a grand adventure with Uncle Matthew. Just like being a real cowboy. I'd even write about it in my journal. Please, Ma?"

"I don't think that's—"

"Come on, Lizzie," Matthew implored, "why not let JT come with me? He's good on a horse and good company too."

"And we can take Flax with us," JT said eagerly. "Flax is a good herder and watchdog."

"And if'n you don't mind, ma'am, I'd like to go too." Brady looked up from his whittling. "Bein' I can't swim, I ain't too keen on all that river travel myself."

"You really want to come with me?" Matthew looked hopefully at him. "I'd be pleased to have you along, Brady, but are you sure you're—"

"Wait, wait, just a minute…" Elizabeth held up her hands. "Next thing you know, you'll have everyone going by land with you." She turned to Asa. "What do you think of all this?"

"I think it's a fine idea. Our animals will be in excellent hands. Truth is I was tempted to go along with them myself, 'ceptin' I feel responsible for our unit while they're on the river. Can't be in two places at once."

"You really think it's a fine idea?" Elizabeth frowned at him. "The three of them and Flax, setting off like that without a scout or guide or anything to get them to where they need—"

"Elizabeth," Matthew said with impatience. "All we do is follow the river. It's not that hard."

"But I've heard it's a terribly rough trail," she reminded him.

"Sure it's rough and slow going when you're taking a wagon, but not so rough and not so slow when you're on a horse. And you do want your livestock safely delivered, don't you?"

Elizabeth was torn. She did want her animals to make it in one piece. "I want my son safely delivered too," she told him.

"I promise you, Lizzie, I will guard JT with my life."

JT snickered. "And I'll guard Uncle Matthew with my life."

"And I'll guard both of them for you," Brady added with a twinkle in his eye. "And the dog too."

Now they all laughed.

Elizabeth looked to her mother. "What do you think of this?"

"I think they're going to have a good adventure together."

"What about Indians?" Elizabeth ventured.

"Look, Lizzie." Matthew glanced over at Jess. "I don't like saying this, but you folks on the raft…well, you're in more danger of an Indian attack than we are. We've got brush and rocks to hide behind. But you'll be out there floating in the river with nothing to hide behind."

"But don't you worry," Asa said quickly. "We'll arrange our wagons so that we have a space between them to take cover if needed. And by my tally, we've got at least a dozen adults who know how to shoot. That's like a small infantry. We'll have regular guard duty and keep our guns ready to defend ourselves if necessary. However, according to the captain, that is unlikely."

Elizabeth looked longingly at JT. "It'll be hard to part ways."

JT stood and came over to her. Taking her hand in his, he looked into her eyes. "But we'll be together again, Ma. I promise we will."

Her boy looked so much like a man that she felt her eyes getting misty. And she knew she had no more argument. "Well, I guess there's nothing left to do but agree."

JT hugged her. "Thanks, Ma. I won't let you down."

Just like that, Matthew gathered Brady and JT and immediately began making lists of supplies they'd need. They agreed to leave as soon as possible in the morning.

"When can *we* leave?" Elizabeth asked Asa.

"Not for a few days," Asa said.

"A few days?" Suddenly she felt impatient. "Why the delay?"

"That's the soonest the men in charge of the raft will be ready to leave," he explained. "They need to shore up the raft. I promised to make it worth their while to do their best job. Trust me, it'll be time well spent. Once we're on that river, we want the raft to be as strong as can be."

"I'm grateful for the time," Clara said. "We'll do some laundering and other preparations for the river trip."

"I suppose we'll have time to gather berries and such," Elizabeth said.

"And I'll take some of the men hunting," Asa told them. "We'll have plenty of time to get some game smoked for the river trip."

They all continued to talk with enthusiasm, making plans for all that needed to be done in preparation for parting ways and for the next couple weeks of their journey.

Elizabeth got up early the next morning. She wanted to do everything she could to ensure that JT had everything he would need for his "grand adventure." She still had reservations about this plan, but she knew he was determined. And Matthew's words about having no place to hide on the river had been sobering. She realized that no one on this journey was truly safe. In the middle of the night, she decided that the best they could do was to be wise and to trust God.

JT was down on his knees, rolling up his bedroll, when she saw a couple of large holes in the soles of his boots. "JT..." She knelt down to look more closely. "These boots are really worn out."

"I know, Ma." He stood with the bedroll in his arms. "But I already wore out the other ones." He stuck out a dusty boot. "These will just have to make it the rest of the way."

"Unless..." She remembered packing some of James' things for when JT grew bigger. "Wait here." She climbed back into the wagon, relieved to see that Mrs. Taylor was already awake. "I need to get into a box beneath the bed," she told her. Together they struggled to move and shift things, finally unearthing the box Elizabeth wanted. She pried open the top and then dug down until she found a pair of boots, holding them up in victory. "Just what we need," she proclaimed as she hurried back down to JT. "Try them on," she told him, and to her delight they were only a bit too big.

"And my feet might grow while I'm helping Uncle Matthew," JT assured her with boy-like faith.

Elizabeth chuckled. "I have no doubt of that." Next she reviewed the list Matthew had made for him, adding a few things she thought would be necessary. Then finally, she pulled out her canteen—the one Eli had swapped and never swapped back—and handed it to JT. "This looks like a cowboy canteen."

"Really, Ma?" His eyes lit up. "You want me to take Eli's canteen?"

"Yes. I'll keep yours with me, and we can trade back in Fort Vancouver."

He held up his Bowie knife. "Remember when Eli gave me this?"

She nodded, feeling a lump growing in her throat. She told herself it was because of JT leaving like this, but she knew it was partly due to Eli as well.

"Matthew said there won't be room for my guitar. But Brady and I are both taking our harmonicas."

"That's good." She put her arm around his shoulders. "I know you'll be all right out there, son. But I'll be praying for you—all of you—just the same."

"I know you will. I'll be praying for you too."

"Let's go over to Grandma's now…see what we need to pack in the way of food stuff."

Clara and Jess were already at work, measuring out enough rations of food to get the three of them to Fort Vancouver.

"And don't forget we'll hunt along the way," JT assured them. "I'll bet we'll be eating better than you folks stuck on the river raft."

"We can catch fish," Jess reminded him.

"I have good news," Matthew said as he and Brady led some of their horses into camp in order to load them. "We've picked up a couple more cowhands."

"What?" Elizabeth felt hopeful. "Does that mean JT won't need to go?"

"*Ma?*" His voice was laced with pleading.

Matthew came over to stand by JT. "JT is my right-hand man. You can't take him away from me just because Jeremiah and Julius have thrown their hats in the ring."

"Really?" Elizabeth was surprised. "Jeremiah and Julius are going with you?"

"Their families were going to leave their teams behind in the hopes they could replace them in Empire City or Coos Bay, which might not be likely. So when they heard we were doing this, they asked to come along with us."

"Perhaps there will be safety in numbers," Elizabeth conceded, and JT looked relieved. And really, it was some comfort to think that the Bramfords and Prescotts were willing to send their sons on a trek like this. Before long, everything was gathered and bundled and loaded onto the horses and mules, and Matthew announced it was time to leave.

"Who knows…" he said as they were climbing into their saddles. "We might even reach Fort Vancouver before you river folks."

"Well, if that happens, you know what to do," Asa told him.

Matthew patted his vest pocket. "I've got all the instructions you copied down for me right here, Pa."

Before the livestock drivers left, their family members all gathered round them, and Asa said a brief prayer for their safety and Godspeed. Elizabeth tried to hide her tears as she called out her farewells. She knew that these fellows—in fact, all of the pioneers—were in God's hands. It was futile to surrender herself to worry and fear. Even so, it was hard to watch them go. But JT sat tall in his saddle, and before they were out of sight, he removed his hat to give her one last wave.

Chapter Twenty-Three

After a successful hunting trip, Asa and the other men in their unit set up a large makeshift smoker with canvas and evergreen branches, and it was Mrs. Taylor's job to keep the smoldering fire burning throughout the day—and to make sure no one pilfered the smoked meat. Clara and Elizabeth washed clothing in the river. They also shook dust out of all the bedding and gave their wagons a thorough cleaning. Then they organized the food and kitchen supplies so that it would be easier to prepare food on the river.

"Why don't we invite Lavinia and Matilda to combine their food stuff with ours," Elizabeth suggested. "That way we can do all the cooking together, and everyone can help out."

Clara nodded. "Many hands make light work."

The other women were relieved to combine their kitchens, although Matilda was concerned that her meager provisions were unworthy. "I'm worried we might not even have enough beans to make it all the way to Fort Vancouver."

"Just remember the boy who brought Jesus his fishes and bread," Elizabeth said to cheer her. "In the end, everyone had more than enough."

And Lavinia happily volunteered Evelyn and Belinda and Amelia to help with the cooking. "They've all gotten to be much better cooks than I am," she confessed to Elizabeth. "Thanks to you and Clara."

When they gathered all the food together, Elizabeth and Clara were surprised at how much they had. Even when they figured it out, planning on three meals a day for seventeen people, they seemed to have more than enough.

"And we aren't even taking the smoked meat into account," Elizabeth pointed out.

"And Asa and the men are trying to catch salmon today," Clara told her. "Your father plans to smoke that as well."

"And right now Jess and Ruth are out gathering more berries. We already have enough to make a fair amount of jam."

"Ruthie wants to make some pies."

Elizabeth sighed. "And yet a lot of folks from the wagon train seem to be suffering from hunger."

Clara nodded sadly. "Asa and the captain have encouraged them to make use of all the food this land has to offer, but not everyone is good at hunting and fishing."

Elizabeth knew this was true. Unfortunately, not all the pioneers had the kind of experience they needed to succeed in the West. She just hoped that by the time they settled, they'd improved these survival skills. Although nothing had been said about it, Elizabeth suspected that Asa had selected a campsite for unit one that was separate from the others because he was concerned about theft. They all knew that the desperation of some of the travelers was causing some to steal. For that reason, Asa had instructed them to never leave their campsite alone or unguarded.

"Also, I suppose the men are busy falling timber to make their own rafts to get their families down the river. It's difficult to hunt and build at the same time."

"Mother," Elizabeth began carefully. "Do you think we should share some of our food with the others?"

Clara nodded eagerly. "I have been thinking that very thing, but we'd have to speak to the others first."

"The Bentleys shouldn't mind because they were short on supplies anyway. Our surpluses will help to feed them."

"And I doubt Ruby and Doris would be opposed to generosity," Clara said. "But I'm not so sure about Lavinia."

Elizabeth knew her mother was right. Lavinia might balk at this idea. "What if I invite her to come see how much we have and show her how much we expect to need for the duration of our trip?"

"Yes." Clara made an uneasy smile. "But you know as well as I do that charity doesn't come naturally to Lavinia. I suppose that's because she's a businesswoman."

"But maybe I can convince her that we have more than enough." Elizabeth looked at the barrels and tins. "Perhaps we should go over it again just to be certain." And so they went through the supplies one more time, listing out how many meals for how many days for how many people, and they clearly seemed to be overstocked.

"And we'll be able to restock in Fort Vancouver," Elizabeth pointed out. "Yet some of our fellow travelers are going hungry." She described a young mother she'd seen while washing clothes yesterday. "She was so thin that I could see her ribs through her threadbare camisole. And her children were skin and bones."

"Oh, dear." Clara sadly shook her head. "I've seen some things too." She held up a bag of cornmeal. "We could easily get by without this. We have more than enough...and we won't even be walking. Somehow we need to convince Lavinia."

"I have a plan," Elizabeth said suddenly. "I'll invite her to take a little walk with me...a little sightseeing tour." Winking at her mother, she tucked a couple of leftover breakfast biscuits into her skirt pocket and then hurried over to Lavinia. She was sitting in her rocker with her feet resting on a barrel, reading a book she'd borrowed from Asa.

"Good afternoon, neighbor," Lavinia said cheerfully. "Will you look at me—I have become a woman of leisure."

"I see that." Elizabeth pointed to where damp clothes were hanging on several lines strung between the wagon and a nearby tree. "But it seems that someone's been hard at work."

"Yes, the girls and I finally finished the last of the laundry." She let out a weary sigh. "And now the young ladies are out gathering berries and firewood."

"Good for them. And I wondered if you'd like to take a stroll with me."

Lavinia looked unsure, but then she closed the book and slowly stood. "Yes, I suppose a leisurely walk might do me good. And it is a lovely day. Besides, I haven't had a good conversation with you since we reached the Columbia. I suppose it's time to catch up." She called over her shoulder now. "Augustus, you stay in camp until I get back, you hear?"

"Yes, Ma," he called from the back of the wagon.

Lavinia chuckled. "All of Augustus' clothes are drying on the line at the moment, so he is confined in the wagon with a book."

Elizabeth laughed. "I felt badly that I was unable to wash JT's clothing before he left. It was hard watching him set out in his dusty trail clothes."

"Oh, don't worry about that. He will only get dustier and dirtier."

Elizabeth linked arms with Lavinia. "Let's walk past our old traveling companions..." she said. "See how they are faring."

"Hugh tells me that some of the smaller rafts are nearly ready to float, but they're only big enough for passengers and limited goods. Many wagons will be left behind."

"We're fortunate that we can take ours." Elizabeth noticed a skinny pair of barefoot boys in raggedy clothes trying to catch something with their hands in a nearby creek. "It looks like they're fishing," she said quietly.

"Haven't they heard of a fishing pole?"

"Perhaps they're too poor to have one," Elizabeth whispered. "Look how skinny they are. I'll bet they haven't eaten today."

"Truly?" Lavinia frowned. "That's not good."

Elizabeth now led Lavinia toward them. "Let's do a good deed." She slipped Lavinia one of the biscuits and then called out to the boys. "Young men," she said to them. "Are you having any luck with your fishing?"

The boys looked up at her with grubby faces. "Nah," the bigger one said. "They're too fast."

Now Elizabeth held out a biscuit. "Would you like this?"

His eyes grew wide as he hurried to her. "Thank you, ma'am."

"You too," Lavinia called out now. "Come and get yours, little man."

"Hurry, Levi," the bigger boy called. "Come get a biscuit."

Elizabeth knelt down to look into their faces. "Now, don't tell the other children about this because we don't have enough for everyone."

The taller boy shook his head as he gobbled up the biscuit.

"Good luck with your fishing," Elizabeth called out as she linked arms with Lavinia again, walking her away.

"Those poor dirty little urchins," Lavinia said. "What kind of mother lets her children go around looking like that?"

"Some children on this train have lost their mothers," Elizabeth reminded her. "Some have lost their fathers."

"Oh, yes…I suppose that could be the problem with those poor waifs."

Elizabeth continued walking Lavinia past the various camps. Some seemed to be faring well, but others looked fatigued and hungry…and hopeless.

"Let's go back to our camp," Lavinia told Elizabeth. "This is making me uncomfortable."

As they walked back, Elizabeth explained that she and Clara had done an inventory and made lists. "It appears we have surplus food."

"Surplus food?" Lavinia looked skeptical. "That hardly seems possible."

"We checked the supplies twice," she told her. "And we didn't even take into account the smoked venison and salmon the men are providing."

"Well, even if we do have surplus, we will need more provisions for the remainder of our journey."

"Yes, I know. But we should be able to replace some things in Fort Vancouver."

"Maybe...but they may only have foods like beans and cornmeal." She made a face. "And I am sorely tired of beans and cornmeal."

"Then perhaps we could donate some of our beans and cornmeal," Elizabeth suggested.

Lavinia tipped her head to one side as if considering this. "I suppose I could agree to that. But only after I see our supplies and your lists. I will not risk my family's welfare."

"We wouldn't expect you to."

By the end of the day, it was agreed that unit one would donate some surplus food to be administered by Captain Brownlee and shared among needy families with children who were going hungry. "But please don't reveal where the food came from," Asa told the captain that evening as they all gathered at their campsite.

"This is very generous," the captain said as he eyed the tins and boxes of beans, cornmeal, and rice. "And I have some good news for unit one. Your raft is ready to go. First thing in the morning, I'll bring one of the spare oxen teams, and we'll start getting your wagons loaded."

⁂

With their six wagons secured and everyone aboard, the large log raft, with two hired men poling, began to drift down the Columbia River. The canvas coverings had been removed from the wagons in order to prevent them from acting as sails that could hamper the navigation of the raft.

"Isn't this exciting, Mama?" Ruth grasped Elizabeth's hand.

"Yes." Elizabeth looked out at the water. "Just don't get too close to the edge, Ruthie. If the raft hits rough water or a rock, you might fall in."

"But I can swim," Ruth reminded her.

"Yes, but this water is swift, and you could be swept away. Besides that, you need to stay out of the men's way. They need to be able to get around easily on the raft with their poles. They might not see you and accidentally knock you overboard."

"I'll be very careful, Mama."

Elizabeth smiled. "I know you will." She also knew that with Ruth being the youngest traveler and friendly to everyone, she had many sets of loving eyes on her. Still it was a little unsettling to see all that river and no railing to keep a person from tumbling over.

"I'm going to draw pictures of what we see going down the river." Ruth pulled her pencils and tablet from the back of their wagon. Because her paper was limited, Ruth had worked hard to squeeze several drawings on each page. She already had a nice collection of pictures.

"Look, Mama." She held the tablet for Elizabeth to see. "That's the Indian woman who sold us the moccasins. Remember her?"

Elizabeth lifted the hem of her skirt to point at a moccasin-shod toe. "I certainly do." They had both decided to give their shoes and feet a rest by wearing their moccasins to float down the river. Elizabeth had nearly forgotten how comfortable the soft shoes were.

With little room to move about the raft, people eventually made themselves comfortable in and about the wagons. Some napped on piles of bedding. A few read books or wrote in journals. Others, like Elizabeth, were perfectly content to sit and watch the landscape floating by. She'd never seen such majestic rolling hills before. Truly, they were probably mountains, but they had such soft, graceful curves that they seemed more like gigantic rolling hills. They were the color of a straw field before harvest—a warm golden tone. But the color seemed to change as clouds rolled by. It was really nothing short of glorious, and she felt she could happily sit and watch it all day.

"Look!" Ruth pointed to the south side of the river. "Those animals—what are they, Mama?"

Elizabeth peered at the herd. "They don't look like antelope," she told her.

"Those are bighorn sheep," Asa hollered from the other side of the boat.

"There must be thirty or more of them," Elizabeth observed. "Aren't they majestic looking?"

Of course, the men were already talking about hunting and mutton roasts, but fortunately for that particular herd, it was far too early in the day to stop the raft.

By the end of the day, when the shadows grew long and the hired men said it was time to stop, Elizabeth was grateful to get back onto solid ground. Despite the beautiful scenery, she was tired of the confinement of the raft and always having people so close around her. She was eager to stretch her legs.

It took several trips to unload what they'd need for the night. And Adam and Matilda, who had no tent, opted to sleep on the raft. They planned to rig a tent of sorts by running a tarp between the wagons. Asa agreed this was a good idea. "Just keep your rifle handy," he told Adam. "If we hear shots, we'll all come a runnin'."

Again, Elizabeth was reminded of the dangers of being out here like this in the wilderness. However, she tried to believe that just as the captain and Eli had said, the Indians in these parts were relatively peaceful. At the same time she knew that the situation could change and deteriorate quickly. And she tried not to think of the scenes that Malinda had described.

They made camp right on the river, which made collecting water for cooking and cleaning much handier. Truly, of all the days on the trail, this had been one of the easiest.

"I'm not sure if I can get used to doing so little during the day," Elizabeth admitted to the other women as they worked together to prepare supper.

"Perhaps my mother can give you lessons," Evelyn told her.

Belinda giggled. "Yes, Aunt Lavinia is quite good at doing nothing."

"I beg your pardon?" Lavinia looked up from her book. "I *am* doing something. I am reading a book. Furthermore, you young girls have all made it perfectly clear that your outdoor cooking skills are far superior to mine. Why would you want me to interfere?"

Elizabeth chuckled, wondering if Lavinia hadn't pulled the wool over everyone's eyes by pretending to be so useless over a cooking fire.

"Perhaps you should read aloud to us," Ruby called out.

"Yes, yes," they all agreed, begging her to read.

"All right. I am reading *Essays* by Ralph Waldo Emerson," she told them. "It was published in 1849, I believe." She cleared her throat and began to read.

> To go into solitude, a man needs to retire as much from his chamber as from society. I am not solitary whilst I read and write, though nobody is with me. But if a man would be alone, let him look at the stars. The rays that come from those heavenly worlds, will separate between him and what he touches. One might think the atmosphere was made transparent with this design, to give man, in the heavenly bodies, the perpetual presence of the sublime. Seen in the streets of cities, how great they are! If the stars should appear one night in a thousand years, how would men believe and adore; and preserve for many generations the remembrance of the city of God which had been shown! But every night come out these envoys of beauty, and light the universe with their admonishing smile.

"Oh, my!" Doris sighed. "Isn't that beautiful."

"And how fitting that Emerson was writing about appreciating solitude," Elizabeth declared. "After being contained so closely together all day, unable to escape each other's company while our little boat floated downriver, I can relate to his words."

"You wanted to escape our company?" Lavinia demanded.

"No, no, not actually." Elizabeth realized how this sounded. "I only meant that after having the freedom of walking out in the open so much, often being on one's own, well, I suppose we'll have to get used to dwelling in such close quarters." She poured the cornbread batter into the Dutch oven and found a spot on the fire for it. Even though Belinda was making a lot of biscuits, they'd decided to make a large batch of cornbread as well. Whatever leftovers they had would get them through their midday meal tomorrow.

Now seeing that everyone else was occupied and that nothing more needing doing, Elizabeth decided to excuse herself. "I'm going to take a short walk and see if there are any berries nearby."

"I would come too," Ruth told her, "but Amelia and I are going to make some huckleberry pies for dessert tonight."

"With the trout the men caught today and huckleberry pie, we are truly eating like kings," Elizabeth proclaimed as she left. It was already getting dusky, but the sky reflecting on the river made it seem lighter, and she found a rock by the water's edge and sat down. She was close enough to hear the sounds of the women working to prepare supper, and she could see some of the men just past the big raft with fishing poles. Truly, this scene was idyllic, especially compared to the rugged wearing days of the past.

She leaned her head back, and looking up at the sky, which was just turning a dark periwinkle blue, she prayed for the safety of JT and Matthew and the rest of them. Then she prayed for the wagon train travelers on the various trails and the ones waiting to ride the river. Finally, she prayed for Malinda and her family. She had no idea if they were still on their homestead or heading right now back to Kentucky.

"Hello?"

Elizabeth jumped to her feet. "Oh, it's only you."

"*Only* me?" Will looked deflated.

"I'm sorry," she told him. "I didn't mean it like that. It's just that you startled me, and then I was relieved you weren't a Cayuse Indian out on the warpath."

"Ah…the Cayuse…weren't they responsible for the Whitman Massacre up near Fort Nez Percé?"

"That's what I read a year or two ago. But it's not something I particularly cared to bring up in these parts. Especially when we're not that far from where it happened. That story would frighten poor Ruthie to no end, and I'm sure your daughters wouldn't care to hear of it either."

"So is that what you were so intently thinking on just now?"

"No, not actually." She frowned to remember Malinda's accounts about Indians. "But I suppose it was similar in some ways. I was just imagining how Malinda and her children might be eastbound for Kentucky and how she might be thinking she will find us there…and we are headed west, hoping to reunite with her."

"Do you think that's what she's doing right now?"

She looked out over the horizon. "I don't know…I certainly hope not. But can you imagine?" She used her hands to show him, passing each other in opposite directions.

"Ships that pass in the night."

"Isn't that Longfellow?" she said. "I can barely remember that poem."

"Yes. The great Henry Wadsworth Longfellow. Let's see how much I can recall.

> Ships that pass in the night, and speak each other in passing,
>> Only a signal shown and a distant voice in the darkness;
>> So on the ocean of life we pass and speak one another,
> Only a look and a voice, then darkness again and a silence.

She sighed. "That is sad…and beautiful."

"Sorry. I didn't mean to make you feel worse."

"No, it doesn't make me feel worse. And if Malinda is heading east right now…well, there's nothing to do about it, is there?"

"Look," he pointed up the river and into the sky. "The first star. Perhaps you should make a wish."

She smiled. "I've already prayed a prayer. That should suffice."

"All right then, I'll make a wish." He stared at the star intently as if he was thinking hard about something.

"What's your wish?" she asked.

"I can't tell you."

"Why not?"

"Surely you know that a wish can't come true if you tell someone."

She laughed. "I thought only children believed in wishing on stars."

Now he looked at her with nearly the same intensity that he had looked at the star. "I suppose there is still a child living within me. Just ask my daughters."

"Speaking of your daughters, I should probably go back and help with dinner."

"I'll walk with you," he offered. "Just in case there are any Cayuse lurking about."

She wished she could make light of this, but thoughts of Malinda's letter extinguished any humor. And so as they strolled she changed the subject. "Today was a perfectly lovely day," she said. "I wonder if all our days on the river will be so pleasant."

"The men piloting the boat say September weather is usually quite nice. But it's possible a summer storm could stir up. Also, we'll have some rough waters to go through here and there. It won't all be smooth sailing."

"No, of course, not." Did he really think she thought it would be?

"I'd been meaning to tell you something."

She paused to pick some wildflowers, avoiding his eyes and hoping he wasn't about to say something they would both regret.

"I spoke to Brady."

She stood up with some flowers in her hand. "To Brady?"

"I felt it was only fair that he be informed as to Oregon laws in regard to slavery and land ownership. I asked him if you'd mentioned any of this to him, and he told me you hadn't."

Elizabeth frowned. "I know...I had been meaning to...but how does one say something like that? And after all Brady's been through recently. Nearly drowning and then getting beat up like that. How could I tell him about these new Oregon laws?"

"Yes, that's what I was worried about. And I didn't want him riding through Oregon with our young men and perhaps meeting up with some unsavory types, if you get my meaning."

She nodded grimly. "I'm sorry to say that I do."

"So I wanted Brady and the others to be warned. And I took it upon myself to do so."

"What did you tell Brady?"

"I told him that if he wanted to be safe, he should simply pretend that he was their slave and act the part."

"Oh." She felt a rush of bitterness at the injustice of this.

"I know. It seems unfair to me as well. But as I explained to Brady, it could be the difference between life and death." He shook his head. "Also, Brady out there riding as a free man could put our boys in harm's way...I mean if their group was discovered by the wrong sort of men.

So until we reach our destination, I have advised Brady to simply play the part."

"And what did Brady say?"

"He seemed to understand." Will winked. "And I told him that I would be proud to be his legal counsel should he need it."

"That's generous." Elizabeth felt a new pang of pity and concern. "Did you tell him…about the other law too? About not being able to own land?"

"I saw no reason to mention that."

She felt a smidgeon of relief. "I would like to break that to him myself. Once we're in Fort Vancouver. It's possible he'll want to make other plans." She sighed as they walked a bit farther. "Although I can't imagine being without Brady. I've known him for so long…he feels like family."

Now Will stopped, bending down to pick a few purple wildflowers that she hadn't even seen. "And in case I haven't said so before, Elizabeth…" He handed her several flowers to add to her bouquet. "The company of you and your family certainly makes the trip more pleasurable. I cannot even imagine how bleak this experience might have been if we hadn't been fortunate enough to travel with you folks."

She smiled. "Oh, I'm sure you would have met some other fine folks. Your children are quite good at making friends."

"But that wouldn't have been the same." He handed her one more flower with a wistful smile. "I don't think the trail is the best place to go courting, but once we're settled, I'd be obliged if you'd let me go about it properly."

She started walking again. With each step she was trying to think of an honest yet gracious answer, but no words came to her. The truth was that she didn't know how to answer him. She knew she enjoyed his company. She liked the conversations they shared. And yet…she was unsure.

"I'm sorry," he said gently. "I told myself I wasn't going to say another word along these lines. But seeing you in the dusky light…the flowers in your hands…well, you'll have to forgive me, but it just gets a fellow to dreaming."

They were nearly in camp, and she still couldn't think of a proper response. But hearing the voices of the women growing louder, she knew she needed to say something quickly. "Thank you for seeing me back to camp," she told him. "I'm obliged." Then she excused herself and hurried over, pretending to be fascinated by how the pie making was progressing. As she chatted with Ruth and Belinda, she felt the female eyes watching her. She knew they had seen the two of them walking into camp together. And they could obviously see the flowers she was now putting into a tin of water. She knew what they were thinking. The problem was that she didn't really know what she thought yet.

Chapter Twenty-Four

The farther they traveled west on the Columbia River, the more stunning the landscape became. Towering evergreen trees contrasted against the brilliant sapphire blue river. The abundance of colorful waterfowl and birds of prey made them easy to spot. Interesting rock formations looked as if they'd sprung right out of the ground, reaching toward the clear blue sky and rolling clouds. And they even got glimpses of pointed snowcapped peaks towering majestically on both sides of the river. All so pristine and amazing that the beauty sometimes brought actual tears to Elizabeth's eyes.

She peered over Ruth's shoulder, watching as Ruth attempted to capture the natural splendor of this region. Today she was drawing a mountain peak with evergreens and the river, complete with ducks.

"You have become quite an artist," Elizabeth told her.

"Thank you." Ruth beamed up at her. "Do you think someday I'll show these pictures to my own little girl? And tell her about when we came out here to Oregon?"

Elizabeth laughed. "I certainly hope so."

"That's what I heard Belinda saying the other day," Ruth admitted.

"It sounds like Belinda looks forward to getting married."

"Is Belinda old enough to get married?"

"I suppose she is." Elizabeth glanced over her shoulder to see if any of their traveling companions were listening, but most of them were on the back end of the raft at the moment, watching as some of the men fished. "I guess that's up to Belinda and her parents...and the lucky young man, of course."

"Who *is* the lucky young man?"

Elizabeth tweaked one of Ruth's braids. "I don't know that there is one yet. But I'm sure Belinda will figure it all out when the time is right. And the man who gets her will be lucky indeed."

"What about you, Mama?" Ruth looked up with bright eyes.

"What about me?"

"What about your lucky man?"

"My what?" Elizabeth looked around nervously again, worried that someone might overhear them.

"When will you get married again, Mama?"

"I...uh...I don't know."

"Belinda says that her father wants to marry you."

"*Ruth.*" Elizabeth put her forefinger to her lips. "Some things are best spoken of in private."

Ruth looked confused. "*Private?*"

"Not on this raft, Ruth. Not with everyone else around to hear. In *private.*"

Ruth nodded with a knowing look. "All right, Mama. I'll wait and talk to you about getting married later—in private."

Elizabeth just shook her head. "I'm going to go check on Grandma now."

Of course, on the other side of the wagon, Clara had heard every word. And like Ruth, she wanted to talk about it. However, she had the sensibility to keep her voice low.

"It's become rather obvious that Will is courting you," she whispered. "The question on everyone's mind is, how do you feel about it, Lizzie?"

Elizabeth let out a loud sigh.

"I don't wish to intrude," Clara continued. "But he is a good man, Elizabeth. And if you want him to court you, there's no reason you shouldn't let it be known." She laughed. "You certainly aren't lacking for chaperones. No one here would be concerned about impropriety."

"Excuse me, Mother." Elizabeth stood back up. "I think I will go speak to Lavinia now."

But Lavinia seemed to have the same thing on her mind as everyone else. And eventually, Elizabeth found a quiet corner between the wagons where she could sit by herself without being forced to converse with anyone. But then Mrs. Taylor joined her. "Afternoon, Elizabeth," she said as she pulled a chair next to her. "I just enjoyed a nice little nap."

"Good for you." Elizabeth smiled. "I think many of us have been catching up on sleep."

"Isn't this beautiful country?" Mrs. Taylor looked toward the tall trees along the river. "I hear we have only one more day on this raft."

"Yes, can you believe it?"

"I spoke to your father in regard to my fare for the ship's passage."

Elizabeth was caught off guard now. She hadn't even considered this. As far as she knew, Mrs. Taylor had no money.

"I have offered my services as a schoolteacher for the children when we settle," she told Elizabeth. "In repayment for my fare."

"Oh…?" Elizabeth was still unsure. "What did my father say?"

"He thought it was a good idea."

Elizabeth smiled. "Well, so do I." Elizabeth didn't have the heart to tell Mrs. Taylor that Malinda had written of a school and church already there. She assumed that meant a teacher too. However, if life was in as much upheaval as Malinda described, perhaps they would need a teacher. Anyway, it didn't really matter. It wasn't as if she and her family could leave this poor woman stranded and on her own in Fort Vancouver. And certainly not after she'd assured Mrs. Taylor that she was family.

"I used to teach," Mrs. Taylor told her. "And I played the organ in church too."

"I doubt that there will be an organ where we are going, but you never know."

"No…you never know."

❧

Elizabeth felt exceedingly thankful when they stepped off of the raft at Fort Vancouver. But her gratitude was suppressed by her anxious concerns regarding her son. Seeing livestock held in a nearby corral gave her hope. Was it possible they had already arrived? But on closer inspection, she realized those were not their animals. Still, they could have them penned up somewhere else. She looked out toward the fort, realizing this was a big place.

"Do you think Matthew and JT are here yet?" she asked her father. They were all waiting on the dock. Soldiers were bringing a team of oxen in order to help them remove their wagons from the raft.

"I don't know." Asa glanced around the busy dock. "But if they're here, we'll soon find out."

Adam and Matilda Bentley were coming over now, carrying large bundles on their backs and in their arms. "We just want to thank you," Adam told Asa and Elizabeth. "You've been a fine unit leader, and it was a privilege to ride the river with you folks."

"Do you have people here?" Elizabeth asked Matilda. "Someone to stay with until you get settled?"

"Yes," Matilda assured her. "Adam's uncle has been expecting us."

They exchanged hugs, and the young couple continued on their way.

"Imagine carrying everything you owned like that," Elizabeth said to her father as she watched the couple walking toward the fort.

"At least they made it to their destination," he told her. "Not all the emigrants on our wagon train were so lucky."

"Yes, I suppose you're right."

Now he nodded over to where Lavinia and Mrs. Taylor and some of the girls were peering up at a large boat. Happily chattering away, they were unaware that they were in the way of the stevedores unloading supplies. "Elizabeth," Asa said quietly. "Why don't you send all those females over to the fort?"

"You want to get them out of harm's way?"

"Yes, and before someone gets knocked into the river." He winced to see Mrs. Taylor nearly toppling off the dock, but Lavinia grabbed her arm. "It'd be a shame to make it all the way without anyone falling overboard, only to lose someone here. Tell them that anyone who's not directly responsible for a wagon better just clear on out of here."

Elizabeth went over to the women, explaining Asa's plan. "We'll meet up with you at the fort," she assured them. "After we get the wagons relocated." She locked eyes with Ruth now. "And the fort's a big busy place, so I expect you to stay with Grandma until I get there."

"Do you want us to go to the post office for you, Mama?"

"Yes." Elizabeth nodded. "I would appreciate that."

Sharing two teams of oxen, it took longer than expected to get the six wagons parked in a holding area, where they would be ready to be loaded onto the ship. Then they worked together to put the canvas coverings back over their wagons to protect them against elements in case the weather changed. "Be sure to take what you and your family need for the night," Asa instructed them. "And we'll have access to the wagons until they're loaded onto the ship. After that, they'll be in a hold. So you'll want to get out anything you'll need for the sea journey as well."

It was just getting dusky as Elizabeth, Jess, and Ruby, followed by Asa, Hugh, and Will, walked toward the fort.

"Isn't it beautiful here?" Ruby commented.

"I think this is the prettiest fort I've ever seen," Jess said.

"It's no wonder so many folks want to settle here," Elizabeth added.

"Would you want to settle here?" Jess asked quietly. "I mean, if you found out your sister-in-law had returned to Kentucky?"

Elizabeth took in a deep breath. Although everyone was well aware of the situation with Malinda, no one had spoken of it much. And for that, Elizabeth was grateful. "I honestly don't know," Elizabeth confessed.

"Maybe there will be a letter here," Ruby told her.

"Yes." Elizabeth nodded. "That's what I'm hoping for."

"Do you think Matthew and the others are here at the fort?" Jess asked hopefully.

"I don't know." Elizabeth shifted her bag to her other hand and then reached over and squeezed Jess' hand. "But I'm sure it won't be long until we see them again."

Jess just nodded.

"Can you believe it?" Ruby said loudly.

"What?" Jess and Elizabeth both asked.

"We made it! We got all the way to Fort Vancouver. At long last—we're here!"

This amazing realization seemed to hit all six of them at once, and out there in the dusky light of the moon rising in the east, not far from the tall log walls of the fort, they all let out some happy whoops of delight—loud enough that they might have worried the soldiers if they thought there were hostile Indians nearby.

"Well done," Will told Asa. "You've been a fine leader, and I thank you for it."

"That's right," Hugh told him. "We couldn't have done it without you."

"You Bostonians turned out to be a stronger, savvier lot than I ever imagined," Asa admitted. "I'm proud to have had you in my unit."

"And how about Ruby?" Elizabeth said. "When we started out, we didn't know quite what to make of her and her lady friends. But now…" She clasped Ruby's hand. "We are family."

Asa nodded. "And you were fine at driving your wagon, Ruby. Just fine."

They continued as they walked up to the fort, congratulating and slapping backs and shaking hands. Everyone was in high spirits.

"If Matthew and the others were here, we could have music to commemorate this happy occasion," Ruby said.

"We'll celebrate," Elizabeth assured them. "In due time, we'll celebrate."

Despite her confident words, Elizabeth said a silent prayer for JT, Matthew, Brady, and the rest of their group. She prayed for God's protection…for Godspeed…and for God to safely get them here.

The fort was busy and noisy inside with soldiers and settlers and even a few Indians, which Elizabeth found reassuring. She wanted to continue picturing Indians as peaceful and friendly, the way Eli had attempted to paint them. Or at least most of them. But she knew that they were no different from the white man—some were good, and some were not.

"There's Clara and Ruth," Jess told Elizabeth.

Ruth came running up with a piece of paper in her hand. "A letter, Mama! It's from Aunt Malinda!"

"Oh!" Elizabeth took the letter and then moved them over to a less busy spot. Setting down her bag, she eagerly opened the envelope, quickly scanning the letter.

"Read it out loud, Mama."

"Yes." Elizabeth nodded. "I will."

> *Dear Elizabeth,*
>
> *I received your second letter today, informing me that you and your family are already traveling on the Oregon Trail. This confirms to me that you did not receive my letter warning against this very thing. I addressed that letter to your farm in Kentucky, and I'm afraid it arrived too late. However, upon receiving your letter this morning, I must confess that I became quite giddy. It is entirely selfish on my part, but I am so very happy to know that you are coming. I can think of nothing that would please me more. Yet at the same time, you need to be forewarned that there are problems in my part of the world. Yes, it is just as beautiful as I've ever described to you, but alas, this land comes with its own troubles. I must also inform you that my John has passed away, leaving me, like you, a widow. I am keeping my message to you brief in the hopes of sending it back with the mail carrier on morrow. I will address it to the last stop that I expect you will be making in Fort Vancouver. If you get this letter, please, know that you and*

your family are most welcome to stay with me. I wish you all a safe ocean voyage, and I will look forward to seeing your sweet face in late September.

> *Sincerely and affectionately yours,*
> *Malinda Martin*

Chapter Twenty-Five

The next few days at the fort passed very slowly for Elizabeth. There were plenty of distractions and chores to be done as they shopped for needed supplies, preparing for the last leg of their journey. But always, she wondered about JT and the others. No one spoke of it much, but she suspected that they were all preoccupied with similar thoughts. Why were they not here yet?

"I wonder if I was mistaken to let Jeremiah go with them," Will confided to her on their fourth day of waiting for the livestock drivers to arrive.

"Why is that?" she asked.

"Jeremiah is the least experienced rider. Julius has taken riding lessons since he was a tot. But Jeremiah took it up only a couple of years ago."

"He seemed an accomplished rider to me."

"Thank you. But my imagination has been playing havoc with me. And if anything has happened to him...I will never forgive myself."

"I'm sure he and the others are just fine." Elizabeth waved to where the others were coming over to join them now. The plan was for everyone to walk out to where the wagons were stored. It would be their last chance to load the supplies they'd purchased and to get anything they needed for the voyage—which was now only three days away.

"What will we do if JT and Uncle Matthew and Brady don't make it here on time?" Ruth asked Elizabeth as they were walking toward the docks and their wagons.

"Some of us will go on the ship with our wagons." Elizabeth explained Asa's plan. "And some of us will remain behind to wait for them. The ship will return in two weeks and take the same route again."

"Oh...I hope that's not what happens." Ruth's voice was filled with disappointment. "I miss my brother and my uncle and Brady and Flax."

"I know." Elizabeth sighed. "I miss them too."

They all worked together, packing the wagons and taking what they needed while aboard the ship. Fortunately, their voyage would stop at a couple of ports along the way and last only a few days. And then, at Asa's suggestion, they removed the canvases and the wooden bows. Tucking everything flat inside their wagons, they wrapped the canvases snugly over their goods and tied them down with ropes. It took a couple of hours, but everyone helped until all six wagons were secured. Among some of the things Elizabeth had pulled out of her wagon were JT's good go-to-meeting clothes. She'd done the same for her and Ruth, thinking that once they were on the ship, they might need them. However, she knew that there was also the chance she'd have to leave JT's behind with her father. Asa had made it clear that if anyone in their family stayed behind, it would be him. Of course, she hoped and prayed that would not happen.

They were just traipsing back to the fort when Ruth let out a scream. And imagining rattlesnakes or Indian attacks or something terribly gone wrong, Elizabeth turned and dashed back to where Ruth had been walking with Amelia and Belinda. But Ruth seemed fine and in fact had a huge grin on her face as she pointed up the river. "That's them!" she cried. "Mama, that's *them*!"

"What?" Elizabeth squinted, shading her eyes from the sun to see a group of animals moving toward them from a distance. Perhaps some of the soldiers bringing cattle to the fort. "Well, it certainly does look like someone driving a herd," she admitted. "But how do you know it's—"

"*Look, Mama!*" Ruth grabbed her by the arm. "That's Beau and Bella—see those tall black horses? And there's—"

"You're right, Ruth Anne!" Elizabeth took Ruth's hand, and they both began rushing toward them. "That's our men and our animals!"

The rest of them started running too—even Lavinia and Mrs. Taylor. And although Elizabeth knew they must look a sight for whoever was on watch back at the fort—a bunch of emigrants dashing out to meet some cowboys—for the life of her she just could not stop herself. And soon they were all together again, everyone laughing and hugging and talking all at once.

"JT," Elizabeth said to her dust-encrusted son. "You look like you grew several inches since I last saw you!"

He laughed. "It's just these boots, Ma. They got higher heels than my old ones."

She firmly shook her head. "No, son, I'm sure you grew. And you look just like a man now."

"All right, everyone," Asa called out. "Let's get these animals to the corral over by the docks. They need to be watered and fed. And then we'll get these hardworking cattle drivers to a bathhouse. I reckon we might be able to get them cleaned up just in time for supper."

"We'll go on ahead," Lavinia suggested, "and make sure the bathhouse has plenty of hot water for all of you."

Instead of going with the other women back to the fort, Elizabeth sent Ruth with her mother and then went along with the men to tend to the livestock. She wanted to make sure her animals were well cared for and in good shape for the short ocean voyage awaiting them. And perhaps more importantly, she wanted to have a word with Brady.

She worked, feeding and watering and checking hooves and hides and mouths and ears of her animals, until finally it was just Brady and Matthew and her.

"Brady and I plan to camp here with the livestock," Matthew told her. "But we'll walk you back to the fort and get cleaned up some and eat."

So while they walked together, Elizabeth explained the law that had been recently passed. "I know Will explained part of it to you," she said.

"He told me to act like a slave," Brady said. "So I done that."

"I'm not sure it mattered much," Matthew told her. "The only folks we ran across didn't seem to care one way or the other."

"I hope that's how it will be here, but the new laws are complicated. Although they voted to oppose slavery, they also voted to keep Negroes out of Oregon."

"Less'n they act like they's already a slave," Brady filled in.

"Yes, if a settler has slaves, they're allowed to stay for three years."

"For three years?" Matthew sounded shocked.

"That's what Will told me. But he also said that law might be unenforceable." She looked at Brady, seeing he was confused. "Or the law might get changed," she told him. "Right now lots of laws about slavery and abolition are changing. So Will thinks you'll be all right if you stay with us, Brady. The problem is that you won't be able to own your own land." She felt a lump in her throat. "You don't know how sorry it makes me to tell you that. More than anything I wanted to see you settled with your own farm."

Brady looked down at the ground, saying nothing.

"I am so sorry." Elizabeth exchanged glances with Matthew and could see that he looked angry.

"That is so unfair!" He swung a fist in the air. "It makes no sense."

"I agree," she told him. "I couldn't believe it when Will explained it to me. How can voters be abolitionists and then oppose Negroes as well? Where do they think folks like Brady are going to go?"

"California?" Matthew said sadly. "Unless their laws are just as ridiculous."

Elizabeth looked back at Brady now. She could tell he was hurting. "So I don't know what to tell you, Brady. You are a free man. You know that. You can make up your mind to do whatever you think is best. Father and I both owe you for all the work you did and—"

"And I owe you too," Matthew said.

"We can pay you and you can choose where you want to go." Elizabeth felt tears coming.

"Is that what you think I should do?" Brady's brow was furrowed deep. "Just go on my way? By myself?"

"I don't know what's best for you, Brady," she confessed. "I wish you could stay with us. But I don't want to tell you what to do. It's your decision."

"As much as I'd hate to see you go, I'd understand," Matthew told him. "There are opportunities out there. Mining and cowboying, which you're good at. And I hear the railroad's going to be coming this way."

"I just don't know what to say." Brady let out a weary sigh. "I s'pect I'm too old for some of that. But then I rode with you youngins, and I think I done all right."

"You were better than all right," Matthew assured him. "We needed you."

"Anyway, you don't have to say anything right now," she told Brady. "Just get yourself cleaned up and get some food, and then you can sleep on it. The ship doesn't leave for a couple more days."

᠅

Elizabeth knew she was trying to avoid Will Bramford. And knowing this made her feel both guilty and confused. She felt guilty because she genuinely liked Will. She enjoyed his company and felt they had established a good friendship…but one didn't usually run the opposite direction when a friend was approaching. The confusion came every time she remembered what he'd said about wanting to court her. Any widow in her right mind should welcome such attention. And yet Elizabeth did not.

"You seem troubled," Clara said to her on the morning they were preparing to board the clipper. Everyone had stood out on the docks the night before, marveling at the enormous boat and watching in fascination as the crew began taking their wagons aboard. The men were down there right now, helping to load the livestock. And the ship was set to sail at noon.

"I'm not troubled." Elizabeth smiled as she packed Ruth's sweater on the top of her bag, keeping it handy in case the sea air turned chilly. "You must be imagining things."

"So it must be my imagination that whenever Will Bramford comes your way, you distract yourself by speaking to someone else, or sometimes you simply turn and walk away?" Clara sat down on a cot, carefully studying her daughter.

"Mother." Elizabeth shook her head. "I think your imagination is running away with you."

"Elizabeth, I might be old, but I'm not blind."

Elizabeth looked around the room that the women had been sharing the past few nights. The others had already gone down to the docks to watch the goings-on, so it was only Clara and Elizabeth now.

"Sit down." Clara patted the cot next to her. "If you can't talk openly to your own mother, who, pray tell, can you talk to?"

Elizabeth reluctantly sat, folding her hands in her lap and suddenly feeling as if she were Ruth's age again—about to get a scolding from her mother.

"When I've heard you and Will in conversation, you always sound quite friendly, and it's obvious to me that you both like and respect each other."

"That's true."

"And I suspect that Will's interest in you is sincere."

Elizabeth simply nodded.

"You do like him, don't you?"

"Yes. I already said that, Mother." Elizabeth heard the impatience in her answer.

"Has he done something offensive? Has he made improper advances?"

Elizabeth looked up at her mother, and seeing her creased brow and parental concern, she knew it was time to speak openly. "No, he has done nothing wrong. Well, not exactly. He has expressed his interest in courting me—after we get settled."

Clara smiled. "I hoped that was where this was all leading. I'm so happy for you."

"Why?" Elizabeth smoothed the folds in her skirt, pressing them with her fingers.

"Because I think you and Will are a wonderful match, darling. He is intelligent and interesting and—"

"But I have no feelings for him, Mother. Not like that."

"Oh…" Clara nodded with a somber expression.

"I know what you're thinking," Elizabeth said quickly. "You want to tell me that what I had with James was something that only comes once in a lifetime. And that for some people, like Aunt Rebekkah, it never came at all." Elizabeth didn't need to remind her mother that she'd heard this all before. They'd had that conversation more times than Elizabeth cared to recall back in Kentucky, back when her mother was always trying to find Elizabeth a new husband.

"Elizabeth." Clara's voice grew firm. "In the frontier, where you will be trying to build a new life, create a new home, and start your farm, a man like Will Bramford could be a very handy thing."

Elizabeth couldn't help but laugh.

"I am not trying to be humorous."

"I'm sorry, Mother."

"Listen to me, Elizabeth, your father is getting older. Your brother has his own wife. And now even Malinda is without a husband. Do you honestly think you would be wise to reject Will Bramford's offer of marriage if he were to ask you?"

Elizabeth bit her lip and then slowly shook her head. "No, that would probably not be considered wise…by anyone."

"You know I would not tell you what to do, especially in matters of the heart. But I will say this—you could do much worse than Will Bramford, dear daughter." Clara peered into her eyes. "Can you not be thankful that you had true love with James? Isn't that enough?"

"What if it were possible to feel that again, Mother?"

Clara looked confused.

"Never mind."

"I do think it's possible to feel that way again," Clara told her. "The friendship you feel for Will could grow into love. I believe it."

Elizabeth looked away now.

"That was not what you meant, was it?"

"I am going to tell you something, Mother. But only if you promise to never speak of this to me again. Not unless I initiate the conversation."

Clara simply nodded.

"I have those feelings for Eli."

Clara looked shocked. "Eli Kincaid?"

"Do I know any other Eli?"

Clara seemed truly speechless now.

"And I realize it's futile. Eli is not the kind of man who wants to settle down. He loves his freedom and independence. He is married to the trail."

Clara sighed. "I did like him, Elizabeth. He seemed a truly fine man. But I fear you're right. He does not seem like a marrying man. In fact, I sometimes felt worried when I saw you with him. I was afraid he might break your heart."

Elizabeth felt tears burning in her eyes. "I suppose I didn't realize that was even possible."

Now Clara put her arms around her, holding her tightly. "I don't know what to tell you, Lizzie. But perhaps...well, if you could feel that way about Eli...perhaps you can feel that way about Will too...if you would only just give it a chance."

"I will try to keep my heart open," Elizabeth finally said. "I know you're right—it will be difficult settling in the frontier without a man by my side, and I can't expect Matthew and Father to continue helping as they did back home. We'll all have our hands full now. And I realize that it's perfectly foolish to pass up a fine man like Will Bramford in the hopes of an unattainable dream."

Without further ado they gathered their bags and went outside to where the autumnal sun was shining warmly. Then without speaking, they quietly strolled toward the docks—as if all was well and Elizabeth hadn't just cried like a baby in her mother's arms. Despite her assurances to her mother, Elizabeth still felt torn inside. Was it truly better to settle for a marriage that would provide her with security and comfort, or to hold out for the improbable...the impractical...and most likely the impossible? Of course, she knew the answer to this. A widow with two children trying to settle out here in the wilderness...how much more obvious could it be?

Chapter Twenty-Six

It wasn't until the day they were to depart that Brady spoke to Elizabeth regarding his decision. She was helping to tend to the livestock, wanting to be sure her horses got some exercise before being boarded in the hold of the ship.

"I been givin' it plenty of thought," Brady began slowly. "And I think I come to a decision. But first I want you to know how obliged I am that I got to come with you and your folks, ma'am. I never knew that I would get such pleasure out of crossing over the land like I did. But it was the best thing I ever done. I know that for sure."

"I'm so very glad, Brady." However, she was also very worried. Unless she was mistaken, he was about to tell her that they were soon to part ways. She wasn't sure she could bear it. Especially after the talk with her mother, reminding her that Matthew and Asa would be busy settling their own land. What would she do without Brady?

"I got ta see plenty o' things I mighta not seen," he continued.

"That's for sure. But you also had some bad experiences on the trail. I'm sorry for that."

"Oh, yeah, I saw some bad—for sure. But I also saw some good. And I saw that some of the bad wasn't so bad. And some of the good that wasn't so good." He chuckled. "I reckon that's just how it is."

She nodded. "You're probably right."

"So if you still want me to go with you and your family, ma'am, I'd be much obliged."

She blinked. "You would?"

"I sure would. If'n you want me."

"Oh, Brady, I'm so glad! I was so worried you were going to leave us. I'm so thankful!" She controlled herself from hugging him because she knew it would make him uncomfortable. But she was certain her ear-to-ear grin said it all.

"I thought and I thought about it," he told her. "And I kept thinking that you folks is like my family. I ain't never gonna get another family like you been to me. I'm too old for that. So even if I have to play like I'm your slave, I'd druther do that than be free as the wind and lonely."

"Well, you will always have a home with us, Brady. And I don't see any reason why you can't build your own house and have your own spot of land on my farm. No one needs to know all the whys and wherefores. Besides, Will said he'd be your legal counsel, should you ever need it."

He nodded. "He told me that."

<hr/>

The traveling time they had saved by floating the raft on the river seemed small in comparison to the time they were saving on this ship. They'd stopped at Fort Astoria for a couple of hours on their second day out, but they were still making excellent time. Elizabeth was showing Ruth and JT the map, trying to estimate where they were.

"We already went from there to there?" Ruth exclaimed as she traced her finger from Fort Vancouver to Astoria. "In just one day?"

"This is a fast ship," Elizabeth told her.

"We should have taken this ship all the way from Kentucky."

JT let out a loud hoot. "No ship goes from Kentucky to Oregon."

"That's partially true," Will said from where he was standing not far away, peering out toward the horizon as they were. "But if you'd come up to Boston harbor, you could have boarded a ship to bring you out here. We thought about doing that—and it's how some of our goods are coming. But going round the horn takes a mighty long time. Besides, you wouldn't get to see all the amazing country we saw."

"And besides that, Aunt Lavinia gets so terribly seasick," Belinda added. "She'd probably have died going by ship the whole way."

"How is she doing now?" Elizabeth asked with concern.

"Not too well." Belinda shook her head. "It's Amelia's turn to sit with her."

"Poor Lavinia. I truly think she would improve if she would come out here in the open air. The breeze is a bit brisk, but I feel so much better up here than I do when I go down below."

"I told her you said that, but she still won't hear of it. No one can pry her out of that bed."

"Fortunately, we only have one more day," Elizabeth reminded her. She looked down at the deep blue waves as the clipper sliced through the ocean. She wondered if she had ever traveled this fast. Possibly when she was a reckless youth, riding on the back of her father's fastest horse. But those were the kinds of risks she didn't take anymore as a mother and a widow. She glanced over at Will, trying to imagine what it might be like to be married to such a man. Twelve years her senior, with graying hair, he wasn't unattractive, although she had never been fond of such side-whiskers. Perhaps she would be able to convince him to take a razor to them. But the mere thought of trying to remake a man even before they wed...well, it was a bit disconcerting to say the least.

Because her mind and heart were so torn on this matter, she continued to do her best to avoid being alone with Will. Fortunately, that was not difficult on this boat. There always seemed to be someone about, ensuring that they never had a private conversation.

Because the only two state rooms had gone to Hugh and Lavinia and Asa and Clara, Elizabeth was sharing a berth with Ruth, Jess, and Mrs. Taylor. JT was staying with Julius, Jeremiah, and Augustus. And

Matthew and Brady insisted on staying down below with the livestock. How they could stand it was a mystery to Elizabeth, especially since she was feeling woozy tonight. However, everyone else in her berth seemed to be sleeping soundly. Afraid she was going to become ill and wake everyone up, she decided to go on deck and see if some fresh air would settle her stomach.

Pulling a coat over her nightgown and a shawl over her head, she tiptoed out and up the gangway and emerged into the chilly night air. It took a few minutes and some long deep breaths before the fresh sea wind cleansed all thoughts of seasickness from her. Leaning over the railing, she peered at the three-quarter moon that was just coming over the horizon, illuminating the land and the ocean with a cool beam of pale blue light.

"Beautiful, isn't it?"

Elizabeth jumped, grabbing onto the rail to keep herself from tumbling.

"Careful there." Will put a hand on her shoulder to steady her. "I didn't mean to scare you like that. I thought you'd seen me."

"No," she gasped. "I didn't see anyone." Then she explained trying to avoid being sick down below.

He nodded. "I didn't want to admit it, especially to my daughters since they make fun of Lavinia so, but I've discovered I get a little queasy too."

She chuckled. "I'm sure your girls wouldn't tease you for that."

He laughed. "And I thought you knew them better than that."

"They are fine girls."

"Yes. But spirited. And I'm afraid that I've given them free rein. They express themselves quite liberally. I suppose it's fortunate we're going to live in the Wild West. They may appear a bit more civilized and cultured here than back in Boston."

"Yes, I have a feeling that the Western frontier needs strong-willed women."

"You seem to be well suited for it, Elizabeth."

She could hear the tenderness in his tone, and it made her uneasy.

"I know I promised not to attempt to court you until we reached

Elk Creek," he said quietly, "but seeing you out here in the moonlight...
well, it's not easy to hold my tongue."

She continued looking toward the land, to where the moon was
steadily rising, trying to think of something gracious yet noncommit-
tal to say. Nothing came to her.

"It won't be long now," he said more lightly. "The captain said we'll
make Coos Bay by midmorning. And we'll be unloaded in time to
have several hours of traveling time before we make camp for the night."

She nodded. "And it will be only two days' journey after that. If all
goes well, that is. But the weather does seem to be in our favor. And we
did have a gorgeous sunset tonight. You know what they say about red
sky at night and—"

"*Elizabeth.*"

She could hear the emotion in his voice...the wistful longing. And
yet she felt no such longing in her own heart, no romantic stirrings
whatsoever. All she felt was an extreme uneasiness, which felt more disturbing than seasickness.

How could she lead this good man down a road that she knew she
would never travel? It was not only unfair, it was unkind. And Will had
been a good friend to her. He deserved better. Hard as it was, and even
if she was burning a bridge, she had to make her feelings known.

"Will," she said in a firm tone. "May I be very honest with you?"

"Please, do."

She turned to look directly at him. "You are a fine man, and I have
enjoyed your companionship and our conversations immensely."

"As I have yours, Elizabeth." He smiled. "I never dreamed I'd meet
someone like you on the Oregon Trail."

"And I truly value your friendship. And I hope that we can continue
to be friends."

His smile faded. "But...?"

"But I just don't have those kinds of feelings for you. The kinds of
feelings that a woman should have for a man, the kinds of feelings that
you deserve in a wife, Will."

He frowned. "You don't think your feelings could change? Or that
my feelings could make up for it?"

She knew her mother would be greatly dismayed to see what her daughter was so easily tossing aside. Elizabeth herself might one day regret this decision. But right here and right now, it was the only choice she could honestly make. "I don't think my feelings will change. And I've tried to make them change. Believe me, I've tried. I've tried to convince myself that we would be a good match. I wanted to believe it was possible. But I would be a hypocrite and a liar to pretend that I loved you like that."

Will didn't respond but just looked out across the moon's reflection slicing through the ocean.

"And I'm so sorry to tell you this because I know it's a disappointment. And the honest truth is that I'm feeling very scared right now."

"Scared?"

"That I could be making an enormous mistake. I realize my situation. I'm a widow settling in the frontier with two children." She paused to look at the moon. "They say looking at the moon can make you mad. What if I've lost my senses because of the moonlight?"

"You're not making sense to me," he said dully.

"The moon is making me feel strong," she confessed. "Like I can take on this great challenge. But at the same time, underneath it all, I'm very frightened. I'm worried I could wake up tomorrow or the next day or the next...and I could completely regret this conversation."

He slowly shook his head, emitting a sad sigh.

"I hope you don't feel I've misled you, Will. I felt confused because I truly enjoyed your friendship...and I suppose I hoped my feelings would blossom into something more."

"I don't feel misled, Elizabeth. Just disappointed. Now if you'll excuse me, I think I shall go down below."

"Yes...of course...good night." As she watched him going, she suspected he would prefer to be seasick down below than to remain with her on deck. "Dear God," she prayed, "I hope I haven't made a most regrettable mistake."

Chapter Twenty-Seven

Elizabeth and her family gathered together near the bow, watching as the ship sailed into Coos Bay. A sea breeze blew steadily, filling the sails and driving the vessel farther inland.

"Isn't it beautiful," Clara said. "Have you ever seen so many trees?"

"Oregon is timber country," Asa declared. "We will have no shortage of wood for building houses and barns and fences."

"Malinda said the weather this time of year is some of the very best," Elizabeth told them. "The rains don't usually start for a few weeks."

"Let's hope she's right," Asa told her. "From what I've heard about the trail we need to take from here, it'll be a bear if it rains."

It seemed no time at all until the big ship lowered its sails and finally came to a graceful stop next to the docks. "This is it," Elizabeth told her children. "We're nearly there."

Everyone was excited as they disembarked from the ship, chattering among themselves and pointing out colorful waterfowl and a nearby sawmill and other interesting sights. While wandering about the docks and waiting for the unloading, they also saw a number of Indians who looked entirely peaceable. Ruth, with tablet and pencils handy, found a pile of crates to sit on while she attempted to make a sketch of their ship, and Mrs. Taylor seemed perfectly content to sit and watch her. All were happy to get their feet on solid ground again—or as solid as the gently rocking docks could be. Especially Lavinia.

"Is that Empire City?" JT asked Elizabeth.

"I think it must be," she told him. "Remember Aunt Malinda wrote that it's the county seat. Just a few years ago, I believe."

"And it's called Coos County," JT added. "I wonder what Coos means."

"It's the name of the Indians who live here." She glanced over to where several Indians were huddled together in conversation.

"I think Asa said that Coos means lake and pines," Clara told them. "Or something like that."

"It seems the Prescotts have a problem," Asa told Clara and Elizabeth when he joined them. "The ship with their cargo went on down to San Francisco first, planning to stop on the way back here, but they haven't arrived yet."

"What does that mean?" Clara asked. "Has the ship sunk?"

"Oh, no, I don't think so." Asa glanced over to where Lavinia, Hugh, and Will were conversing. "But they want to stay here and wait for that ship so they can bring everything out there with them. Lavinia hopes to open up a store before winter."

"Yes, I know." Elizabeth nodded. "But does that mean we have to wait here with them?"

"They told us to go on ahead. They have their map and know where to meet up with us. So unless you have objections, I think we should head on out as soon as our wagons and animals are unloaded from the boat."

Before they left, they took their time saying goodbyes. Even though they knew it would be for only a few days or a week at most, it was difficult telling their dear friends farewell—except for one of them. Elizabeth had no problem telling Will a stiff goodbye. They shook hands as if they barely knew each other and then quickly moved on.

Unfortunately, that didn't miss her mother's watchful eye. But thankfully, she didn't ask questions.

Truly, there was no time for questions because once the teams were unloaded, everyone was busy hitching the wagons and preparing to go. And suddenly, with the sun high in the sky, Elizabeth and her family were on the wagon trail, heading southwest. At first, the trail was fairly well traveled and smooth. But after a couple of hours and numerous turnoffs to other various destinations, the trail become more uneven. Finally, they reached a nice meadow, and with the sun dipping low into the sky, they decided to make camp.

"What a pretty place," Elizabeth said as they prepared to fix supper. "I wouldn't mind settling right here."

"But you wouldn't be neighbors with Malinda," Clara pointed out.

"That's true." Elizabeth sighed. "I cannot wait to see my dear friend's face."

"I don't remember what she looks like," Ruth said as she laid some firewood down.

"That's because you were a baby when they left," Elizabeth reminded her. "But the last time I saw her, she was a little shorter than me. Her auburn hair was braided and pinned around her head. And her eyes, which were just the color of the clouds before a thunderstorm, were filled with tears."

"Because she was sad to leave?" Ruth asked.

Elizabeth nodded. "We both cried."

"She was your best friend?"

"She was." Elizabeth stirred the cornbread batter.

"And her children are Todd—he's the oldest—and Emily and Bart and Susannah." Ruth recited the list happily. "And Susannah is the youngest, like me, and she's only a year older than me. Right, Mama?"

"That's right." Elizabeth poured the batter into the cast-iron pan.

"Do you think Susannah will be my best friend, Mama?"

"I know you'll be friends, Ruth."

"Will Bart be JT's best friend?"

"Well, they're about the same age." Elizabeth smiled. "I guess we'll just have to wait and see. Besides, don't forget about Tumbleweed Tillie.

She was your best friend on the wagon train. And it won't be long until they get here too."

"I'll have all kinds of friends, won't I?"

"And I'll have enough children to get a school started," Mrs. Taylor declared. Now she and Ruth, using their fingers, attempted to count how many children would be among the settlers.

Elizabeth felt her mother watching her as they worked together preparing food and organizing the kitchen things that hadn't been used much for the last week or so. She knew that Clara had questions about Will. But Elizabeth wasn't sure she wanted to answer them. Not yet anyway. Instead, she busied herself with rearranging her wagon and checking on her animals. And then, claiming she was tired from not sleeping well on the boat, she excused herself to bed. But instead of going to sleep, her mind began to race. They were so near their destination, she had every reason to be excited. But at the same time she felt increasingly uneasy. What if she'd made a huge mistake by saying those things to Will last night? Why couldn't she have simply remained quiet?

But she realized she had done what she had to do. It was not in her to be false. Not to anyone. And especially not to someone she would be bound to spend the rest of her earthly days with. No, if she was going to have to scrape out a new life for herself and her children, working harder than she'd ever done before, she wanted to do it on her own terms. And that would not include a marriage of convenience.

The following day, everyone was up at the crack of dawn, and after a quick breakfast, the three wagons were ready to roll. "We're a very short wagon train," Ruth said as the women walked together in the cool of the morning.

"At least we don't have to wait so much for everyone," Jess replied. "That was one of the things I disliked most about the wagon train. Waiting, waiting, waiting…and then it was hurry up and 'wagons ho' and everyone scrambling."

"I can hardly believe that tomorrow will be the last day of this long, long journey," Clara said gratefully. "But I'm so relieved. I suppose if I had to, I could walk the rest of the way."

"The wagon journey might be over, but it will be the beginning of another kind of journey," Elizabeth pointed out. "Our work will just be starting."

"I suppose that's true." Clara sighed. "But Asa promised me that he'd set up our tent and that he'd put our bed and my rocker inside it...and that I wouldn't be expected to leave it for at least a week."

"Oh, Grandma." Ruth laughed. "You wouldn't really stay in your tent for a whole week without coming out, would you?"

"I might."

"Well, I'm sure Malinda will have some sort of accommodations for us too. At least that's what she used to say back when James and I were planning to come."

"I will just be thankful not to keep moving," Mrs. Taylor said. "Moving and moving and moving. I understand Clara's sentiments completely. I would like to just sit down in one place and stay put for about a week too."

"I'll tell Asa to put two chairs in the tent," Clara told her. "One for you and one for me."

Elizabeth did not share their sentiments. Seeing this beautiful land with lush green meadows alongside the curving river and tall trees of all kinds growing abundantly, all she could think was, how soon would they get there so she could ride her horse around and pick the perfect spot to build her house? At the same time, she felt a little uneasy as she wondered how this lovely fertile land could really be claimed for little more than a dollar an acre. Land like this in Kentucky would not only be difficult to find, it would be costly. In some ways it all seemed too good to be true right now.

But then she remembered when land claims had been completely free in Oregon—when she and James originally nurtured this dream together. That had seemed too good to be true too. But they had still believed it...believed in the dream. She wondered if James could see them now. And if so, what was he thinking? Was he pleased and proud of how well they had all handled the trail, of how they'd made it safely all the way out here? Or would he be concerned that Elizabeth had taken on too much? Of course, she would never know these things. But she did remember those winter nights back in Kentucky, those times she'd felt James' presence urging her, pushing her, exhorting her to pursue the old dream.

❧❦❧

On their last day of travel, after stopping for the midday meal, Elizabeth announced that she planned to saddle up Molly and ride the rest of the way. They estimated it was about four miles to Elk Creek, but Elizabeth knew she could get there in a fraction of the time it would take the wagons.

"That way I can warn Malinda that she'll soon have a small wagon train parked in front of her home," she told them.

"Can I ride with you, Ma?" JT asked eagerly.

She looked at Brady. "Do you mind driving the rest of the way?"

He smiled wide, revealing that broken tooth. "Not at all, ma'am."

She pointed to Ruth. "I know Mrs. Taylor wants to rest in the back, but I'll bet you can ride with Grandma and Grandpa if you like."

It wasn't long before both JT and Elizabeth had the horses ready. "I'm going to let Molly stretch her legs a little," Elizabeth told him. "After she warms up, I'll let her run. But you go at whatever pace feels comfortable to you."

"Are you saying you want to race me to Elk Creek?" His eyes twinkled as he swung up into the saddle.

"No, of course, not." She gave him a sly look and then pressed her heels into Molly's withers. "Gid-up!" And she took off in a canter. But after a while, she slowed down, and she and JT walked the horses together. She knew there was no need to run the horses too hard. She simply wanted to beat the wagons there and to have Malinda to herself for a spell. So much to say.

"Do you think our land will look like this?" JT asked as they went around a particularly pretty curve in the river.

"I sure hope so. It all seems like good farmland to me. Good grass for raising cattle and horses." By now they had seen a couple of cabins and were certain they were in Elk Creek, but Elizabeth knew they hadn't reached Malinda's yet because she knew Malinda and John had built a barn several years ago. Finally, they came into another sweet meadow where Elizabeth saw a cabin and a barn, and somehow she knew this was it.

"Look, JT," she said happily. And now they both urged their horses into a gallop. But Elizabeth slowed Molly down, allowing JT be the first one there. She couldn't wait to see Malinda's reaction. He was just hopping off Asa's horse when Malinda and a girl came rushing out of the house.

Elizabeth slid off her horse with a big smile, and running directly to Malinda, she hugged her long and hard. "We're finally here!" she cried. "We made it!"

"Welcome to Elk Creek!" Malinda spread her arms wide, and after a long hug and a few tears, Malinda and Elizabeth held each other at arm's length, just staring at each other in wonder. "I know I've gotten old," Malinda said.

"No, you're even more beautiful," Elizabeth insisted. Ignoring the lines on her friend's face, Elizabeth touched a strand of auburn hair. "Not a bit of gray."

"And look at you." Malinda just shook her head. "You haven't changed a bit."

Elizabeth looked down at her worn and dusty riding outfit and the boots that were now being held together with rawhide strips. "I'm afraid I'm a mess."

"A beautiful mess," Malinda assured her, and they both burst out laughing.

Just then another girl and a boy came out and shyly joined them, and Malinda, after exclaiming over how much JT had grown, introduced everyone. "This is Emily," she started with the older girl. "She'll be fourteen soon. And this is Bart, he's just a little older than JT. And this is Susannah. She's nine."

"And Todd's the oldest," Emily told them, "but he's working out in the field."

"The rest of my family will be here in a couple of hours," Elizabeth explained. "But I was so excited to see you, I couldn't wait."

"Bart, why don't you help tend the horses and then show JT around?"

Malinda said. "And girls, how about if you go put on some water for tea?"

"Can we make the cake now?" Emily asked eagerly.

Malinda chuckled. "Yes, dear, you can make the cake now." She winked at Elizabeth as the two girls dashed back into the cabin. "They've had it all ready for several days now. I told them they couldn't start it until we saw the whites of your eyes."

Elizabeth laughed. "I can hardly believe we're really here." And now she remembered something…something sobering. "Oh, Malinda, I'm so sorry about John. I didn't get your letter until it was too late. I suppose if I had received it back in Kentucky…well, I reckon I wouldn't be standing here right now."

Malinda put her arm around Elizabeth's shoulders as they strolled through the yard. "I'm so glad it missed you. And I couldn't be happier that you're here. Oh my—I have missed you so much! So I take it that you did get my letter then—the one where I warned you not to come?"

Elizabeth nodded. "But we were well on our way."

"I wrote that letter in such a frenzy, Elizabeth." She sighed. "I can't even remember what I said."

"You sounded very distraught. There were Indian uprisings…and you hadn't been without John for very long."

"Let's take a walk around the place so we can talk."

"I'd love that."

Malinda showed her the improvements she and John had made over the past eight years. And truly, it was impressive. But Malinda explained how the pioneers helped each other. "And as you can see, there is no shortage of timber."

"And there's a lumber mill at Empire City."

"Yes, things are changing fast." She looked toward the south. "Do you want to see the parcel of land that John had picked out for you and James?"

"No one's claimed it yet?"

"It's still waiting for you."

As they walked, Malinda explained about how the past few years had been frightening with a number of Indian battles. "But I'm sure I made it out to be worse than it is. And now it's been very quiet these past nine months. I've been assured that since the military stepped in, the worst of our troubles are over."

"That's a relief."

"I hadn't really intended to hide the truth from you," Malinda confessed. "But you wrote to me of how my letters cheered you and the children...after James passed on."

"Yes, we loved your letters. It helped us pass many a winter evening. And we would reread them again and again."

"That's why I shied away from serious topics. And after you lost James, well, I never dreamed you'd do this." Malinda shook her head. "I was so shocked when I got your first letter. I couldn't believe you would take on something so difficult. But then I realized you didn't know how hard the Oregon Trail truly was. And I had painted such pretty and romanticized pictures of the West. I hope you'll forgive me."

"There's nothing to forgive. Every word you said about the West is true." Elizabeth waved her hand. "Look at this land. It's beautiful!"

They were standing on a small hill now, looking out on the river and the meadows that seemed to stretch for miles. "See that rise over there to the west?" Malinda used her finger to draw a line. "Across there and to the edge of the river and then on up to the grove of trees?"

"Yes." Elizabeth nodded. "It's all very lovely."

"It can be yours." She waved her hand. "Well, unless you don't want to claim a whole unit. John had walked it out back when James was alive, back when we thought you were coming...he felt you'd want a full unit. Now that you're not married you may only want a half. Perhaps that's all you'll qualify for. To be honest, I'm not sure how the laws work now. The land was free when we came. But already so much has changed." She sighed. "Even we have changed."

"Not so very much." Elizabeth smiled happily.

"But you and I are both widows now. Isn't it hard to believe?"

Suddenly Elizabeth felt the desperate need to speak to a confidante. And so without really thinking, almost like she used to do when they were girls, her story poured out. She told Malinda all about Will and his attempts at romance and his hopes for marriage. "But just a few days ago, I made my position clear to him."

"Your position?"

"That I cannot marry him."

"Why not?"

"Because I don't love him, Malinda. I just don't have those feel-ings...like I had for James. Like you had for John. I felt sure you would understand."

"I'm not so certain I do." Malinda frowned. "Let me see if I under-stand this correctly. You have a widower lawyer, and you enjoyed his company, and he and his family have followed you out here—and he wanted to marry you?"

"Yes," Elizabeth answered meekly.

Malinda looked stunned. "And you told him no?"

Elizabeth merely nodded.

"Oh, Lizzie, Lizzie, Lizzie." Malinda shook her head in a dismal way. "I hope you won't regret this."

"I suppose you agree with my mother on this...and you think I'm very foolish."

"No. You are not foolish. You are a strong woman with good judg-ment. I have all faith that you know what you're doing, my dear friend. And to think you made it all the way out here. And, my goodness, how many people did you entice to come along with you?"

Elizabeth chuckled. "I did not entice them. We simply spoke fondly of this Promised Land that you had written to us about, and well, it seemed that people were listening." Now she began to tell Malinda about the Bostonians. "Lavinia and Hugh plan to open a mercantile."

"A mercantile?" Malinda clapped her hands. "Oh, Elizabeth, that's wonderful!"

"They were waiting for a shipment of goods that they wanted to bring with them, but we think they should be here within the week."

"You are a miracle worker. And tell me, who else have you brought to our frontier land?"

"Mrs. Taylor." Elizabeth quickly explained how they had adopted the widow. "And she wants to teach school."

"That would be lovely. I had been teaching at our tiny school of only six children, counting my own four. But after John passed...well, I lost interest. The children will have some catching up to do."

"And there will be plenty of children." Now Elizabeth told about the other families traveling the Applegate Trail.

"Oh, my! We may become a township yet."

Elizabeth laughed. "We are going to populate this region, Malinda. I hope you don't mind."

"Mind? I'm thrilled. We need settlers." She waved her hand again. "Look at all this land just waiting for folks to come live here. When will the folks on the Applegate Trail arrive?"

"I'm not sure. I think I heard the middle of October, although I hope it's sooner. And I hope they're not having any troubles because there's someone..." She was about to tell Malinda about Eli but stopped herself. Already she appeared foolish for turning down Will Bramford. She didn't want to seem like a silly schoolgirl—not at this stage of life.

"What is it?" Malinda demanded. "There is a glint in your eyes, Elizabeth Anne. A glint that tells me something is going on."

"Oh, it's nothing." Elizabeth looked back over the land. "I can't wait to see my livestock partaking of this luscious—"

"Lizzie." Malinda turned her back around. "I know you. And I know that look. You better tell me the truth. Is there someone special who's traveling on the Applegate Trail right now?"

Despite her resolve not to act like a schoolgirl, Elizabeth giggled. Then she linked her arm into Malinda's. "Shouldn't we get back to the house now?"

"Come on, Lizzie. I've known you since we were smaller than Susannah and Ruth. Out with it. Who is on the Applegate Trail right now? I will venture to guess that it's a man. And it must be a man that your friend Will is not terribly pleased over. Am I right?"

"No one...well, besides James...but no one else has ever known me as well as you do, Malinda."

"Tell me everything," Malinda insisted as they walked back.

And so Elizabeth obliged her. She even told her about the kiss. "I was completely shocked…but at the same time I wasn't."

"I can't wait to meet this Eli."

"You might not get the chance."

"But you said he was coming—"

"He was guiding them on the Applegate Trail. But that doesn't mean he'll come all the way out here. In fact, I would be surprised if he did. For all I know he could have plans to guide another group on up to the Willamette Valley. I heard mention that settlers are flocking there like fleas on a dog."

"Oh, I suspect your Eli will come by here," Malinda said.

Now Elizabeth spoke very frankly and honestly, explaining how Eli was not a marrying man. "He loves his life on the trail…I fear he loves his freedom even more than he loves me."

"But he does love you?"

Elizabeth shrugged. "I'm not even sure of that. But there were moments when I felt that he did."

"Well, he did kiss you." Malinda nodded firmly. "That's almost like saying he loves you."

"Or simply toying with my affections." Elizabeth laughed, but she could hear the hollowness to it. Then, as they neared the house, Elizabeth made Malinda swear to secrecy in regard to Eli.

"Quite frankly, it's doubtful that anything will ever come of it," she said finally, "but now you know…that is the reason I had to disappoint Will."

"Poor Will." She made a tsk-tsk sound.

Elizabeth gave her old friend a furtive glance. Was it possible that Malinda might be a good match for Will Bramford? Yet in the same instant, Elizabeth remembered that Malinda had not been widowed for a full year yet. Elizabeth remembered how long it took her to even consider remarrying. Surely this was much too early for Malinda as well. However, she had also noticed that Malinda wasn't wearing black.

"Have you been unable to find widow's weeds out here in the wilderness?" Elizabeth asked quietly.

"Oh, certainly, I had them. Mrs. Levine saw to that—you'll meet her soon. But when the heat of summer came and it had been more than six months, I put that ghastly woolen black dress away."

"I see." Elizabeth wasn't going to admit to her that she'd worn black for years.

"Besides, there's far too much to be done around here without worrying about such conventions. This is the West, Elizabeth. Life is different here. You'll see."

Elizabeth just nodded. "I'm sure I've had a good sampling of that already on the Oregon Trail."

Malinda laughed. "Yes, of course, you have. Sometimes I forget the hardships of the trail myself. I suppose it's a bit like giving birth—horrible when you're in the midst of it, but after it's over with, you put it all behind you."

Now Elizabeth laughed. "I never thought of it in that way, but I think you've gotten it just right." Already, she was beginning to forget the hardships and deprivations of crossing the country in a wagon and on foot. It truly was not so much different from how she'd felt after the pain of giving birth followed by the joy of holding her newborn baby in her arms. One did tend to forget the difficulties…in time.

Chapter Twenty-Eight

Malinda's farm became an even busier place when the Prescotts and Bramfords arrived. But by then, Elizabeth had already parked her own wagon as well as her livestock on the unit of land John had picked out for them. After walking the boundaries and studying the soil and the river, her parents had decided to take the unit west of her. And Matthew and Jess had their eye on the unit to the south. But Elizabeth was happy to remain on the land that abutted Malinda's.

It was surprising how quickly everyone made up their minds about claiming units. Perhaps it was because they saw the natural beauty of the land, or perhaps it was because they were concerned about the families still coming on the Applegate Trail.

The Prescotts and Bramfords decided to claim three and a half units. Because some of their children were eighteen or older, they were able to make more claims. But all the property they'd decided upon was to the east and, to Elizabeth's relief, a good distance from her land.

However, she was somewhat surprised when Lavinia and Hugh

hired some local men to help them put up a small building, right next to the church, to contain the mercantile. And when other settlers in these parts heard the news, the Prescotts were already in business.

"Perhaps we should have brought goods to sell instead of livestock," Elizabeth teased her father one evening as they gathered outside of his tent for a family meal. Although Malinda had offered to share her home with Elizabeth's family, they were all determined to get cabins up—if it was possible. Already, Jess and Matthew had made good progress. Because of the news that Jess was with child, everyone in the family had been eager to help them get a small cabin built.

"If the weather turns bad, we'll move in with Malinda," Elizabeth had told her parents. Malinda had made it clear that Elizabeth and the children were more than welcome in their home. And she'd even offered the same to Asa and Clara, but Asa seemed determined to get a cabin up. "Even if it's just one room," he told Elizabeth. "Your mother said as long as it doesn't have wheels on it, she will be happy."

One week after the Bostonians had arrived, everyone gathered at Malinda's barn for an evening of music and food and getting acquainted with the neighboring settlers. It was the first time they'd all been together like this—simply for fun—since their days on the wagon train. Of course, Elizabeth felt slightly uneasy around Will. And she couldn't help but notice he was much more serious and taciturn than before. Was it because of her? Finally, she could stand it no longer, and despite her sensibilities, she grabbed hold of Malinda's hand. "Come with me," she said. "I want you to meet someone."

"I thought I knew everyone here," Malinda said.

"Maybe so." Elizabeth continued walking Malinda across the room to where Will was sitting alone on a crate. "Excuse me," she told him in an overly loud voice. "But I would like you to meet Malinda."

"We've already met," Will told her in a cool tone.

"Yes. Well, maybe you met her. But you don't really *know* her." She made a very stiff smile. "Malinda is my very best friend. She is smart and interesting and fun to talk with." She gave Will a determined look. "A lot like you." Now she turned to Malinda. "Will is smart and interesting and fun to talk with."

"Yes, but I—"

Elizabeth interrupted Malinda. "And I hope you two will enjoy getting acquainted." Then, just like that, Elizabeth turned and walked away. She couldn't help but chuckle as she hurried back to where her mother and father were standing, probably watching the whole thing.

"So much for social conventions," she said as she joined them. "Malinda said that the rules changed out here in the West."

"It looked to me like you were foisting your oldest and dearest friend upon the poor man that you recently jilted," Clara whispered in Elizabeth's ear.

Elizabeth frowned. "Really, Mother. 'Jilted' is a very strong word."

Clara's lips curled into a smile. "You know what I mean. Besides, didn't you just insinuate that social conventions were out of style here in the West?"

"Look," Elizabeth said quietly. "They are actually talking."

"And unless I'm mistaken," Asa added, "they are enjoying it."

❧

All through the valley, Elizabeth could hear the twang of axes as her family and friends felled trees to use for their cabins. Elizabeth was the only one who had made no progress in building. However, she had chosen what she felt was the best site for a home, marking it off with stones and hoping that eventually, after her parents and brother finished their cabins, they might be able to help on hers. Brady, Asa, Matthew, and even JT were taking turns on the two cabins—one day at one and one day at the next—and they were already beginning to look habitable. Or nearly. There was still much to be done. But it amazed Elizabeth how quickly it was going with all of them working together.

As she walked to Malinda's, she wondered if it might perhaps be best if she and the children did plan to winter with her. As Malinda had said, she had plenty of room. Ruth could share the girls' bedroom with Emily and Susannah, JT could bunk with the boys in the loft, and Elizabeth could sleep with Malinda. It would be cozy but nice.

Even Mrs. Taylor had found lodging. Ironically, it was with Mrs.

Levine, a pioneer widow with four grown sons. Mrs. Levine had been here longer than anyone and was actively lobbying for a school and post office. When she learned that Mrs. Taylor hoped to teach settlers' children, she immediately invited her into her home. And Mrs. Levine had been pleased as punch to learn that Prescotts' Mercantile would soon open for business.

"There you are," Malinda said as Elizabeth came onto the porch. "I was just wishing you'd stop by."

Elizabeth set her basket down. "I heard there were edible mushrooms down by the marsh. Do you know anything about them?"

"I sure do. Let me get my bonnet and tell the girls and I'll be right along." When Malinda returned, a basket over her arm, she looked so happy that Elizabeth thought she was actually glowing. Or perhaps she was radiant.

"You seem in exceptionally good spirits today," Elizabeth said.

"Oh, yes, I am." Malinda's basket swung cheerily back and forth as they walked.

"Is it because you're so pleased to have new neighbors?"

Malinda chuckled. "Yes, I suppose that has much to do with it."

"I'm glad you're not feeling overly crowded. I was worried that it might be a bit much for you."

She waved her hand. "No, not at all." She stopped walking, turning to peer at Elizabeth. "Do you want to know the truth of the matter?"

Elizabeth blinked. "I certainly do."

"Well...I've been trying to think of a way to tell you this..."

"What?"

"Will Bramford has been stopping by my place..." She giggled. "Just being neighborly. At least that's what I thought."

Suddenly Elizabeth felt an unwanted jolt go through her. Was Will courting Malinda? However, she couldn't bring herself to form that question.

"Oh, Elizabeth, it is so wonderful." She peered into her eyes. "And I realize I have you to thank. Will said as much last night."

"Last night?"

"Before he went home—or back to their camp. Poor things, they haven't made much progress on their cabin, although Jeremiah is determined to get it up before winter because he wants to stay in it—even if it is by himself."

"I'm sorry," Elizabeth interrupted. "You are losing me, Malinda. What are you actually saying?"

"I'm saying that I do believe Will is going to propose marriage to me."

"You do?"

"Oh, it's too soon to be certain, but the conversation has definitely drifted in that direction, and I have made it clear in no uncertain terms that I am most in favor."

"You want to marry Will?"

Malinda put a finger over her lips. "Please, Elizabeth, keep it down. I'm sure the children are coming to their own conclusions, but it's premature to say anything."

Elizabeth felt dumbfounded. Malinda and Will were getting married? Already? Oh, she knew that it was something she'd actually tried to help along. But she had never imagined it would take off so quickly. "Are you saying that you're truly ready to consider marrying again?" she asked Malinda. "I don't want to sound overly prudent, but you have not even been a year without John."

"This is the frontier, Elizabeth."

"Fewer social conventions here...I remember." Elizabeth felt slightly lost now. It wasn't so much the idea of Will wanting to marry someone else—although that was a bit disconcerting—but the idea of her best friend partnering with another, someone besides John...well, that was troubling.

Malinda studied her closely. "You haven't changed your mind, have you? Do you have feelings for Will?"

"No, not at all."

Malinda let out a relieved sigh.

"I'm very happy for you."

"I hoped you would stand up with me...if we do decide to wed."

"Of course," she said quickly. "I'm happy to do that...Just like the first time."

"You think it's too soon, don't you?"

"I honestly don't know," Elizabeth confessed. "For me it would have been too soon. But everyone is different."

They had reached a spot where mushrooms were growing, and Malinda showed Elizabeth how to identify them. So for a while neither of them spoke but simply gathered. Finally, when they were done, Malinda told Elizabeth how to dry and store them. Then without saying much, they walked back to the clearing between their properties and parted ways. But as Elizabeth walked back to her camp, she felt slightly lost. It was almost as if her mother's words were coming back to haunt her now. Everyone seemed to have someone to partner with. Everyone except Elizabeth. Not only had she lost Will, she had lost Malinda too. And if Malinda and Will married, Elizabeth and her children would have to find someplace else to live.

As Elizabeth walked to her parents' unit, where they had decided to continue doing the cooking together, she wondered how she would be feeling right now if she was the one planning to marry Will, not Malinda. But truly it seemed to make no difference. Her biggest concern now was that she needed to have a place for herself and the children to live. And neither her parents' nor her brother's tiny one-room cabins were going to offer much.

She set the basket of mushrooms on the table with a *thunk* and then sat down on one of the chairs, letting out a loud sigh. The makeshift dining room was set up under the tarp to protect it from sun and rain.

"Is something wrong?" Clara looked up from her sewing, studying Elizabeth curiously.

"Perhaps."

"Do you want to talk about it?" Clara glanced around their campsite. "The men folk are at Matthew's until suppertime. And Ruth finished her chores and is playing with Susannah. The children are making the most of their time since Mrs. Taylor announced that school will officially begin next Monday."

"That means one less hand working on the houses," Elizabeth said quietly. "JT will need to be in school."

"Yes, but Asa says they're coming along just fine. He expects they'll both be finished by late November."

"And will that be too late to start a house for me?"

"I thought you were going to stay with Malinda."

So now Elizabeth spilled the story of Will and Malinda, and Clara actually had the audacity to laugh.

"I fail to see the humor," Elizabeth told her.

"That was just happy laughter, Lizzie. And it's only because you helped bring those two together. And I'm just so happy for the both of them. They will make a fine couple—don't you think?"

"I'm not sure what to think."

"Surely you're glad for them…"

Elizabeth made a sad sorry excuse of a nod. "Yes, of course."

"But you're feeling a bit put out?"

She shrugged. "Where will the kids and I stay now?"

"With us…or Matthew."

Elizabeth wanted to protest that neither option was ideal. But that seemed silly considering that nothing in the frontier was particularly ideal. Well, except for the land. She pointed to the basket of mushrooms, explaining what Malinda had said. "And now I think I'll go look around my own property…try to come up with a plan for getting a roof over my own head."

"Don't worry, dear, your family will help you when the time comes."

That was just the problem, Elizabeth thought, as she walked over to her piece of land. When would the time come? Next summer? When everyone was busy with crops or building barns? Or maybe it would be the year after that? Elizabeth had never been the most patient person—she knew this. But it seemed unfair that she would have to wait longer than everyone else to get her cabin. After all, it had been her idea to come here in the first place. Besides that, Brady was her hired man—he was supposed to be helping her. And JT her own son. She knew she was being silly and selfish and childish as she continued to rant and rave in the privacy of her own mind.

If this was what life on the frontier was going to be like, isolated and lonely and at the mercy of her family to help her, maybe she wasn't cut out for it after all. Suddenly she remembered being on the wagon train, and as crazy as it seemed, she missed it. She missed the simplicity of packing up each morning and rolling along. She missed the thrill of exploring new places, and she missed having people nearby. Mostly she missed the freedom of having only two goals—to survive and to keep moving forward.

Of course, she knew that life here wasn't all that much different. Like all things, it would take some getting used to…and some patience.

She reached her homesite and walked the perimeter that she'd mapped out. She tried to regain some composure as she imagined where a window might go someday—if it was possible to get window glass out here. And as she stood where she wanted the front door to be situated, it hit her. She realized that she was going about this all wrong. With everything else, whenever she got frustrated and impatient like this, she knew that it was simply a signal. It was time to give her worries and anxieties over to God.

She knew that just as he clothed the flowers and fed the birds, he was going to take care of her and her children. She just needed to trust him. She sat down on one of the stones she was using as a marker. In due time, it would all get done. In the meantime, she and her children would be just fine because, as always, God would take care of them.

"Mama! Mama! Mama!" screamed Ruth's voice, causing Elizabeth to jump to her feet, her heart in her throat.

"Over here!" she yelled as she ran toward the sound of Ruth's voice. Suddenly she was imagining Indians on the attack, just as Malinda had described. But when she saw only Ruth racing toward her, she figured she was wrong.

"What is it?" Elizabeth cried out as she continued running to Ruth. "Has JT been hurt? Did he fall off the roof or did Grandpa—"

"No, no, Mama." Ruth paused to catch her breath. "It's nothing like that." She held onto her sides, puffing.

"What is it, child? Tell me."

"The rest of the wagon train…" Ruth huffed. "They made it!"

"The rest of the wagon train?"

"The ones on the Applegate Trail, Mama. They're here right now. At Malinda's farm. Come and see."

Elizabeth grabbed onto Ruth's hand. She too was tempted to run, but Ruth already seemed out of breath. "Did you see them all?" Elizabeth asked.

"I saw the Flanders and Tumbleweed Tillie," Ruth said happily. "Her hair is almost long enough for pigtails now."

Elizabeth laughed. She wanted to ask Ruth if she'd seen Eli, but she also didn't want to get Ruth's curiosity aroused. Besides, Elizabeth assured herself, she would know soon enough.

When they got there, they exchanged hugs and welcomes with the Flanders and the McIntires and some of the others, but Elizabeth did not see any sign of Eli. And truly, why would he come this far?

"So you had no problems on the Applegate Trail?" Elizabeth asked Flo. "No Indian troubles?"

"Not at all." Flo looked around and nodded. "This truly is beautiful country, Elizabeth. We're so glad to be here."

"No problems finding the place?" Elizabeth was glancing around the wagons and animals, still hoping to spy a certain Appaloosa…and a man in a fringed buckskin.

"Not at all." Flo removed her bonnet, shaking the dust off. "Eli took us right to the road that comes alongside this pretty river. And he told us it would take three days. And here we are."

"And welcome you are." Elizabeth hugged her again.

"Well, Bert's bound and determined to have a look around before dark," Flo told her. "And Malinda has offered us one of her boys to show us some of the land. If Bert has his way, we'll be staking a claim before the sun sets."

"Don't be in too much of a hurry," Elizabeth told her. "There's plenty of land for everyone."

"I know, but we gotta hurry if we want to get a cabin up before winter," Flo said.

"From what I hear, winters aren't too harsh in these parts," Elizabeth assured her.

"Yeah, I heard the same, but I also heard it can get mighty wet. 'Specially if you ain't got a roof overhead."

Now Susannah had joined Ruth and Tillie, all three holding hands in a circle, doing a merry little jig and acting like they were old friends.

"Mama," Ruth came over with a hopeful expression. "Susannah is asking if Tillie and me can spend the night at her house. Can we, Mama?"

"Can we?" Tillie asked Flo.

"Makes no difference to me," Flo told her. "Makes more space in the wagon."

"Mama?" Ruth asked eagerly. "Please?"

"Did your mother give you permission?" Elizabeth asked Susannah.

She nodded with the same serious gray eyes as her mother. "Mama said we girls can sleep in the loft and the boys will sleep in the barn. She told Bart to go and ask JT if he wants to come too."

"Maybe Walter can come too," Ruth said, referring to Tillie's brother.

Before long it was all arranged, and the children were thrilled at the prospects of an evening of fun and games, celebrating their new friends and the news that school would start on Monday. The Flanders and the McIntires set off to explore the countryside, and Elizabeth went back to her own land...to think.

It was reassuring to know that she would have even more neighbors now. The school would certainly be a lively place for Mrs. Taylor. She hoped she was up to it. In some ways their little settlement would be similar to the wagon train—except that they wouldn't be moving every day. And truly, Elizabeth reminded herself, that had gotten wearisome at times. How often she had wished to simply stay put. And now she could do just that.

Elizabeth knew she should count her blessings...and that she should be content and thankful. But as she checked on her horses and livestock, and as she roamed around her wagon and tent, which seemed strangely empty, she felt lonelier than she'd felt in ages—and she had the distinct feeling that she'd made an enormous mistake. First she thought she was simply having regrets about Will...about letting the chance for companionship slip away. But then she realized that she was only trying to fool herself into thinking it was about Will.

The truth was niggling away in the back of her mind, and as much as she tried to dismiss it, she knew that her sadness was over Eli. She went up to the site of her house and sat down on one of the cornerstones. She knew it was over. She would never see Eli again, and the sooner she got over it, the better off she would be. And yet memories of him seemed to be haunting her now, filling her with nearly as much sadness as she'd felt when she'd lost James.

"This is ridiculous," she told herself as she wiped hot tears with the hem of her skirt. Now she stood, and with great resolve, she walked down to Elk Creek and picked up a rock that was about the size of a large loaf of bread. Lugging the heavy wet stone back up to the home-site, she placed it along the line of what would one day be the foundation wall. Then she went back to the creek and got another. And another. And another.

Chapter Twenty-Nine

The children had been in school for a full two weeks now, and Elizabeth's stone foundation wall was nearly a foot tall and just as wide. Oh, she realized that it would take some maneuvering and fitting of the rocks as well as some sort of mortar or mud to make the wall secure enough to support the heavy log walls of her cabin. But it made her happy to see it taking shape. Not only that, but she'd used a shovel and a broom to smooth out and level the dirt floor on the inside. With a bit of moisture and packing, it was slowly becoming fairly solid beneath her feet.

She knew dirt floors were not uncommon in the frontier, but she hoped that they would eventually have a wooden one. But more importantly, they would have a roof above their heads. For now, she got true pleasure just standing inside what would one day be the front room of the house and looking out over the meadow, past the creek, and down to the river below. Her animals looked contented, already making themselves at home in the lush grasses and ample creek water. A sight better than Devil's Backbone, she sometimes reminded herself. And Flax did his best to see that the livestock didn't stray, but she longed for the day when she could put up some rail fences to contain them securely. Perhaps she'd even have a barn someday…although that probably wouldn't become a reality for years to come.

At least they had a henhouse now. She and the children had started building it from leftover pieces of logs that JT brought home after working on Asa and Matthew's houses. Using twine and wire to hold it together, they had managed to create a very rustic sort of henhouse. And they hoped it wouldn't be too long until the hens began to lay. She was also working on a stick fence to go around the spot where she hoped to plant a garden next spring. She and the children had been gathering sticks that they wove together to make fencing to keep the critters out. She knew her improvements were minor compared to what others were doing. But it was the best she could do under the circumstances, and it was satisfying to see even the smallest project to completion.

Her brother's and her parents' houses were both slowly but surely coming along—small, sturdy boxes made of logs that they were falling themselves and moving with oxen. Just yesterday, when she was admiring the walls of Matthew and Jess' cabin, which were already nearly four feet high, her brother had assured her that they would begin work on her cabin by early November. She had teasingly told him that if she had no house by the time winter came, she and her children would simply be sleeping with him and Jess. She could tell by the look in his eyes that her jovial threat might have actually put a spark beneath him. Anyway, she hoped so.

Everyone was busier than ever these days. And fortunately the autumn rains seemed to be holding off. The most recent newcomers had quickly found land to claim. However, the Flanders and McIntires, due to their limited funds, were only able to file for half units. That was all that Elizabeth, as a single woman, had been allowed to file for as well. However, the west half of her unit was still unclaimed. She had considered mentioning it to the Flanders, but Bert was pleased with the location they had found. It was on the east section of Elk Creek and not too far from the mercantile and church. "A right handy spot for a blacksmith shop," Flo had happily told her. "And close enough to the school that the youngins can't complain too much. And just think, Elizabeth, maybe we'll have a real town there someday, and you and me can say we helped to start this place."

The biggest news in Elk Creek was that Malinda and Will had officially announced their engagement last Sunday after the church service. Everyone seemed surprised at how quickly it all happened—everyone except Elizabeth, now that she'd had time to think on it. Will was a man who was ready to get married. And Malinda was a good woman. And neither of them was getting any younger. The wedding date was set for December. Malinda had confided to Elizabeth that conventions or no conventions, it seemed only proper and respectful not to wed until a full year had passed since John's death.

Tomorrow night, there would be a barn dance at Malinda's to celebrate the engagement, and everyone in Elk Creek would be there. The women were bringing the food, and Matthew, JT, Brady, and the McIntires would be providing the music. It would be a joyous occasion, and Elizabeth was as pleased about the engagement as anyone. In fact, she planned to wear one of her best dresses and to kick up her heels—which reminded her she needed to check the clothes on the line to make sure the sun wasn't fading them. She'd spent most of the morning laundering nearly every garment they'd brought with them. She wanted it all clean and dry before the first rains came, which could be any day now according to Malinda.

She was just unpegging Ruth's best red gingham dress when she heard the sound of horse's hooves not too far off and getting closer. It was too early for the children to be coming home, although she'd let them ride Molly this morning. She reasoned that it was just one of her neighbors or Asa or Matthew. But the sound of someone approaching caught her off guard, sending a chill down her spine. Being alone like this in an area that had experienced Indian troubles not so long ago, she considered running out to the wagon and grabbing her gun, which remained loaded, but she decided against it. Still, she was curious as to who was riding out here in the middle of the day, especially when everyone seemed to be busy working on cabins or other chores.

With Ruth's dress hanging loosely over an arm, she crept around the wide trunk of the maple tree and, remaining hidden, peered out in the direction of the horse and rider. But what she saw coming was so startling that she nearly fell to the ground. Not Indians, thank the good Lord, but the rider approaching on a tall Appaloosa wore fringed buckskins and a big smile.

"Elizabeth!" Eli called out. "I was told I would find you up here."

Clutching Ruth's dress to her chest and with wobbly knees, Elizabeth slowly walked toward him. Was this real, or was she simply imagining things?

"*Eli?*" Her voice came out in a hoarse sounding whisper.

He slid down from the horse and then paused to untie something from the saddle horn. "I have something of yours," he called over his shoulder.

She laid Ruth's dress on the stone foundation of her unbuilt house and then, resisting the urge to pat her windblown hair into place, she went closer to see, still disbelieving that it was really him and not just a daydream.

He held out her old canteen toward her. "I do believe this belongs to you."

Was he serious? "Honestly, you came all the way out here just to bring me *that?*"

A grin lit up his face.

Now she folded her arms across her front, pretending to be offended though she was mostly just suffering from shock. "What if I refuse to trade back with you? What if I've decided that I prefer your fancy canteen to my old beat-up one?"

He continued approaching, only stopping when he was just inches from her. "I was hoping you did." He reached over and cupped her chin in his hand, looking deeply into her eyes. "I have missed you."

Suddenly it felt like her secure little world was slipping sideways. And she knew deep inside of her that if she let him kiss her again...and if he left her again...she would never be able to pull herself back together. Or it would take a long, long time. And so she stepped back, and his hand fell to his side. But the look on his face showed he was perplexed.

"Eli…" she began carefully. "I have missed you too. More than I care to say. But here is the truth of the matter. I cannot play games with you. And I fear my heart is not strong enough to be toyed with again."

"Can we talk?"

She sighed. "Certainly. I would love to talk." She waved over to her stone foundation. "Come on in." Because the weather had been continuing warm and sunny—a real Indian summer, Malinda was calling it—Elizabeth had set her chairs and table on the rug. And at Ruth's suggestion, she'd even put a vase of flowers on the table. The general effect was actually quite charming. "I'm playing house," she told him.

"Nice place you got here," he said as they sat down across from each other. "Open and airy."

She nodded. "We like it."

"Good view too." He tipped his head toward what would one day be a front room window—if she could get ahold of some glass, which Lavinia had assured her would not be a problem.

"My father and brother and Brady are working on the other cabins first. We thought I was going to stay with my dear friend Malinda." Now she explained to him that Malinda had been widowed. "It seemed a good arrangement for me to spend the winter with her. Two widows and their children sharing a home together. I was looking forward to it." She sighed. "But now it's not to be." She pointed to the stone foundation. "So, as you can see, I've been doing my best to get my house started. Trying to be patient as I wait for the men to come and help me."

"What went wrong with your friend Malinda?"

"Oh, nothing went wrong. In fact, something went very right. My friend Malinda is getting married."

He nodded. "I see. But that leaves you and your children in the lurch."

She made a half smile. "It was actually my own fault. I introduced the happy couple to each other." She chuckled to remember that night. "In fact I nearly forced them on one another."

"You did?"

"It was Will Bramford, and he had—"

"Will Bramford?" Eli's brow creased. "But I thought Will wanted to marry you."

"Well, yes…he did. But I turned him down."

Eli's eyes lit up. "You did?"

"Yes. Everyone, including my mother and even Malinda, thought I was a perfect fool to pass up such an opportunity. But I told Will that although he was a good friend, I did not have those sorts of feelings for him…the kind of feelings a woman wants to have for her husband." She looked directly into his eyes and then, embarrassed at her own boldness, looked down at the small pink flowers in the vase.

When Eli didn't respond she looked back up.

"Do you think I made a mistake too?" she asked him.

He just shook his head. "I don't think so, Elizabeth."

"So may I ask you a question now?"

"Sure." He waited.

"Why did you come here?"

"To see you."

"It was a long way to come…to see me."

He nodded. "Longer than you know."

"What does that mean?"

"I was headed to California after delivering the Applegate Trail folks up here. I had thought about coming on out and saying hello to you, but I was afraid that…well, I just felt uneasy about something."

"I see."

"But the farther I got away from here…it seemed like with each passing mile…well, it was like something had ahold of me and was pulling me back."

Elizabeth frowned. "That sounds a bit uncomfortable."

He smiled. "I don't mean to make it sound like that."

"So what was it, Eli? What had ahold of you?"

"I think you know."

She shrugged. "I'm not so sure I do."

"Elizabeth, you must know that I love you. I think you've known that from the beginning. Haven't you?"

She felt her resolve melting. "Maybe…"

"You know how I've struggled with it."

She gave him a sad smile. "I know that you enjoy your freedom."

He frowned. "The problem is, I'm not sure I can enjoy it anymore."

Hearing him say that was not comforting. In fact, it made her feel a tinge of guilt. Was it her fault that he was unhappy? Did he expect her to do something to make this right? To apologize to him? "Do you know what's truly ironic?" she finally said.

"I haven't a clue."

"I was barely settled in here and, as you can see, not even a roof over my head, and I suddenly found myself missing the wagon train. I missed being out there on the trail. I missed being on the move." She slapped her hand on the table. "Can you believe that?"

His eyes lit up. "So you *do* understand my dilemma."

"I think I do. Just a little."

There was a long pause now with only the sound of the breeze rustling the drying leaves on the trees and a pair of doves making their mournful calls.

"Elizabeth, I've told you how I feel. But you seem determined to play your cards close to your chest. Can't you help me out a little here?"

"Whatever do you mean?" Oh, she knew she was being coquettish. But hadn't he accused her of making him unhappy?

"I told you, Elizabeth. I've confessed to loving you. I knew it from the day we met. And I know it now."

"Oh..." She knew that he wanted her to declare her love too. And part of her wanted to, but another part wanted to hold back, to play it safe and protect her heart. Most of all, she wanted to be honest. What more could she do?

"Eli, I never would have admitted it back then, when we first met, but I did feel something inside of me. It happened almost in the same moment that I first saw you. Something inside of me seemed to fall into place. It was almost like I heard it go *click*. And yet it was terribly unsettling because I wasn't ready for such feelings again. I felt it would be untrue to James."

"I understand."

"It took me most of the Oregon Trail to get to the place where I could accept that James is gone and my life with him is over. I finally realized that it's all right for me to have a new life...a new love..." She held up her palms up in a helpless gesture. "Unfortunately, about the same time that I figured it out, you took off down a different trail."

"I couldn't really help that."

"You couldn't?" She studied him closely.

He smirked back at her. "You're right. Maybe I could have. But I think I needed to go down that trail, away from you...to figure it out for myself."

"Did you figure it out?"

He nodded as he reached for her hands, gently holding them in his. "I figured out that everything I've been wanting, everything I've been searching for, all that I've been dreaming about...it's all right here with you."

She felt her heart in her throat. "Are you sure?"

He squeezed her hands. "I'm absolutely certain. But I still need to hear you say it, Elizabeth. I've declared my love for you, but you're holding out on me."

She took in a deep breath. "All right, Eli, I will tell you. Yes, I love you. I do. There, I've said it. And it hasn't been easy loving you."

"I'm sorry about that."

She felt a rush of relief now. It felt so good to have her feelings out there in the open. "I honestly did not believe I would ever experience this kind of love again."

"I know. I felt the same way."

"And it was because of my feelings for you that I knew I could never marry Will. Do you know that my love for you has the power to make me lonely and miserable for the rest of my life?" She searched his blue eyes. "And if you should decide to leave me again..." Even saying these words aloud filled her with sorrow.

"I am not going to do that, Elizabeth."

"You're not?"

"I'll admit I was a wandering man. I think I was looking for something...a place to come home to. But now I believe I've found it. I know that my home is with you…this is where my heart is. I'm ready for us to build something together here."

"You are?"

"Elizabeth Martin, I'm asking you to marry me."

Tears of joy were filling her eyes—and she was speechless. Was this truly happening? It seemed too good to be real.

"Are you going to answer me?" He squeezed her fingertips.

"I'm sorry. Yes, of course, I'll marry you, Eli Kincaid. I will gladly marry you!"

And now he stood, and pulling her to him, he kissed her again. This time it was with as much passion as before, the time when he'd kissed her goodbye. But as he held her tightly and as she relaxed in his arms, she knew that this kiss was only the beginning.

Discussion Questions

1. Some of the pioneers had difficulties lightening their wagonloads. What one possession would be hard for you to let go of? Explain how you would feel leaving it behind.

2. Describe your reaction when Mr. Taylor lost his life.

3. Mrs. Taylor isn't always easy to like. Is someone in your life like that? Compare your real person to Mrs. Taylor.

4. Elizabeth found herself in the middle of a love triangle. Which man were you rooting for? Why?

5. How did you feel when Brady took a thrashing after rescuing the boy in the river? Do you see a spiritual metaphor in that scene?

6. Why do you think the dance hall girl refused to let Elizabeth send her money in payment for her kindness to Brady?

7. Why do you think Elizabeth was so certain that Eli was not the kind of man to settle down? Was she being realistic or just trying to protect her own heart?

8. Malinda's first letter (warning Elizabeth not to come) was alarming. Describe an instance in your life when you expected a disaster but it turned out all right.

9. What did you think when Mrs. Taylor changed her mind at the last minute, pleading to continue on with Elizabeth and her family?

10. Were you surprised that Elizabeth rejected Will's attempts to court her? Do you think that was realistic (for that time period) or not? Describe.

11. After all her hard work and planning and helpfulness, Elizabeth feels a bit left out once her family is actually on the frontier. Describe a time you felt like that.

12. What was your favorite part of this story and why?

Chapter One

Elizabeth walked Eli around the perimeters of the whole unit of land. "John and Malinda had been saving it for us…" She stopped herself. "I mean for James and me."

He nodded. "I understand."

"But now both John and James are gone." She didn't want to think too much on this sad fact. It seemed more important to go forward than to look back. "Anyway, you can see where my half unit ends." She waved her hand. "And where yours would begin."

"It's hard to believe the government is selling this land for so cheap." Eli frowned. "But they want it settled." He glanced over to the Coquille River. "Are there any Indians around here? I heard the Coquille Indians are friendly. This looks like the kind of place a tribe would be comfortable in."

"I haven't seen a single Indian since we were in Coos Bay," she told him. "But Malinda said there had been trouble in these parts. Perhaps they've moved on."

"I know the ocean isn't too far away. It's possible they've gone over there to fish or to collect clams."

"I'm looking forward to seeing the ocean," she told him.

He grinned. "Yes, we'll have to do that together." He looked intently into her eyes. "Now that you've agreed to become my bride, is there anyone I should see to get permission? Asa perhaps?"

She laughed. "No, I don't need my father's permission to marry, but I would like his blessing. However, there is someone you should ask. Rather, two someones. School let out a bit ago, so I'm sure they'll be here soon."

"I can't wait to see them."

Now she told him about JT helping to drive the livestock along the Columbia River. "It was almost as if he left a boy and grew into a man while he was gone. He's still talking about the adventures they had."

"Did he take his Bowie knife?"

"He certainly did. And I let him take your canteen as well."

Eli chuckled. "I'm glad you did."

"And Ruth is turning into quite an artist. You'll have to ask her to show you the drawings she did while we floated down the Columbia. She says she's saving them for her children." She laughed. "Can you imagine?"

"I think we would make fine grandparents."

Elizabeth pointed over to where JT and Ruth were just coming in sight on her horse. "There they are." Suddenly she felt nervous. Perhaps this was a conversation she should have privately with her children. What if they were unhappy about this? And hadn't she always promised them that they would be the first to know? "Oh, dear," she said quietly as she waved to them. "I'm feeling extremely nervous right now."

"So am I," Eli admitted.

"Eli!" JT yelled from the horse, nudging Molly to go faster.

Eli went to meet them, helping Ruth from the horse as JT hopped down. As both children hugged him, JT asked where he'd been and Ruth asked how long he planned to stay.

"That depends," he told them.

"On what?" Ruth asked curiously.

"Well, your mother and I want to ask you about something." He tossed her an uneasy glance.

"That's right," she told them. "Eli has asked me a very important question." She looked back at him, hoping he'd take it from here.

"I came here to ask your mother to become my wife," he told them.

JT looked stunned, but Ruth just grinned. "I knew it!" she told Eli.

"But your mother said she cannot marry without her children's approval. What do you think about me marrying your mother...and hopefully becoming your father?" He cleared his throat. "Someday."

"I like it!" Ruth told him. "I wanted Mama to marry you a long time ago, back on the wagon train. Didn't I, Mama?"

Elizabeth just chuckled and nodded. But her eyes were on JT. He was being awfully quiet. And his expression was very somber and hard to read. What was he thinking?

"I appreciate you giving your consent, Ruth. But we need the approval of both of you." Eli looked at JT now. "What do you think about this, JT? I realize you've been the man of the house." Eli glanced over to the stone foundation. "Well, there's not much house yet, but you've been playing the role of the man in this family. And doing a good job too." He grinned. "Your ma told me about how you helped drive the livestock through the Columbia Gorge. Takes a man to do that."

JT nodded proudly. "I know."

"So, JT," Elizabeth began, "what do you think?"

JT looked from Eli to Elizabeth, and a smile slowly broke over his face. "I think it's a good idea. I approve." He stuck out his hand to Eli, and they shook on it.

"I appreciate that," Eli told him. "You had me worried there for a bit."

JT chuckled. "Sorry. I just wanted to give it my careful consideration."

Elizabeth laughed now, patting him on the back. "I appreciate that, son."

"Does anyone else know about this?" Ruth asked. "Grandma and Grandpa or—"

"Nobody but you two," Elizabeth assured her. "Remember what I told you—you and JT would be the first to know."

"Can we go tell them now?" Ruth asked.

Elizabeth glanced at Eli, and he just shrugged. "Don't see why not."

"Yes, but let's ask them to keep it to themselves until after Malinda and Will's party tomorrow. I don't want to steal their thunder."

"Good thinking," Eli agreed.

And so they all headed over to share the good news with Asa and Clara and Matthew and Jess and Brady. Naturally, everyone was nearly as happy as Elizabeth and Eli, and they all promised to keep it under their hats.

Book 1 in the HOMEWARD on the OREGON TRAIL series...

Westward Hearts

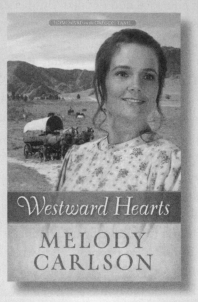

The Oregon Trail—
Hardship or Happiness? Loneliness or Love?

Kentucky, 1856—Elizabeth Martin has mourned her husband's death for three years, but now she feels ready to fulfill the dream they had shared—to take their two children west. The dream becomes reality when her middle-aged parents and bachelor brother surprise her with the news that they want to go as well.

After converting three of their best wagons for an overland journey and thoroughly outfitting them with ample supplies and tools, the family travels from Kentucky to Kansas City, where they join a substantial wagon train. Elizabeth soon draws attention from fellow traveler Will Bramford as well as Eli Kincaid, the group's handsome but mysterious guide.

Will Elizabeth's close-knit family survive the challenges they face on the Oregon Trail? And is this young widow truly ready for new love—even as she pursues the dream once shared with her late husband?

Angel of the Cove

Book 1 in Sandra Robbins'
Smoky Mountain Dreams series

It's 1894, and Anna Prentiss has never wanted to be anything but a nurse. But before she can start school in New York, her brother sends her to Cades Cove, deep in the Smoky Mountains, to spend a summer apprenticing to the local midwife. Anna is determined to prove herself and then head to the big city.

But nothing could have prepared Anna for the beauty of the Cove or the community and friendships she finds there. And she certainly wasn't prepared for Simon Martin, the handsome young minister, or the feelings he arouses in her. Has God's plan for Anna changed? Or is she just starting to hear Him clearly?

Love Blooms in Winter

Book 1 of Lori Copeland's *Dakota Diaries*

North Dakota, 1892—Mae Wilkey's sweet next-door neighbor, Pauline, is suffering from old age and dementia and desperately needs family to come help her. But Pauline can't recall having kin remaining. Mae searches through her desk and finds a name— Tom Curtis, who may just be the answer to their prayers.

Tom can't remember an old aunt named Pauline, but after two desperate letters from Mae, he decides to pay a visit. An engagement, a runaway train, and a town of quirky, lovable people make for more of an adventure than Tom is expecting. But it is amazing what can bloom in winter when God is in charge of things.